Abby Green spent her teens reading Mills & Boon romances. She then spent many years working in the Film and TV industry as an Assistant Director. One day while standing outside an actor's trailer in the rain, she thought: *there has to be more than this*. So she sent off a partial to Mills & Boon. After many rewrites, they accepted her first book and an author was born. She lives in Dublin, Ireland and you can find out more here: www.abby-green.com

Susanna Carr has been an avid romance reader since she read her first Mills & Boon at the age of ten. She written sexy contemporary romances for several ...lishers and her work has been honoured with ...rds for contemporary and sensual romance.

...anna lives in the Pacific Northwest with her family. ...en she isn't writing, Susanna enjoys reading ...mance and connecting with readers online. Visit her ...bsite at susannacarr.com

Caitlin Crews discovered her first romance novel at ...e age of twelve and has since conducted a life-long ...ve affair with romance novels, many of which she ...sists on keeping near her at all times. She currently ...ves in the Pacific Northwest, with her animator/comic ...ook artist husband and ...imals.

The Mistresses

COLLECTION

Mistresses: Claimed for The Royal Bed

ABBY GREEN

SUSANNA CARR

CAITLIN CREWS

MILLS & BOON

First Published in Great Britain 2020
By Mills & Boon, an imprint of HarperCollins*Publishers*
1 London Bridge Street, London, SE1 9GF

Mistresses: Claimed for the Royal Bed © 2020 Harlequin Books S.A.

A Diamond for the Sheikh's Mistress © 2017 Abby Green
Prince Hafiz's Only Vice © 2014 Susanna Carr
Majesty, Mistress… Missing Heir © 2010 Caitlin Crews

ISBN: 978-0-263-28135-4

MIX
Paper from
responsible sources
FSC **FSC™ C007454**
www.fsc.org

This book is produced from independently certified FSC™ paper to ensure responsible forest management.

For more information visit: www.harpercollins.co.uk/green

Printed and bound in Spain
by CPI, Barcelona

A DIAMOND FOR THE SHEIKH'S MISTRESS

ABBY GREEN

CHAPTER ONE

SHEIKH ZAFIR IBN HAFIZ AL-NOURY, King of Jandor, was oblivious to the exquisite mosaics on the path under his feet as he paced restlessly, and he was equally oblivious to the water burbling from the ornate central fountain. The tiny multicoloured birds darting between the lush exotic blooms also went unnoticed in this, just one of the many stunning courtyards of his royal palace in Jahor, the imposing capital city of his kingdom, which ran from snow-capped mountains in the east, across a vast desert to the sea in the west.

Zafir was oblivious to it all because all he could think about was *her*. It was getting worse. He'd had to call an important meeting to a premature end because he'd felt constricted and claustrophobic, aware of the heat in his blood and the ache in his core. An ache he'd largely managed to ignore for the last eighteen months.

Liar, whispered a voice, *those first three months were hell*.

Zafir scowled in remembrance. But then his father had died, and all his time and attention since then had been taken up with his accession to the throne and taking control of his country.

But now it was as if he finally had time to breathe again, and she was back. Infiltrating his thoughts and dreams. Haunting him.

Zafir loosened his robe at his neck with jerky movements. *Sexual frustration*, he told himself, momentarily coming to a halt on the path. It was just sexual frustration. After all, he hadn't taken a woman to bed since... *her*, and that incensed him even more now.

It wasn't due to lack of interest from women. It was due to Zafir's single-minded focus on his job and his commitment to his people. But he was aware of the growing pressure from his council and his people to find a suitable Queen and provide heirs, so they would have faith and feel secure in their King and future.

Zafir issued a loud curse, scattering the birds around him in a flurry. *Enough.* He whirled around and strode back out of the courtyard, determined to set in motion the search for an appropriate match and put *her* out of his head once and for all.

He stopped in his tracks, though, as he passed the overgrown entrance to the high-walled garden nearby. None of the gardeners had touched it in years, and Zafir hadn't had the heart to enforce its clean-up since taking power. He knew that his staff viewed it almost superstitiously; some believed it was haunted.

Maybe it was, he thought bleakly, his thoughts momentarily diverted.

He went and stood at the entrance and looked at the wildly overgrown space and realised with a jolt that today was the anniversary. The anniversary of his sister's death. Nineteen years ago. He'd been thirteen and she'd been just eleven. He stepped in, almost without realising what he was doing.

Unlike the rest of the pristinely manicured grounds, there was no water trickling into the circular pool that could barely be seen under greedy weeds. There were no lush flowers or exotic birds. It was dormant. Still. Dead.

He could still remember hearing the almost otherworldly scream of his brother Salim, Sara's twin. When Zafir had burst into the garden he'd found his brother cradling Sara's limp body, her head dangling over his arm at an unnatural angle. Her face had been whiter than white, her long black hair matted with the blood which had been dripping into the fountain's pool behind them, staining the water.

Salim had screamed at him to do something... *Save her*... But Zafir had known instinctively that she was gone. He'd tried to take Sara out of Salim's arms to carry her into the palace, to find help, see if there was any chance, but Salim, sensing Zafir's grim assessment, had only tightened his hold on his twin sister's body and shouted hoarsely, 'If you can't help, then don't touch her... Leave us alone!'

Sara had died from a massive head and neck injury after falling from the high wall around this garden where they'd used to play and climb, in spite of Zafir's protests. Salim hadn't spoken for weeks afterwards...

To Zafir's shame, the dominating thing he now recalled was the awfully familiar disconnect between him and his siblings. The sense of isolation that had pervaded his whole life. He'd always been envious of Salim and Sara's very special and close bond, which had been to the exclusion of everyone else. But right then he would have gladly given up his own life to see his sister's brought back...

'*Ahem*... Sire?'

Zafir tensed. Very few people managed to catch him unawares and he didn't appreciate this intrusion into such a private moment.

He didn't turn around as he responded curtly, 'Yes?'

There was some throat-clearing. 'The...ah... Heart of Jandor diamond, Sire. There are things we need to discuss about it, and the upcoming diplomatic tour.'

Zafir closed his eyes briefly, letting the painful past fade back to where it belonged, and when he was ready turned around to survey the young aide he'd taken on after his father's death almost fifteen months ago—much to his council's disapproval. They'd wanted him to keep his father's old guard and not rock the boat, but Zafir favoured a more modern outlook for his country's future and was slowly but surely implementing his ways.

He started walking back towards the palace, his aide hurrying alongside him, used to keeping up with his demanding King by now.

The Heart of Jandor diamond was a mythically rare gem. Thought for years to have been either stolen or lost, it had been found recently during archaeological excavations outside the palace walls. There had been much rejoicing and fervent whispering of it being a good omen. It was the largest known red diamond in the world, famed for its beauty. When it had first been discovered it had had a natural heart shape, and so had been cut and refined into its current incarnation, retaining its distinctive shape.

It had originally been unearthed in the eastern mountains of Jandor and given as a gift to woo Zafir's French great-grandmother. The fact that her marriage to his great-grandfather was the only one in his family history which had allegedly been a happy one merely confirmed for Zafir that love within marriage was as much of a rarity as the diamond itself—and about as improbable.

Irritated to find his mind deviating like this, Zafir said now, 'Well? What are your thoughts, Rahul?'

'We are starting the diplomatic tour in New York next week, as discussed.'

New York.

No one else would have noticed the slightest misstep in Zafir's authoritative stride. But *he* noticed. And he despised himself for it. Suddenly all thoughts of his sister and the lingering grief he felt were eclipsed by *her* again. The ease with which she could get to him after all this time only made him angrier.

What the hell was wrong with him today?

Manhattan was primarily where their relationship had played out over several months. And in spite of his best efforts his blood simmered, reminding him of just how far under her spell he'd fallen. Until it had been almost too late.

Zafir's strides got longer, as if he could outrun the past nipping at his heels, but even by the time he'd reached his palatial offices she was still there, those amber-hazel eyes looking up at him slumberously while a sinful smile made that famously sexy and lush mouth curve upwards. As if she'd known exactly what she was doing to him, drawing him deeper and deeper into—

'Sire?'

Zafir gritted his jaw against the onslaught of memories and turned around to focus on his aide. 'Yes, Rahul.'

The young man looked nervous. 'I…ah…have a suggestion to make regarding the jewel.'

'Go on,' Zafir bit out, curbing his impatience. His aide was not to know that he'd unwittingly precipitated the storm currently raging inside him.

'The diamond is being brought on your diplomatic tour as an exhibit and a stunning example of Jandor's many attractions in a bid to promote business and tourism.'

Zafir's impatience spiked in spite of his best efforts. 'I know very well why we're bringing it on the diplomatic tour. It was my idea.'

The man swallowed, visibly nervous. 'Yes, and we'd planned on displaying it in each city in a protected glass case.'

'Rahul…' Zafir said warningly, coming close to the end of his tether.

His aide spoke quickly now. 'The suggestion I want to make is this—rather than show it off in a sterile and protected environment, I thought it might prove to be far more dynamic if it were seen up close… We could let people see how accessible it is and yet still exclusive and mysterious.'

Now he had Zafir's attention. 'What are you talking about?'

'I'm talking about hiring someone—a model—someone who will actually wear the jewel and come with us on the tour. Someone who will walk with us among the guests at each function, so they can appreciate the jewel's full beauty, see how it lives and breathes—just like Jandor's beauty.'

Zafir looked at Rahul for a long moment. This was why he'd hired the younger man after all—to inject new blood into his father's archaic council.

The idea had merit, and Zafir assessed it in seconds. However he was about to dismiss it for various reasons—not least of which were to do with security—but just as he opened his mouth to speak an image exploded into his head, turning his words to dust.

He immediately turned away from the younger man, for fear that something would show on his face. All he could see was *her*, lying on a bed, with her long, sinuous limbs and her treacherously hypnotic beauty, naked but for the jewel that nestled between her high, full breasts. It would glow fiery red against that perfect pale skin.

As red as his blood—which wasn't simmering now. It had boiled over.

He'd allowed the floodgates to open, and right at that moment Zafir knew there was only one way to rid himself of this ache and move on. And he *had* to move on. His country depended on it.

Zafir's mind reeled as the idea took root and embedded itself deep inside him. Was he really considering revisiting the past and the one person he'd vowed never to think or speak of again?

A spurt of rebelliousness and something much more ambiguous ignited inside him.

Why not?

This could be the perfect opportunity to sate his desires before he committed to his full responsibilities and the people of Jandor owned him completely. And there was only one woman Zafir wanted.

She owed him, he told himself grimly. She'd lied to him. She'd betrayed him by not revealing her true self, her true nature. She'd walked out of his life eighteen months ago and he hadn't had enough of her. She'd left him aching and cursing her.

The fact that he'd once considered her suitable to be in his long-term future was a reminder that was unwelcome. This time when he took her he would know exactly who she was. And he would feel nothing but lust and desire. He would have her long legs wrapped around him again and he would sink deep enough inside her to burn away this irritating lingering lust.

He turned back to Rahul, who was looking nervous again.

'Sire, it was just a—'

Zafir cut him off. 'It was a brilliant suggestion and I know exactly who will be our model.'

Rahul frowned. 'Who, Sire?'

Zafir's pulse thundered in his veins. 'Kat Winters—the American supermodel. Find out where she is. Now.'

A week later, Queens, New York

Zafir observed her from the back of his car, with the window rolled down. He couldn't quite believe his eyes—that Kat Winters was working in a busy midrange restaurant in Queens. But, yes…one of the world's arguably most beautiful women was currently wearing skinny jeans and a white T-shirt with a black apron around her small waist. Her hair was piled up in a messy knot on her head and there was a pencil stuck through it, which she was now fumbling for as she took an order.

Everything in Zafir recoiled from this very banal scenario—except it wasn't disgust he was feeling, seeing her again. It was something much hotter and more urgent. Even dressed like this and without a scrap of make-up she was exquisite. A jewel such as she could not be hidden in a place like this. What the *hell* was she doing here? And what the hell was she doing going under another name—Kaycee Smith? And how dared she refuse to even consider the offer he'd sent to her via her agent?

Her agent had sent back a terse response:

Kat Winters is no longer available for modelling assignments.
Please do not pursue this request.

No one refused Zafir. Or warned him off. Least of all an ex-lover.

He issued a curt instruction to his driver now, and his window rolled up silently as he got out of the car and stretched to his full height of six foot four. He recalled Kat in vertiginous heels, the way it had put her mouth well within kissing distance. The way her added height had aligned their bodies so perfectly. He watched her walk away from the table and grimaced when he saw she was wearing sneakers.

Not for long, he vowed as he moved forward to the door of the restaurant. Soon she would be in heels again, and soon that lush mouth would be his again. All of her would be his again.

He had no idea what she was playing at, with this meek little game of being a waitress, but he was certain that once she heard what he had to say she'd be demonstrating her gratitude that he was prepared to give her another chance to be in his life and in his bed again, even just for a few brief weeks, in the most satisfactory way.

'Kat.'

It took a second for the significance of that word to sink in. No one here called her Kat. They called her Kaycee. And then there was the voice. Impossibly deep. And the way *Kat* had been pronounced, with the flat inflection that had always made it sound exotic. And authoritative—as if her name was a command to look at him, give him her attention.

It took another second for the realisation to hit her that there was only one person who could have spoken.

With the utmost reluctance, vying with disbelief, she looked up from the countertop.

Zafir.

For a moment she simply didn't believe it. He couldn't be here. Not against this very dull backdrop of a restaurant in Queens. He inhabited five-star zones. He breathed rarefied air. He moved in circles far removed from this place. This man was royalty.

He was a King now.

And yet her agent had told her only a couple of days ago that he'd asked for her, so she should have been prepared. But she'd blocked out any possibility of this happening. And now she was sorry, because she wasn't remotely prepared to see the man she'd loved with such intensity that it had sometimes scared her.

She blinked, but he didn't disappear. He seemed to grow in stature. Had he always been so tall? So broad? But she knew he had. He was imprinted on her brain and her memory like a brand. The hard-boned aristocratic features. The deep-set dark grey eyes that stood out against his dark olive skin. The thick dark hair swept back off his high forehead. That perfect hard-muscled body without an ounce of excess fat, its power evident even under a suit and overcoat.

He was clean-shaven now, instead of with the short beard he'd worn when she'd known him, and it should have made him look somehow *less*. But it didn't. It seemed to enhance his virility in a way that was almost overwhelming.

She hadn't even realised she'd spoken his name out loud until the sensual curve of those beautifully sculpted lips curved up slightly on one side and he said, 'You remember my name, then?'

The mocking tone which implied that it was laughable she could have possibly forgotten finally broke Kat out of her dangerous reverie and shock. He *was* here. In her space. The man she'd had dreams and nightmares about meeting again now that her life had changed beyond all recognition.

In her nightmares he looked at her with disgust and horror, and to her mortification she woke up crying more often than not. Her dreams were no less humiliating—they were X-rated, and she'd wake up sweating, believing for a second that she was still whole...still his.

But she was neither of those things. Not by a long shot.

Her pulse quickened treacherously, even though his presence heralded an emotional pain she'd hoped had been relegated to the past but which she was now discovering not to be the case.

She spoke sharply. 'What are you doing here, Zafir? Didn't you get my agent's message?'

He arched a brow and Kat flushed, suddenly aware of how she'd just addressed a man before whom most people would be genuflecting. A man who had two conspicuous bodyguards dressed in black just outside the main door.

She refused to be intimidated. It was almost too much to take in, thinking of the last time she'd seen him and how upset she'd been, and then what had happened…the most catastrophic event of her life.

'I got her message and chose to ignore it,' Zafir said easily, his tone belying the curious punch to his gut when he registered Kat's obvious reluctance to see him again.

Kat folded her arms, as if that could protect her from his all too devastating charisma. Typical arrogant Zafir. He hadn't changed.

Tersely she said, 'I'm working, so unless you've come here to eat this isn't appropriate.' *It'll never be appropriate.* But she stopped herself from saying that with some desperation.

Zafir's smile faded and those unusual dark grey eyes flashed. 'You refused to engage with my offer, which I do not accept.'

'No,' Kat said, feeling the bitterness that was a residue from their last tumultuous meeting, when she'd left him. 'I can well imagine that you don't accept it, Zafir, because you're used to everyone falling over themselves to please you. But I'm afraid I feel no such compulsion.'

His eyes narrowed on her and she immediately felt threatened. She'd always felt as if he could see right through her—through the desperate façade she'd put up to try and convince people she wasn't a girl who had grown up in a trailer with a drug-addicted, mentally unstable mother. A girl who hadn't even graduated from high school.

Yet Zafir hadn't—for all that she'd thought he might. Until he'd had the evidence shoved under his nose and he'd looked at her with cold, unforgiving eyes and had judged and condemned her out of his life.

'You've changed.'

His words slammed into her like a physical blow. He

was right. She *had* changed. Utterly. And this was her worst nightmare coming to life. Meeting Zafir again. And him finding out—

He wouldn't, she assured herself now, feeling panicky. He couldn't.

'Is this gentleman looking for a table for one, Kaycee?'

Kat looked blankly at her boss for a second, but she didn't mistake the gleam of very feminine appreciation in the older woman's eyes as she ogled Zafir unashamedly.

Galvanised into action, she took the menu out of her boss's hands and said firmly, 'No, he's not. He was just looking for directions and now he knows where to go.' She looked at Zafir, and if she could have vaporised him on the spot she would have. 'Don't you, sir?'

Her boss was pulled aside at that moment by another member of staff, and Zafir just looked at Kat for a long moment, before saying silkily, 'I'll be waiting for you, *Kat*. This isn't over.'

And then he turned and walked out.

Kat really didn't want to leave the restaurant when her shift was over, because Zafir's car was still outside. As was the very conspicuous black four-by-four undoubtedly carrying his security team.

She was more than a little shocked that he was still waiting for her. Two hours later. The Zafir she'd known a year and a half ago had never waited for anyone—he'd been famously restless and impatient. Fools had suffered in his presence. He'd cut down anyone wasting his time with a glacial look from those pewter-coloured eyes.

As Kat dragged on her coat and belted it she felt a sense of fatalism settle over her. If Zafir had ignored her agent and tracked her down this far, then he wouldn't give up easily. She should know more than anyone that when he wanted something he pursued it until he got it.

After all, he'd pursued *her* until he'd got her. Until he'd dismantled every defence she'd erected to keep people from getting too close. Until she'd been prepared to give up everything for him. Until she'd been prepared to try and mould herself into what he'd wanted her to be—even though she'd known that she couldn't possibly fulfil everything he expected of her.

Her hands tightened on her belt for a moment. He'd asked her to be his Queen. Even now she felt the same mix of terror and awe at the very thought. But it hadn't taken much to persuade him of her unsuitability in the end.

She steeled herself before walking out through the door, telling herself that she was infinitely stronger now. Able to resist Zafir. He had no idea of what she'd faced since she'd seen him last...

As soon as she walked outside though, the back door of Zafir's sleek car opened and he emerged, uncoiling to his full impressive height. Kat's bravado felt very shaky all of a sudden.

He stood back and indicated with a hand for her to get in. Incensed that he might think it could be this easy, she walked over to him, mindful of her limp, even though disguising it after a long evening on her feet put pressure on her leg.

'I'm not getting into a car with you, Zafir. You've had a wasted evening. Please leave.'

She turned to walk away and she heard him say,

'Either we talk here on the sidewalk, with lots of ears about us, or you let me take you home and we talk there.'

Kat gritted her jaw and looked longingly down the street that would take her to her apartment, just a couple of blocks away. But if she walked away she could well imagine Zafir's very noticeable car moving at a snail's pace beside her. And his security team. Drawing lots of attention. As he was doing now, just by standing there, drawing lingering glances. Whispers.

A group of giggling girls finally made Kat turn around. 'Fine,' she bit out. 'But once I've listened to what you have to say you'll leave.'

Zafir's eyes gleamed in a way that made all the hard and cold parts of Kat feel dangerously soft and warm.

'By all means. If you want me to leave then, I'll leave.'

His tone once again told Kat that that was about as likely as a snowstorm in the middle of the brutally hot Jandor desert, and that only made her even more determined to resist him, hating that his visit was bringing up memories long buried. Memories of his beautiful and exotic country and how out of her depth she'd felt—both there and in their relationship. Zafir had been like the sun—brilliant, all-consuming and mesmerising, but fatal if one got too close. And she had let herself get too close. Close enough to be burnt alive once she'd discovered that the love she'd felt had been unrequited.

She'd been prepared to marry him, buoyed up by his proposal, only to discover too late that for him it had never been a romantic proposal. It had been purely because he'd deemed her 'perfect.' Her humiliation was still vivid.

She stalked past him now and got into the car, burningly aware of his gaze on her and wondering what on earth he must make of her—a shadow of her former self. The fact that she didn't seem to be repelling him irritated her intensely.

Zafir shut the door once her legs were in the car and came round and got in the other side, immediately dwarfing the expansive confines of the luxurious car. For a moment Kat felt herself sinking back into the seat, relishing the decadent luxury, but as soon as she realised what she was doing she stiffened against it. This wasn't her life any more. Never would be again.

'Kat?'

She looked at Zafir, who had a familiar expression of impatience on his face. She realised she hadn't heard what he'd said.

'Directions? For my driver?'

She swallowed, suddenly bombarded with a memory of being in the back of a very similar car with Zafir, when he'd asked his driver to put up the privacy window and drive around until he gave further instructions. Then he'd pulled Kat over to straddle his lap, pulled up her dress and—

She slammed the lid shut on that memory and leaned forward to tell the driver where to go before she lost her composure completely.

She refused to look at Zafir again, and within a couple of minutes they were pulling up outside her very modest apartment block. Kat managed to scramble inelegantly out of the car before Zafir could help her. She didn't want him to touch her—not even fleetingly. The thin threads holding her composure together might snap completely.

Her apartment was just inside the main doors of the apartment block, on the ground floor, and Kat could feel Zafir behind her. Tall, commanding. Totally incongruous.

As if to underline it she heard him say a little incredulously, 'No concierge?'

Kat would have bitten back a smile if she'd felt like smiling. 'No.'

She opened her door and went into her studio apartment. What had become a place of refuge for the past year was now anything but as she put her keys down and turned around to face her biggest threat.

Zafir closed the door behind him and Kat folded her arms. 'Well, Zafir? What is it you have to say?'

He was looking around the small space with unmistakable curiosity, and finally that dark grey gaze came to land on her. To her horror, he started to shrug off his overcoat, revealing a bespoke suit that clung lovingly to his powerful body.

When he spoke he sounded grim. 'I have plenty to say, Kat, so why don't you make us both a coffee? Because I'm not going anywhere any time soon.'

Kat stared mutinously at Zafir for a moment, and for those few seconds he was transfixed by her stunningly unusual eyes—amber from a distance, but actually green and gold from up close, surrounded by long dark lashes. They were almond-shaped, and Zafir's blood rushed south as he recalled how she'd look at him after making love, the expression in her gaze one of wonderment that had never failed to catch him like a punch to his gut.

Lies.

It had all been lies. She might have been a virgin, but she'd been no innocent. It had been an elaborate act to hide her murky past. Suddenly he felt exposed. What was he doing here?

But just then something in Kat's stance seemed to droop and she said in a resigned voice, 'Fine, I'll make coffee.'

She disappeared into a tiny galley kitchen and Zafir had to admit that he knew very well why he was here—he still wanted her. Even more so after seeing her again. But questions buzzed in his brain. He put down his overcoat on the back of a worn armchair and took in the clean but colourless furnishings of the tiny space she now called home.

He'd never been in the apartment she'd shared with three other models when he'd known her before, but it had been a loft in SoHo—a long way from here.

She emerged a couple of minutes later with two steaming cups and handed one to Zafir. He noticed that she was careful not to come too close, and it made something within him snarl and snap.

She'd taken off her coat and now wore a long-sleeved jumper over the T-shirt. Even her plain clothes couldn't hide that perfect body, though. High firm breasts. A small waist, generous hips. And legs that went on for ever...

He could still feel them, wrapped around his back, her heels digging into his buttocks as she urged him deeper, harder—

Dammit. He struggled to rein in his libido.

'Take a seat,' she said, with almost palpable reluctance.

Zafir took the opportunity to disguise his uncontrollable response, not welcoming it one bit. He put it down to his recent sexual drought.

She sat on a threadbare couch on the other side of a coffee table. Zafir took a sip of coffee, noting with some level of satisfaction that she hadn't forgotten how he liked it. Strong and black. But then he frowned, noticing something. 'Your hair is different.'

She touched a hand to the unruly knot on her head self-consciously. 'This is my natural colour.'

Zafir felt something inside him go cold when he observed that her 'natural colour' was a slightly darker brown, with enticing glints of copper. Wasn't this just more evidence of her duplicitous nature? Her hair had used to be a tawny golden colour, adding to her all-American, girl-next-door appeal, but in reality she'd made a mockery of that image.

He put down his cup. 'So, Kat, what happened? Why did you disappear off the international modelling scene and who is Kaycee Smith?'

CHAPTER TWO

ALL KAT HEARD WAS, 'Why did you disappear off the international modelling scene?' For a moment she couldn't breathe. The thought of letting exactly what had happened tumble out of her mouth and watching Zafir's reaction terrified her.

She'd come a long way in eighteen months, but some things she wasn't sure she'd ever be ready for…namely revealing to him the full reality of why she was no longer a model, or who she was now. The graceful long-legged stride she'd become famous for on catwalks all over the world was a distant memory now, never to be resurrected.

She breathed in shakily. *Answer his questions and then he'll be gone.* She couldn't imagine him wanting to hang around in these insalubrious surroundings for too long.

'What happened?' she said, in a carefully neutral voice. 'You know what happened, Zafir—after all you're the one who broke it to me that I'd been dropped from nearly every contract and that the fashion houses couldn't distance themselves fast enough from the girl who had fallen from grace.'

Kat had been blissfully unaware of the storm headed her way. She'd been packing for her new life with her fiancé—filled with trepidation, yes, but also hope that she would make him proud of her… What a naive fool she'd been.

Zafir's face darkened. 'There were *naked* pictures of you when you were seventeen years old, Kat. They spoke pretty eloquently for themselves. Not to mention the not inconsequential fact of the huge personal debt you'd been hiding from me. And the real story of your upbringing—enabling a drug-addicted mother to find her next fix.'

Kat's hands tightened on her cup as she remembered the vicious headline Zafir had thrust under her nose. It had labelled her 'a white trash gold-digger.' A man like Zafir—privileged and richer than Croesus—could never have begun to understand the challenges she'd faced growing up.

Kat felt a surge of white-hot anger but also—far more betrayingly—she felt hurt all over again. The fact that he still had this ability to affect her almost killed her. Feeling too agitated to stay sitting, she put down her cup and stood up, moving to stand behind the couch, as if that could offer some scant protection.

Zafir was sitting forward, hands locked loosely between his legs. He looked perfectly at ease, but Kat wasn't fooled by his stance. He was never more dangerous than when he gave off an air of nonchalance.

'Look,' she said, as calmly as she could, 'if you've just come here to re-enact our last meeting, then I can't see how that will serve any purpose. I really don't need to be reminded of how once my so-called perfect image was tarnished you deemed me no longer acceptable in your life. We said all we had to say that night.'

Her hands instinctively dug into the top of the couch as she remembered that cataclysmic night—stumbling out of Zafir's apartment building into the dark streets, the pain of betrayal in her heart, her tear-blurred vision and then... Nothing but blackness and more pain, the like of which she hadn't known existed.

Zafir stood up too, dislodging the sickening memory, reminding her that this was the present and apparently not much had changed.

'Did we, really? As far as I recall you said far too little

and then left. You certainly didn't apologise for misleading me the whole time we were together.'

Struggling to control herself as she remembered the awful shock of that night, Kat said, 'You saw that article and you looked at those pictures and you judged and condemned me. You weren't prepared to listen to anything I had to say in my defence.'

Kat's conscience pricked when she recalled how she'd always put off telling Zafir the unvarnished truth of her background. And as for the debt... She'd never wanted to reveal that ugliness, or the awful powerlessness she'd felt. Not to someone like Zafir, who set such an exacting standard for moral strength and integrity.

'Dammit, Kat, you told me nothing about yourself— when were you going to reveal the truth? If ever?' He shook his head before she could respond, and repeated his accusation of that night. 'You were obviously hoping that I'd marry you before the sordid details came out and then you'd be secured for life even if we divorced.'

Kat felt breathless, and nausea rose inside her. 'It wasn't like that...'

Zafir looked impossibly stern. As unforgiving as he had been that night. He changed tack, asking her again, 'Who is Kaycee Smith?'

Kat swallowed painfully, not remotely prepared for her past transgressions to be visited upon her again like this. 'Kaycee Smith is the name on my birth certificate.'

A dark brow arched over one eye. 'A pertinent detail missed by the papers?'

She refused to let Zafir do this to her again. Humiliate her. Annihilate her.

Kat tipped up her chin. 'It was about the only thing they did miss.'

Thankfully, she thought now. Otherwise she would never have been able to fade away from view as she had.

'We have nothing to say to each other, Zafir. *Nothing.* Now, get out—before I call the police and tell them you're harassing me.'

Kat moved decisively from her spot behind the sofa towards the door, powered by anger and the tumult inside her, only to be stopped in her tracks before she reached it when Zafir asked sharply, 'Why are you limping?'

Immediately the adrenalin rush faded, to be replaced with a very unwelcome sense of exposure. There was nothing to hold on to nearby and it reminded her of how vulnerable she was now.

She turned around slowly and realised that she was far too close to Zafir. Every part of her body seemed to hum with electricity. It was as if her libido had merely been waiting for his presence again, and now it was no longer dormant but very much awake and sizzling back to life.

His scent wound around her like a siren call to lean closer...to breathe in his uniquely male smell. It had always fascinated her—the mixture of earthy musk and something indescribably exotic which instantly brought her back to her first and last visit to Jahor, with its awe-inspiring palace on a hill overlooking the teeming ancient city on the edge of the ocean.

She'd felt so awed and intimidated at the prospect of becoming a Queen of that land, and yet deep within her she'd thrilled to the challenge. But when Zafir had deemed her unsuitable to be his wife she'd realised what a fool she'd been to indulge in such a fantasy. She was no Queen, and she had no right to the ache of loss that still had the power to surprise her when she wasn't vigilant.

Her head snapped up. Zafir was still frowning. She moved back, aghast that her body could betray her like this. And then she remembered what he'd asked: *Why are you limping?*

Everything inside Kat recoiled from revealing herself to Zafir. The urge to self-protect was huge. He had no idea of the extent of the devastation in her life since she'd seen him—not all of which had to do with him. It also had to do with events totally beyond him.

But she knew that giving him nothing would only pique his interest even more, so reluctantly she said, 'I was involved in a road traffic accident a while ago. I injured my leg and I was out of circulation for some time.'

Try at least a year, Kat thought to herself, and held her breath, praying he wouldn't ask for more details.

Zafir looked at her assessingly. 'Is that why you haven't returned to modelling? And is that why you're living like this? Because you still haven't cleared your debts? You're obviously recovered now though, and I can't imagine the fashion world wouldn't have renewed your contracts eventually, once the story had died down.'

Kat hid her reflexive flinch at *'you're obviously recovered now.'* But she wasn't about to explain anything—not when Zafir was clearly no more ready to hear the truth now than he had been back then. And he was right—except when the fashion houses *had* come calling again she'd been in no position to consider going back…

Kat breathed out unsteadily. She avoided answering his questions directly and said, 'I do some hand modelling, but that's about it. And the waitressing.'

Zafir came closer, standing beside the chair. His gaze was far too keen on her and incisive. She could almost hear his brain working, trying to join the dots.

Kat just wanted him gone. He'd upended her world once before and she wouldn't survive him doing it again.

'Look,' she said now, trying to hide the desperation in her voice, 'did you really come here to rake over old ground, Zafir?'

She stopped and bit her lip as a dangerous thought

occurred to her—perhaps in spite of everything he *had* come to listen to her side of the story? Even belatedly?

For a moment Kat felt something very delicate flower deep inside her, but after a moment Zafir shook his head and said curtly, 'No. Of course not. That's in the past and I've no wish to revisit it any further.'

Kat's heart thumped. Hard. Of course he hadn't come here to hear her side of things. Apparently she was as pathetically susceptible to this man as she'd ever been, and in spite of everything she'd been through that was somehow more devastating than anything else. She felt a dart of panic at the knowledge that time had done little to diminish her feelings or her attraction to him. If anything, everything felt more acute than it had before.

She forced out words through a tight jaw. 'Then if you wouldn't mind leaving? We had a past and you pretty definitively ruled out any future, so what more could there possibly be to say?'

She regretted asking the question as soon as she saw the calculating gleam come into those slate-grey eyes.

'Our future is exactly what I'm here to talk about. A different future to the one previously envisaged, yes, but I don't see why we can't leave that in the past and move on.'

Kat's insides tightened as if warding off a blow. 'I'm not interested in discussing any kind of future or *moving on* with you, Zafir.'

Zafir's jaw clenched and he had to consciously relax it. He wasn't used to anyone talking to him like this—and he couldn't remember Kat ever being so combative. But he couldn't deny that somewhere deep inside him he thrilled to it. She *had* changed, and yet she was still intriguingly familiar. Achingly familiar. His whole body hummed with frustration to be so close and yet have her hold him at arm's length and look at him as if he was an unwelcome stranger.

In truth, he hadn't expected her to be so antagonistic towards him. He knew things had ended badly before, but she was the one who had kept the truth from him, clearly in a bid to avoid risking his commitment to marry her—which was exactly what had happened. Yet she was acting as if she was the injured party!

He cursed himself. He hadn't planned on rehashing the past, but obviously it had been inevitable. But, as he'd said, he was done talking about the past now—it was time for him to lay out his plans for Kat. For *them*.

In spite of everything, and even though he knew there were a thousand reasons for him to turn and walk away from Kat and forget he'd ever seen her again, he *couldn't*. Not now. But he assured himself that he could have what he wanted and get on with his life. And he fully intended to.

'I'm not leaving until I've said what I came to say, Kat.'

Dismayed, Kat watched as Zafir illustrated his point by sitting down again. He was an immovable force, and she recognised that steely determination all too well. The last thing she wanted was for him to see how raw she felt, so she schooled her features and sat down opposite him, as if this visit wasn't tearing her apart.

She looked pointedly at her watch and then back to him, 'It's getting late and I've got work early in the morning. I'd appreciate it if you could keep this short.'

Zafir inspected the bland expression on Kat's face. For a moment he'd caught a glimpse of something much more fiery, but it was gone now. She seemed to be determined to treat him as if he was someone she hadn't been intimately acquainted with. Soon, Zafir vowed, they would be intimately acquainted again, and she'd be moaning his name in ecstasy as her release threw them both over the edge and purged him of this ache.

He forced his mind out of his fantasies with effort and said, 'Did you even listen to the proposition I sent your agent?'

Kat shook her head, a long tendril of hair dropping from the knot on top of her head to curl around her neck. Zafir wanted to undo her hair and let it fall in a luxurious curtain down her naked back, the way it had before. He gritted his jaw at the image. This was ridiculous—he could barely conduct a coherent conversation without X-rated images flooding his mind.

Calling on every ounce of control he possessed, he said, 'What I'm proposing is a modelling assignment—'

He stopped and put up his hand as soon as he saw Kat's mouth open, presumably to protest. She closed it again, her lush lips compressing into a tight line. Zafir ignored the pulse throbbing in his groin.

He tried another tack. 'You might recall me telling you once about the famed missing jewel, the Heart of Jandor, the biggest red diamond in the world?'

Kat tensed opposite him, and then he saw a flush tinge her cheeks pink as if she too was remembering that moment—lying in her bed in Jahor, her limbs sprawled over his in sated abandon as he'd told her the story of the gem. He'd had to sneak into her rooms like a teenager, even though they'd been unofficially engaged at the time. His people would have been scandalised by such liaisons.

Kat had lifted her head from his chest and said huskily, 'That's so romantic... I hope they find it some day.'

Zafir could recall how a vague feeling of dread mixed with fear had washed over him on hearing the wistful tone in Kat's voice, and how he'd felt the urge to say something, *anything*, to take the dreamy look from her eyes, to tell her that such a thing as romance had no place in his life. Duty trumped emotion. Always. There would be no room for romance when he became King and she was Queen.

But then she'd reached up and kissed him…and he couldn't remember anything else.

'I remember something…vaguely,' she said tightly now, and Zafir desisted from arguing that she clearly remembered very well.

There was a curt edge to his voice after that memory. 'They found the diamond recently, during an archaeological dig. It was a cause of much celebration and my people have seen it as a good omen for the future.'

Kat's hands were clasped in her lap. 'I'm very happy for you…and them…but I fail to see what this has to do with me.'

Zafir said carefully, 'It has everything to do with you, Kat, because I've chosen you to be the model who will wear the diamond on our worldwide diplomatic tour to promote Jandor.'

The sheer arrogance of Zafir's pronouncement rendered Kat speechless for a moment. And then she spluttered, 'But that's ridiculous. I'm working here. I have a life here. I have no intention of going anywhere with you.'

Zafir stood up, and as if she hadn't spoken he said, 'It's a very select tour. The first function is the evening after tomorrow, at the Metropolitan Museum of Art. Then we and the diamond go to London, then Paris and then back to Jandor, where it will be put on permanent display.'

Kat stood up, quivering all over with volatile emotions. 'There is no *we* in this, Zafir.'

'If it had gone according to my plan, then, yes, I agree—I would have no need of you. But my chief aide came up with the idea of showing off the diamond in an infinitely more accessible way—instead of keeping it in a sterile environment, we will display it on a beautiful woman and have her meet and greet specially selected guests with us at each function, so that they can see how the gem really glows with a life force. It will bring the gem—and Jandor—alive.'

Kat folded her arms against the terrifying thought of people clamouring around her, too close, staring at her, pawing at her to get to the stone. One of the side effects of the accident she'd been involved in was that she felt claustrophobic in certain situations where she felt trapped.

She shook her head. 'No way, Zafir. I'm not interested. And surely if this is to promote your country, then you should be using a model from Jandor.'

Kat saw the steely glint in Zafir's eyes. It meant that he'd most likely anticipated every one of her arguments and was ready to counter them.

'We don't yet have a modelling agency in Jandor, but we *do* have aspiring fashion designers who are eager to showcase some of their designs during this tour. Also, I want someone who has the poise and grace of an experienced model—and they don't come more experienced than you.'

Feeling desperate, she said, 'There are a million models just as experienced as me—if not more.' A hint of bitterness crept into her voice. 'Models who don't come with negative baggage. If I appear in public with you as Kat Winters, the press will have a field day and all those stories will get raked up again.'

Kat sent up silent thanks now that their break-up had occurred before the official public announcement of their engagement had been made.

'Yes, they might,' he conceded, 'and I've considered that. But I have an excellent PR team, who will field any of the old stories and drown them out with this new one.

Resurrecting Kat Winters to wear the most famous re-discovered gem in the world will be an irresistible story.'

Kat went cold inside as the full extent of Zafir's cool calculation sank in. Her involvement would be purely to provide an angle. Something to fire up the headlines even at the expense of negativity. Everything Zafir was outlining was literally her worst nightmare. She felt panicky. She wasn't prepared to step back into the world of Kat Winters again—not for anyone.

She shook her head. 'The answer is no, Zafir. Now, please leave. I'm tired.'

But of course Zafir didn't turn around to leave, much as Kat wished he would. Even as she felt the betraying hum of awareness that flowed like illicit nectar through her blood.

'Obviously I wouldn't expect you to do this for free, Kat. I would be willing to pay handsomely for one of the world's most sought-after and elusive models. I'm well aware of the fees you once commanded, and as your credit history shows a lack of ability to hang on to your earnings, it looks like you're not really in a position to turn down such a lucrative contract.'

He illustrated his point with a sweeping glance around her studio apartment.

Kat's hands curled into fists. *Of all the patronising—* She stopped just as she was about to blurt something out. Something that would make those far too incisive eyes narrow on her and make him start asking questions again.

It was the last thing she wanted to bring up, but she had to. Maybe it was the thing that would finally push Zafir to leave. 'Have you considered the speculation that would inevitably be sparked about *us* again?'

He waited a beat and then said, 'Yes, I have, and I see no harm in it—not when it's likely to be confined to the duration of the tour and then it'll die away again.'

There was a rough quality to Zafir's voice that sent a rush of awareness through Kat's blood—as if her body was already reacting to some secret signal. For a moment she couldn't really comprehend the way he was suddenly so watchful, but then it sank in with horrifying clarity.

'You can't seriously mean for us to—' She stopped, afraid to speak the words out loud. Afraid to make herself look a fool again. Afraid she might be right.

Afraid she might be wrong.

'Can't seriously mean for us to what, Kat?'

Zafir moved closer and she was rooted to the spot. He stopped within reaching distance, the harsh lighting of her apartment doing nothing to leach away any of his sheer gorgeousness.

'I can't seriously mean for us to be together again?'

Kat looked at him, horrified and excited in equal measure. She half shook and nodded her head.

Zafir's face suddenly took on a harsh aspect. 'That's exactly what I mean. I want you back in my bed, Kat. We have unfinished business. When you walked out—'

'You mean when you cast me aside!' Anger flooded Kat's veins again, giving her the impetus to move back out of Zafir's dangerous proximity, crossing her arms defensively over her chest.

'We're not going to rake over that ground again,' Zafir said harshly. 'Suffice it to say that our engagement might have been over—there was no way I could have presented you as my future Queen after those headlines and pictures—but our relationship didn't have to be over.'

Shock mixed with affront, and hurt poured through Kat, making her tremble. She was back in time, standing before Zafir in far more luxurious surroundings saying incredulously, 'You don't love me.'

He'd slashed a hand through the air. 'This isn't about *love*, Kat. It's never been about love. It's about mutual respect and desire and the fact that I believed—mistakenly—that you were the perfect choice to be my wife and future Queen.'

'*Perfect*...' She'd half-whispered it to herself, never hating a word as much as she had then.

Her whole life she'd been told she had to be *perfect*. To win the next competition. To get the commercial over the other pretty girl. To get enough money to save her mother... Except she'd failed—miserably.

She'd looked at Zafir and said in a hollow voice, 'Well, I'm not perfect, Zafir. Far from it.'

And she'd walked out, leaving her engagement ring on the hall table. And now she was glad—because clearly he would have demoted her from the position of future wife, but kept her in his life as his mistress.

And she'd never been further from perfect than she was right now.

'Get out, Zafir, this conversation is over.'

But her words bounced off him as if an invisible shield protected him.

'Think about what you're turning down, Kat. A chance to restart your life and return to where you belong. Have you thought about what you'd be turning down?'

He mentioned a sum of money and it was literally life-changing. Kat felt her blood drain south.

He reached into an inside pocket and took out a card, holding it out to her. She unlocked her arms from her chest and took it reluctantly.

'That's my private number. I'll be staying at my penthouse apartment. I'll give you till tomorrow morning, Kat. If I don't hear from you I *will* find someone else and you will never hear from me again.'

She looked at him and marvelled that she'd once believed that he loved her because he'd asked her to marry him. Because she'd always had a romantic notion that that was what people did when they loved someone, in spite of being brought up as the only child of a single parent with no clue as to her father's whereabouts.

But Zafir's motives had been so much more strategic than that. She'd been scrutinised and deemed suitable. *Perfect.* And now he was asking her to step back into a world that had chewed her up and spat her out. Not only that, he was asking her to lay herself bare to him again, to let him carve out the last remaining part of her heart that still functioned and let him crush it until there was nothing left.

Kat was stronger now than she'd ever been, considering the trials she'd faced in the past eighteen months, but she was still only human and she wasn't strong enough for this. No matter how much money he was offering.

Without taking her eyes off Zafir's, as if some small, treacherous part of her wanted to commit them to her memory, she held up the card and ripped it in half, letting the pieces fall to the floor.

'Goodbye, Zafir.'

His eyes flashed and his jaw clenched. Kat could feel the waves of energy flowing like electricity between them, but after a tense moment he just stepped back and said, 'As you wish. Goodbye, Kat.'

But to Kat's dismay, when Zafir finally turned and walked out, picking up his overcoat as he did so, and when the door had shut behind him, the last thing she felt was triumph.

She found her feet moving towards the door instinctively, as if to rush after him and beg him not to go. She stopped in her tracks, shocked at the profound sense of loss that pervaded her whole body, and she wrapped her arms around herself as if that could hold back all the turmoil she was feeling.

Zafir had devastated her once before. She couldn't let it happen again.

So she stayed resolutely where she was, and after she'd heard the sound of his vehicles leaving from outside the apartment she breathed in shakily and sank down onto the couch behind her.

She looked around her, as if seeing the space for the first time again. She'd grown used to the bare furnishings and the sparse décor. It was all she'd been able to afford after the accident and her lengthy rehabilitation, even though the largest part of her debt had finally been gone.

And the reason it had been gone was because once those pictures of Kat had gone public, her blackmailer—the photographer who had taken them in the first place—had had no further means with which to blackmail her. After all, everything he'd always threatened her with had come true—her career had imploded in spectacular style.

Perversely, Kat had been grateful to whoever had found and leaked the pictures, because they had freed her from a malignant threat she'd had no idea how to deal with.

On numerous occasions she'd wanted to confide in Zafir, but then she'd feel too intimidated, or too scared of his reaction. How could a man like him, who had grown up in such a rarefied world, possibly understand why she would do such a thing? The thought of revealing all that ugly poison had pulled her back from the brink each time.

And in the end hadn't she been vindicated? She'd never forget the look of disgust and horror on his face as he'd confronted her with her past.

Kat stood up again, restless, as Zafir's visit sank in properly. She told herself that it was his arrogance that still left her breathless, but really it was the knowledge that he still wanted her, and the even more shattering knowledge that she still wanted him. The core of her body felt hot and achy, and her blood felt thick and heavy in her veins.

Damn him.

She paced back and forth, and as she did so her eye snagged on something in the corner of the room and she stopped. Zafir hadn't noticed them. Crutches and a folded-up wheelchair. She hadn't needed the wheelchair for some time now, but she would never *not* need one to hand. And she'd always need the crutches.

To Kat's shame, she knew that *this* was as much of a reason as any other as to why she'd all but pushed Zafir out through the door. Because she couldn't bear for him to know what had happened to her. Because she couldn't bear to think about the fact that, even if she *was* to ever be with Zafir again, he would not want to be with her.

Because she was irrevocably altered.

Kat picked up the crutches and went into her tiny bedroom. She took off her sneakers, undid her jeans and pulled them off, then stood in front of her mirror, inspecting herself critically.

At first glance Zafir might not notice anything different about Kat—after all she stood on two legs, and was the same height she'd always been, with the same straight back. But then she imagined his gaze travelling down and stopping on her left leg. Specifically on the prosthetic limb that now made up her lower left leg, with its mechanical ankle and fake foot.

Even now Kat couldn't recall anything about the accident itself on that fateful night. She only knew that one minute she'd been crossing the street and the next she'd been waking up, a day later, in a hospital, with a doctor informing her that they'd had to amputate below the knee to save her leg—which was kind of ironic, considering half of it was now gone.

She'd had flashbacks however, since then, of regaining consciousness and realising that her foot was trapped under the heaviest weight. People had crowded around her but she hadn't been able to move or speak. And then she'd slipped back into darkness.

That was why she got claustrophobic now.

Sometimes people gave her a second glance, but they soon dismissed her when they saw her slightly limping gait and figured this woman with darker hair and no make-up couldn't possibly be *the* Kat Winters.

A ball of emotion lodged itself in Kat's chest, and before she could stop them hot tears blurred her vision. But she dashed them away angrily as she sat down on her bed and set about removing her prosthetic limb with an efficiency born of habit.

It had been a long time since she'd indulged in self-pity. That had been in the dark early days, when she'd fallen down in many graceless heaps while trying to get to the bathroom during the night, when she'd hurled her crutches across the room in a rising tide of fury at the hand she'd been dealt. Or when she'd locked herself away for long days, sunk in such a black depression that she'd thought she might never emerge into daylight again.

It was her oldest friend, Julie, who was also her agent, who had finally saved her. And the local rehabilitation centre. It was there that she'd learnt how to deal with her new reality and had been able to start putting things into perspective after meeting a man who had lost both his legs in a war, and a woman who had lost an arm, and an endlessly cheerful little girl who'd lost her limbs after meningitis… They, and many more, had humbled her, and reminded her that she was one of the luckier ones.

And gradually she'd clawed her way out of the mire to a place of acceptance, where this was her new reality and she just had to get on with it. And she *had* been getting on with it, perfectly well, until a Zafir-shaped storm had blown everything up again.

Kat could be honest enough with herself to acknowledge that—as much as the accident and its consequences had made her feel as if her life had shrunk—she'd been living in a kind of limbo, taking one day at a time. The accident had been so catastrophic that she'd been able to block out that last night with Zafir for a long time, but recently it had been creeping back, as if now she was ready to deal with it...

Maybe he was right, whispered a coaxing voice. *Maybe you do have unfinished business. Perhaps if you took on the assignment you could lay more than one ghost to rest.*

The ghost of the relationship she'd *thought* she had with Zafir, but which had never really existed...only in her romantic fantasies.

The ghost of the Kat Winters she'd been before—in awe and intimidated by nearly everything and everyone around her in spite of her high-flying career, and by none more so than Sheikh Zafir Ibn Hafiz Al-Noury. The ghost of her mother's death and the constant feeling of failure Kat had grown up with when she hadn't been able to save a mother who hadn't wanted to be saved.

The thought lodged in Kat's head, and as much as she wanted to dismiss it out of hand she was afraid that she couldn't go back to fooling herself that Zafir was firmly in her past. She'd been too scared to really look at the repercussions of what had happened between them, but seeing him again this evening had roused more than one dormant part of her.

Not least of which was the reawakening of her sexual awareness. It was terrifying. The prospect of intimacy and what it would mean now was something she'd found easy to bury deep inside her since the accident. If she'd thought about it at all, she'd imagined that it would be with someone gentle, kind…patient.

Zafir was a force of nature—above such benign human virtues. He didn't have to deal with imperfection. He walked amongst the brightest, the best, the most beautiful. He was one of them.

Panic skittered up Kat's spine. There was no way she felt ready to trust Zafir on an intimate level again with her *new* self.

Resolutely shutting her mind to that scenario, she thought again of that fateful night and their fight.

Her conscience pricked when she remembered rushing out of his apartment—had she been too hasty? But once she'd known that he didn't love her, the last thing she'd wanted to do was try to defend herself to someone who had only ever seen her as some kind of a commodity.

That's how her mother had seen her—as a means to make money, capitalising on her daughter's beauty. Zafir had been no different—he'd all but admitted he'd only proposed because she'd fitted into his life on a superficial level and nothing more. It had driven home to Kat how much she hungered to be loved for her whole self.

But she had the sinking feeling that her secret wounds would remain raw until she confronted Zafir properly and forced him to listen to her side of the story behind those lurid headlines.

Not that she wanted anything more than that… The prospect of *more* made panic surge again even as her blood grew hot.

She would deny that her attraction to him was as strong as ever with every breath in her body—she had no intention of ever letting Zafir see her like this. She looked down at her residual limb and ran a hand over it almost protectively.

Yet even as she entertained the possibility of acqui-

escing to his demand—purely on a professional basis—
she balked at the thought. The prospect of going back
into that world and being scrutinised terrified her. And
doing it all with Zafir by her side? Scrambling her brain
to pieces? Making all the cold parts of her melt again
after she'd spent so much time rebuilding her defences?

No way. She couldn't. She wasn't strong enough yet.

At that moment Kat caught sight of her reflection in
the mirror as she sat on the bed. Her eyes were huge. She
looked panicked and pale... Something inside her resisted that. She sat up straight and took in the full reality
of who she was now. A damaged woman, yes, and less
whole than she'd once been, but actually in many ways
more whole than she'd ever been.

She'd always known on some level that she wasn't prepared to hide away as Kaycee Smith for ever, and Julie
had been putting more and more pressure on her to come
out of her protective cocoon, to let herself be seen again.

And now Zafir was asking her to take on a modelling assignment. That was all. *No, it's not*, whispered a
snide voice, and Kat's heart thumped in response. Zafir
had wanted perfection before, and he'd rejected her because she'd fallen from grace. She would never give him
a chance to do that to her again.

She thought of the sum of money he'd mentioned and
realised with a churning gut that it would allow her to pay
Julie back. Her friend had helped support Kat through
not only the first six months of her rehabilitation, but
since then too, because Kat had only had the most basic
of insurance. But also—and maybe more important—
she realised that she would be able to help the rehabilitation centre that had been so instrumental in her recovery.

The St Patrick's Medical Centre for Traumatic Inju-
ries was currently facing the prospect of closure due to
lack of funds and resources. Kat would be in a position to

give them enough money to avoid imminent closure until they could get back on their feet and raise more funds for their long-term future.

If she accepted Zafir's job offer.

Her heart sped up with a mixture of terror and illicit excitement—if she said yes, then she could use it as an exercise to prove to herself just how ill-suited she and Zafir had always been, in spite of the insane chemistry between them. Never more evident than now. She was no longer a wide-eyed virgin being initiated into a world that had moved at a terrifying pace—too fast for her to shout, *'Stop!'* and get off.

She was strong enough to take on Zafir and walk away with her head high.

Are you really, though?

Kat assured herself that, yes, she was.

This would be purely a professional transaction. Zafir would never touch her emotions again—or her body. He was the kind of man who relished the conquest, who relished making a woman acquiesce to him of her own volition, and she had no intention of acquiescing to an affair.

The walls Kat had had to build just to survive since the accident were impenetrable. He wouldn't break through. She could do this.

She picked up her mobile from the table near the bed before she lost her nerve, focusing on anything but the terror she felt at the thought of what she was about to do. And how it would affect her life.

This wasn't just about her. Not when she now knew she could put that money to good use. Vital use.

Zafir had made it clear that he would walk away, and if Kat knew anything about him it was that he meant what he said. He was a proud man. He wouldn't ask again and he certainly wouldn't beg.

As Kat dialled her friend's number and waited for her

to answer, she caught sight of her reflection in the mirror again. She scowled at her flushed face and the too-bright eyes that whispered that her decision had a lot less to do with altruism and more to do with something much darker and far more ambiguous deep inside her.

And then Julie answered and Kat had a split second to decide whether to take a step into a dangerous future or remain safe in the past.

CHAPTER THREE

ZAFIR STOOD AT the window of his penthouse study and looked out over Manhattan, sparkling under the autumn sun, with Central Park in the distance. He was trying not to acknowledge the sense of triumph and satisfaction rushing through his blood, but it was hard.

Along with it, though, had come something far more contradictory—a kind of disappointment—and Zafir realised that it was because when he'd walked away from Kat last night she'd seemed so resolute. And, as much as it had irritated him intensely, he'd admired it on some level. It was rare to find anyone going against him in anything—especially since he'd become King.

He recalled getting into his car last night and how stunned he'd been that she'd turned him down. And then how he'd had to physically restrain himself from instructing his driver to turn around so that he could go back to Kat's apartment and shatter that cooler than cool reception by reminding her in a very explicit way of just how good it had been between them. How good it could be again.

And yet before 8:00 a.m. this morning his personal phone had rung and it had been her agent, confirming that Kat had decided to take on the assignment after all.

At this very moment she was with her agent and his legal advisors, signing the contract, and then she was due to spend the rest of the day and tomorrow in preparation for the tour with a team of stylists. Rahul would go through the itinerary with her and make sure her passport and travel documents were in order for when they left the United States.

So her cold stonewalling and reluctance last night had been an act. Much like the act she'd fooled everyone with when he'd first met her, projecting a false persona of someone who was honest and hard-working, making the most of the opportunities presented to her.

She'd been honest, at least, about coming from a poor background—which in Zafir's eyes had only made her more commendable. She'd epitomised the American dream of grit and ambition and achieving success no matter what your circumstances were.

But in actual fact her story had been a lot darker and murkier. She'd had a huge personal debt she'd never revealed—in spite of commanding eye-wateringly high fees as one of the most in-demand models of her time. She'd had a drug-addicted mother, no father to speak of, and barely any education. Not to mention the coup de grâce—those provocative pictures taken when she was only seventeen years old, apparently in a bid to make money so her mother could score her next fix.

Even now when Zafir thought of those explicit pictures he felt his vision cloud over with a red mist and his hands curl to fists in his pockets. Kat had been so young, and yet she'd looked at the camera almost defiantly. The rage he'd felt towards the person behind the camera had scared him with its intensity. But what he'd felt towards Kat had been much more complicated—anger, disappointment. Protectiveness. *Betrayal.*

When he'd confronted her with the headlines due to hit the news stands within hours, he'd wanted to hear her say that she'd been an unwilling victim, so that he could apportion blame to someone else and not her... But she'd agreed with him that she was not perfect. That she was flawed. And then she'd walked out of his apartment and disappeared, leaving him with a futile anger that had corroded his insides as he'd gone over it in his head again and again, trying to make sense of how he could have been so naive...

It had made him doubt if she'd even been a virgin, or if that had been part of an elaborate ruse to attract his jaded interest. Certainly her innocence had shocked him at the time when she'd admitted it; he'd believed virgins in their twenties to be as mythical as unicorns, and it had dissolved some of Zafir's very cynical defences.

And yet in spite of that history he was bringing her back into his world. *Because he had to have her.* Zafir's jaw clenched. He did not like being at the mercy of desires he couldn't control. Maybe it had something to do with the fact that he'd been her first lover, making his connection to her feel somehow more primal...

But, he reasoned to himself, now he knew all Kat's secrets. Now he knew that she was suitable only to sate this fever burning in his body. He would never put her on a pedestal again, or imagine for a second that she could be the woman who would stand alongside him in front of his people.

Kat took in her reflection in the floor-length mirror. At that moment she was almost glad that Julie had had to leave her with the team of stylists and hair and make-up artists and go back to work. She needed to be alone right now.

She was dressed from head to toe in a black velvet sleeveless haute couture gown with a deep vee that ran almost down to her navel, exposing more skin than she had in years. Her hair was pulled back in a rough chignon. The heavy make-up felt strange on her face after not wearing any for so long. And she was wearing heels— albeit only two-inch heels.

Her critical gaze travelled down her body and she lifted up the bottom of the dress. Her breath caught. To the untrained eye her legs looked absolutely normal. As they'd always looked.

In the place of her habitual prosthetic limb was the cosmetic one that Julie had insisted on Kat being fitted for some months ago. It had been specially made for her in a factory in the UK, in a bid to show Kat that perhaps embarking on more than hand modelling was possible, but this was the first time she'd put it to use. And luckily the fit was still fine.

Kat looked down. It was remarkable. Her toenails were painted. She could even see veins. No one would notice a thing. A bubble of emotion rose up from her chest and she looked up again, letting the dress fall back, blinking her eyes rapidly to get rid of the sudden and mortifying onset of tears.

She was slightly ashamed of how overcome she felt to see herself like this, when she'd never expected to see herself like this again. When she'd thought she'd closed the door firmly on her old life. When she'd told herself that she'd never *really* felt a part of that world.

And yet here she was, feeling such a mix of emotions that it only proved to her that she was more tied to her old life than she'd realised.

A sharp rap sounded on the door to the bedroom in the lavish suite where she'd been changing into count-less outfits and she called out hurriedly, 'Just a second.'

No doubt the stylists were eager to see the dress on her, as it was the one she'd wear on the first night of the tour, chosen for its clean lines so that the diamond would be shown to its best advantage.

She composed herself and held the dress to her chest where it was still a little loose. As she opened the door she said, 'The fit is fine. I just need to be zipped—'

The words died on her tongue and she had to look up and up again at the man filling the doorway. *Zafir.* She hadn't seen him when they'd arrived earlier to sign the contract, and she'd felt jittery with nerves, waiting for him to appear at any moment. When he hadn't, she'd almost fooled herself into thinking that this assignment was not at his behest.

But it was. And here he was, wearing a shirt and dark trousers, his top button open and sleeves rolled up. She guessed that he'd just come from his office. He always had been a workaholic.

He was as leanly muscled as she remembered, the power in his body evident in a provocatively subtle way that was mesmerising and made her think of how he'd looked in his traditional Jandori robes—like a fierce warrior.

His voice broke her out of her embarrassing trance. 'You'd like me to zip you up?'

Anyone but you.

Kat clutched the dress to her breasts even more tightly, suddenly feeling as shy as the virgin she'd once been, in front of him.

She tried to look past him. 'I can ask one of the stylists…' Then she realised how quiet it was. 'Where is everyone?'

'I sent them away for the evening.' Zafir looked at his watch. 'It's 4:30 p.m. They've been working all day and so have you.'

Kat looked at him a little stupidly. She hadn't even realised how late it had got.

He lifted his hands. 'The dress? I'd like to see how it looks with the diamond.'

Kat balked. 'You have it with you now?'

Zafir nodded.

With the utmost reluctance Kat moved closer and turned around, presenting her bare back to him. She'd never before realised how vulnerable it felt—exposing the most defenceless part of your body to someone you didn't trust.

Yet even as she told herself that she didn't trust him she had to suppress the betraying shiver of anticipation that ran through her body as she waited for Zafir to pull up the zip. It didn't help when countless memories bombarded her of similar moments, when he had pressed close behind her and moved his hands around and under her dress to cup her breasts, pressing a hot kiss to her neck.

She hadn't felt vulnerable or defenceless then. Far from it.

She'd trusted him.

Her nerves were jangling painfully when she finally felt his hands on the zip, just above her buttocks, and then its far too slow ascent up her back, pulling the dress tighter around her torso, so that her breasts were pushed together under the discreet boning, creating a voluptuous cleavage. Something that wouldn't have bothered her too much in the past, but which felt positively indecent now.

When the zip was up she quickly turned around and moved out of touching distance. Zafir's eyes were a dark grey. To her relief he moved back and stood aside so she could walk out of the bedroom and into the suite. The unsteadiness of her legs had nothing to do with her prosthetic limb.

Kat stopped in her tracks, though, when a young woman dressed in a sober black suit, with her dark hair pulled back, stepped out of the shadows to stand beside the table where a large black box sat.

She'd thought they were alone, but they weren't. Perversely, that didn't seem to be of any comfort.

Zafir walked over to the table with his innately masculine grace, saying as he did so, 'I'd like you to meet Noor Qureshi. She's going to be your personal bodyguard for the duration of the tour while you wear the diamond.'

Kat put out her hand, slightly in awe of the female bodyguard. 'It's nice to meet you.'

They shook hands, but Zafir was drawing Kat's attention to the box, where he had his hand on the open lid. Kat came forward as Zafir said something to Noor, and the woman nodded before slipping discreetly out of the main suite door, presumably to wait outside.

Kat barely noticed. She fancied she could almost see the red-hued glow before she saw the actual diamond, and when she stepped close enough to see the stone resting against the black silk she gasped.

It was literally breathtaking. A stone about the size of a golf ball, in a heart shape. It seemed to glow and emit some kind of luminosity. Kat could imagine how it must have appeared when it was first discovered, deep in the mines, even in its rough state.

Zafir lifted it out and Kat saw that the gem sat in a thick collar-style platinum setting, and that the platinum was inscribed with what looked like Arabic script. The diamond dropped from the collar, stark and hypnotic.

Zafir held the necklace up, clearly indicating that he wanted to put it on Kat, and once again she stood in front of him, and shivered slightly as his arms came around her and the red diamond necklace appeared in her eye-line. She could feel him behind her, the heat and strength of his body.

It was one of the things that had drawn her to him like a helpless moth to a bright burning flame. His very masculinity. And it had surprised her, because ever since she'd been tiny she'd been aware of men and their strength, and how they could use it against a woman, after witnessing her mother bringing home one abusive male after another.

But Zafir was the first physically powerful man who had connected with Kat on another level and she hadn't instinctively shied away from him. To the contrary. And now she was feeling that same pull—as if her body was a magnet, aligned only to his and no one else's.

She closed her eyes for a second, as if that would help fight his pull, and then she felt the weight of the stone land on her upper chest. It was warm, not cold, and she instinctively reached up to touch it, feeling the pointed end. The metal of the collar was cool where it touched her skin.

Zafir's fingers brushed the back of her neck as he closed the clasp and then they were gone, and the necklace felt heavy around Kat's neck. He came and stood in front of her, looking at the stone and then at her, critically.

'Move back,' he commanded.

Kat felt an urge to resist his autocratic demand, but she did as he asked, taking a step back.

This is just a job and he's your employer, she repeated to herself like a mantra.

Those impenetrable grey eyes raked her up and down. He walked around her, and even though she'd endured years of people inspecting her like a brood mare, she felt restless under Zafir's intense gaze. Self-conscious. The top of the liner which sat between her leg and the prosthesis suddenly felt itchy, and she had to stop herself from reaching down to touch it.

Zafir came and stood in front of her again, that gaze boring into her, making her skin heat up.

'Stunning,' he pronounced. 'You're per—'

'Don't say that word!' Kat interrupted in a rush, immediately regretting it when Zafir's eyes narrowed on her.

Of course Zafir ignored her. '*Perfect?* Well, you are.'

Kat felt very aware of her leg, and the discomfort of getting used to the new prosthesis. She felt like a fraud, and longed to pull the necklace off. The weight of it was oppressive now, and a panicky sensation was rising.

She couldn't do this.

She turned around and bent her head forward, saying tightly, 'Can you take it off, please?'

There was no movement for a second, but then Zafir's hands were at the back of her neck. She caught the diamond in her hands when the clasp was undone and turned around, holding it out to Zafir.

He was too close. Kat held up the necklace, silently begging Zafir to take it and put some space between them. Finally he did, and stepped aside to put it back safely in the box.

Kat immediately walked over to a window, needing the illusion of air at least. She put her hand to her throat and felt for a moment as if she wouldn't be surprised to see that the necklace had left some kind of a mark.

Like the mark Zafir left on you? Inside where no one can see?

The panic rose. Kat turned around and looked at Zafir, who was shutting the box again but watching her. So far they'd exchanged only a handful of words, but the silent communication between them was almost deafening. It was too much.

'I'm sorry,' she blurted out. 'I don't think I can do this after all.'

Zafir put his hands in his pockets, unperturbed by her outburst. 'You're a professional model. This is probably one of the easiest jobs you've ever been asked to do—walk amongst a crowd for a few hours over a handful of evenings.'

It was so much more than that.

Zafir's easy dismissal made Kat see red. 'I'm not a model any more, Zafir. I haven't done this in—' She stopped short of saying exactly how long and amended it to, 'Months.'

'I'm sure it's just like riding a bike,' he drawled infuriatingly.

Kat had to force oxygen to her brain by taking a big deep breath. Zafir had no idea what he was really asking of her, and she had no intention of revealing all to the man who had so casually stepped on her heart.

Thank God, she thought now, *I never actually told him I loved him.*

'Anyway,' he said, prowling closer to where she stood in fight-or-flight mode, 'it's too late. You've signed the contract and, as per your request, a sizeable sum of upfront money has been already wired to your nominated account. No doubt to fill the black hole your debt created. Unless, of course,' he added silkily, 'you want to give the money back?'

Kat sagged. For a moment she'd forgotten. The money wasn't to fill a debt hole—it was going straight to the rehabilitation clinic, whom she'd already informed about their unexpected windfall, much to their delight and relief. And to Julie, to reimburse her for what she'd paid for the cosmetic limb. Kat had insisted, in spite of Julie's protests, wanting to feel as if she was at least starting to make her own way again.

So, yes, it *was* too late.

Straightening her shoulders, she called upon the inner strength she'd never known she possessed until recently and said, 'No, I'm not giving the money back and, yes, I've agreed to the job so I'll keep my word. I'm going to change into my own clothes now, and then I'd like to go home.'

Zafir frowned. 'I've booked this suite for you for tonight and tomorrow night—until we leave for Europe.'

Kat shook her head firmly. 'No. I'm going back to my apartment tonight. There are still some things I need to pack, and I've got one last shift at the restaurant this evening.'

Zafir's eyes flashed. 'You are *not* working in that restaurant another minute. And my driver can wait for you and bring you back here when you're ready.'

This was what Zafir had done before, and she'd been too awed to say no.

'You're moving in with me, I want you in my bed when I wake up in the morning, Kat.'

A summons she'd been only too happy to comply with.

'Please do not tell me what I can and can't do, Zafir. I'm not officially working for you until tomorrow, when I will be here at the appropriate time to start preparing for the first function.'

She tore her gaze away from his and walked with as much grace as she could muster to the bedroom, shutting the door firmly behind her and resting against it for a moment.

Her heart was pounding. Underneath all Zafir's arrogance she could feel his compelling pull, asking her for so much more. It had been explicit in the way he'd looked at her wearing the diamond. As if he wanted to devour her. No wonder she'd panicked for a moment.

Was that why he'd dismissed all his staff? Had he really believed that that's all it would take? Seeing him, being enticed with the rarest jewel in the world, she'd fall back into his bed—except this time without any illusion that he wanted more than a finite affair.

This time there would be no marriage proposal to kick the earth from under her legs, making her feel for the first time in her life as if she truly was worth something to someone… She'd believed that Zafir had really wanted her and loved her for herself, and not just for the aesthetically pleasing sum of her parts.

Kat struggled with the zip on the dress, but she was damned if she was going to emit so much as a squeak to let Zafir know she might need help. Eventually she managed to get it down, after some serious body contortions, and stripped off to get back into her own clothes.

She caught a glimpse of herself in a mirror and stopped for a moment, reminded of the fact that at first glance no one would see anything amiss but that on closer inspection they'd see her leg, and frown, and think, *Wait a second...*

Kat went cold all over as she contemplated Zafir ever seeing her like this—naked and exposed, her wounds visible.

Suddenly conscious that he was mere feet away, and separated from her only by a door, Kat stopped dithering and got dressed in her own clothes again, before going into the bathroom to wash off the make-up.

When her face was clean she straightened up and looked at herself. This was her now. Unadorned. She was naturally pale, and her hair tumbled around her shoulders, messy after she'd brushed it so roughly and darker in hue than she'd had it before, with natural copper highlights. She could see the faint lines wrought on her face already—the marks of her experience. Marks of her new strength, which she'd never needed more than now.

Zafir only wanted her when she appeared as she just had—when she was Kat the Supermodel.

As long as she could keep him at arm's length and show him that she wasn't the same woman, he'd soon lose interest and move on to someone far easier and more docile. As she'd once been. And when Zafir did lose interest and move on she'd finally be able to let go of the ties that still bound her to him like a spider's resilient silken threads, because his behaviour would confirm for her that all he'd ever been interested in was the illusion of the perfect woman.

A small voice whispered to Kat that all she had to do was take off her jeans, walk out of the bedroom and show

Zafir exactly who she was. He'd never want anything to do with her when he saw that she wasn't everything she'd once been. He could handle the potentially negative PR fallout, but he surely wouldn't want to seduce an ex-lover who was now an amputee.

So why don't you just do it, then? crowed that inner voice. *Go on—walk out of here and show him who you are now.*

Kat's hands gripped the sink hard. Her gut churned. If she did, it would all be over. She'd have to give the money back. She'd have to go to the rehab centre and apologise for getting their hopes up.

She took a deep breath, forcing herself to be calm. She was overreacting. Panicking. She didn't owe Zafir anything. She didn't owe him any explanations. He would lose interest once he realised that Kat would resist him no matter what. A man like Zafir didn't want a strong, opinionated woman. He wanted someone who wouldn't challenge him.

She could do this. She *would* do this. And when she walked away from Zafir after this was over, it would be for good.

Zafir handed over the diamond in its box to Noor and her security team. When he'd closed the door behind them he paced up and down restlessly.

Kat was seriously perplexing him. The fact that she'd choose going back to her rundown neighbourhood over sleeping in luxury was simply inexplicable. Not to mention wanting to fulfil one last shift at that excuse for a restaurant.

Once he'd known that she'd acquiesced to the job, he'd assumed it meant that she was also agreeing to share his bed again. After all, he'd made it explicitly clear that he wanted her. And he knew she still wanted him—it throbbed in the air between them like live electricity.

He scowled at the closed bedroom door. So what was she up to? The sum of money she'd already received was enough for her to seriously upgrade her life. And yet just now, when he'd reminded her that it was too late for her to walk away, it had almost seemed as if she was reluctantly agreeing to commit to something burdensome—not embarking on a journey to one of the easiest paydays she'd ever had in her life.

He had to admit to a niggle of doubt that it was the money she was really interested in, even though he'd long ago come to the conclusion that Kat had refrained from telling him about her massive debt because she'd figured that once they were married he'd have no choice but to clear it for her.

He'd lavished her with gifts, yes, but she'd never seemed as enthralled by them as other women had. She'd get embarrassed, or try to convince him she didn't need whatever trinket he'd given her. When he'd given her underwear she'd blushed—and just thinking of that now made his body hard.

He went over to the window to look out broodingly. In the aftermath of their last bitter argument he'd summed their relationship up as nothing more than an elaborate act. Kat had been canny enough to try and secure a permanent position in his life before revealing the skeletons in her closet. In a way, with her coming from the background she had, he couldn't really blame her for developing such survival instincts...

He heard the bedroom door open and turned around to see her emerging, dressed down in a plaid shirt and faded jeans. Sneakers. Her hair was loose, the luxuriant waves tumbling around her shoulders, and his blood leapt. He realised that he preferred it like this—darker. It made her beauty somehow more dramatic, mature.

She was pulling a wheelie suitcase behind her and she caught his look and said defensively, 'I'm not staying. This is full of the accessories I told the stylists I'd bring from home.'

The uncomfortable assertion that she really wasn't playing hard to get made Zafir's skin prickle. He walked across the room and saw how she tensed visibly, her hand clutching the handle of the suitcase. It made something deep inside him roar like an animal. He knew this woman intimately. He'd been her first lover...the first man to bring her to orgasm...

A sense of extreme exposure that he wanted her so much—so much that he'd brought her back into his life and precipitated all these questions—propelled Zafir forward until he had both Kat's arms in his hands. He barely noticed the suitcase fall to the side because she was no longer holding it.

She was looking up at him, two spots of pink in her cheeks, her eyes huge and wary. Gold and green.

Something dark rose up inside him and he couldn't hold it back.

'How many have there been, Kat? How many men have you lain down for and fooled into believing that you're just a regular woman? Did they know who they were sleeping with? That the woman with her legs wrapped around their hips was really—'

'*Stop it.*'

Kat was as rigid as a board under his hands. 'How dare you? Who I have or haven't slept with is none of your business. I don't want the sordid details of your lovers, who I've no doubt you made sure met your exacting standards of moral integrity.'

Zafir's pulse thundered as Kat's sweetly evocative

scent tantalised him. The only woman he wanted was glaring at him and shooting gold sparks from her eyes.

He forced out through the hunger raging in his blood, 'Quite frankly, I'm a lot less fixated on moral integrity this time around.'

A shiver ran through Kat's body and Zafir felt it.

'There is no *this time*. This is just a job for me—that's all. I'm not interested in anything else.'

Everything in Zafir rejected that, and he lifted one hand to cup Kat's delicate jawline. Just the silken brush of her hair against the back of his hand had his body hardening all over again.

'Why are you denying this, Kat? Whatever is between us, it's mutual. And it's even stronger than before.'

She shook her head. 'It's not mutual.'

'Liar,' Zafir breathed, as every part of his body went on fire with an urgent and undeniable desire to prove Kat wrong. And along with that desire he felt something much more dangerous: *emotion*.

To block it out, deny it, Zafir cupped his hand behind Kat's neck and drew her to him until he could feel the length of her willowy body pressed against his.

Her hands came up between them to his chest. The wariness and anger was gone, to be replaced by something far more like panic. And why would she be panicky unless he was about to prove her very wrong?

'Zafir, what are you doing?'

His blood was pounding. 'I'm proving that once a liar, always a liar…'

And then he bent his head and covered Kat's mouth with his, and for the first time in eighteen months the roaring savage heat inside him was momentarily soothed.

Under the intense carnal satisfaction to be tasting her again was that emotion and a kind of relief. As if he'd found his way back to some place he'd been looking for.

It was so profound and overwhelming that for long seconds Zafir didn't even deepen the kiss—he just relished the sensation of Kat's soft, lush mouth under his.

And then she made a soft mewling sound and Zafir fell over the brink of his control and hauled Kat even closer, kissing her deep enough to see stars.

Time stood still. The earth might have stopped rotating. All Zafir was aware of was the feel of Kat's curves against his body, the stiffness of his arousal cushioned against her soft belly…and the desire to stop at nothing until he was deeply embedded between her legs and she was crying out his name as her climax sent them both into orbit.

It took a second for Zafir to realise that Kat had torn her mouth away and was pushing against his chest, breathing heavily enough for him to feel her breasts move against him. He almost growled. He felt feral.

She pushed hard and dislodged Zafir's arms, stumbling slightly as she stepped back. Her eyes were molten, her mouth was swollen and her cheeks were flushed, and the only thing keeping Zafir from reaching for her again was the knowledge that he'd already exposed himself.

'I do not want this, Zafir. I won't deny that the attraction between us is still there—'

Zafir snorted at the understatement and Kat's eyes turned steely.

'But I am not going there with you again. We had our moment and it's over. And unless you can promise to keep things between us on a professional footing I'll have no choice but to back out of our agreement and return the money you've already paid me. Don't think I won't, Zafir. The money is important to me, but not as important as not making the same mistake twice.'

No one spoke to Zafir like this. No one considered him a mistake.

But then an echo of his brother's voice whispered from the past, angry...

'Sara was a mistake, Zafir, our parents didn't even pretend to grieve when she died. Her life had no value because she couldn't rule when she came of age. They betrayed her more than you'll ever understand...'

Zafir pushed the past away, and with it the familiar ache of longing and disconnection. That ache shamed him, because he was above such weakness, or should be. He had to be. And he also ruthlessly shut out the niggling pain that his brother hadn't confided in him more.

Salim had shut Zafir out long ago, pursuing a life of debauched irresponsibility. Laughing in the face of his responsibilities. It was love that had done that to his brother—albeit sibling love. The twins had had their own little world, exclusive to everyone around them—even Zafir. And after Sara had died Salim had never been the same.

Seeing his brother's reaction to Sara's death, witnessing the pain of losing that intense bond, had bred within Zafir a lifelong desire to protect himself against such deep investment in another person. It appalled him that you could lose yourself like that.

Kat was looking at him now, and Zafir took a step back—as much from the intensity flowing between them as from his unwelcome reflections. He didn't appreciate Kat's ultimatum, but at the same time he didn't want to reveal the extent of his need. He'd already revealed too much. However, he could not let her rewrite their history.

He folded his arms. 'What happened between us was not a mistake, Kat. We were both adults, acting on mutual desire. The fact that it ended as it did was as much your responsibility as it was mine. You kept truths from me and I shouldn't have trusted you so easily.'

Kat seemed to go pale in the low lights of the room. 'Let's just leave it at that, then.'

Something in Zafir rebelled at that. 'By all means—if you think we can leave the past in the past. I, however, happen to believe that sooner or later you'll have to admit we have a present too.'

Kat bent down and picked up the handle of her suitcase. She looked at Zafir. 'The only present we have is a professional one, Zafir.'

For now, he told himself silently as he came forward and took Kat's suitcase out of her hand, leading her out of the suite and to his car downstairs.

She got into the car without looking at him once, keeping her face averted. Only that lingering sense of exposure stopped him from pulling her back out of the car to show her what a mockery this *professionalism* was.

He'd arrogantly assumed resuming a physical relationship with Kat would be easy. He couldn't have been more wrong. And yet he wasn't dissuaded. If anything, this pared down and feisty Kat was sparking his desire in a far deeper way than she ever had before.

As he watched his car slide away from the kerb and into the evening traffic he told himself that she wouldn't be able to hold out against this insane chemistry for long.

CHAPTER FOUR

'KAT, YOU LOOK...AMAZING.'

Kat heard the thickness in her friend's voice and tried not to let it affect her. She was having a hard enough time just breathing, and said shakily, 'Jules, I really don't know if I'm ready for this.'

Julie came and stood between Kat and the full-length mirror in the hotel suite bedroom, where Kat had returned some hours ago with her bags packed for the trip. They would leave tomorrow for London.

Kat was wearing the black velvet dress again. Her hair was in the chignon and her make-up had just been completed. Everyone had left, so now it was just the two of them.

Her petite blonde friend took Kat's hand in a firm grip and looked up at her steadily. 'I wouldn't push you if you weren't ready, Kat. But you are. You can't keep hiding from the world.'

Kat bit her lip to stop herself asking plaintively, *But this job? Now?* She looked at her reflection over her friend's head and saw the panicked look in her eyes, and forced herself to take in a breath.

Just then there was a knock on the door. Kat loved her friend for not jumping to answer it immediately, waiting to get a nod from Kat first. Gratitude made her chest swell because she knew that if she truly wanted to walk out of here right now her friend would support her. But she didn't want to let her down. And she didn't want to let the rehab centre down.

She could do this.

Before Julie had even opened the door Kat knew who it

was. Heat prickled over her skin. And, sure enough, when it swung back Zafir was there, filling the space effortlessly. He was dressed in a tuxedo and he was ridiculously gorgeous. And, even though Kat had seen him dressed like this before, it was still a shock to the system to behold such a formidable specimen of masculine perfection.

It was also the first time she'd seen him since yesterday, and the memory of that kiss made her pulse pound unevenly. Coming to terms with the resurrection of her sexual awareness was something she really hadn't expected to have to deal with for a long time. And yet it rushed through her now like an unstoppable wave.

Zafir was holding the necklace in his hand and he lifted it up. 'May I?'

Kat nodded dumbly and tensed against Zafir's effect on her as he walked in and came behind her, raising his hands up and over her head so that he could tie the clasp at the back of her neck.

The necklace felt warm and heavy against her skin and Kat touched it unconsciously. Julie's blue eyes had grown comically large and round as she took in the gem nestling against Kat's skin.

Kat looked at her reflection in the mirror and for a moment she was mesmerised too by the glowing red heart-shaped jewel. It did look somehow *alive*.

And then she raised her eyes and her gaze snagged on Zafir's. Those dark grey depths were focused solely on her. Not even looking at the gem. She swallowed. He was very close behind her, she could feel his heat, and only for the fact that Julie was still there, effectively acting as chaperone, stopped Kat from taking a step away.

He was the one finally to step back, and Kat breathed in shakily.

He went and stood beside Julie. 'You look stunning.' She was glad he hadn't said *perfect*.

He extended his arm towards the door. 'Shall we? My driver is waiting.'

As Kat stepped forward her friend touched her arm and mouthed *good luck*. And then it was just Kat and Zafir, stepping out of the suite to where the security team were waiting, looking serious and alert.

Noor got into the elevator with them, and Kat was relieved not to be alone in the small space with Zafir. When they got out on ground level they were ushered straight to Zafir's car, and Kat instinctively arranged the long dress over her left leg, conscious of her prosthetic limb. It had been a long time since she'd felt so undressed.

Thankfully Zafir had to take a call on his mobile as they cut through the early-evening Manhattan traffic, giving Kat time to gather herself before entering back into the fray in spectacular fashion.

By the time they pulled up in front of the iconic Metropolitan Museum Zafir was off his phone, and the palms of her hands were clammy with sweat. It got worse when she saw the hordes of paparazzi and reporters and other people already lining the red carpet in their finery.

Zafir touched her bare arm and she looked at him.

'Okay?'

Kat nodded jerkily. 'Fine.'

She'd never been less fine in her life.

'Just follow my lead.'

Zafir got out of the car then, and came around to Kat's side, opening the door and helping her out. Once again she was glad of the dress disguising her leg as she stood up and wobbled for a moment. Zafir's hand was on her arm again, holding her steady.

She stepped up onto the sidewalk and they moved forward. As people noticed who they were a hush seemed to fall over the crowd for a split-second, and then all hell broke loose as they walked onto the red carpet.

Zafir had tucked Kat's arm over his and she wasn't aware of how tightly she was holding on, she was being blinded by all the bright flashes going off in her face.

For a moment she was paralysed, and then Zafir's deep voice sounded in her ear, saying calmly, 'Start walking and smile—that's all you have to do.'

And suddenly she was moving, propelled forward by Zafir. They stopped periodically to let photographers take pictures, and Zafir stood back to let Kat be photographed on her own.

After a few long torturous minutes Kat found herself relaxing slightly, as if a long unused muscle was coming back to life. She knew how to do this—how to project a smiling façade. She'd done it for years. And slowly the ability returned.

And then someone shouted out, 'Where have you been, Kat? Are you and Zafir back together?' and all her fragile confidence shattered.

She stumbled, but Zafir was there in an instant, steadying her again. He replied to the questions smoothly and authoritatively.

'Persuading Kat Winters out of retirement was an unexpected coup and we're delighted she's working with us for this diplomatic trip. As for our relationship—that's none of anyone's business except our own.'

Eventually they reached the end of the red carpet. Kat was ready to crawl under a rock, but the evening hadn't even started yet. And she was angry.

She pulled away from Zafir and looked up at him, saying in a low voice, 'You could have shut down their questions about our relationship more comprehensively.'

Zafir just looked at her explicitly. 'I could have.'

But I didn't.

He didn't have to bother saying that part. Before she could react, though, he put her arm firmly in his again and propelled her forward to the main entrance of the function room. Her anger dissolved into panic at the sight of the packed room.

He stopped there for a second and looked at her again. 'Ready?'

No! she wanted to blurt out, but if she turned and ran she'd only have to face the red carpet again. There was literally nowhere to go except forward.

Not liking how symbolic this moment felt, Kat nodded jerkily and they stepped over the threshold of the room, its doors being held open by pristinely uniformed butlers.

Much like the hush outside when they'd arrived, as soon as they stepped in through the doorway everyone turned to look and there was an audible intake of breath. Kat realised that a spotlight rested on her—undoubtedly it was to showcase the diamond, not her, but she still felt utterly exposed.

Zafir took her arm from his and stepped to the side, leaving her feeling ridiculously bereft for a second. Then she heard his strong voice say, 'May I present to you Kat Winters and the Heart of Jandor?'

The enthusiastic clapping and gasps of wonder at the sight of Kat and the gem had faded away, to be replaced by the excited chatter of hundreds of VIP guests.

Zafir noted the presence of high-ranking politicians mixed with award-winning actors and actresses, world champion athletes, prize-winning authors and everyone who was anyone with satisfaction. And yet his feeling of satisfaction somehow fell short.

He found he was more interested in where Kat was and with whom. Currently she was standing a few feet away from him, surrounded by a small goggle-eyed crowd. Irritated by this dent in his sense of satisfaction, Zafir cursed himself.

This was exactly what he'd envisaged, wasn't it? To have one of the most beautiful women in the world standing amongst an awed crowd as she showcased his country's famed jewel?

But if anything she outshone the diamond. The inky black of the dress and its clean lines showcased the perfection of Kat's body. No other jewellery. Understated make-up. And not a bump or a mark or a blemish to mar that lustrous skin.

Zafir didn't recall her being so pale before, but presumably if she hadn't been travelling to exotic locations for fashion shoots, as she'd used to, then she'd lost her natural golden tan. And yet her skin seemed to glow even more. Like a pearl.

She was in profile to him now, and his gaze scanned down from the abundant dark hair artfully arranged in its chignon, to her high forehead, straight nose, lush mouth, delicate jaw and long, graceful neck.

The rare gem sat just below her collarbone, glowing as if lit from within by fire. Her shoulders were slim and straight. And then, as if compelled by the beat of his blood, his hungry gaze dropped to the voluptuous swells of her breasts.

Blood rushed to his groin and Zafir had to grit his jaw and use all of his control to stop making a complete fool of himself. He snapped his gaze back to her face, which he could see now was tense. Smiling, but tense.

He recalled how tightly she'd gripped his arm while on the red carpet, and how she'd wobbled precariously a couple of times as if her legs were unsteady. And the strangest thing... When he'd announced her arrival a short while before and watched her stand tall but alone, bathed in the spotlight, he'd felt a curious sense of pride, without even knowing why, exactly.

She turned her head then, as if sensing his intense regard, and looked at him, and before Zafir was even aware of what he was doing he ignored the veritable queue of people Rahul had lined up to speak to him and walked to Kat's side.

Hours later Kat ached all over, and she sank down into the hot bath as much as she could, wishing she could submerge herself completely and forget how exposed she'd felt as she'd been paraded through that enormous room like a thoroughbred horse at a bloodstock auction.

And yet, to her surprise, Zafir had stayed by her side more or less constantly—even though she'd seen the frustration on his aide Rahul's face as he'd tried to entreat Zafir to talk to this person or that person.

She didn't like to admit that his presence had steadied her as much as it had unnerved her, and made her feel more capable of bearing up to the scrutiny—which had been of *her* as much as the gem. And that had been Zafir's cynical plan all along, hadn't it? To get the most out of bringing the notorious Kat Winters out of the woodwork?

Yet, a small voice pointed out, he hadn't had to stay by her side like that. He could have quite easily ignored her all night...

But before she went down the dangerous path of believing that he'd stayed by her side out of concern or anything more, she reminded herself that Zafir's motivations had undoubtedly been to make sure that she didn't damage the Jandor 'brand' or upstage the diamond. And also because he was still messing with her head, not letting her forget the sensual threat he'd made.

At the end of the evening Zafir had been pulled aside to talk to an emissary from the American foreign office, and Rahul had come to let Kat know that she could hand back the gem if she so wished. Like a coward, she'd seized the opportunity, and he'd accompanied her to an anteroom where Noor had overseen the return of the gem to its box and it had been whisked safely away.

Then, when they'd re-emerged into the function room and Kat had seen that Zafir was still in conversation, she'd told Rahul that she was ready to leave.

Immediately he'd looked worried and said nervously, 'I should check with the King—'

Kat had cut in more firmly than she'd felt, 'I'm quite tired, and we have an early start to get to London in time for the function tomorrow evening, I'm sure you wouldn't want the King to be displeased because I don't appear rested.'

She'd almost felt sorry for how conflicted Rahul had looked, but eventually he'd agreed and had accompanied her down to the car and seen her off.

She'd just been breathing a sigh of relief when she'd received a text from Zafir while still in the car.

Next time, we leave together, Kat. Get some rest for tomorrow. Rahul will escort you to the royal plane in the morning and I'll meet you there.

Kat hadn't appreciated being made to feel like an admonished child, and yet now her mind drifted back to how Zafir had looked amongst the crowd earlier, how effortlessly he'd stood out with his height and dark good looks.

She couldn't stop a pulse fluttering between her legs as she recalled how she'd caught him looking at her with something raw in his eyes. Raw, and hungry. It had leapt across the space from him to her, and she'd felt it as strongly as if he'd physically reached out and touched her.

The pulse between Kat's legs intensified and she shifted in the bath, putting her hand down there, almost as if she could try to stop it. But once her fingers came

into contact with her sensitised skin and she felt how slip-
pery she was she sucked in a pained breath.

She'd been on a knife-edge of desire all evening, as
much as she'd tried to ignore it. But she couldn't any
more, and her fingers moved tentatively but far too easily against herself, helped by the water and her own slick
arousal.

She'd never touched herself like this…not until Zafir
had shown her how and had instructed her to do it for
him. She thought of that now—how he'd sat naked in a
chair and told her to get on the bed and spread her legs,
to show herself to him, and then to touch herself. He'd
held himself in his hand as she'd done his bidding, his
fist moving up and down the stiff column of flesh in a
slow, relentless rhythm.

It had been the singularly most indecent and erotic
thing she'd ever experienced, and just as she'd exploded
into pieces around her own fingers Zafir had surged up,
taken her hand away, seated himself between her legs
and thrust into her, deep and hard, and had kept her falling over the edge again and again until she'd screamed
herself hoarse.

Kat could feel herself quickening now, tightening, as
her movements became more feverish and desperate…
and yet in the same moment she realised that Zafir wasn't
watching her this time. She was alone in a bath…dream-
ing of the past and a scenario that would never be repeated.

Disgusted with herself, she took her hand away and
opened her eyes, breathing harshly, ignoring the ache
between her legs and the way her nipples were so tight
they hurt. The truth was that she knew she would find
no real satisfaction like this, and it killed her to admit it.

Kat pushed herself upright from the water and bal-
anced on one leg. She sat on the edge of the bath, swing-

ing herself over before drying herself roughly and reaching for the crutches she had nearby. Then she manoeuvred herself to standing, excess water dripping onto the towels she'd placed on the floor to stop herself from slipping and sliding when she got out.

Getting out of a bath was a process that was second nature now, but it had taken many months to perfect. It never ceased to amaze and humble her how much she'd taken for granted before.

She deliberately avoided her reflection in the countless bathroom mirrors, feeling like a coward. But right now she didn't need a reminder of exactly why Zafir would never look at her with that same hungry raw need again.

And the sooner she shut down these inappropriate fantasies, the better. Or she wouldn't survive another day, never mind another couple of weeks.

The following day Zafir was still stewing over the fact that Kat had left the function without him last night.

They'd departed from New York early in the morning, nearly six hours ago, so their landing in London was imminent.

Rahul had brought her to the plane and Kat had looked pale and tight-lipped, answering any questions Zafir had posed with monosyllabic answers. And then, when he'd suggested that she take advantage of the bedroom to rest, she'd disappeared for the rest of the flight.

Zafir sighed moodily and took in the sea of endless clouds outside his window. He really wasn't used to being thwarted like this. Especially not when the sexual tension between them was off the charts. He'd seen the way her gaze had roved over him hungrily when she'd first stepped into the plane, as if she wasn't even aware of her impulse. Which was the same as his. To devour her with his eyes at every opportunity.

He heard a noise from the back and that ever-present desire spiked as Kat's evocative scent reached him just before she did. She sat down in her seat again, asking huskily, 'We're nearly there?'

Zafir did his best to clamp down on the need to reach over and pluck her bodily from her seat and into his lap. 'Yes,' he gritted out. 'Within the next half hour. We've started our descent.'

Rahul's staff were at the front of the plane—out of sight and earshot—and his greedy gaze took in Kat's soft jeans and the loose, unstructured top that somehow still managed to mould itself to her curves. Her hair was down, and Zafir wanted to wrap it around his hand and force her to look at him.

'You won't turn to stone if you look at me, Kat.'

He couldn't disguise the irritation lacing his words. He saw how she tensed, but then eventually she turned her head and those glorious golden, amber and green eyes settled on him. Cool. Unreadable. *Why* was she so reluctant to take what he was offering? A no-strings-attached, very adult exorcism of this palpable connection between them.

He turned in his seat more fully, to face her. 'You must be hungry. You haven't eaten because you were sleeping.'

Before she could say anything he'd called for a steward, who materialised immediately. Zafir looked at Kat expressively. For a moment a mutinous expression crossed her face, but then she seemed to give in and said to the staff member, 'I'll just have something light...like an omelette, if you have it?'

Zafir added an order for coffee for both of them and the steward left.

Looking disgruntled, Kat said, 'You're still too bossy. And arrogant.'

Zafir shrugged, unperturbed. 'I'm a King now. I have a licence to be as bossy and arrogant as I want.'

Suddenly Kat looked stricken, and those eyes which had been so unreadable were now full of something far more readable. Sympathy.

'I never mentioned your father. I'm sorry for your loss. I know you weren't particularly close, but still it can't have been easy.'

Zafir's insides clenched. Plenty of people had offered empty platitudes when his father had died, but few had known just how barren their relationship had been. But he'd told Kat. And her simple sincerity now tugged on a deep part of him that *had* mourned his father—or at least mourned the fact that he'd never been a father in the real sense. The loving sense.

The steward arrived then, with Kat's food and the coffees, and Zafir said gruffly, 'Eat. We'll be landing soon and we have a busy schedule this evening.'

After a few moments Kat picked up her cutlery and ate with single-minded absorption.

When she'd finished, he mused out loud, 'You always did have a good appetite.'

Kat went still and pushed the plate away from her before taking up her cup of coffee. She glanced at Zafir without letting him see her eyes properly. Her mouth had gone tight and she said, 'When you grow up hungry it gives you an appreciation of food that others might not have.'

'Was it really that bad, Kat?'

She glared at him. 'You read that article along with everyone else in America, didn't you? The lurid details of my life in a trailer park?'

Zafir shook his head, his irritation mounting. 'I still don't know why you couldn't tell me the full details. There's no shame in growing up poor, *or* in a trailer park.'

'No,' she said, avoiding his eyes again. 'Only in the choices we make to survive.'

Kat felt bitterness corrode her insides even as she knew that this was her chance to spill it all out to Zafir. He was listening and receptive, and she'd always wanted to tell him, hadn't she? But suddenly the thought of laying it all out felt too huge. She still felt vulnerable after appearing in public again for the first time last night, and like a coward she clammed up, avoiding the opportunity.

Instead she looked at him and said, 'You called me a liar the other day, but I never lied to you. I just…didn't tell you everything.'

'A distinction that hardly exonerates you,' Zafir pointed out.

He felt frustration mount when she didn't respond, aware of a niggling sensation that she was still hiding things from him.

Just then the air steward arrived to clear Kat's plate and inform them that they'd be landing shortly, and to make sure they were ready. The tension dissipated and Kat broke their staring contest to turn her head and look out of her window.

The plane circled lower and lower over the private London airfield and Zafir addressed his question to the back of Kat's glossy head, unable to resist pushing her for a response. 'You never told me why you didn't go back into modelling full-time once you'd recovered.'

Zafir could feel her reluctance as she finally turned to look at him again, eyes guarded.

'It wasn't a career I'd ever really chosen for myself, and I discovered that if I had the choice I wouldn't necessarily step back into it.'

Which was more or less the truth, Kat reassured herself as Zafir's incisive gaze seemed to laser all the way into her soul. Even if she hadn't lost her leg she wouldn't have wanted to step back into that vacuous world. Being forced out of her old existence and into a new one had revealed a desire to find a more meaningful role in her life. What that might be, she wasn't even sure herself yet. She only knew that she wanted to help people as she had been helped…

The plane touched down with a brief jolt and Zafir finally looked away. Released from that compelling gaze, Kat took a breath. She'd tried to rest earlier, in the plane's luxurious bedroom, but sleep had proved elusive. She was too wound up after those illicit fantasies in her bath last night and the prospect of another public exhibition this evening.

Perhaps, she thought to herself a little hysterically, this was Zafir's retribution? Expose Kat to the ravenous judgmental hordes who would pick her over until there was nothing left?

Although, from what she'd seen of the headlines in the papers that Rahul had been poring over in the car earlier, there didn't seem to be much dredging up of the past— only feverish speculation as to why Kat had re-emerged and where she'd been and the nature of her relationship with Zafir. Kat wasn't sure whether to be relieved or even more anxious at the thought that someone from the rehabilitation clinic might recognise her and sell the story of what had really happened to her.

Before she could dwell on that too much Zafir was standing, holding her bag in one hand and his other hand out to her. She looked at it for a moment, and then realised how futile it would be to try and resist. She put her hand in Zafir's and let him pull her up. She stumbled slightly, falling against Zafir's chest. His eyes flared and his hand came up to steady her, curling around her arm tightly.

For a moment their bodies were welded together and the heat between them surged.

Roughly he said, 'Kat, why can't you just admit—'

'Sire, the cars are ready.'

Zafir clamped his mouth shut and didn't look around at Rahul, their interrupter.

Relief flooded Kat, because she realised that if Zafir had kissed her in that moment she'd have responded helplessly. She pulled free and walked to the entrance of the plane, taking care on the steps down, telling herself it was her prosthetic limb and not the throbbing arousal rushing through her body making her feel wobbly.

The event in London was even more impressive than the one in New York. Because of Zafir's royal status, senior members of the British royal family were present, imbuing the classic surroundings of one of London's oldest and most exclusive hotels with an elegance and gravitas Kat had never experienced before.

The ornate furnishings glittered under the flickering glow of hundreds of candles. A string quartet played on a dais at one end of the room. Pristine waiters moved silently and discreetly through the crowd, offering tantalising, exotic hors d'oeuvres prepared by Zafir's Jandori chef and glasses of priceless champagne.

Tonight Kat was dressed in a long strapless white dress. A sheath of simplicity which helped to show the red diamond to its best advantage. Zafir hadn't arrived at her suite to put the diamond around her neck earlier—it had been a stylist who had taken it from one of Noor's guards to place around her neck—and Kat denied furiously to herself that she'd missed his presence and his touch.

When Rahul had met her to walk her down to the function room, which was in the same hotel where they would stay the night, he'd explained that Zafir had had to take an important conference call and sent his apologies.

She'd denied the little dart of disappointment and

she'd ruthlessly quashed the relief she'd felt to see Zafir waiting outside the function room—pacing, actually—dressed once again in a classic tuxedo that did nothing to disguise his virile masculinity and everything to enhance it.

His gaze had swept her up and down. This evening her hair was tamed into a sleek bun, low at the back of her head, and she'd seen Zafir's gaze rest on it and how his eyes had flared with something unreadable. In that moment she'd gone breathless, imagining that she could almost feel his desire to undo it and let her hair fall down in its habitual unruly tumble of waves. He'd always loved it down…and the memory of that had made her weak.

But then he'd extended his arm, and she'd walked forward as the doors had opened and they'd stepped through.

And now Kat was standing beside Zafir on a small podium as he spoke to the hushed crowd and told them of the myriad opportunities available for business and recreation in his country. Kat found herself forgetting that she was under a spotlight while Zafir's deep and hypnotic voice painted a seductive picture of a land steeped in history and with boundless opportunities.

His love for his people and his country was evident in the passion in his voice, and she couldn't stop a dart of surprise and pride because she'd had no idea that Zafir was so determined to be a force for change in his country. The vision he outlined was modern and progressive, and was now being met with resounding applause.

She'd underestimated him, and that unsettled her as he stepped off the podium and held out a hand to help her down. She wasn't thinking, and she landed on her left leg a little awkwardly, wincing as the movement jarred her prosthesis. Any kind of steps, up or down, were more of a challenge than before.

Immediately he was sharp. 'Are you okay?'

'Fine—I just turned my ankle for a moment,' she embellished quickly.

Zafir frowned. 'Maybe we should have someone check it.'

Instant panic flooded her veins, turning her blood cold. 'No, I'm fine. Really.'

She spent the rest of the evening with a bright smile plastered on her face, even as her discomfort increased. She needed to take her prosthesis off to adjust it, but Zafir wouldn't leave her side and she was loath to attract his attention.

Finally, when she was wondering if the evening would ever end, the crowd thinned out and Zafir said, 'I'll take you to your suite and you can give the necklace back to the security guards for the night.'

Relief made her almost dizzy as he accompanied her out of the room and up in the elevator, with the ever-present Noor. Kat could be thankful for at least that much. As long as she wore the diamond, she wouldn't be alone with Zafir.

Once in Kat's suite, Noor stood at a respectful distance as Zafir took off the necklace and placed it into the box before handing it over.

Noor bowed her head. 'Good night, Sire… Miss Winters.'

She left the room and they were alone. Before Kat could say a word, though, Zafir put his hands on her shoulders and turned her around so she had her back to him. Then his hands were on her hair, plucking out the pins that had been holding the tight bun in place. As she felt it loosen and start to unravel, the discomfort of her limb was forgotten momentarily at the sheer bliss of *this*… Zafir's hands moving through her hair, massaging her skull.

His voice was low, husky. 'I've imagined doing this all evening.'

His body was close behind her and she could feel his heat and the whipcord strength of him. So close. So seductive. Treacherously, something gave way inside her, as if it was too strong for her to keep holding it back. Almost without realising what she was doing, she turned and looked up.

Zafir went still. Kat was looking up at him, eyes wide and molten, cheeks flushed. Every instinct within him called for him to claim her—finally. But something stopped him…a memory, brutally vivid and brutally exposing.

Kat sensed the chill even before she saw the heat in Zafir's eyes disappear. He dropped his hands and stepped back. She blinked, feeling vulnerable and hating herself for that small moment when he must have seen her desire laid bare.

When Zafir spoke he sounded harsh. 'Go to bed, Kat. I have some meetings here in the morning. Rahul will accompany you to the airport after lunch.'

And then he turned and walked out, the door closing behind him with an incongruously soft click.

Kat felt a little dazed, not sure what had just happened. She looked around and sank down onto the nearest chair. She could feel the discomfort in her leg again, and pulled up her dress in order to start taking off her prosthetic limb. But then she stopped, realising she needed to get her crutches first.

Feeling seriously on edge and irritable, she went into the bedroom, cursing Zafir for scrambling her brain so much that she forgot the fundamental basics.

But what irritated her the most, as she retrieved her crutches and started to undress so she could take off her prosthesis, was the fact that if he hadn't pulled back just

now she'd most likely be on the nearest horizontal surface, giving up all her secrets to Zafir in the most humiliating way possible.

And that wasn't even the worst thing—because the
worst thing was the insidious need to know, why had
he stopped?

CHAPTER FIVE

LONDON UNDER MOONLIGHT twinkled benignly outside Zafir's suite window, with all of the famous landmarks lit up: the London Eye, the Shard, the dome and spires of St Paul's cathedral. But he couldn't care less about any of them. Or the fact that so far his diplomatic tour was a resounding success.

His head was filled with only one thing. Recrimination for letting a mere memory stop him from seeking the relief his body ached for. That was the past—this was the present. And yet the two were colliding far too vividly for his liking.

But when Kat had looked at him just now the sense of déjà vu had been strong enough to propel him out of her orbit. Déjà vu of the moment he'd proposed to her...

As much as Zafir would have liked to believe his proposal had been a well thought out and strategic move, it hadn't been. It had been spontaneous—not a behaviour that usually dictated his actions. They'd been travelling in his private jet, from London back to New York, and as he'd watched Kat across the aisle, staring dreamily out of the window, with his blood still humming after an overload of recent carnal satisfaction, she'd turned her head to look at him and he'd been overcome with a desperate and inexplicable need to ensure she never left his sight. And so he'd proposed, surprising her as much as himself.

He cursed himself now and turned from the view not liking the reminder that his proposal had been far less strategic than he liked to admit. He strode into the bedroom, shedding clothes as he went until he was naked.

When he reached the bathroom he stepped into the shower and turned it on. To cold.

He cursed volubly as the freezing water hit his skin, but it did little to douse the fever in his blood or the unwelcome memories in his head. He should have just followed his instincts and taken her. She wouldn't have stopped him this time—he felt it deep in his gut. And lower, where he still ached in spite of the cold water.

If anything, Kat had only proved that her defiance and reluctance were an act, and that she was biding her time before giving in. It was a little power play…she was messing with his head.

Next time he wouldn't let anything stop him, and when this tour was over and he'd slaked his lust he *would* walk away from Kat, and he would not feel the slightest ounce of regret because she'd be relegated to the past for good.

'Dinner, Kat. It's a social construct designed for people to sit down together and make conversation. Break bread together.'

Kat looked at Zafir suspiciously where he stood on the other side of her Parisian hotel suite's door. The Paris event wasn't due to take place until the following evening, and Kat had been savouring the thought of some breathing space while Zafir had meetings at the Jandor consulate nearby. She'd been looking forward to an early evening in bed, with a view of the Eiffel tower outside her window, watching old movies and eating ice-cream— her comfort staples. But now her peace was shattered.

'I know what dinner is.' She tried to keep her tone even. 'But what do you want to talk about? We have nothing to discuss.'

Zafir leaned a shoulder against the doorframe, supremely relaxed. Supremely dangerous. 'We're friends at least—aren't we, Kat?'

She scowled. 'You're my employer and I'm your employee.'

'We have history,' he countered.

'*Ancient* history,' she blasted back, panic rising as she realised that the past felt far too close for comfort. This Zafir was the one she remembered and feared. Relentless, seductive. Impossible to resist.

'We're ex-lovers,' he said silkily. 'I'd say we have plenty to talk about.'

And just like that a slideshow of explicit images bombarded Kat's memory banks, rendering her speechless.

As if sensing her momentary weakness, Zafir straightened from the door and said, 'I'll come back for you in an hour, Kat. Be ready.'

He was leaving before she could wrap her tongue around another word, but then he stopped abruptly and came back. 'Actually, I was going to go for a run, if you'd like to join me?'

A sharp pain lanced Kat right in the gut. She and Zafir used to jog together all the time. She'd taken great delight in keeping up with his punishing regular five-mile regime.

She felt hollow inside as she shook her head firmly. 'No, thank you.'

Zafir shrugged minutely and backed away again, oblivious to the turmoil caused by his easy invitation. 'As you wish—see you in an hour.'

She finally shut the door on his retreating back, and leant against it, an awful poignancy making her chest swell with emotion. Before it could turn into anything more she issued an unladylike curse and pushed herself away from the door.

The prospect of an evening with Zafir loomed large. The hollow feeling dissipated, to be replaced with a predictable array of physical reactions at the thought of sitting down with him one on one. Her skin grew hot, her pulse tripled and butterflies swarmed into her belly against her best efforts to quell his effect on her.

He was chipping away at the walls she'd erected around herself and he wasn't even aware of it. Yesterday evening she'd come so close to succumbing, and only because of *his* self-control she'd been saved from outright humiliation.

Damn him and his games. Damn him and his easy invitation to do something she'd never easily do again.

But he doesn't know about your leg, reminded a chiding voice.

And he never would, she vowed now. Because if he did it would mean he'd breached her last defences.

She walked over to the closet and opened the doors, purposely picking out the most casual clothes she possessed.

But when Zafir appeared at her door again, in exactly an hour's time, he looked smart and gorgeous in a dark suit, with his shirt open at the neck, and she felt like a rebellious teenager. His explicit look told her what he thought of the soft leather trousers, flat ankle boots and the loose, unstructured grey top. She'd left her hair down, wore minimal make-up, and reached for her light wraparound jacket and bag before coming into the hall and closing the door behind her.

Zafir appeared amused, which made her feel even more exposed and silly. 'Don't worry, Kat. I won't get the wrong idea, if that's what you're afraid of.'

He stood back to let her precede him into the elevator, and as it descended he leant against one mirrored wall with his hands in his pockets.

'You used to love wearing short skirts and high heels,' he observed. 'Is this some new feminist stance or is it just to ward me off?'

Kat's insides turned to ice. She *had* loved wearing the highest of heels and the shortest of dresses and skirts. And only ever for this man, because the carnal hunger and appreciation in his gaze had used to make her feel sexy and desired.

Relief warred confusingly with disappointment to hear that Zafir would obviously prefer to see her dressing as she'd used to.

Feeling exposed, she rounded on him, saying heatedly, 'No, it's not a feminist stance, actually. Women *should* be able to wear whatever they want—and not to entice a man. For themselves.'

He wasn't perturbed by her outburst. As the elevator doors opened he said easily, 'I was merely making an observation, not stating a preference, and I agree with you one hundred per cent. For what it's worth, Kat, you could wear a sack from head to toe and it wouldn't diminish how much I want you.'

Before she could respond to that, he took her arm in a loose but proprietorial hold to guide her across the exclusive Paris hotel lobby and out through the doors to his chauffeur-driven car.

She barely noticed the ubiquitous security vehicle waiting to tail their every move. Zafir had blindsided her a little. She'd always pegged him as being unremittingly traditional and conservative because he was so effortlessly alpha, but maybe that wasn't fair.

When they were settled in the back of his car she asked, 'Where are we going?'

He looked at her, his face cast into shadow, making it stern and even more compelling. 'It's a surprise.'

Kat's insides clenched. She had a feeling she knew exactly where, and if she was right she wanted to jump out of the car right now. Zafir had introduced her to a restaurant here on their first trip to Paris, shortly after they'd started seeing each other, and the experience was seared into her memory.

It was one of the city's oldest establishments, famous for its decadent furnishings and for its private dining rooms, which had been used in previous centuries for clandestine assignations of a very carnal nature. Zafir had, of course, booked one of those rooms, and Kat's memories of the evening had nothing to do with the food they'd eaten and everything to do with the wicked pleasures he'd subjected her to in the intimate and luxuriously furnished space...

She refused to let Zafir guess how agitated she was by these memories and looked out of the window, taking in the glittering lights and beautiful buildings. She'd always loved Paris as it had been the first place she'd visited outside of America in her early modelling days. Its beauty and history had astounded her, and nowhere else had ever had the same effect on her.

Her conscience twinged... Except for Jahor, the awe-inspiring capital city of Zafir's country, Jandor. It sprawled across a series of hills, overlooking the sparkling sea, and the skyline was made up of minarets and flat roofs, with children flying multicoloured kites as the sun went down. Overlooking it all was the golden-hued grand palace.

'We're here.'

Kat came out of the past and frantically checked where they were, a sigh of relief moving through her when she realised they weren't at the restaurant she'd been thinking of. Instead, as Zafir came around and helped her out of the car, she saw that they were in a small street on Île de la Cité—one of Paris's many small islands in the Seine.

Intrigued in spite of herself, she let Zafir lead her over to a small restaurant tucked between two tall buildings. From the outside it looked inviting, with golden light spilling out onto the street. And it was not like anywhere Zafir had ever brought her before.

In fact when he spoke he sounded almost…uncertain. 'This is one of Paris's best kept secrets.'

Kat looked at him and said drily, 'Were you expecting me to throw a tantrum because it's not a restaurant three hundred storeys up with a view of the Eiffel Tower?'

Zafir was unreadable, 'I'm not sure what to expect any more.'

Before she could respond, he was leading her into the restaurant. She was surprised to see that he got a warm welcome from the proprietor, who greeted Zafir like a long-lost son and her like an old friend.

Within seconds their coats had been taken and they were seated in a discreet corner, tucked away but able to see everything. The table was small, but exquisitely set with a white tablecloth and silver cutlery. Soft music played in the background and every other table was full, everyone engrossed in each other. It was achingly and effortlessly romantic.

Feeling vulnerable and defensive, Kat said, 'I wouldn't have thought this was your kind of place.'

Zafir shook out his napkin and laid it across his lap before reaching for a bread roll. 'I worked here in the kitchen as an apprentice chef while I was at the Sorbonne for a semester.'

Kat's jaw dropped. Zafir looked at her and smiled.

'Good to know I'm still capable of surprising you.'

Feeling even more vulnerable now, Kat said testily, 'You accused me of lying, but you weren't exactly forthcoming with information yourself.'

Zafir's smile faded and air between them crackled. 'It wasn't talking about myself I was most interested in where you were concerned.'

A waiter appeared then, and took their order, and he

was quickly followed by a sommelier who took their wine order. When the wine had been poured and they were alone again, Kat felt ridiculously self-conscious and aware of Zafir, his long legs bracketing hers beneath the table.

He sat back, the delicate stem of his wine glass between long fingers. 'Why did you do it, Kat?'

She looked at him, feeling panicked. 'What?'

His face was stark. 'The pictures. Why did you let a man see you like that when you were so young? Why weren't you in school?'

Kat's hand tightened on her glass. She hated that she still didn't feel ready to tell Zafir everything. She wondered if she ever would. '*Now* you want to know? It won't change anything.'

Their starter arrived—deliciously creamy mushroom soup with truffle oil. To Kat's relief, Zafir seemed happy to let the question go while they ate, and he told her some stories of working there under a famously mercurial chef.

She said, 'I had no idea you were interested in cooking. And why take a job when you didn't have to?'

'I may be privileged—'

Kat snorted indelicately at that understatement.

Zafir continued. 'But I soon got bored when I wasn't studying. I was walking past this place one day and saw a sign in the window advertising for kitchen help, so I applied. No one here knew who I was. To them I was just Zafir Noury, a foreign student. It was only when my bodyguards made themselves a little too noticeable that questions were asked. But they let me stay working here and protected my identity. When Marcel, the owner, got into financial difficulty some years ago I was able to help him out, so now I have a stake in the business too.'

Kat's jaw would have dropped again, but she kept her mouth firmly shut. This was a side to Zafir she'd never known existed. Happy to be anonymous. Not afraid of menial work. When she'd known him he'd been feted as the Crown Prince of Jandor, King in Waiting. Influential and imposing. Overwhelming.

To her surprise they fell into an easy conversation for the rest of the impeccably prepared meal. So when their plates had been cleared, and Kat was feeling semirelaxed in Zafir's company for the first time since she'd seen him again, and he repeated his question about those photos she felt almost betrayed. As if he'd been lulling her into a false sense of security on purpose.

Feeling prickly, because she knew she was being a coward, she said, 'What purpose will this serve, Zafir? You weren't interested in knowing before. Why now?'

He shrugged minutely. 'Let's just say that when you ran out of my apartment that night you left more questions than answers.'

Kat bit back the accusation that he'd not been remotely interested in hearing any explanations that night, because truly, how hard had she tried to get him to listen to her? Not hard at all. Not once she'd known how he really felt. Or *didn't* feel.

But she realised now that the time had come—ready or not—to tell him what she would have told him that night if she hadn't felt so betrayed by his admission that he didn't love her.

She took a breath and forced herself to look at him. 'By the time I was seventeen I was the main breadwinner. Thanks to the endless round of beauty pageants I'd been entered into ever since my mother realised my looks had currency, I was working almost full-time as a model and supporting us both. I badly needed money for her medical bills.'

Zafir frowned. 'Her drug use.'

Kat refused to let him intimidate her again. She said in a low, fierce voice, '*No.* I never funded her drug use. But no matter what I did, or how many rehab programmes I tried to get her onto, she always relapsed.' Kat could feel her cheeks grow hot with shame as she said, 'She used to steal from me to buy her drugs. No matter how careful I was, she always found the money.'

'But surely you had a bank account?'

'Yes,' Kat said tightly, 'but I was a minor, so she was the joint account holder. That was no safer place to hide my money than underneath my bed.'

Zafir's eyes flashed. 'You were a minor when that man took those photos.'

Kat felt bile rise when she thought of that awful day. A day when she'd crossed a line and knew she'd never feel clean again.

'My mother was in a bad way. She'd taken all my money and she'd almost overdosed to death. She was in hospital. My last resort was to try and get her into a private rehab facility...but it was expensive. This man—the photographer—he wasn't anyone I'd met before, but one of the girls I modelled with told me about him and about the money I could make...'

'If you took your clothes off.' Zafir's voice sounded cold and austere, and the look on his face was one of disgust.

Kat threw her napkin down and stood up, emotion making her voice shake. 'I am not here to be judged and condemned by you for a second time, Zafir. What I did, I did because I had no other choice. And it didn't do much good anyway, because the day before she was due to go to the facility my mother managed to do what she'd been trying to do for years—she successfully overdosed herself to death.'

Kat left the restaurant, weaving unsteadily through the tables, desperately trying to stem the onset of tears. Once out in the street, she hugged her arms around herself, suddenly cold. The bodyguards were alert, watching her from their car nearby. Noor didn't seem to be with them this evening, and Kat almost missed the other woman's presence.

She started to walk in the other direction, cursing her leg for a moment because she couldn't just run. The street was cobblestoned, and any uneven surface was treacherous for her now.

She heard steps close behind her and tensed, but then she felt something big and warm land on her shoulders and turned around to see a grim-looking Zafir holding her jacket and bag. He'd given her his coat.

She would have reached for her things, but she was afraid her hands would shake, so she clutched Zafir's coat around her, hating the fact that it felt so comforting and smelled so enticingly of him.

'I'm sorry,' he said abruptly.

Stunned by his apology, Kat responded unevenly, 'I... it's okay.'

Zafir ran a hand through his hair, his grim look being replaced by something close to anger. 'Dammit, Kat, if I'd known what had happened to you...why you were in that position...' He trailed off.

Old injury resurfaced and Kat said, 'You believed I didn't tell you because I was afraid you wouldn't marry me. That wasn't the reason at all, Zafir. I didn't tell you because I was ashamed of the choice I'd had to make. And because my world was so far removed from yours.'

'I might have at least been able to understand, though...'

Disgust crossed his face again, but this time Kat recognised it wasn't directed at her.

'That man took advantage of you when you were at your most vulnerable.'

She shook her head. 'He didn't take advantage of me,

Zafir. I made a choice to take up his job offer and earned a lot more money than I would have through a more traditional route. I have to take responsibility for that.'

Kat thought of telling Zafir everything—how the photographer had gone on to blackmail her once she'd become well-known—but something stopped her. It was an unwillingness to let him see just how far-reaching that bad choice had been, sending poisonous tendrils into her life for a long time afterwards. Better to let Zafir believe she'd just been bad with money than utterly naive. Because she'd been naive where he'd been concerned too. And the last thing she wanted was for him to know that.

Zafir's car pulled up alongside them with a low, sleek purr. They didn't go back into the restaurant and Kat felt bad now for rushing out, wondering what Zafir's friend and business partner must think.

As they drove silently back through the Paris streets Kat realised that the evening—apart from that abrupt ending—had been very pleasant. More than pleasant.

She said now, before she could censor herself, 'I liked that restaurant. Why did we never go there before?'

Zafir's face was cast into shadow and his voice sounded rueful. 'I liked to show you off...and, to be honest, I didn't think it was your scene.'

Kat fell silent, realising that she'd been so busy trying to live up to what she believed to be Zafir's high expectations of glamour and sophistication that she'd presented a largely false persona the whole time they'd been together.

Just before they reached the hotel, Zafir turned to her and asked, 'What was his name, Kat?'

Confused for a moment, she said, 'Who?'

'The man who took those pictures.'

Kat was shocked at the steel in Zafir's voice. She shook her head. 'It won't make any difference now—'

'Kat.' He cut her off. 'Either you tell me now or I'll find out my own way. All you'll be doing is saving my team some unnecessary work.'

She looked at him and knew it would be futile to deny Zafir when he was like this. 'What are you going to do?'

His mouth tightened. 'His name, Kat.'

Realising he'd only find out eventually anyway, she told him.

Satisfaction gleamed in Zafir's eyes as he got out of the car and came round to help her out. His hand was tight on hers, and he didn't let her go all the way up in the elevator and until he walked her to her door.

Her heart was thudding against her breastbone. She still had Zafir's coat around her shoulders and she shrugged it off now, handing it back. He took it, handing her her things.

Reluctant to look into those grey eyes, because it felt as if something fundamental had shifted between them and she wasn't sure where she stood any more, Kat turned to the door, inserting her key. It clicked and she pushed it open. She turned back at the last moment and forced herself to look at Zafir. His face was expressionless, but something burned deep in his eyes. Something that scared her as much as it excited her.

Her hand tightened on the door handle. 'Good night, Zafir.'

For a heart-stopping moment she thought he was about to step forward and kiss her, and she knew that if he did that she wouldn't be able to resist. She felt as if an outer layer of protective skin had been removed.

But Zafir just took a step back and said, 'Good night, Kat. Get some rest.'

Kat watched him leave, and a minute later she was still rooted to the spot and trembling all over. That explicit look had been hot enough to make her feel scorched all over. And hot enough to confuse the hell out of her. Because he'd walked away again.

She was also still reeling from his sincere apology. And his anger on her behalf at the photographer. He still didn't know the half of it. About the blackmail...

An insidious though sneaked into her head... Maybe she'd finally done it. Maybe the truth of her past had been enough to drive him away.

Realising she was still standing outside her room, Kat quickly went inside and rested her back against the door, doing her best to ignore her thumping pulse and the betraying feeling of disappointment.

But it was clear now: her past was a passion-killer. Zafir might still be attracted to her, but he didn't really want the whole unvarnished truth of her past getting in the way. She told herself that she should be happy. Relieved. This is what she wanted, wasn't it? To prove to herself that Zafir only wanted the superficial and nothing deeper.

But she wasn't happy—or relieved. She was in more turmoil than ever.

A short while later, in his own suite, Zafir paced up and down, his head reeling with what Kat had told him.

He knew he wouldn't be able to rest until he'd started a search for the man who had taken such advantage of her. Despite her insistence that she had been just as responsible.

Zafir had had no idea how erroneous those salacious newspaper reports had been, or how cruel. And when he thought of a much younger Kat, in dire straits, needing help, he felt a helpless raw fury rise up within him.

She hadn't kept all this from him for fear he'd break the engagement and because she'd sought financial security—it had been because she hadn't trusted him enough to accept her past. And she'd been right.

Recrimination blasted him. He'd judged and condemned her before she'd had a chance to say anything.

There was so much more to her than he'd ever given her credit for, and this insight was proving yet again that something he'd thought would be easy—seducing Kat into his bed again—was anything but. And yet he'd never wanted her more.

When Zafir met Kat at the door of her room, early the following evening, he stopped in his tracks. For a heart-stopping, pulse-pounding moment he thought she was naked. But then he realised that she was wearing a flesh-coloured dress that moulded to her every curve, dip and hollow. It had a high neck and long sleeves, so she was effectively covered up, and yet he'd never seen anything more provocative.

Her hair was up again, and she already wore the diamond. It sat, glittering, over the dress against her breastbone. Only the presence of the stylist and Noor and her guards stopped Zafir from overreacting and sending Kat back into her suite to change into a sack that would cover her from head to toe.

He was the one, after all, who had specified a wardrobe of clothes designed to show off the diamond to best advantage, and this dress did it perfectly. The problem was that it set Kat off to best advantage too, and the truth was that once again she effortlessly outshone the rare stone.

His eyes met hers and something clenched tight inside him when he saw a hint of vulnerability before she quickly masked it.

Willing the heat in his body down to a dull roar, he held out his arm to her and said, 'Shall we?'

* * *

The function was taking place in a ballroom at the very top of the hotel in which they were staying. It was sumptuous and decadent—and a blur to Kat. As was the view of Paris visible through open French doors on this unseasonably warm autumn evening. Apparently the rolling bank of clouds on the horizon heralded a storm, and Kat didn't appreciate the irony that the weather was mirroring her feelings so accurately.

She'd barely slept a wink last night, tossing and turning, wondering if she *had* driven Zafir away. As dawn had risen she'd felt gritty-eyed and hollow. Fully expecting that the next time she saw Zafir he would be looking at her with pity, or a kind of cool reserve.

But he hadn't. He'd looked at her with explicit heat in his eyes. And now she hated him for doing this to her, making her feel so confused and on edge.

Compounding her inner storm was the fact that Zafir had barely left her side. He was touching her constantly, either taking her arm or her hand, or placing his hand low on her back, just above her buttocks. She was hot all over and between her legs there was a merciless throb. Her breasts felt full and heavy, her nipples pressing against the material of the dress, but thankfully not glaringly obvious under the heavy material of the gown.

He'd turned away from her for a brief moment, and she was relishing the chance to get her breath and try to bring her heart rate under control again. But just as she was relaxing slightly a vaguely familiar voice called out.

'Kat! It's really you!'

Kat turned and a jolt of pure shock ran through her to see one of the only models she'd been relatively close with.

Her old friend stepped forward and enveloped Kat

in a huge hug. When she pulled back Kat saw the body-guards hovering protectively and said faintly, 'It's fine… I know her…'

She looked back at her friend and to her horror felt emotion threaten as remorse gripped her. Remorse for cutting her friend off after the accident. Cassidy had tried to contact her on numerous occasions, but Kat hadn't been capable of talking to anyone.

'I'm so sorry, Cass… I should have been in touch…'

Her friend took her hand and shook her head, 'No, Kat, you don't have to say anything. It's enough to see you now…' The stunningly beautiful Irish model, with her dark red hair, pale skin and blue eyes, smiled crookedly, 'But, *God*, I've missed you on the circuit.'

Kat smiled back, squeezing her friend's hand, appreciating this acceptance of her behaviour. She knew it was down to Zafir that her emotions were closer to the surface than usual, but that didn't help much.

Far too belatedly she spotted a tall, imposing man at her friend's side. He was dark and stern-looking, with compelling dark brown eyes. He also looked vaguely familiar… It was only when Zafir stepped up to Kat's side again that she saw it—a distinct resemblance.

She also noted how this man slid his arm possessively around her friend's waist. Clearly they were lovers. He was looking at Kat's necklace and said in a deep and slightly accented voice, 'So this is the famous Heart of Jandor?'

Kat resisted the urge to touch the stone. 'Yes, it is.'

Then Zafir surprised her by saying, 'Welcome, Riad. Kat, this is my very distant cousin, Riad Arnaud, a descendant of my French great-grandmother who was gifted this very diamond. And this is Kat Winters, who I'm sure needs no introduction.'

Riad inclined his head towards Kat, and then he drawled, 'Some might say I have a claim on this diamond.'

Zafir responded, sounding unperturbed. 'It belongs to Jandor—as you very well know. Left to us by your ancestor.'

Zafir's cousin looked as if he was considering this, but then he smiled and his face was transformed from stern to gorgeous. The tension dissipated as he clapped Zafir on his shoulder and said, 'You do know how I like to wind you up about the diamond, and it never fails.'

Zafir let out a short laugh. 'It's good to see you, Riad. It's been far too long.'

Kat turned to Zafir then, and said, 'This is Cassidy O'Connor—an old friend of mine. We modelled together.'

Cassidy stepped out of Riad's embrace to shake Zafir's hand. Kat noted with interest how Riad's face tightened as he watched the two greet each other. There was something very proprietorial in his dark gaze and he quickly drew Cassidy back to his side. For a moment Kat felt a twinge of envy.

Riad was saying something about arranging a meeting and stepping back, but Kat's friend stepped forward to hug her again. She whispered into Kat's ear, 'Is everything okay? You look great, but…different.'

Kat pulled back and smiled weakly. 'I have a lot to tell you, Cass. I'll call you when I get home?'

Cass took her hand and squeezed it. 'Promise me you will. I don't want to lose touch again.'

Kat nodded and said, 'Promise.' Then she added impulsively, 'And you, Cass, are you okay? Are you both…?' She trailed off ineffectually.

To her surprise her friend paled slightly, but then she smiled brightly and said, 'I'm fine. And we…well, I'm not quite sure what we are, to be honest.'

And then her friend was gone, sucked back into the crowd with her brooding and enigmatic lover by her side, leaving Kat pondering that perhaps all was not as straightforward as it had seemed between them.

A while later, after a seemingly endless round of being introduced to people and being stared at, Kat's nerves were on end and she felt close to breaking point—physically and emotionally.

As if sensing her vulnerability, Zafir took advantage of a moment when they were alone and bent down to say, sotto voce, 'It's going to happen, Kat. Tonight.'

Those words…said with such implacable arrogance after his mixed messages pushed Kat over the edge of her control. She hissed up at him. 'No, it's not, Zafir. It's really not.'

She walked away as steadily as she could and felt his gaze boring into her from behind. She went through the open French doors and breathed in deep, hoping the cool air would calm her down.

Dark storm clouds were gathering on the horizon and she heard a distant crack of thunder. She was aware of someone hovering nearby—a bodyguard. And now she felt foolish for stalking off.

She wished in that moment that Zafir had never reappeared in her life. And then the thought of that made her suck in a pained breath and put a hand to her belly as if someone had just punched her.

Taking another deep breath, and assuring herself that she still had everything under control, Kat turned around and walked back into the room—only to see Zafir smiling indulgently down into the upturned face of a famous French actress, a renowned beauty, who had her scarlet-tipped nails firmly on Zafir's arm as she told him something undoubtedly scintillating and hilarious.

As if feeling the weight of her gaze, Zafir turned his head for a second and looked straight at her, with no expression on his face, and then he deliberately turned his back on her and his attention to the other woman.

The speed with which Kat became engulfed in a red mist of jealousy shocked her. As did the speed with which she could already imagine that Zafir had decided she was too much trouble to pursue, and was now turning to an easier and far more accommodating prospect.

Kat had made Zafir wait before finally agreeing to date him that first time. He'd been too overwhelming... intimidating. But a woman like that wouldn't make him wait. He'd give and she'd take and then move on...not like Kat, who'd never really moved on.

She turned away from the sight just as Rahul passed close by. Kat caught his arm impulsively. 'I've got a headache—do you think it'd be okay if I left now?' She crossed her fingers at the white lie.

Rahul immediately looked concerned and anxious. 'Let me just check...'

He was gone before she could stop him, and suddenly Kat couldn't bear to watch Zafir's face change expression as he was told that she wanted to leave early. She threaded her way through the crowd to where another of Noor's men was waiting and told him she was ready to give the necklace back. He looked unsure, but took her aside to a secure area and waited as she removed it and handed it over.

He and his colleague had it boxed up and whisked away within seconds. Discreet and efficient.

When Kat stepped back into the room she let out a sigh of relief that she couldn't see Zafir or Rahul. She pressed the button for the elevator, wanting to get out of Zafir's orbit before she made a complete fool of herself.

It finally arrived with a soft *ping* and the doors opened. She'd stepped in, and had just pressed the button to go down when a hand inserted itself into the closing doors, forcing them open again.

Zafir.

CHAPTER SIX

ZAFIR WAS ANGRY. 'Leaving so soon?'

Kat forced herself to sound cool. 'I have a headache.'
She wasn't even lying now. She could feel a throbbing
at her temples.

He frowned and stepped into the elevator with her
as the doors closed. Instantly the space was dwarfed by
his tall and broad masculine form. 'I'll see you down to
your room.'

Panic surged. 'You don't have to—you shouldn't leave
the function.'

Zafir shrugged even as his eyes stayed on her, alert.
'They'll hardly notice now, the champagne and cocktails
have been flowing for a couple of hours. The object of the
evening has been achieved. Jandor will be indelibly imprinted on their minds, thanks to you and the diamond.'

Zafir pressed the button and the elevator started moving with a little jolt. It was enough to make Kat sway and
go off balance, falling backwards. As quick as lightning
Zafir reached for her, taking her arms and hauling her
against him.

They both sucked in a breath at the contact, and with
a muttered curse Zafir reached out and slammed a hand
on the stop button. Kat's hands were pressed against his
chest as the elevator came to a juddering halt.

'What are you doing?'

'Do you really have a headache, Kat?'

She looked up at him helplessly. She knew if she tried
to move he'd only pull her even closer, and as it was she
could feel every hard plane of his chest, and down lower

the unmistakable thrust of something much more potent. His arousal. For her? Or for that woman?

Heat and self-disgust flooded her body. She pushed herself away, stepping back until she hit the wall and could go no further.

Zafir took a step closer. 'You don't have a headache, do you?'

Kat bit her lip, but the sharp pain made no difference. Images of him laughing down at that woman, made her say rashly, 'What do you even care, Zafir? I'm just a living, breathing mannequin. Your guests will be missing your presence.'

Zafir's eyes flashed and then narrowed on her, and he came even closer. So close that she could see the beginnings of stubble along his hard jaw. The darker flecks of grey in those mesmerising eyes.

Softly he asked, 'You wouldn't be jealous, would you, Kat? Jealous that I was giving attention to a woman who made it obvious that she'd welcome me to her bed if I just said the word?'

Aghast that she'd exposed herself so easily and quickly, Kat blurted out, 'Don't be ridiculous. I don't care who you sleep with.'

Zafir stepped even closer. Close enough to touch. 'Liar,' he breathed. 'I think you do care.'

The expression on his face was fierce now. He put his hands on the wall, either side of her head, enclosing her with his whole body.

Kat was barely breathing. The tension was thick enough to cut with a knife. Her hands were balled into fists at her sides in an effort to stop herself from grabbing him—or smacking him.

'The truth is that you've reduced me to crude methods not even used by hapless teenage boys.'

Kat shook her head, finding it hard to focus. 'What are you talking about?'

Zafir's jaw clenched. 'I'm talking about making you jealous, Kat. I wanted to make you jealous. I wanted to provoke you into showing me something…anything…so that I don't feel as if I'm the only one going crazy here.'

Kat swallowed, all her turmoil dissolving and being replaced by a dangerous tenderness. She whispered unevenly, 'You're not going crazy…'

'The problem is,' he said, as if she hadn't spoken, his voice rough, 'that I *do* care who I sleep with, and unfortunately there's only one woman I want to sleep with. She's haunted me for months and I can't get her out of my head…not till I've tasted every inch of her again.'

Kat felt a dangerous languor steal over her. She was oblivious to the fact that they were in a stalled elevator. 'Who…?' she managed to croak out. 'Who is this woman?'

Zafir lowered his hands from beside her head and expertly wrapped one arm around her waist, pulling her into him. His other hand found and started plucking the pins from her hair as he said throatily, 'You know it's you, Kat…it's always been you.'

It's always been you…

Kat could feel tendrils of her hair falling down around her shoulders. She didn't have the strength to resist Zafir any more. She wanted him with an ache that was painful. And when his mouth touched hers she couldn't stop a helpless whimper of need escaping. Her hands were already unfurling and climbing up to wrap around his neck.

The kiss quickly became carnal and explicit. This was no gentle exploration. This was months of hunger and frustration. Months of X-rated dreams. Zafir demanded Kat's response and she gave it, arching her whole body into his as if they could just fuse there and then.

She was dizzy, ravenous for the taste of Zafir's mouth, sucking his tongue deep, nipping with her teeth. He was hot and hard against her belly, and she longed to wrap her hand around him and squeeze his flesh, remembering the way his breath would hiss between his teeth.

His hands roved over her back, slipping over her dress, feeling her curves. She felt constricted, her breasts pushing against the heavy fabric, nipples tingling with need.

Zafir's hands went lower, covering her buttocks, squeezing with his big hands, pulling her dress up. It was the sensation of air on her bare leg that finally managed to cut through the heated haze in Kat's brain, and with a stark feeling of sheer panic and dread she realised that Zafir was about to expose her in more ways than one.

She broke away from his kiss and opened her eyes. It took a second for her to focus, and her breathing was as jagged as her heart rate. The fact that Zafir looked similarly dishevelled was no consolation.

She'd almost forgotten…

She stepped to the side, her dress falling down around her legs. Covering her again. Her mouth felt swollen. Other parts of her felt sensitive. Slick. *God.* He'd been moments away from lifting her up so she could wrap her legs around his waist.

'What is it, Kat?'

She couldn't look at him. Her hair was half up, half down, and she raised trembling hands, trying to repair the damage. 'Please…just take me back to my room.'

For a long moment there was only the sound of harsh breathing in the small space, and then Zafir turned away and pressed a button. The elevator started moving again, and this time Kat put a hand on the wall to steady herself. She saw her clutch bag on the floor, where she must have dropped it, and bent down to pick it up with nerveless fingers.

Zafir's back was impossibly broad and remote in front of her. She longed to say something. Anything. But her tongue was frozen.

When the elevator doors opened Zafir stepped out. Kat followed him down the corridor to her room. She opened her clutch to get her key, but her hand was shaking too much to put it in the door. Any hope of disguising his effect on her was well and truly gone.

Her key was plucked out of her hand by a much bigger one and Zafir opened the door efficiently, waiting for her to go in. Kat wanted to sag down into a chair and take the weight off her quivering legs, but Zafir followed her in, closing the door behind him.

She faced him, heart thumping. 'Zafir, I didn't mean for you to—'

'Continue what we just started?' he inserted harshly.

He folded his arms. He'd never looked more formidable or gorgeous.

'Well, tough,' he said. 'Because I have every intention of finishing what we started.'

Kat shook her head and forced herself to speak as calmly as possible. 'I'm sorry, Zafir, if I gave you the impression…'

But the words dried up in her throat under his quelling look. She knew Zafir was more sophisticated than that. Just because they'd kissed, he wouldn't expect more now. But it wasn't about that. She'd felt the conflagration between them. It was unique. Unprecedented. Undeniable.

He unlocked his arms and shed his jacket, tossing it on a nearby chair. Then he reached for his bow tie and undid it with jerky moves, yanking open his top button.

He looked around. 'Do you have anything to drink in here?'

Kat lifted her hand and pointed to the drinks tray on a table near the window. Zafir strode over, more animal than man. He poured himself a shot of something and drank it back in one.

Then he looked at her. 'Do you want anything?'

Kat was shocked. It was as if a layer of civility had been stripped away. She'd never seen him like this. Not even that night when her world had crumbled to pieces around her.

She shook her head, even though her mouth was dry. 'No, I'm fine.'

Zafir slugged back another shot and turned around to face her. 'You're not, though, are you?'

Kat could feel herself pale.

How did he know?

'What do you mean?'

'What I mean is that for some reason you're determined to deny us this closure.'

Relief warred with anger.

He didn't know.

'You're so certain that resuming our physical relationship will end with everything neatly tied up in a bow?'

Hurt lanced her that Zafir could believe it would be so simple. But it would be...for him. Because he had no feelings involved. Only lust. She wished it could be so easy for her.

His mouth was a tight line. 'It's inevitable, Kat. We can't be within two feet of each other without going up in flames. Can you handle another week of this? Because I know I can't.'

One week. Surely she could survive one more week and then walk away, heart and soul still intact?

She lifted her chin. 'I can, Zafir. I'm sorry for what just happened...' A sudden flash of their two bodies welded together and how good it had felt to have him kiss her made her falter, but then she regained her composure and said, 'But it was a mistake.'

'A word I've heard more times than I care for lately,' Zafir said.

He started to pace then, and that only drew Kat's hungry eyes to his lean form.

He stopped suddenly to look at her. 'What is it, Kat? Is this punishment for what happened before? This is your retribution? Because I didn't give you a chance to explain your past? Because I judged you too harshly?'

Kat's eyes widened. It was so much more than that. That had been just the tip of the iceberg.

He hadn't loved her.

She backed away. '*No*, Zafir. I'm not that petty.'

She whirled away from him, afraid he'd see something of the emotion she was feeling on her face.

A bleak, futile anger rose up and she turned around again. 'It's not all about you, you know. There are things…things you don't understand.'

He frowned, and then his gaze moved over Kat's shoulder to something behind her and he frowned even harder.

She only had the barest moment of premonition before he said, 'Why are there crutches in your room?'

Kat wanted to close her eyes. She wanted to be on her own so she could curl up in a ball and pretend she'd never seen Zafir again. Pretend that her body wasn't pulsating with awareness just to be near him.

This was the moment of truth. It had been spectacularly naive or stupid of her to believe that she could keep her secret from Zafir. It was amazing that he hadn't found out already. And she'd never been less ready to tell him. Especially not after that moment in the elevator, reminding her of just how explosive it had always been between them. And how it could never be again. Not after this.

'Kat?' There was something stark in his voice. 'Who do the crutches belong to?'

She looked at him and swallowed painfully. 'Me. Because I need them.'

Zafir shook his head. Not understanding. And why would he?

'Tell me why you need them when you're standing in front of me right now.' He sounded harsh now.

It was time to stop hiding. Kat reached down and caught her dress in one hand. She pulled it up, revealing her prosthetic limb and the joint where it met her leg.

Even so, it took a few seconds for Zafir to understand what he was looking at—and when it finally registered he went pale. Eventually his gaze lifted back to her face. The room was so silent it felt like time had stopped.

'What are you showing me?' Zafir's voice was hoarse.

The dress fell from nerveless fingers to cover her leg again. She started to tremble and felt cold. She was going into shock. 'The accident…the one I mentioned. It was worse than I let you believe. They had to amputate… My foot…was crushed.'

She must have swayed or something, because suddenly Zafir was there, hands on her shoulders, pushing her down into a chair. He disappeared for a moment and then reappeared with a glass in his hand.

He held it up to her mouth. 'Drink some of this.'

Kat's eyes were on his as she lifted shaking hands to the glass and tipped back her head. The liquid burned down her throat and she coughed. Zafir took the glass away as fire bloomed in her chest, having an almost immediate effect on the numb coldness that had gripped her.

He put down the glass. His hands were on the chair's armrests either side of her. He looked as if he'd just been punched in the gut.

'Why didn't you tell me?'

Because I was using it as a crude defence to resist you.

Kat opened her mouth and shut it again uselessly, before saying finally, 'At first I didn't see that it was any of your business. And then...when you offered all that money to do the job... I couldn't afford to say no and I was afraid if you knew you'd think I couldn't do it.'

Zafir's grey gaze bored all the way through her. 'I don't think that's it at all—or not all of it.'

Feeling threatened, and horribly exposed, Kat pushed herself up out of the chair, forcing Zafir to stand. She stalked away from him, acutely aware of her limp now.

She whirled back, the truth spilling out. 'I'm different now, Zafir. You want the Kat I was before, and she doesn't exist any more. I didn't want to see you look at me the way others do—with horror and pity.'

She'd dreaded this moment ever materialising, and she feared that she'd avoided it for so long for the most basic reasons of vanity more than anything more noble. And that killed her when she knew she was so much stronger than that. But standing here now, in front of the only man who'd ever made her feel truly alive, she couldn't bear it. Tears weren't far away, and that would be the worst humiliation.

'You know where the door is, Zafir. Please, just go.'

But he didn't go. He came closer, and Kat held herself rigid for fear she'd shatter into a million pieces before she was alone again, when she could lick her wounds without that devastating gaze on her.

When Zafir spoke, he sounded harsh. 'You really think I hadn't realised that you'd changed in some very fundamental way? Have you not noticed that if anything it's only made me want you more?'

Kat blinked. She'd expected to be looking at a retreating back and a closing door. Not listening to Zafir sounding almost...hurt.

'You really think I'm that shallow?' he asked.

She might have before, when he'd more or less admitted he'd only proposed because she embodied some physical ideal, but now everything she'd thought she'd known about this man was jumbled up and contradictory.

She couldn't speak. The fact that he was still here was too much. The tears she was desperately holding back filled her eyes. She heard a curse, and then Zafir's white shirt became a blur in her vision as she was enveloped in strong arms and held tight against his body.

It was heaven and hell as a storm took hold of Kat that she had no control over and no choice but to give in to it. She wept for everything: her heartbreak, the loss of her leg, for her deceased and damaged mother and for the fact that she'd longed for Zafir's arms around her so many times…even though she'd denied it to herself.

For a long time she stood in the harbour of Zafir's arms as his hands moved soothingly over her back. *Compassion.* Another facet to this man she hadn't seen before, adding to the complexity she felt around him now.

When her sobs had finally died away she pulled back and looked with horror at Zafir's wet shirt. She could see the darkness of his skin underneath, and despite her paroxysm of emotion she felt awareness sizzle deep inside. Mortified—because any desire Zafir had ever felt for her must have been incinerated by now—she pulled herself free of his arms completely, wiping the backs of her hands across her hot, wet cheeks.

He was the last person in whose arms she'd expected to find solace. Her eyes felt swollen. She must have rivers of mascara down her cheeks. This truly was her lowest moment. And that was saying a lot, considering what she'd been through.

'I'm sorry,' she said thickly, avoiding his eyes, 'I don't know what came over me.'

He took her by the hand and led her over to a chair, pushing her down gently. He reappeared with a tissue, and another shot of alcohol in a glass. He crouched down before her and made her take a sip of the drink, until gradually she felt seminormal again.

He dipped another tissue in a glass of water and gently rubbed at her cheeks.

She was mortified at the emotional storm she'd just unleashed all over him—and at the way he was tending to her so easily.

When he'd put the tissue down she forced herself to look up from his damp shirt to his face, which was tense and unreadable. 'Your shirt is ruined.'

His mouth tightened. 'I couldn't care less about my shirt. In fact—' He broke off and stood up, starting to undo his buttons.

Kat's mouth opened as his impressive chest was revealed, bit by bit. 'What are you doing?' she squeaked, holding the glass to her like some sort of shield.

Zafir's shirt was open now, and he made short work of the cufflinks, throwing them on a nearby table before he let the shirt drop to the ground and then he knelt down in front of her again.

His naked and very masculine chest filled her vision. It was deliciously broad, with dark hair dusting defined muscles. And dark, flat nipples that she remembered were sensitive to the touch, earning her a hiss through his teeth whenever she'd lavished attention on them...

She felt bewildered and exposed. 'Zafir—'

'I want to see it, Kat. Show me your leg.'

Her insides clenched hard in rejection of that. But he looked determined. 'Why would you want to see it?'

Zafir couldn't exactly articulate why he needed to see Kat's leg, but it came from a visceral place deep within him that was boiling over with a mixture of volatile emotions. Reverberating shock, futile anger, and a kind of grief he'd only ever felt before for his sister.

'I want to see what happened to you.'

He could see the myriad expressions crossing her face, dominated by clear reluctance, and it made him want to go out and smash whoever had done this to her into tiny pieces. But then something else crossed her face that he couldn't decipher—something like resignation—and she put her hands on her dress, pulling it up over her knees.

The sparkling folds of the dress were gathered on her smooth thighs and he could see now where thick material like a sock came halfway up the thigh of her left leg. It was flesh-coloured. So it wouldn't be too noticeable? That sent another spurt of raw emotion through Zafir.

He moved back to give Kat room, watching as she pressed a button at the bottom of the prosthetic limb and then she pushed at it firmly, so that the whole apparatus slid down and off.

He absorbed fresh shock seeing her amputated leg, which now ended just a few inches below her knee. The thick, sock-like liner stretched from above her knee, to the bottom of her limb, where it was rounded and had a pin, which obviously slotted into the prosthetic leg to help keep it in place.

Her hands moved to the liner covering her leg and he could see that they were trembling. He moved forward and covered her hands, forcing her to meet his gaze by sheer will.

When she eventually looked at him he said, 'Let me?'

She bit her lip, and it looked so painful that Zafir wanted to reach out and rescue it, but then she said hoarsely, 'You don't have to do this.'

He reminded her, with an arrogance that felt hollow now, 'I don't have to do anything.' There was a heavy weight in his chest, an ache he'd never felt before.

Eventually she lifted her hands from under his and Zafir looked down and took a breath before carefully rolling the liner down Kat's thigh, over her knee and off, taking in the enormity of the moment as her naked leg was revealed.

He put both hands on her leg, cupping it, feeling the skin where it was so brutally cut short. The scar was a jagged but neat line, and he ached even harder to imagine the pain she must have gone through. The weeks and months of rehabilitation. The fact that he hadn't noticed anything before now was testament to her sheer will.

The earth could have stopped revolving outside, he was so focused on Kat and this moment. He looked at her. 'Tell me what happened?'

Her hands were tightly clasped in her lap, knuckles white. Her face was pale, eyes huge. 'It was dark. I was crossing a road… There was a truck and a motorcycle. They told me afterwards that the truck's brakes failed and it went out of control, hitting the motorcycle. I ended up in the middle. My foot…was crushed.'

Zafir thought of her broken, lying still on the road, and felt a dizzying surge of panic. It took him a moment to compose himself, but then he said, 'I'm so sorry, Kat… that this happened to you.'

She half shrugged, as if it was no big deal, but he could see the vulnerability in her eyes.

'The man on the motorcycle died, Zafir. He was only twenty-two. When you consider that… I was lucky.'

For a second Zafir's mind blanked as he thought of how easily it might have been Kat who had lost her life.

Bitterly he said, 'It sounds like the truck driver was the lucky one.'

Kat shook her head. 'He has to live with the guilt he feels every day. He came to visit me and I've never seen anyone so haunted.'

Zafir was humbled by her compassion. He realised now where her new steely strength came from, and he felt something like awe. He also felt a very sharp pang at the assertion that he should have been there for her.

But he hadn't—because he'd judged her on the basis of lurid headlines without really giving her a chance to explain her side. For the first time, Zafir felt a rush of remorse and regret. Everything had changed and yet, conversely, nothing had changed.

Kat felt so delicate and vulnerable under his hands, and yet strong. It made his blood pulse faster through his veins. Acting on pure instinct and need, Zafir spread his hands out, encompassing Kat's leg completely. He bent forward and pressed a kiss to her knee, then lower, to the top of her shin, his hands moving down and cupping her residual limb.

He heard her sucked-in breath and a strangled-sounding, 'What are you doing?'

He lifted his head and looked at her with explicit intention. He moved both hands up her leg at the same time, until they encircled her bare thigh. Blood thundered in his veins.

'What do you think I'm doing, Kat? I'm finishing what we started.'

CHAPTER SEVEN

KAT COULDN'T BREATHE. Again. It was a miracle that any oxygen was reaching her brain. Somehow, from somewhere, she managed to suck in a breath. And another one. Her heart rate wouldn't slow, though. She felt flayed alive. Raw. But deep within her core burnt a fire that not even her turmoil could quench.

She'd expected Zafir to be long gone by now. But he wasn't. He was kneeling at her feet, looking up at her with that molten silver gaze. It was uncompromisingly direct, leaving her nowhere to hide.

And yet her mind reeled. He'd just looked at her... touched her leg. Inspected it. Cupped it reverently. Kissed it.

Emotion threatened again. The only people who'd touched her there since the accident had been medical professionals, or herself when she'd had the nerve to, and it had taken a long time to do it without crying.

Yet Zafir had just done it, and he hadn't looked remotely horrified or disgusted. He'd looked sad. Angry. Fierce. And there'd been something unmistakably possessive in his touch too—as if he was claiming some kind of ownership of her damaged limb. Which was obviously just a figment of her overwrought brain.

She shook her head, forcing herself to articulate her scattered thoughts. 'You don't mean that...'

Something struck her then, and she went cold all over. Zafir was a proud man. A very alpha man. A man full of integrity.

She recoiled back in the seat. 'You don't have to prove

anything, Zafir. If you stand up and walk away it won't make you less of a man.'

His hands tightened on her thigh and his eyes widened. A look of affront came over his hard-boned face. 'First you think I'm too shallow to handle this news and now you're accusing me of being too proud to walk away from something I don't want to do?'

Kat swallowed. She'd never seen Zafir look more stern.

His voice resonated deep within her. 'I would have thought that the least you know about me by now, Kat, is that I don't ever do anything I don't want to. I want something and I go after it. Do I need to remind you of how I went after you?'

She shook her head quickly. She did not need a reminder of that all-consuming seduction right now—her brain was addled enough as it was.

'I am here,' he said, 'because I want you, Kat. I tracked you down because I couldn't get you out of my head. Because I believe we have unfinished business. Because I believe that I won't be able to get on with my life until I've tasted you again…until I'm buried so deep inside you that I might finally be able to think clearly again. What happened to you changes nothing about how much I want you.'

All Kat heard was 'until I'm buried so deep inside you' and her whole lower body clenched, as if it was already anticipating taking his body into hers. As if some muscle memory was already reacting just to his words.

She clamped her thighs together, trapping Zafir's hand. His eyes flashed. He knew. He could sense her helpless response. But insecurity warred with desire. Did he really still want her?

With gentle but remorseless force, Zafir pushed her knees until they were spread apart and he was between them. Her dress was ruched up around her thighs, and if he looked he would see her very plain white panties.

As if reading her mind, his hands moved upwards, and Kat's breathing grew ragged and fast. Within seconds he would know just how badly she ached for him. She'd be utterly exposed.

She reached down and covered his hands, stopping their progress, and shifted, sitting up straighter in the chair, trying to put some space between them. She seized on something, *anything*, that might restore sanity, even though the blood rushing through her body wasn't asking for sanity at all. The opposite…

'I haven't been with anyone since—' She stopped. She'd been about to say *since you*, but she didn't want Zafir to know that. It would mean too much. She hoped he'd assume she'd meant to say *since the accident*.

Zafir shook his head. 'None of that matters. What matters is here and now.'

He rested his arms on the armrests of her chair and just looked at her. Her thighs were bracketing his chest…she could feel the tiny abrasions of his chest hair against the delicate skin of her inner thighs. Between her legs she was so damp and hot it was embarrassing.

'You're so beautiful,' he said simply.

Kat wanted to duck her head, avoid that blistering gaze, but she couldn't. She couldn't speak.

Zafir bent forward and touched his mouth to hers.

Kat closed her eyes and a helpless sound of need flowed from her mouth to his as the kiss hardened and deepened. It was too late for sanity. She couldn't resist this. *This* was what she wanted and needed to make all of the questions and doubts and insecurities fade away. When Zafir touched her she couldn't think of anything else. And she didn't want to.

On every level he'd defeated her. Kat's whole body

arched towards his, her arms finding and twining their way around his neck as his kiss got deeper and darker, and so explicit that it sent electric shocks all the way through her core, against which Zafir's taut belly provided a delicious friction.

His hands were on her thighs, lifting them up to hook around his hips. Kat didn't have time to think about how she looked, or how the lack of her limb felt. Zafir was too all-consuming.

One hand was on her back now, finding the top of the zip at her neck. He tugged it down and she felt air touch her bare skin as the dress slackened around her breasts. Zafir took his mouth off hers to pull back. They were both breathing harshly.

Without taking his eyes off hers, he pulled her dress forward and down, easing it off her shoulders and down her arms until she was naked from the waist up. The design of the dress had precluded the need for a bra.

Then he looked down at her.

She saw the way his eyes grew even darker, and colour slashed across his cheeks as he took in her bare breasts.

He said something guttural in Arabic. And then he brought his hands to her flesh, cupping her and squeezing. Her nipples were hard, stinging points, and when Zafir passed a thumb over each of them she almost cried out, they were so sensitive.

He looked at her and said raggedly, 'I've dreamt of this. Of you…'

He put one hand on her back, encouraging her to arch towards his mouth. He cupped her breast with his other hand, and then surrounded first one nipple and then the other in hot sucking heat. Kat's hands were buried in his hair, clinging on for dear life as he stoked her arousal to painful levels.

It was as if a wire was directly connecting Zafir's

mouth on her breasts to her core. The deliciously wicked combination of his rough tongue and teeth on her sensitive flesh pushed her right over an edge she didn't see coming, and she found herself shuddering in his arms as an orgasm gripped her and threw her high, before letting her float back down to earth.

She stiffened and pulled back in mortification, her cheeks burning. Her body had just betrayed her spectacularly. She shook her head. 'I'm sorry... I—'

He stopped her with a finger to her mouth. He looked wild. 'Don't you dare apologise. If I don't get inside you soon, Kat, I'm in danger of disgracing myself in a way that only used to happen when I was a boy and unable to control my body.'

Her eyes widened as comprehension sank in. 'You mean you—'

'Yes,' he said succinctly. And then, 'Where's the bedroom?'

All semblance of civility was gone now. And it was the sexiest thing Kat had ever seen.

'Behind you.'

With effortless strength, Zafir stood and scooped Kat up against his chest. Her arms went around his neck as he kicked open the bedroom door and brought her into the dimly lit room.

The gathering storm clouds outside went unnoticed as Zafir lowered Kat to the bed. So did the jagged fork of lightning and the first drops of heavy rain.

A part of Kat couldn't believe this was happening, and she needed a moment to assimilate everything and analyse the consequences. And yet, in spite of this knowledge, she couldn't bring herself to utter a word as she lay back and watched Zafir strip off the rest of his clothes with all the natural-born confidence of a spectacularly beautiful, sexually virile man.

Kat's eyes widened as she took in a sight she'd thought she'd never see again. A very aroused Zafir. Her greedy gaze avidly took in his whole body, noting that his muscles seemed even harder than before. His body bigger. And yet he was leaner. As if he'd shed some softer layer. Maybe becoming a King had done that to him.

'You, Kat,' he said gutturally. 'I want to see you too.'

He started to tug at her dress, pulling it down over her hips and off completely. Now she only wore her plain white panties, and she felt embarrassed. She'd always made an effort before, aware that Zafir had once liked wispy concoctions of lingerie—usually sent to her by him. But as he came down beside her on the bed now, his eyes gleamed with a hunger that turned any doubts to dust.

His hand smoothed over her chest and belly, which contracted with need. When his hand reached her underwear and his fingers slid underneath to explore she put a hand down instinctively. He looked at her. Once again she bit her lip. Unsure. As if she hadn't ever lain with this man before. As if he hadn't just seen her fall apart after barely touching her.

'I haven't… I don't look after myself down there like I used to.' Her cheeks burned.

Zafir's nostrils flared. 'Kat…when are you going to get it? *Nothing* about you could turn me off.'

His words unleashed a fresh flood of heat, and she realised now how careful she'd always been to live up to some ideal that she'd thought he wanted. His hand explored further, over the curls she'd always been told she had to remove for the sake of lingerie modelling contracts.

When his fingers touched her very core she arched her back off the bed. Within seconds her panties were gone and her legs were splayed. Zafir clamped big hands on her thighs, holding her captive as he bent his head and proceeded to explore her drenched sex with a thoroughness that rendered her insensible.

Her first orgasm had taken her by surprise. This one built and built until she almost screamed with the need to release the tension—and then Zafir circled her clitoris with his tongue, sucking it roughly, and she exploded into a million pieces.

When he loomed up over her he looked like a god. A dark, sexy, dangerous god. His muscles gleamed with sweat and she could smell his arousal—and hers. And even though her body wanted to float on a sea of bliss after that orgasm, when she heard the snap of latex and looked down to see Zafir's hands on his straining erection, need gripped her like a vice again. He made her insatiable. Greedy. She felt as if she'd been starved of some vital thing and was only now realising how empty she'd been.

He came down over her and aligned their bodies. She could see nothing else but him, feel nothing else but him. He surrounded her utterly.

After a breath he thrust into her body, deep and hard and unequivocal. As if stamping his brand on her. Kat breathed in the sheer expanse of him, awed at the way he filled her so completely. It was all at once familiar and altogether new. It was exquisite.

For a heart-pounding moment Zafir stayed embedded in her like that, as if he too was savouring the moment. And then something inside Kat broke apart. She reached for him, wrapping her arms around his neck, arching upwards. And as he started to move in long slow strokes in and out of her body's tight clasp, she gave herself over to the sensations racing through her body, rendering her mute.

His movements quickened and became less controlled,

he reached for her left thigh and brought it up, holding it firmly, deepening his penetration. Kat was only aware of the pinnacle of pleasure beckoning. It came at them like a steam train, blasting them apart and then welding them back together as Zafir's big body slumped over hers. They were so joined at every possible point, Kat wasn't sure she'd ever been a separate entity.

She fell into an exhausted slumber under Zafir's weight, unaware of him moving off her and standing up from the bed, looking at her as though he'd never seen her before.

Zafir was still reeling a few hours later as he looked out at the dawn breaking over the Paris skyline. The storm had passed—a storm he'd only been peripherally aware of. He felt as if a bigger storm had just happened in this hotel room.

In him.

He could see the shape of Kat on the bed in the reflection of the window, her elegant curves, her breasts...

He turned around and looked at her properly, his gaze inevitably tracking to her left leg, where it ended so cruelly short. He could see the faint imprint of his hand on the pale skin of her thigh, where he'd obviously gripped her in the throes of the most urgent lust that had ever gripped him.

As if hearing his thoughts, she moved minutely on the bed, and Zafir's chest tightened when he saw how her left leg instinctively wanted to stretch out. He wondered if she experienced the 'phantom limb' that people spoke of, when they could feel the pain of their amputated limb even though it wasn't there any more.

Seeing her like this... It made him feel so many different emotions he wasn't sure where one started and the other ended. But mostly he felt angry that she hadn't trusted him enough to tell him. And, worse, that she'd clearly expected him to turn tail and run.

But then, he had to concede heavily, why would she have thought otherwise? After all, he'd pursued her relentlessly after seeing her model lingerie on a catwalk. Why wouldn't she believe that he was shallow enough to value physical perfection over anything else?

He shook his head. Sex with Kat had always been amazing. So amazing that it had prompted him to track her down again. But this…what they'd just shared…had reached a whole new level. He didn't remember it ever being so carnal or so visceral. He'd literally had to have her…or die. Sinking into her that first time had impacted on him on a level where sex never usually did.

He went cold as the significance of that sank in. It had felt like coming home. But not in the way that returning to Jandor always felt like coming home… This had been far more profound and disturbing. It had felt like coming back to a place he'd longed for without even realising it.

Zafir's immediate reaction was to negate this revelation as a lust-induced delusion, but the truth was harder to deny.

Things with Kat had morphed out of all recognition. And it had nothing to do with the fact that she'd been hiding the truth that she was an amputee. It had everything to do with the fact that after having sex with this woman closure had never seemed more distant.

He dragged his gaze back up her body to her face. She was awake now, and looking at him with wide golden eyes. And just like that desire returned—urgent and swift.

Her gaze tracked down his body, obviously taking in his helpless physical reaction. Her cheeks coloured as she said in a sleepily husky voice, 'You showered…'

For a second Zafir warred with his emotions and tendrils of panic growing inside him. This was so far beyond what he'd expected to experience with Kat again that he wanted to tell her that last night had been enough. He wanted to walk out through the door and never look back. Because suddenly things weren't as simple as he'd thought they would be.

But that urge to leave curdled in his belly.

He didn't want to leave. He wanted her.

Compelled by a force stronger than he could deny, he twitched his towel off his hips and stalked back to the bed. He lay down alongside Kat and touched her thigh, seeing how something in her eyes veiled itself.

'I marked you...'

She looked down and saw his handprint. Her hair hid her face as she said in a slightly breathless voice, 'It's okay...it doesn't hurt.'

Zafir scooped her hair over her shoulder and tipped her chin up so she had to look at him. She was wary, but he could see the heat in her eyes. He kept his eyes on hers as he moved so that he was between her thighs... his erection notched against the place where she was hot and wet. Ready for him.

It was too much. Zafir didn't have a hope as he gave in to the raging desire inside him, blocked out all the warning voices and slid home. Again. And again. Until he was reduced to rubble and the voices were mercifully quiet.

Kat woke up surrounded by steel and heat. She couldn't breathe. Panic gripped her and she instinctively thrashed out, flailing uncontrollably.

She vaguely heard a sound, but it took long seconds for her to realise that Zafir had all but pinned her to the bed and was now looming over her saying, 'Kat, relax— it's me... You're okay.'

She went still, even though panic still raced through

her blood. Eventually it dissipated and she asked shakily, 'What happened?'

'You were lashing out...screaming. "Get it off me! Get it off..."'

The first tendrils of understanding sank in, quickly followed by embarrassment. She breathed deep. Zafir's very naked body was over hers, but even that couldn't distract her from the fact that she'd just had the same nightmare she'd had for months after the accident.

She pulled back from Zafir's embrace and he let her go reluctantly, as if he knew she needed space but didn't want to allow it.

She struggled to find a way to explain herself. 'I'm sorry... If I feel claustrophobic it brings back the accident...when I was trapped under the truck.'

Zafir reared back. 'I make you feel claustrophobic?'

Kat was shocked at the hurt she heard in Zafir's voice. 'No...no. I'm just not used to waking up in bed with someone.'

Kat realised that part of it was disbelief that Zafir was still here—that she'd woken in his arms. The claustrophobia lingered, but it had nothing to do now with traumatic memories and everything to do with feelings rising inside her that she didn't want to analyse, like a coward.

She sat up and avoided his eye. 'I think I'll take a bath. Could you pass me my robe, please?'

Zafir said nothing for a long moment, and then he got out of the bed, unashamedly naked, and handed her a silken robe. Kat watched him walk into the bathroom and registered the sound of water running. She quickly pulled on the robe, covering her own nakedness, and scooted to the edge of the bed.

Zafir reappeared in the doorway, still naked. Ridiculously, Kat felt like blushing and she blurted out, 'Could you hand me my crutches?'

Zafir strode over, saying, 'You don't need your crutches.'

He was about to bend down and pick her up into his arms but Kat put out her hands, heart thumping treacherously at the innately masculine reaction.

'No, Zafir, I can do it myself.'

He drew back and looked down at her, a muscle pulsing in his jaw. 'Very well.'

He went and retrieved her crutches from the other room and Kat pulled herself upright on them, making her way into the bathroom, burning with self-consciousness. The only people who had seen her like this were medical professionals and Julie. Not a lover. Not Zafir.

She didn't want to turn around to see what might be on his face and she shut the bathroom door behind her, feeling alternately stronger than she'd ever felt but also weak. As if she'd scored some useless point.

She turned off the taps of the bath and disrobed, carefully stowing the crutches and lowering herself into the steaming, fragrant water.

The water lapped around her and a sense of déjà vu struck her as she recalled the last time she'd had a bath and where her mind had gone. She couldn't stop the images of the night they'd just shared from circling in her head like a lurid movie.

When he'd come back to the bed as dawn had broken they'd made love again. He'd pulled her over his body so that she was straddling him, and just before he'd thrust up into her body he'd asked, 'Is this okay? Are you comfortable?'

She'd nodded, aghast at how overcome she'd felt in that moment. She'd never seen this far more tender and gentle side to Zafir before. Even though there was nothing tender or gentle about their lovemaking.

She'd been so…uninhibited. Sex with Zafir had never felt like this. Before, she'd always felt somehow…aware of herself. Aware of all the women he'd been with before her and of her inexperience. It was as if a wall of glass had separated them, and no matter how skilful Zafir had been Kat had never lost herself completely, always holding some part of herself back.

But last night had been different. She'd lost herself completely. There'd been nothing between them but heat and lust and desperate need. It was as if she'd undergone some seismic shift.

There was a knock on the door, making her jerk upright. 'Kat, are you all right?'

Her voice sounded strangled as she called out, 'Fine. I'm fine.'

Zafir scowled on the other side of the door. Everything in him burned to go to her. He could imagine Kat's naked body all too well—slick and wet, droplets of water beading on her nipples...

He paced back and forth, aware of his body responding to his imagination. Cursing softly, he pulled a towel around his waist, as if that could douse his desire.

She'd looked so proud just now, walking into the bathroom on her crutches, back straight and tall. The stark reality of what she'd gone through had impacted on him all over again. It had almost but not quite eclipsed what he'd felt when she'd told him she felt claustrophobic. *Hurt.* An emotion he'd only ever felt around his siblings when they'd used to shut him out.

Hurt was not an emotion he welcomed. He'd always liked and respected Kat, but he'd never claimed to love her. He wanted no part of that—not after seeing his brother so destroyed by it.

Once again Zafir felt the urge to just walk away. Consign this to the status of a one-night stand. A slaking of lust. But even as he thought that he knew it was a lie. His body burned for her. One night would never be enough.

Just then there was the sound of splashing and a muffled curse. Zafir didn't even think. He walked straight into the bathroom.

Kat was sitting up in the bath and she looked at him. All he saw was gleaming pale skin and those glorious breasts rising from the water.

'I heard…something…' he said, feeling ridiculous.

'I just dropped the soap.'

Kat's cheeks were pink. Her hair was piled high, but long tendrils clung to her skin. Giving up the fight, Zafir muttered a curse and dropped the towel from around his hips, seeing Kat's eyes widen as she took in his helplessly rampant response.

Zafir was climbing into the bath before Kat could react. She squeaked as he settled himself behind her, making water slosh over the edge of the bath. 'What are you doing?'

His arms were around her, pulling her back against his broad chest, and the past and present meshed painfully for a moment, reminding of her of many such shared moments before.

'Zafir…' she protested weakly.

'Yes?' Zafir started to lather his hands with soap and then spread them over her body.

'You don't have to do this…' Kat tensed her body, trying to hold back the emotion she was feeling.

Zafir's hands stilled. He angled himself around to see her face. 'What is it?'

Kat shrugged, as if this wasn't a big deal. 'I just… This kind of thing has been so far from my mind… I certainly never expected that when the time came it would be you…'

Her heart beat fast. This was the closest she could come to trying to articulate the tangled feelings in her breast.

'And are you glad it's me?'

Kat knew now that she was in serious trouble, because experiencing this reawakening with him was more profound than she liked to admit. Not that she could tell him that. Not when to him this was just an affair to gain *closure*.

She shrugged again and said—as nonchalantly as she could when he was at her back, surrounding her in heat and desire, 'You're a good lover, Zafir...'

A good lover.

Zafir curbed his tongue. How did she manage to make that sound almost insulting? As for the thought that she would have let some other man see her for the first time as she was now... Zafir didn't even want to contemplate that scenario.

He concentrated instead on washing Kat's body with an explorative zeal that would soon make her admit that—*what?* What did he want her to admit? Zafir suddenly wasn't sure...

But then he felt Kat start to soften against him, her back arching against his chest, her body moving restlessly under the water, and as he found the slick centre of her body and made her moan he told himself he didn't care. *This* was all he cared about. Here and now.

It was enough. It would be enough.

CHAPTER EIGHT

SOME HOURS LATER Kat was dressed and ready to go, but she was delaying her exit from the bedroom to join Zafir in the suite, where he'd gone to make some calls, because the full significance of the previous night and everything that had happened was sinking in fully—and very belatedly. As if she'd been blocking it out until now.

Just thinking of Zafir's easy acceptance of her secret and how tender he'd been was overwhelming. At every step when she'd expected him to look at her in horror, turn and walk away…reject her…he'd done the opposite.

A flashback came of sweaty limbs entwined, his hand hard on her thigh, clamping her in place so he could thrust even deeper…

Kat felt a fine sweat break out over her body.

To say she was raw and exposed was an understatement. She hadn't felt like this since the aftermath of the accident. It was as if he'd torn her apart and put her back together, and now she wasn't sure who she was any more.

The thought of that grey gaze narrowing on her made her pace back and forth now, gnawing at a nail. A bad habit she'd cut out years before.

Zafir had effectively demolished every wall she'd erected around herself last night, and now there was nothing left to hide behind. The knowledge that she'd been using her leg as a defence mechanism to keep him at a distance was not welcome. And the thought of another night like last night was terrifying.

She was very much afraid he'd effortlessly expose things that she wasn't even ready to admit to herself yet. Like how far he'd burrowed under her skin again. Like how much she yearned for him to look at her as he had before, when she'd done no wrong in his eyes.

He'd used to look at her and say, 'I can't believe someone like you exists in this world…'

A curt rap on the door stopped Kat in her tracks.

'Kat? Are you ready? My car is waiting to take us to the airport.'

To take them to Jandor. Back to the place where Kat had realised just how ill-suited she was to become a permanent part of Zafir's life. And yet she'd tried to convince herself it would be all right.

Her recent thoughts and revelations still reverberating in her head sickeningly, she walked to the door and opened it. Zafir filled her vision. He'd changed into a charcoal suit and looked regal and impressive.

Before she could stop herself, she blurted out, 'There's something I need to say before we leave.'

Unfazed, even though Kat could imagine the veritable army of people waiting for them to leave, he just said, 'Okay.'

She was glad of her slim-fitting trousers and silk shirt. She wanted to send out a no-nonsense vibe.

She walked into the suite and turned around to face Zafir, steeling herself. 'What happened last night won't be happening again.'

Even as she said it she could feel her heart give a betraying lurch. And between her legs pulsed as if in protest.

Zafir leant his shoulder against the doorframe and folded his arms. He raised a brow. 'And why would that be?'

Kat wanted to pace, but forced herself to stand still and sound cool and blasé. 'Because last night was enough for me. And, in any case, Jandor is hardly an appropriate location for the King to be conducting an illicit affair with someone who is eminently unsuitable.'

Zafir straightened up from the wall, his gaze narrowing on her just as she'd feared. 'You never did like Jandor.'

Kat thought she detected a note of bitterness in his voice, and she responded defensively. 'That's *not* true. From the moment I first saw it from the plane I thought it was magical…'

Zafir looked sceptical.

'It's true,' Kat said, less vehemently now, afraid of revealing too much. 'I loved Jahor too. It was just… The palace was so huge and intimidating.'

She shivered now, remembering the massive empty corridors. The hushed reverence. Her fear of doing something wrong. The feeling of hundreds of eyes on her that she couldn't see.

'And you were so busy. I hardly saw you.' Kat hated the accusing note in her voice.

To her surprise, Zafir unfolded his arms and ran a hand through his hair.

He sighed. 'Maybe you're right. My father monopolised my attention.' Those grey eyes pinned her to the spot. 'I shouldn't have left you alone so much.'

Kat broke eye contact, not wanting him to see how much that impacted on her. 'It wouldn't have changed anything in the end,' she said. She had to keep reminding herself of that fact. If not him.

'I'm sorry I hurt you, Kat. I never meant to do that.'

Kat went very still. *This* was why they couldn't sleep together again. Zafir was getting far too close to the beating heart of her, and she didn't want him to suspect that that was why she couldn't repeat last night.

She looked at him and said, very deliberately, 'I was infatuated with you, Zafir. Not in love. It was for the best. I wasn't ready to step into such a hugely responsible role. I would have disappointed you. And, even though I know you would have been happy with a marriage based on respect and chemistry, it wouldn't have been enough for me in the end.'

She knew that much now—indelibly. She needed to be loved in a way that had eluded her all her life. For herself. Not just because she represented some ideal and as such could be used as a commodity, as her mother had used her so shamelessly. And as she had used herself when she'd had to.

An impulse rose from deep inside her at that moment, a desire to unsettle Zafir as much as he unsettled her. 'What about you, Zafir?' she asked before she could stop herself. 'Would a marriage in little more than name really have been enough for you? Are you so cold?'

Zafir was silent for a long moment, and then he said, almost harshly, 'Yes, I am that cold. I was brought up to rule a country, not to fall in love. My parents' marriage was borne out of a need to unite two warring countries. There was no love lost between them, and yet together they brought peace to a region. Surely that's more important than the selfish desires of one person to indulge in the myth of a fairy tale?'

Kat tried to hide her shock. 'I know things are different for you…that you're not the same as the average person…' *Not remotely*, said a little voice. 'But I don't think it's too much to ask, Zafir…even for you.'

He started to pace, and as much as Kat had wished to unsettle him, now she regretted it. He stopped and looked at her accusingly. 'Love tore my brother apart. Destroyed him.'

Kat put a hand on the back of a chair near to her, as if that might steady her. 'What do you mean?'

Zafir had never really talked about his younger brother before, but she knew he existed. He had a reputation as a debauched playboy, and from the photos she'd seen of him in passing, in the gossip pages, he was as tall, dark and handsome as his brother, with a roguish edge that had earned him a place as one of the world's most elusive bachelors.

Zafir said, 'I had a younger sister—Sara. She was Salim's twin. They were playing one day in a walled garden. They were messing about as usual...' Zafir lifted a hand and let it drop. 'I heard Salim scream and I ran to them. She was dead when I got there...a massive head injury... She'd fallen from the high wall...'

Kat wanted to go and touch Zafir as anguish filled her chest, but it was as if he was still surrounded by that wall. 'Oh, Zafir... I'm so sorry. How old was she?'

He looked bleak. 'Just eleven.'

He went over to a window and looked out, his back to Kat. She sat down in the chair.

'They were so close, the two of them. From the moment they were born they had their own little world. Even spoke a language no one else could decipher. When she died...and when Salim realised how little our parents had valued Sara because she'd been a girl and not a boy... something broke inside him.'

After a long moment Zafir turned around. He was expressionless.

'I saw what loving someone and losing them did to Salim. It changed him for ever. I have no intention of ever investing so much in one person that they have the power to destroy you.'

A million things crowded onto Kat's tongue. She wanted to say to Zafir that Salim and Sara had obviously had a very strong twin bond, and of course Salim had taken her death hard, but that was no reason to believe Zafir would experience the same thing. But Kat's tongue wouldn't work. She guessed that whatever she said would be met with deep cynicism.

She stood up and tried to ignore the tightness in her chest. 'I'm sorry you had to experience losing your sister like that, Zafir. I think I would have liked to know her…'

'Yes…' he said almost wistfully. 'I often wonder how she would be now. I think she would be formidable.'

No more formidable than her older brother, thought Kat.

There was a sharp rap on the door at that moment, and Kat flinched.

Rahul's anxious voice floated through the door. 'Sire, the cars are waiting.'

Zafir's gaze narrowed on Kat again as he called out, 'Just a minute.'

She felt a frisson of danger as he walked over to where she stood with all the inherent grace and menace of a predatory animal. Their recent conversation was forgotten as that grey gaze skewered her to the spot.

'You meant what you said? You're certain this affair ends here?'

For a heart-jolting moment Kat thought that Zafir might just leave her here in Paris and go on without her. Maybe she'd pushed him too far, asking those questions…

She forced herself to nod.

Zafir snaked a hand around the back of her neck, under her hair. She went on fire.

He shook his head. 'It's not over, Kat—not yet. You can delude yourself that it is, but when you're ready to be honest and admit that it's not I'll be waiting.'

The worst thing, as he stepped back and she struggled to find some pithy response, was the relief rushing through her that he wasn't leaving her behind.

Not yet.

* * *

The setting sun bathed Jahor in warm golden light. Kat couldn't believe how overwhelmed she was to be back here again, but she told herself it had nothing to do with learning about Zafir's sister and brother or her renewed intimacy with Zafir.

She'd once had a very real fantasy of becoming Queen of this land, humbled and awed by Zafir's belief in her, but that fantasy had been cruelly shattered. She felt it keenly now, though—the sense of loss—even though she knew that it was better this way.

She wouldn't have known the first thing about being Queen. She would have let Zafir down. And she went cold now, thinking of how much worse it would have been if her past had come out after she had become Queen.

Zafir was sitting beside her in the back of a chauffeur-driven car, speaking on his phone in a low, deep voice as they wound their way through the ancient streets and up to the palace on the hill, overlooking the ancient city.

She was glad his attention wasn't focused on her for this moment. During the flight from Paris she'd found his gaze resting on her every time she'd looked at him, and by the time they'd disembarked her senses had been jangling with awareness.

She just had to resist him. That was all.

She could see people through the tinted windows of the car, bowing reverently as they passed by. And then a gaggle of gap-toothed boys chased the car, waving manically even though she knew they couldn't see her or Zafir. She felt an impulse to open her window and reach out to touch their hands, and it shocked her.

It was another reminder of how she'd never have had the decorum to be Queen. So why didn't that thought comfort her? Why did it leave her feeling hollow?

They were sweeping through the palace gates now, and

into the majestic forecourt. Nerves fluttered in Kat's belly as Zafir ended his phone call and said enigmatically, 'You might find some things a little changed since last time.'

When she got out of the car she could see several aides waiting, and Rahul, looking as efficient as ever. Staff greeted them, dressed in long, light-coloured tunics and close-fitting trousers. They were smiling as they took her luggage and Zafir's.

The last time she'd been there the staff had been dressed in black, and they'd had a dour air. There'd also been an oppressive atmosphere, but now there was an air of infectious joyousness.

A smiling young woman came forward to greet Kat, saying in perfect English, 'I'm Jasmine. I'll be your maid while you're here, Miss Winters. If you'd like to follow me?'

Kat looked over to where Zafir was still watching her, and he said, 'Go—settle in and rest. I'll come and find you.'

Then he was striding away, his aides and Rahul hurrying in his wake. And, in spite of Kat's intentions to put some distance between herself and Zafir, all she felt right then was bereft. But, she told herself sternly, that this was a good thing if it reminded her of how out of place she'd felt here before. It would help her to resist Zafir.

She was led over to a nearby golf buggy and the younger woman indicated for Kat to get in. Kat did so, and soaked up the glorious lingering heat and the beautifully cultivated gardens as Jasmine carefully drove them round to where Kat's suite was located, at the other side of the palace.

On her first visit, Kat remembered walking miles and miles through vast corridors behind a silent woman as she'd been led to her quarters, feeling as though she was being punished for something she hadn't done.

Her rooms were different this time—which she was grateful for. She had enough memories bombarding her brain without adding more to the mix. Memories of long hot nights when Zafir had crept into her bed and woken her up with his mouth on her...

'You'll see here, Miss Winters, that your wardrobe is fully stocked with clothes from our finest designers.'

Kat's cheeks burned as she diverted her mind away from X-rated memories, and her mouth fell open as she took in the acres of sumptuous fabrics hanging in the massive wardrobe. She put out a hand, touching an emerald-green gown reverently, and breathed, 'This is too much.'

But Jasmine was already opening drawers nearby, showing her a vast collection of brand-new lingerie and more casual wear. Everything and anything Kat could possibly need.

Except Zafir's trust and love.

She cursed herself for even thinking it. She might have had his trust, before she'd broken it, but she'd never had his love.

She thought of what he'd said before they'd left Paris, and wondered with a pang if any woman would be able to entice him out from behind the rigid wall he maintained around his heart.

Jasmine left Kat alone after she'd given her an exhaustive tour of the vast suite and shown her where a tray had been laid out with mouth-watering refreshments and a jug of iced water infused with lemons and limes.

After eating a little, Kat explored the bathroom, and was alternately shocked and moved to find that someone—*Zafir*—had obviously given instructions to have the shower made more accessible for her, with a chair and rails.

After a refreshing shower, she put her prosthesis back

on and slipped into a long kaftan she'd found among the clothes hanging in the wardrobe. It was dark gold, and it glided over her body like a cool breeze. She lifted her hair up and off her neck, twisting it into a knot on her head, and went outside the French doors to explore the grounds.

The sun was setting in a blazing ball of orange on the horizon and Kat watched it for a long moment, a sense of peace she hadn't experienced in a long time stealing over her. She took a deep breath, revelling in the heat and the rich, exotic scents around her.

This place resonated deep within her in a way that she couldn't explain. A familiar refrain popped into her head: she came from a trailer park in one of the poorest parts of Midwest America and she hadn't even completed her high school education. She had no right to feel an affinity with this place.

Kat pushed the assertion down. She could recognise how intimidated she'd been before, but of course she had a right to be here—no matter what her background was. If anything, the last eighteen months had shown her where her true strengths lay, and she wasn't as wide-eyed and naive as she'd once been.

She walked along a path shaded by the overhanging branches of a tree that bore small black fruits like berries. It truly was paradise. She spotted a walled garden ahead, but came to a stop at the entrance when she saw that it was untended and overgrown—in stark contrast to the lush perfection surrounding it.

Something about it called to her, and she stepped inside. She could just make out an empty dry fountain, and beautiful mosaics that were cracked and broken.

She felt as if she was intruding on a private space, and was just turning to go when she heard a noise. She whirled around to see Zafir standing in the entrance to the garden, breathtaking in traditional flowing cream robes.

As soon as she saw the look on his face something clicked in her mind, and she said slowly, 'This is where she died, isn't it? Sara…?'

He nodded once, curtly, and stepped inside the garden.

Kat said, 'I didn't mean to intrude. I was just passing…'

Zafir came and stood near the overgrown fountain. 'It's fine. How were you to know?'

He didn't look at Kat, and impetuously she asked, 'Tell me about Sara. What was she like?'

She held her breath for a moment, not sure if Zafir would indulge her, but then she saw the corner of his mouth twitch.

'She was beautiful and stubborn and mischievous.'

'Did she have your eyes?'

Zafir shook his head. 'No, she had blue eyes—like Salim. Long dark hair. They were inseparable like I told you, from the moment they were born. Like a little unit.'

'What about you?'

Zafir shrugged minutely. 'They didn't need me. They had each other.'

Kat didn't know what to say to that. She was blindsided by an image of a young Zafir, always on the outside of his siblings' intense bond, and how lonely that must have been.

'I can't believe your parents weren't affected when Sara died. They couldn't have been so cruel.'

Zafir turned around then, and the cold look on his face made Kat suck in a breath.

'Yes, they could and they were. Don't you remember meeting them?'

Of course she did. She'd met them on her first visit and endured an excruciating lunch during which they'd spoken their own language and made no attempt to speak with her, directing all their conversation to Zafir. They'd clearly deemed the prospect of her becoming a daughter-in-law a total travesty.

Zafir shook his head. 'I can't believe you still retain such optimism about people when your own mother exploited you so shamelessly.'

Kat's face grew hot. She felt like that naive virgin all over again. Mocked by Zafir's deep well of cynicism.

She lifted up her chin. 'I'd prefer to be optimistic about people rather than believe there's no hope for love or redemption. You're not your brother, Zafir. Or your parents.'

Suddenly acutely aware of the small space, and its air of general decay, Kat felt claustrophobic.

She started to walk out, but Zafir caught her by the arm. 'Where are you going?'

She looked at him, and hated the ease with which he could strike at her very heart. 'Back to my room.'

'I've arranged dinner for us in my private suite.'

Zafir's hand was warm on her arm, and it made her think of how it would feel on other parts of her body. It would be so easy just to say *yes*—to go with Zafir to his suite and let the inevitable happen. Her blood grew hot just from thinking about it. But she couldn't. Not if she wanted to walk away relatively intact when all this was over.

She pulled her arm free. 'No, Zafir. I'm tired and I'd like to go to bed—*alone*. I'm here to complete the job of promoting the diamond and Jandor and that's all I'm interested in.'

Zafir's eyes took on a gleam she didn't want to interpret. But he just said, 'Very well, Kat. I'll see you after lunch tomorrow, then.'

She had turned to walk away again before she stopped and asked suspiciously, 'The function is in two days. What's happening tomorrow?'

Zafir folded his arms and looked powerful and dangerous. 'A little sightseeing tour of my country. I'm making up for the fact that you saw very little of Jandor last time.'

Panic skittered along Kat's skin. 'You really don't have to do that. You're busy. I can sightsee on my own.'

He walked forward and caught her arm again, escorting her out of the garden in a smooth motion. 'Your concern for my schedule is commendable—but, yes, Kat, I am doing this. Jasmine will help you pack for the trip.'

Kat pulled herself free. *'Pack?'*

'I'm taking you into the desert for the night—a unique experience, and one I'd hate for you to miss out on before you leave.'

Before you leave.

Kat stifled the dart of pain. She recognised his look of steely determination. 'Fine, Zafir,' she bit out eventually. 'But don't think that this changes anything—all you'll be doing is wasting your own precious time.'

Zafir watched Kat walk back to her suite of rooms, her slight limp the only hint that there was anything different about her.

When he'd seen her standing in Sara's garden—as he called it—he'd expected to feel a sense of intrusion. But he'd felt the opposite. He'd felt as if a weight was being lifted off his shoulders. He'd found himself avoiding her eye, embarrassingly afraid of the compassion he suspected he'd see in those amber depths and what it might unleash inside him.

And then, when he'd told her about Salim and Sara and their bond, she'd asked, 'What about you?'

Her innocent question had impacted on him like a blow to the gut. No one had ever said that to him before—*What about you?*—because no one had ever really cared.

Zafir's hands curled into fists now, as if that could

halt the rise of something dark and tangled that he didn't want to decipher.

He turned around and strode back to his rooms, irritation and sexual frustration making his movements jerky. Damn her for throwing up more questions than answers. Damn her for not making this as easy as he'd expected it to be. And damn her for looking so right here…as if she belonged.

She couldn't belong here. Zafir had closed the door on that possibility comprehensively and for ever. He had a future to build, and Kat was not a part of that future. Very soon she would be in his past and Zafir would have no regrets.

But in the meantime he would use every skill he possessed to make her acquiesce one last time, and then—*then*—he would be able to let her go, and when he moved on and chose his Queen it would be someone who didn't look at him and make him feel as though she could see all the way to the depths of his soul…

Late the following afternoon Kat was in a helicopter, looking down in awe as they flew over the vast Jandor desert. The spiderlike shape of the helicopter's shadow undulated over high sand dunes as the sun set in the distance. It was magical.

Much as she had intended blocking out Zafir's far too magnetic presence, it was almost impossible. The space in the back of the helicopter was small, and his thigh was pressed firmly along hers. And she didn't like the look in his eye—far too intense and determined. As if he knew something she didn't.

She hated that he'd checked if she'd be okay in the confined space before they'd left, mindful of her claustrophobia. At every point where she was doing her best to rebuild her walls of self-defence, he was just kicking them down again.

After about thirty minutes they landed in a small airfield and Kat saw a fleet of four-by-fours waiting. One for them, and the rest for the security team and entourage. Zafir led Kat to the first four-by-four, and when she was in he got into the driver's seat. They drove out of the airfield and into the desert, surrounded on all sides by nothing but sand and massive dunes.

Kat was surprised to feel a sense of liberation—as if there was nothing but this in the world. She looked at Zafir's proud profile and the inevitable stubble shadowing his jaw. She wanted to reach out and touch it but she kept her hands to herself.

'How do you know where to go?'

Zafir looked up to where the sun was lowering in the sky. 'The position of the sun tells me where to go…and this…' He tapped at a navigation dial on the dashboard. He glanced at her. 'I know this place like the back of my hand. I used to come here a lot as a teenager.'

Kat turned to face him more, curious. 'What did you do out here?'

Zafir looked away and shrugged. 'Dune racing with my bodyguards. Meeting the nomads and hearing their stories. Learning how to fight and shoot. Training my peregrine falcon.'

Kat didn't say it, but she thought it: he'd obviously done all that alone. Her heart ached in spite of her best efforts.

Gradually she could make out a shape in the distance. She squinted, wondering if she was hallucinating, but it got bigger and bigger until she could see that it was green and lush. Trees… A circle of tall palm trees… An oasis!

She'd been to oases before, for fashion shoots, but they had invariably been close to cities. Not like this, in the middle of an ocean of sand, with nothing as far as the eye could see except sky.

When they stopped she got out of the four-by-four, shading her eyes against the setting sun that was burnishing everything red and gold. She stepped forward to join Zafir, who was rounding the bonnet, and stumbled in the sand, her leg momentarily stuck in the soft surface. Before she could take another step Zafir had caught her and swung her up into his arms.

Kat hated how breathless it made her when Zafir lifted her into his arms, and she huffed against his shoulder. 'I hate this aspect of my disability—that I can't just walk where I used to and that I'm so portable.'

Zafir snorted inelegantly. '*Disability?* I've never met anyone more able in my life!'

Kat's chest swelled, and she hated him at that moment for making it so hard to resist him or to stay cool towards him. She felt hot all over now, and it had nothing to do with the temperature of the desert and everything to do with that inner fire Zafir stoked so effortlessly.

The oasis was indeed ringed with palm trees, and when they stepped through the perimeter Kat gasped. Zafir let her stand, as the terrain here was more solid, and she looked around, drinking in the sight of the lush green idyll.

The oasis was carved out of a natural gorge that held a pool of crystal-clear water. There was a small waterfall down at the one end, sending up a spray of white foam. It was breathtaking.

There was one tent set apart from all the others, with a tented domed roof and lanterns outside, already lit. Zafir led her to this tent, and Kat's heart was thumping unevenly.

He had brought her here to seduce her.

How could she resist him in this place of pure fantasy?

Maybe you don't have to, whispered a wicked voice that she tried to quash.

When they got inside the tent a few more of Kat's defences crumbled. The interior was lit only by candles, and it was a sumptuous decadent fantasy, straight out of an Arabian fairy tale. An X-rated fairy tale. Because what dominated the lush scene was an enormous bed, on top of which lay jewel-coloured cushions and satin bedding. Or maybe the bed was all she saw because she couldn't stop thinking about sex with Zafir again.

One last time.

She somehow managed to tear her gaze from the bed and looked at Zafir. He stood near the entrance, watching her with that intent gaze.

Even though she suspected she already knew the answer she asked, 'Where are you sleeping?'

Zafir even allowed his mouth to tip up minutely, as if she merely amused him. 'In here—with you.'

He moved into the tent. Kat panicked even as her insides quivered with anticipation. If he touched her—which she yearned for as much as she feared—he'd surely guess how far she'd fallen for him all over again.

She put up a hand, seizing on *anything* to try and remind Zafir that she wasn't worth pursuing. She blurted out the first thing she could think of. 'You've accused me of having no ability to manage money and you're right!'

Zafir shook his head. 'Kat, we're not here to discuss your credit rating.'

She ploughed on, determined to try and make him turn away in disgust. 'The money you've given me upfront for this job? It's gone. Already.'

She waited with bated breath, but Zafir just kept coming closer and said easily, 'It's none of my business what you do with your money, Kat. But as a matter of interest what did you spend it on?'

Kat was deflated. She wished she could brandish some gaudy bauble under Zafir's nose, but of course she couldn't—and she also couldn't lie.

She avoided his eye. 'I gave it to the rehabilitation centre where I went after my accident because they're in trouble. And some to Julie, because she supported me.'

Zafir's feet came into her line of vision. He put a finger under her chin, tipping her face up. There was an enigmatic look on his face.

'I know, Kat.'

Her eyes widened with shock. 'How did you know?'

'Because whenever such a large sum of money is wired to another account the bank checks to make sure it's a genuine transaction. My accountants had to verify it. If you'd told me your intentions I could have given it directly to them…'

Kat couldn't escape his gaze and she shifted uncomfortably. 'I hadn't told you yet…about my leg.'

She pulled her chin free and stepped back a few paces, sensing the walls of the tent closing in around her—but not in a scary way. It was in a way that made her blood leap with illicit excitement. Still she resisted, though.

She wrapped her arms around herself. 'That's why I agreed to the job, Zafir, because I realised I could use the money for good. I wasn't looking for an affair—or an easy payday.'

His mouth tipped up wryly. 'I think you've made that clear.'

He came towards her again, as if determined not to give her any space, and for a moment Kat might have believed that they'd slipped through time to another age, where he was a medieval warrior king and there was nothing beyond this place but untamed lands and fierce desires.

He put his hands on her arms.

Far too weakly, Kat said, 'Zafir, *no*.'

His eyes were silver in the flickering candlelight. 'Kat, *yes*. All that matters is this moment. Here and now.'

His words impacted on her like little bombs, blasting the last of her shaky defences.

He pulled her so close that she could feel his chest moving against hers, and the blunt thrust of his burgeoning arousal. Then he cupped her face with his hands, tipping it up to his, and as his mouth covered hers Kat stayed tense, even though she knew it was futile. She wanted this as much as he did.

She was fooling herself if she thought that denying herself this would make things easier in the end... Or at least that's how she justified it to herself as she found herself softening, tipping over the edge of resistance, responding to Zafir's expert touch and kisses, letting his strength hold her up because hers was gone...

CHAPTER NINE

HOURS LATER, WHEN the oasis was bathed in silvery moonlight, and after they had gorged themselves on a succulent feast and then made love again, Kat was curled into Zafir's side, one arm across his chest, her hand idly tracing patterns on his skin. He felt sated, languid, and at peace.

Peace?

When that registered, a prickle of panic skated over his skin. He wasn't looking for peace. He had peace—*didn't he?* He was just looking for an end to this insatiable hunger he felt.

So why did you bring her here to this place? asked a snide voice.

To seduce her ruthlessly and get her to admit she still wanted him. That was why. And Zafir had felt ruthless as he'd noted Kat's attempts to ward him off. The fact that she'd done it by trying to remind him of the accusations he'd thrown at her before had impacted on him in a place he didn't like to acknowledge.

He'd wanted to stop her saying those things, stop reminding him of how wrong he'd been about her…

Kat moved beside him then, coming up on one elbow. He looked at her and his chest tightened. She was sexily dishevelled and still flushed. His hunger was like a sharp spike, clawing at his insides all over again.

She looked at him, and he saw how her eyes had turned more green than amber and she seemed concerned. A sense of desperation joined his panic. Everything in him resisted letting her see the pit of emotions he couldn't analyse in his gut. And so, in a crude reflex to avoid hearing what she was thinking, he moved, gently disentangling himself from her to sit up and reach for a robe.

'Where are you going?'

Her voice was husky, and even that had an effect on him. Zafir gritted his jaw.

He handed her another, smaller robe and watched as she sat up and pulled it on. 'I want to show you something.'

She came to the edge of the bed and started to reach for her prosthesis, but Zafir lifted her into his arms, saying gruffly, 'You don't need it.'

'Zafir, I *do* need it,' she said, her breath warming his neck. 'I don't want to get too used to this—it'll make me lazy.'

There was something in her voice—an edge that made Zafir's jaw clench even tighter. Especially when he thought of any other faceless man lifting her into his arms. But he was already walking out through the tent opening and across the oasis.

Kat curled into him and hissed, 'Someone will see us.'

'No, they won't. We're totally private.'

He walked until they reached the edge of the large pool, its surface rippling and glistening under the moonlight. The waterfall fell nearby—a muted roar. Zafir put Kat down on her good leg and held her steady as he let his robe drop. Then he pulled hers off so they were both naked.

He lifted her again, and stepped into the pool. Kat clung on and squeaked as Zafir lowered them both into warm, silky water. He held her until they were deep enough to float, feeling her nipples pebble into hard points against his chest, which almost undid him.

And then he asked, 'Okay?'

She nodded.

Zafir let her go and Kat swam a couple of metres

through the satin water before flipping onto her back, her wet breasts gleaming enticingly above the waterline in the silver light.

Zafir's body was so hard it ached, and he swam towards her like a magnet drawn to true north. He couldn't help smiling when he saw the grin on her face, and the way her hair was spread out around her like skeins of silk.

'You like this?'

She flipped over again, treading water. 'Swimming was my favourite part of rehab... For a moment I could almost forget what had happened, pretend I was whole again...'

Moved by something that scared him with its intensity, Zafir caught her under the arms and pulled her into him, so their bodies were touching. 'You *are* whole, Kat.'

Her eyes were huge and unreadable in the darkness, but even though Zafir couldn't analyse what was in their depths it didn't make him feel any less exposed. He knew now that he'd crossed an emotional line that he'd never wanted to cross with anyone, and he was afraid there was no way back.

'I feel whole when I'm with you.'

Kat immediately bit her lip, as if regretting what she'd just said.

The water lapped around them and Zafir gave in to the carnal dictates of his body with an eagerness that spoke of his desire not to think about emotions. He pulled her close, catching her thighs and wrapping them around his hips.

She reached down a hand and curled it around his erection, making him suck in a breath and see stars. *Witch.*

'Make love to me, Zafir...' she breathed.

He needed no further urging. He walked in the water until Kat could rest her back against the soft grassy bank. She arched towards him, offering herself. It was all Zafir could do not to tremble in the face of such sheer feminine power as he smoothed a hand down over her breasts and belly.

Catching her around her waist, he drew her closer so that his erection nudged against where she was slick and hot. He stroked himself against her body, teasing them both unmercifully until she was begging... Only then did he plant his legs wide and hold her steady as he thrust up into her body, making everything explode around them and finally, mercifully, dulling the tangled voices in his head and soothing the ache in his chest.

At least for now.

Early the following morning Kat tried not to be so aware of Zafir watching her from a slight distance as one of the senior nomads instructed her patiently on how to let the peregrine falcon fly from where it was perched on her arm, protected by a heavy glove.

Her eyes were as wide as saucers as she listened, and she tentatively stroked the belly of the majestic bird. She was terrified of this beautiful creature, with its huge talons, sharp beak and beady eyes, but trying not to show it.

She lifted her arm to let the bird go free, as she'd been instructed, and it flew up into the air before landing on a nearby stand. The old man with the turban on his head, the wrinkled face and kind eyes, put some food on Kat's glove and the bird swooped back to land on her hand again.

She felt a ridiculous sense of triumph, even though she knew the bird had been trained for years to do exactly this. She couldn't stop smiling, and looked at Zafir.

The smile slid from her face when she saw his expression. He looked as if someone had punched him in the gut. He was pale, and staring at her so intently that she instinctively moved towards him, forgetting about the bird until it moved.

She stopped. The nomad took the bird off her glove then, enticing it to hop back onto his own arm, and when Kat looked at Zafir again it was as if she'd imagined it—now he looked completely fine… Well, except for the intense way he was looking at her.

Memories of their X-rated swim in the pool rushed back, and she was glad of the long traditional kaftan she wore that would hopefully hide the effect Zafir had on her body from these strangers who had appeared to pay homage to their King.

He came towards her, his expression inscrutable. 'It's time to leave. We have a busy day ahead of the function this evening.'

Kat forgot about his enigmatic look as she realised that this was the last function and then she'd be free to go. She nodded quickly and avoided Zafir's eye as took off the glove, handing it back to the nomad with a smile that disguised her sorrow that she'd never see this place again.

Sitting in the back of Zafir's car on their way to the palace, an hour later, Kat was trying not to feel needy. She had to keep reminding herself that their night at the oasis hadn't really meant anything other than a lavish attempt on Zafir's part to prove that he could still seduce her.

And he had.

It was all a game to him. A battle of wills. She had told him she wouldn't sleep with him again, and naturally he had done his utmost to prove her wrong.

Self-disgust curled through her that she'd been so easy. And yet could she regret the intensity of their lovemaking in that idyllic fantastical place, where it had felt as if they were the only two people on the planet? Or the magic of that pool at midnight?

No. Already she wanted to hug those memories to her, like a miser protecting her gold. And Zafir hadn't made any great attempt to engage her in conversation since they'd left, so it couldn't be any clearer really…

She was so distracted with her thoughts that it took a second before she heard Zafir calling her name. She turned her head and looked at him, steeling herself. He was holding out his palm tablet and he looked grim.

'There's something you should see.'

It took her a second to absorb the headline.

The Real Reason Kat Winters Disappeared!

She scanned the piece with a growing sense of panic mixed with terror. Apparently 'a source' close to Kat had told the papers all about her accident, and the subsequent amputation and rehabilitation, with some added salacious details about how she'd wanted to hide away from the world because she was so ashamed of what had happened to her.

Anger flooded her veins…

She looked at Zafir, handing back the tablet as if it was poison. 'I was never ashamed—why would someone say that? I was hurt and in pain, struggling to come to terms with a new reality—'

Kat stopped abruptly, realising how close to full-on panic she was. She'd always dreaded this scenario—the story being leaked—and she realised now that she'd always hoped—naively, obviously—that she would be able to control the story before it came out.

The last thing she had ever wanted was for other people who were in a similar situation to feel she was ashamed to be one of them. She *was* one of them. They had helped her to get through it.

Zafir looked angry. 'Do you know who might have leaked it? Your agent?'

Kat drew back. 'No, Julie is my best friend—she wouldn't do something like this.'

Zafir made some remark under his breath about people and money, and Kat said, 'Give me your phone and I'll call her now.'

He handed over his phone and she made the call. Relief flooded her when Julie sounded as upset as she was, and she hated Zafir for infecting her with his cynicism for a moment, making her doubt her friend's loyalty.

When she'd handed back the phone she said, 'Julie thinks it was someone at the hospital I was taken to directly after the accident. That they saw the new pictures of me and put two and two together.' She grimaced. 'When you lose a leg you tend to be a memorable patient—even if I was using another name and was hardly recognisable at the time.'

Zafir still looked livid. Immediately she thought of something, and her belly sank. 'I'm sorry.'

He frowned. 'What do you have to be sorry about?'

Kat swallowed. 'No doubt the last thing you want is for this news to come out now—before the final event and the last showing of the diamond. It's bound to draw negative press.'

There was a sharp rap on Zafir's window, but he ignored it. They'd arrived back at the palace.

He turned to face Kat. 'There will be no negativity. The diamond will become even more famous when your story of courage is revealed. But I won't force you to go out there this evening if you feel it's asking too much of you. You're the one who will be put under more scrutiny than ever now.'

Kat felt alternately comforted by Zafir's words and bereft. He sounded as if he didn't care what she did either way.

She shrugged minutely. 'It's not as if I've got anything

more to hide than this. It was going to come out sooner or later. If you're not afraid of it impacting the campaign negatively, then of course I'll go out there this evening.'

Even as she said that though, she felt flutters of trepidation—but she also had to acknowledge a fledgling sense of liberation, as if a weight was being lifted off her shoulders.

Zafir looked at her enigmatically before saying, 'Very well—as you wish.'

As if he'd sent a psychic message to someone, his door was opened by a waiting attendant and he got out. The driver opened her door, and when she emerged into the sunlight Rahul was walking over to her, looking pale.

'Miss Winters, I am so sorry. I had no idea about… If I'd known…'

He looked so miserable in his inarticulacy that Kat touched his arm. 'Rahul, you don't need to apologise. You did nothing wrong. And no one knew.'

Rahul walked back to Zafir, who broke away from his attendants to come over to where she was standing. The expression on his face reminded her of the enigmatic way he'd looked at her in the desert before they'd left. It was profoundly irritating that she couldn't read it.

Zafir gestured with a hand. 'Jasmine is waiting to go through your wardrobe and she'll help you choose an outfit for this evening.'

Kat looked to where he was indicating, to see Jasmine and the golf buggy nearby.

Zafir stepped back. 'I'll come to your rooms for you at six.'

Kat wanted to cling to his robes and demand of him, *Where are we now? What did last night mean?*

She watched him walk away and chastised herself. Last night had just been a last slaking of lust. No doubt now that the end was in sight Zafir was already casting his mind ahead to the future and lining up suitable candidates to be his Queen.

Kat shoved down the rise of a very uncharacteristic bitterness and forced a smile as she greeted a serious-looking Jasmine, who was unusually quiet on their way back to the suite. Kat surmised that the news had obviously spread like wildfire.

When they got to her rooms Jasmine looked at Kat with big eyes and asked hesitantly, 'Is it really true, Miss Winters?'

Kat took a deep breath and nodded. Then she sat down and pulled up her kaftan, showing the young girl her leg.

Jasmine sank down at Kat's feet. When she looked up at Kat her eyes were brimming over with tears, and for the first time since her accident Kat felt a sense of liberation bubble up inside her as she reached out and wiped Jasmine's tears.

'It's not that bad, really,' she said with a wry smile. 'Here, let me show you…'

That evening, Kat paced back and forth unevenly across her suite. In spite of her bravado earlier, her nerves were intensifying with every moment at the thought that when she was presented tonight everyone would *know*.

Jasmine melted away discreetly when Zafir appeared at the entrance to her main reception room. Kat stopped pacing and looked at him, her nerves dissolving for a moment as she took him in, resplendent in cream and gold robes, every inch the powerful and impressive King of his country.

His grey eyes raked her up and down. 'You look beautiful.'

Kat felt ridiculously shy and half shrugged. 'Jasmine liked this dress the best.'

It was a long traditional Jandori kaftan, with deceptively simple flowing lines and a V-neck that showed off the diamond she was already wearing. Noor had delivered it shortly before. Over the kaftan she wore a long sleeveless robe inlaid with gold embroidery.

She noticed then that she and Zafir were almost matching, as her kaftan was a similar colour to his. For a second her rogue imagination wondered if this was close to what the bride of Zafir would wear on her wedding day.

It took her a second to realise that Zafir had spoken and she hadn't even heard him. Mortified, she said, 'I'm sorry, what did you say?'

She noticed then that he appeared less than his usual composed self.

He ran a hand through his hair and looked at her. 'There's something I need to tell you. I was going to wait until later, but...'

Kat went cold inside. 'What is it?'

He was grim. 'It's something I discovered this afternoon—a couple of things, actually.'

Kat wasn't sure why, but she felt she needed to sit down on a nearby chair. 'What things?'

Zafir started to pace back and forth, exactly where Kat had just been. He stopped and said abruptly, 'My father was the one who leaked those pictures and the story of your background to the press.'

Kat went very still. Zafir's father's cold features came back into her mind's eye. She stood up again. 'I know he didn't approve of me... But how...? Where did he find the pictures?'

Zafir was pacing again, energy crackling around him like a forcefield. 'He hired investigators to look into your past. They found the photographer and paid him a lot of money to hand over some of the photos.' He stopped again and looked stricken. 'I'm sorry, Kat. I had no idea... If I'd known...'

Kat walked blindly over to another chair, and clutched the back of it. Faintly, she said, 'You couldn't have known.'

She looked at Zafir and tried to push down the feeling of betrayal, even though it hadn't had anything to do with him. She'd known his parents hadn't liked her, but to go that far was hurtful in the extreme.

'It's not relevant now, anyway. What's done is done... your father is dead.'

'There's something else too.'

Kat's hand tightened on the chair. She regretted standing up. 'What?'

'I tracked down the photographer—or rather my team did. That's how I found out about my father's involvement.'

He paced again and then stopped. He'd never reminded Kat more of a caged animal than right now.

His face was all stark lines and hard jaw. 'You should have told me everything, Kat. You should have told me that the photographer was blackmailing you.'

She blanched. 'He told you...?'

Zafir nodded. 'I wanted to make sure that he had no more images of you, and I made sure that the ones that did get leaked to the press were destroyed. They'll never surface again. He was still very bitter about having had his payday taken away from him when the pictures were leaked and published. You could have told me, Kat,' Zafir said now, with an almost bewildered tone in his voice. 'Was I such an ogre?'

Her weak heart clenched. 'No, of course not. I didn't tell you because I was ashamed. You weren't an ogre, but you were a Crown Prince, Zafir. You didn't suffer fools lightly. And I felt like a fool for allowing myself to get into that situation. So many times I wanted to tell you what had happened, but at the last second I couldn't… I never wanted you to find out. Not even now.'

Zafir's jaw clenched. 'No, you would have preferred to go into marriage bringing your baggage with you— bleeding us *both* dry.'

Kat's blood drained south. This was proof, if she'd ever needed it, that nothing had changed between them. She was still in disgrace.

Kat lifted her chin and said, as coolly as she could, belying her profound hurt, 'That would never have been my intention, Zafir.'

Zafir cursed and ran a hand through his hair again. 'I'm sorry… You didn't deserve that…'

Kat refused to let his apology impact on her and forced herself to say, 'Even if you'd known the truth it wouldn't have changed anything. I still would have been deemed unsuitable. I broke your trust, Zafir. I know that.'

His mouth tightened into a grim line. The pain cut deeper when he didn't contradict her. As she watched she could see him retreat somewhere, become stiff, expressionless.

'You don't need to go out there this evening if you don't want to, Kat. I know it must terrify you, in spite of what you said earlier. I hired you and put you in front of the world's media again, and it was through your involvement with me that you had to endure your career and reputation being ruined in the first place. It's my fault you're under this renewed scrutiny.'

He sounded like a stranger. A civil stranger. Not the man who had taken her into a magical pool last night and made love to her as if his life depended on it. But then she hardly needed reminding of where this had been headed all along.

Kat stepped out from behind the chair. She said, 'No.

I committed to doing a job and I'm not going to renege on that.'

Just then there was a knock on the door, and Rahul's voice saying, 'Sire, they're ready for you and Miss Winters.'

Zafir looked at Kat. His insides felt as if they were being corroded by acid. He felt tainted by his father's machinations.

He was still reeling from the revelations of the previous few hours, but now he felt something similar to the way he'd felt much earlier that day, when he'd watched Kat with that bird of prey on her arm, clearly scared but determined not to show it. *Proud.* She'd looked regal, and it had impacted on him like a punch to his gut.

She stepped forward now, and she was a vision in gold with the red diamond glowing at her throat.

He said, 'Are you sure, Kat? You really don't have to do it if you don't want to. I've asked enough of you.'

An inner voice mocked him. *You asked for nothing less than her unconditional surrender and you got it.*

'I'm sure.'

And then she walked to the door, straight-backed and proud. Zafir battled an almost feral urge to grab her and shut the door—as if he knew that as soon as she walked through it she would be lost to him in a way he'd never really appreciated before.

But he couldn't stop her.

He followed her out to the corridor, where Noor and Rahul were waiting. Kat was staring straight ahead and he took her arm, leading her towards the ceremonial room. She didn't resist his touch but he could feel her tension.

Just before the doors to the ceremonial room opened Zafir gripped her arm hard and willed her to look at him.

After a few seconds she did—with clear reluctance. He couldn't read anything in those golden eyes. Could see nothing but a distance he'd never seen before.

His bleakness intensified. For the first time in his life he was floundering. The big doors were slowly opening, and with a heavy weight in his chest he said, 'I'm sorry, Kat.'

'I'm sorry, Kat.'

Zafir's words reverberated in Kat's head as she wound her way through the crowd, with Noor hovering protectively at her side. She'd smiled so much she thought she'd never be able to crack a smile again, even while her heart was shattering.

When Zafir had looked at her outside the door and said those words Kat had known then that it was over. It couldn't have been clearer.

Their past had been resurrected in spectacular fashion and now Zafir knew Kat's story—warts and all. Clearly he was taking responsibility for his father's actions and felt guilty, but Kat couldn't let him own all that guilt.

She should have told him everything. She should've have trusted that he wouldn't reject her… And even if he had—well, then she might possibly have saved herself the negative press fallout because he might have pursued the photographer earlier to protect his reputation as much as hers.

But she'd been living in a dream…fantasising that Zafir loved her and that she would make a great Queen… until it had all shattered. The truth was that their bond hadn't been strong enough to hold them together.

Then…or now.

For a moment the crowd seemed to thin around her and she sucked in a breath, relaxing her facial muscles for the first time in hours. Zafir was on the opposite side of the room, and Kat saw that for once there were no body-guards close by. She had the crazy sensation that she wanted to run from the room, taking the diamond with her—as if it was all she had left to bind her to Zafir, and once it was taken off at the end of the evening she'd disappear completely and he wouldn't even notice she'd gone.

Kat looked over to where Zafir was and at that moment, as if feeling the weight of her gaze on him, he turned his head and his gaze zeroed in on her immediately. Not wanting him to read her far too expressive face, Kat turned and took advantage of the lull to escape to a quieter part of the room.

She saw open French doors nearby, and was almost there when she bumped into someone. She started to apologise, but the words died on her tongue as she recognised who it was. Zafir's mother. And suddenly everything she was feeling coalesced into a very familiar sense of inadequacy. The sense of déjà vu was overwhelming.

Zafir's mother was a tall and regal woman, with cold dark eyes and a strong-boned handsome face. Her head was veiled and she wore an elaborate royal blue kaftan. Kat felt ridiculously ill-prepared, and found herself doing what she'd done the first time—bending in an awkward curtsey, with the vague idea that all royalty had to be curtsied to. Not that she'd ever done that to Zafir, of course.

When she stood again the older woman was managing to look down her nose at Kat, even though she was about the same height.

In perfect English she said, 'I hadn't expected to see you here again.'

Kat tried to ignore the dart of hurt at the thought of what this woman's husband, and possibly she too, had done. Kat didn't need to be reminded that she was not of this world and never would be. 'Your son was kind enough to offer me a job opportunity...'

To be in his bed.

Kat didn't say it.

But as if reading her mind, the older woman made a rude sound. 'If you want to call it that.' And then she said, 'Is it true what they're saying? You lost your leg?'

'Yes.' Kat stood tall. 'My left leg—below the knee.'

Someone who looked like a personal maid came forward then, and whispered something in Zafir's mother's ear.

When the maid melted away again she gave Kat a glacial once over and said, 'If you'll excuse me, please?' And then she swept off with a veritable retinue of people in her wake.

Kat was left reeling a little at the woman's ill manners. And then, remembering that she'd wanted to escape Zafir, she quickly walked outside to a blissfully deserted terrace. She went over to the wall overlooking Jahor and sucked in some air. Thousands of lights lit up the city, making it look even more exotic than usual.

For a moment she stood tthere, soaking in the view, because as of tomorrow morning when her flight took off she wouldn't ever see it again.

Her peace was shattered, though, when a group of laughing, chattering people came out to the terrace. Kat tensed and turned around warily, ready to project her model persona again.

When the group of about five men and six women saw who it was they stopped, before smiling and moving forward towards Kat, evidently excited that they had a private audience with her.

Kat smiled, but the wall was at her back and the people were pressing closer. They weren't speaking English and they were all talking at once, crowding around her to see the diamond.

Kat tried to look around them, to see if she could see

Noor or another bodyguard, but there was no sign of anyone from the security team and she cursed herself for fleeing.

Someone reached out to touch the diamond and Kat started to panic, her breath growing choppy. They were closing in on her and she had nowhere to go. She couldn't see past them, and one of the women had very strong perfume, which made it even harder to breathe.

Someone caught at Kat's arm then, in a surprisingly firm grip which only intensified her panic and growing sense of claustrophobia. She pulled her arm free and stepped to the side in a bid to escape—and found she was stepping into nothing as she discovered too late that there must have been a step she hadn't noticed.

She couldn't stop herself falling helplessly, and all she heard at the last minute was a familiar voice saying, *'Kat!'*

She had flashes of being held in Zafir's arms as he strode through the crowd, saying angrily, 'Where the hell were you, Noor? Those people were all over her...'

Kat tried desperately to speak, to say something, but her tongue wouldn't work and then everything faded out.

CHAPTER TEN

A COUPLE OF HOURS later Zafir was still experiencing waves of relief reverberating through his system. Kat had apparently not suffered any major injury apart from a bump to her head when she'd tumbled down those steps that of course she wouldn't have seen with that thick crowd of people pressing around her.

His hands instinctively clenched tighter when he recalled seeing her lying there, so pale and unmoving, the crowd just gaping at her ineffectually.

She'd come round soon after arriving at the hospital, and her first concern had been to tell him that it hadn't been the security team's fault—she'd slipped away from them. Her instinct to protect their incompetence had only increased his ire at them. And made him realise how much he'd underestimated Kat's innate loyalty.

Zafir was standing on the other side of a door with a window in it, looking at Kat, who was sitting on a bed dressed in a hospital gown. She'd had an MRI scan and they were just waiting to hear the results. Even in an unflattering hospital gown she took his breath away.

She wasn't wearing her prosthesis and there was a wheelchair nearby. But she wasn't alone—there was a little girl sitting beside her aged about nine or ten. The little girl was also a below-the-knee amputee.

He couldn't hear what they were saying, but the little girl was looking at Kat with wide eyes. And then suddenly a hesitant smile bloomed across her pretty face. She'd had tear-stained cheeks when a doctor had brought her to see Kat a short while before.

The little girl's doctor came alongside Zafir now, and

said in a low, awestruck voice, 'Thank you for agreeing to let Amira visit with Miss Winters.'

Zafir desisted from saying that as soon as he'd told Kat about the young girl she'd insisted on him letting her come to visit.

The doctor continued, 'Amira lost her leg due to meningitis. She hasn't spoken a word in months to anyone—not even her family. But now look at her...' The doctor shook his head. 'Miss Winters is a remarkable woman.'

Zafir curbed his irritation that the doctor felt the need to point out to him what he already knew. He was on edge and unsettled.

The doctor pushed open the door and went in to get Amira. She hopped off the bed and got into her wheelchair and waved goodbye to Kat.

Zafir got down on his haunches as she was being wheeled out of the room and her eyes grew as round as they'd been when she'd seen and recognised him the first time.

He held out his hand and she put her much smaller one into his. Something completely alien inside him shifted and expanded.

'Hello, Amira. I believe you've been a very brave young lady?'

She nodded soberly, her huge brown eyes wide with an awe that Zafir was sure wasn't solely for him. Then she said something to him in their own language with an endearing lisp and that alien sensation inside him expanded even more, stopping his breath for a second.

He had to stand to let the doctor wheel her out, and he heard Kat ask, 'What is it? You look as if you've seen a ghost. What did she say to you?'

He turned to Kat, and for the first time in his life he knew that he was being a coward when he said, 'Nothing important.' He went over to her. 'How are you feeling?'

Kat grimaced and put her hand up to where she'd hit her head. 'I think I'll have a headache for about a week, but other than that I'm fine.' She looked at him. 'I didn't mean to disrupt the evening so dramatically.'

Zafir shook his head, feeling anger rise again. 'Those people were practically pushing you through the wall.'

Kat tried not to let herself read anything into Zafir's concern—the way he'd stayed by her side from the moment he'd brought her to the hospital. She tried again, saying, 'You really don't have to stay…'

He shook his head and folded his arms. 'I'm not moving.'

Just then the kind doctor arrived, smiling. He closed the door behind him and came over, saying, 'Good news—nothing untoward appeared on the scan. I'm afraid you'll just have a nasty bump for a couple of weeks, but it should go down in time.'

Zafir looked at the doctor. 'You're sure she's okay?'

'Yes. I can let her go home as long as someone keeps an eye on her overnight for signs of concussion.'

Zafir said immediately, 'I'll make sure she's watched tonight.'

Jasmine arrived then, with some clothes for Kat, and helped her to put on her prosthetic limb and get dressed once the men had stepped outside.

The diamond had been dispatched shortly after Kat had arrived at the hospital—taken by a very meek-looking security guard.

Kat was wheeled out of the hospital in a wheelchair, as per regulations, but once outside she stood up, unsteady for a moment.

Zafir took her arm, leading her over to where his car was waiting.

When they were moving through the narrow streets

towards the palace Kat said as lightly as she could, 'I should still be able to make my flight tomorrow morning.'

Zafir looked at her, and the expression on his face brooked no argument. 'I've postponed it, Kat. You need a day to recover. At least.'

Kat's heart thumped at the thought of another day and night here, knowing that Zafir was just biding his time till she was gone. 'But I'm fine.'

He shook his head, and something sparked in his eyes. 'Is one more day really too much, Kat? You want to leave that badly?'

She was shocked. 'No… I love it here.'

But I also love you, and one more minute than necessary is torture.

But of course she didn't say that.

She swallowed her emotion and said, 'It's fine. I'll stay.'

She turned her head to look out of the window. After their explosive conversation before the event, and Zafir's 'I'm sorry,' Kat knew there was nothing more for them to say to each other. The past had been laid to rest. Now she would just have to suck up the fact that Zafir was acting out of a sense of responsibility. And possibly still that misplaced guilt. No doubt he wanted her continued presence here as little as she did.

When they arrived back at the palace Jasmine was waiting for them, and also Rahul, both looking worried. Zafir gave instructions to Jasmine in his own language and she whisked Kat back to her suite, shooting her concerned glances.

When Kat had had a bath and was re-emerging from the bathroom, feeling a little more human again without half a ton of make-up on her face, Jasmine was still there and looking determined.

Before Kat could say anything the younger woman

said, 'I'm not leaving. The King has told me someone needs to watch over you tonight in case of concussion.'

Kat knew that arguing would be futile. 'Very well…'

She got into bed as Jasmine curled up on a large love seat nearby, her pretty face illuminated by the screen of her palm tablet. Kat felt a surge of gratitude at the thought of how much the girl had already come to mean to her.

Before she tried to go to sleep she said, 'Thank you, Jasmine.'

The girl looked up and smiled. 'You're welcome, Miss Winters. Now, get some rest.'

Kat thought she'd toss and turn for a while, but she actually slipped into sleep almost immediately.

When she woke some time later the room was in darkness and her throat was dry. She struggled to sit up in the bed, and immediately saw movement in the corner—something big and dark. A scream stuck in Kat's throat for a second, before she realised with a hammering heart that it was Zafir looming over her in the moonlight.

'What is it?' he asked. 'Are you all right? Is your head hurting?'

'No, I'm just thirsty. Where's Jasmine?'

Zafir sat down on the edge of the bed and turned on a low light. Kat saw that stubble darkened his jaw and that his hair was mussed up as if he'd been running a hand through it.

He reached for some water and handed Kat the glass. She took a few gulps, hating how aware she was of Zafir's big body. Was it only a couple of days ago he'd been making love to her with such zealous passion? Now he couldn't be more distant.

He took the glass and put it back. His body was rigid with tension and something inside Kat broke. Clearly he couldn't stand to be near her any more.

She sank back under the covers. 'You don't need to watch me, Zafir. I'm fine.'

He reached over and turned off the light and said, 'I'm not going anywhere, Kat.'

And then he stood up and retreated back into the shadows.

When Kat woke up the next morning Jasmine was the first person she saw, and she wondered for a moment if she'd imagined Zafir being there during the night. She was too scared to ask.

Kat ate breakfast, and then took a shower and dressed. Jasmine helped her to put on her prosthetic leg—the girl was totally unfazed now by the whole thing.

She'd deliberately chosen from her own clothes, knowing that she'd be leaving all the other gorgeous garments behind. They belonged to a Kat who had lived a stolen dream for a short time.

After packing most of her things she looked up flights from Jahor to America, and saw that there was one late that night. On impulse she booked a seat, even though her flight home was meant to have been on Zafir's private plane.

She stood up then, determined to go and find Zafir and tell him she was leaving and not to let him persuade her otherwise.

Kat made her way slowly to where Zafir's office was located, absorbing the understated finery of the palace for the last time—its ancient murals and hidden inner courtyards covered in mosaics, and the peacocks strutting around loose and free, as if they owned the place.

When she got to the office she was surprised not to see Rahul outside, in his usual spot, but his cell phone sat on the table so presumably he wasn't far away. Then

Kat heard raised voices, and one familiar one sent icicles down her spine.

Zafir's mother.

Instinctively Kat wanted to turn away from that strident voice, but something kept her rooted to the spot, near the half-open door to Zafir's office.

'What are you going to do about Salim? Your brother is out of control, and meanwhile the country he is meant to be ruling—*my* homeland—is falling into chaos.'

Kat recognised the tension in Zafir's voice as he replied.

'I am not my brother's keeper, Mother, and maybe you should have thought of this a long time ago, when you proved how little we all really meant to you when Sara died. But if it's any consolation I'm hiring someone who is an expert in diplomatic relations to help oversee Salim's accession to the throne in Tabat.'

His mother sniffed and said ungraciously, 'That's something, at least.'

Kat's heart clenched for Zafir and his siblings, and then his mother changed tack.

'And what is *she* still doing here? Wasn't she meant to be gone this morning?'

Kat's heart stopped.

There seemed to be a year of silence before Zafir said coldly, 'I presume you're referring to Kat Winters?'

His mother made a rude sound. 'If you're thinking of making her your Queen again, then you've learnt nothing about being a King, Zafir. She is the most singularly unsuitable woman to be Queen of this country. There's her scandalous past to think of—not to mention the fact that she made a complete fool of herself last night and ruined the event!'

Kat somehow managed to take in some oxygen at that point. She whirled around and walked away as fast as she could—before she could hear Zafir assure his mother that of course he wouldn't be making Kat his Queen. She tried not to feel hurt at what Zafir's mother had said, but it was hard when it echoed her own deepest insecurities.

She didn't see Rahul until it was too late and they collided. Kat said sorry and kept going, terrified that he'd see how upset she was.

When she got back to her rooms she was glad to find them empty, and was relieved she'd gone ahead and booked that plane ticket. She continued packing, telling herself she'd go to the airport early. She would wait there.

'What are you doing?'

She whirled around at the deep and familiar voice, holding some trousers up to her chest. Zafir was inside her room, the door closed behind him. He was clean-shaven now, making Kat suspect again that she'd dreamt his presence during the night. He was the *King*! And she was now his inconvenient ex-mistress. Of course he hadn't been there.

She turned around again and forced her voice to sound cool. Unconcerned. 'I'm packing. I've booked a commercial flight home tonight, Zafir, there's no need for me to prolong my stay.'

He came over and took her arm, turning her to face him. 'You said you'd stay another day.'

She pulled free and let the trousers fall to the floor, stepping back. 'I'm fine. I don't need to stay—and you have stuff to do.' She cringed inwardly at *stuff*.

'I want to talk to you.'

Something illicit fluttered in Kat's belly. 'What is there to talk about? I think we've said everything that needs to be said.'

'Rahul told me he bumped into you outside my office just now… You obviously came to talk to me. Why did you leave?'

Kat glanced away. 'You were busy.'

'I suspected as much,' he breathed. 'How much did you hear of my conversation with my mother, Kat?'

She looked back at Zafir and pain scored her insides. She backed away further. He was too close. 'I heard enough,' she said painfully. 'I didn't stick around to hear you agree with her assessment that I'm entirely unsuitable.'

A flush stained Zafir's cheeks. 'Dammit, Kat, you are *not* unsuitable.' Then he stopped. 'You didn't hear what I said to her?'

You are not unsuitable.

She cursed her silly heart for leaping at that. Kat wanted to look anywhere but at him, but she couldn't look away. He was like the sun—blinding and devastating.

She lifted her chin. 'No. I told you. I'd heard enough.'

'So you didn't hear me tell her that I've no intention of letting you go anywhere?'

She just looked at Zafir, her brain moving sluggishly. A tangled mass of sensations roiled in her gut, but worst of all was a kernel of something that felt awfully like hope.

Kat refused to give in to it. 'Why would you want to keep me here? Our liaison is over.'

Zafir stepped closer to her, his eyes intense. 'Is it?'

Kat felt flustered. 'Well, of course it is. It was never going to last beyond this job, and you couldn't have made it more clear after our conversation yesterday that whatever was there is gone...' Kat was breathing jaggedly and tried to compose herself.

Zafir grimaced. 'When I found out about my father... Kat, it was a huge shock. It made me realise how badly I'd judged you...how badly I'd disrupted your life. But it hasn't changed how much I want you. Do you know how hard it was for me not to touch you last night?'

His words were like a punch in the gut. She breathed, 'So you *were* there…'

He frowned. 'Of course I was—who else would it have been?'

Kat shook her head and muttered, 'I thought it was a dream.'

She took another step back, putting her arms around herself. 'So…you're saying you still…' She trailed off.

Zafir nodded and his mouth compressed. 'I don't think I'll ever *not* want you, Kat.'

Something painful gripped her insides. 'So what are you suggesting, Zafir? Are you going to lock me in your harem and make a carnal visit when you feel the urge, while you marry your suitable bride and have a legion of heirs?'

'What are you talking about? There's no such thing as a harem here and there hasn't been for years.'

Mortified, because she was giving herself away spectacularly, she looked away, wishing she had something to hold on to. 'Forget it.'

Zafir came close and put a hand to her chin, forcing her to look at him. He had a fierce light in his eye. 'Do you really think that I would want to set you up as my mistress?'

She swallowed. 'I don't know what to think any more.'

Zafir shook his head. 'I don't want a mistress, Kat. I want a wife—a Queen.'

The pain was excruciating. She pulled away from Zafir and somehow managed to say, 'And that's what you deserve. I'm sure you'll choose the perfect Queen.'

Zafir folded his arms. His eyes were like laser beams now. 'I've already chosen her.'

Kat looked at him and felt a surge of jealousy at the thought of this mystery woman. 'Then how can you not let me go? I can't be here now—it's unconscionable.'

Zafir shook his head. 'It's very consciable, actually, because I want you to be my Queen, Kat. And *that's* what I told my mother—before I told her to get out of my sight and that I wanted her gone from Jandor within a week. She's no longer welcome.'

Kat shook her head. Something was happening inside her…something was cracking open… But she couldn't let it. There was too much at stake, too much not yet said. Too much had happened in the past. There had been too much hurt.

'You wanted to make me your Queen before, so what's changed, Zafir? Is it the fact that the truth of my history is a little more palatable? Or is it because you feel guilty that your father interfered? It doesn't change the fact that I did keep things from you. I'm just as guilty for what happened.'

Zafir looked pale now. 'No, it's not because your history is more palatable, or because of the guilt I feel— which I don't think I'll ever *un*feel.' He said heavily, 'The truth is that I didn't fight hard enough for you before.'

'Because you didn't really want to marry me.'

Kat was trying desperately to get Zafir to admit that he didn't really mean what he said. Because if she believed him and he didn't…she'd never recover.

He looked at her for a long time. And even trapped under that intense gaze Kat couldn't help but be acutely aware of his powerfully lean body in dark trousers and a white shirt.

After a long moment he said, 'I can't deny that.'

She sucked in a painful breath. She hadn't actually expected to hear him agree with her, and it should have been a relief but it wasn't.

'But not because of why you're thinking, Kat.'

Kat's circling thoughts came to a halt.

'I was very careful to keep my feelings for you superficial, Kat. I had you on a pedestal as this perfect para-gon of beauty and morality—a small-town girl who had worked hard to get where she was. A woman who was unbelievably innocent. I put you in a box and I didn't look any deeper. I know it sounds crazy, and contradictory, but by proposing to you and convincing myself it was for those shallow reasons, I was able to keep you with me while not admitting the depth of my emotions—the real reason I wanted to marry you. Because I loved you. You see, I told myself I'd never allow love to impact my life. I was so sure that I wouldn't ever succumb to such an emotion that I arrogantly denied to myself that I felt anything deeper than liking and respect for you.'

Kat wasn't sure she could speak now, even if she wanted to.

Zafir grimaced. 'When those headlines surfaced and I confronted you... I didn't really give you a chance to explain your side because on some cowardly level it was easier for me to break the engagement and tell you I didn't love you than to admit how I really felt. How could I? When I wouldn't even admit it to myself?'

Zafir stepped closer to Kat.

'I love you, Kat. I know that now, and I always did... I was just too scared to admit it before. Seeing how Salim was so destroyed after Sara's death, feeling that loss my-self—it terrified me. I never wanted to love someone so much that it would send my life into a tailspin if some-thing happened to them. And our parents hardly provided us with any kind of healthy example...'

He shook his head, his face paling.

'But when I saw you on the ground last night, lying so still, I realised then that it would be far worse if I'd never told you how I felt than if I'd tried to protect myself from the pain. Even if you don't love me.'

Kat couldn't breathe. She felt as if she was hanging

over a huge abyss by a thread. But as she looked at Zafir, into those slate-grey eyes, the light in them died and he took a step back.

Before she could reach out or say anything he said, 'There's something I've suspected for a while, but I've been too afraid to ask...'

'What?' she managed to croak out.

'The accident...it happened that night, didn't it? The night we fought.'

Kat felt the blood drain from her face, and Zafir's own face paled even more. She'd never seen him look so stricken.

'Kat...what did I do to you?'

He backed away even further, as if he couldn't bear to be near her. Everything in her rebelled at that. He'd told her he loved her. She had to believe. To trust.

She closed the distance between them and took his hands in hers. They felt cold. 'No,' she said, and then more firmly, when she saw his eyes so bleak, '*No*, Zafir. You do not get to do this. What happened that night was no one's fault. It could have just as easily been you. You don't get to take responsibility for an accident.'

She clung onto his hands, willing him to come back to her.

'I was an emotional coward too... As soon as I heard you say you didn't love me I ran—because I wasn't brave enough to fight for myself or for you.'

He shook his head, his face etched with pain. 'I have no right to ask you to stay now. I've brought nothing but destruction into your life.'

He wouldn't look at her, so Kat let one hand go and reached up to touch Zafir's face, smoothing the lines, the tension in his jaw. She turned his face until their eyes met and she said, 'Well, tough, because I'm not going anywhere—unless you didn't mean any of what you said?'

Fire flashed in his eyes and Kat breathed a sigh of relief.

'Of course I meant what I said.'

She took a deep breath. 'I love you too, Zafir. What I felt for you before was immature... I couldn't handle it. It was too much. I don't think either of us were ready to deal with the enormity of how we felt. It killed me to think you'd only valued me for my physical attributes. I felt worthless. I felt like no one had ever really loved me for me—not even my mother.'

Zafir reached out and cupped Kat's jaw. His eyes were suspiciously bright.

'I love all of you, Kat—every bit. I love the little girl who was pushed out in front of cameras and lights at far too young an age. I love the young teenager who struggled to protect her mother and who did something radical to keep her mother alive because she had no other choice. I love the young woman who didn't let her experiences make her bitter, but who clung on to something good in spite of being blackmailed by an arch manipulator... And I love the woman who overcame a massive life event to become even stronger and more proud. You have a huge life ahead of you, and you're going to be an inspiration to so many people.'

Zafir got down on one knee in front of Kat and she stopped breathing. He pulled a black box out of his pocket and looked ridiculously nervous. He opened it to reveal a square-shaped Art Deco ring, with a red stone surrounded by white diamonds.

'Is that...?' She couldn't even finish the question.

Zafir nodded, his eyes on her as he took the ring out of the box. 'It's part of the Heart of Jandor red diamond. My great-grandfather had it made for my great-grandmother out of an offcut of the original stone. It wasn't her engagement ring, but she wore it every day. I wanted to give you a different ring, Kat. To symbolise a fresh start… That is…if you'll have me?'

Kat's chest had swelled so much that her eyes stung. She felt as if she might float away, but Zafir was anchoring her to the ground, waiting for her answer.

At the last moment old insecurities surfaced. 'What if your mother is right, Zafir? I'm not cut out to be Queen… I'll let you down…'

Zafir stood up, looking fierce. 'You will make a great Queen, Kat. You're compassionate and passionate. You're intelligent and endlessly kind—and stronger than anyone else I know. Jasmine adores you and Rahul would die for you. When I saw you holding that falcon you humbled me with your innate grace. It was then that I knew I couldn't let you go. And then I found out about my father and I knew I had no right to ask anything more of you. Do you want to know what Amira said to me at the hospital?'

Kat nodded, feeling overwhelmed at everything he was saying, each word soothing the wounds of her soul.

'She said to me, "Your Queen is beautiful," and she was right. You are beautiful—inside and out. My mother was born and bred to be Queen and she spread nothing but pain and misery… You are more of a Queen than she could ever be.'

Kat eventually held out her hand and said in a choked voice, 'Then, yes, I'll be your Queen. I love you, Zafir.'

He grew blurry in her vision as he put the ring on her finger, and then she was being lifted into his arms and taken over to the bed.

He laid her down and said fervently, 'I need you, Kat, so much…'

She put her arms around him and arched into his body. 'I'll never walk away from you again,' she said emotionally. 'You're my King and my home, Zafir.'

Six months later

Kat stood behind the curtain with Amira's hand tightly clasped in hers. They looked at each other and Kat winked. Amira smiled widely. In the last few months the little girl had been transformed into her normal gregarious self again, with a new prosthetic leg.

A woman stepped forward and whispered, 'Your Majesty, whenever you're ready…'

Kat wasn't sure she'd ever get used to being called *Your Majesty*, but slowly, with each day, it was sinking in that she was a Queen.

She looked at Amira to make sure she was ready, and then took a breath, pushing the curtain aside and stepping forward.

Lights illuminated their path down the long catwalk. They were both dressed in the latest designs from Jandor's best designers for Jahor's inaugural fashion week, with all proceeds from the show going to the global amputee fund that Kat and Zafir had set up in recent months. The fund gave money to all aspects of limb loss, including research into prosthetic limbs.

Kat had been persuaded out of retirement by Julie, but was only agreeing to modelling work that didn't conflict with her role as Queen of Jandor, and work that didn't disguise her limb—and, again, all proceeds were going to charity. She was determined to make her face and her body work for the best causes this time, and she'd never felt more fulfilled or happier.

But then, her work wasn't the most important thing in her life. Not by a long shot.

As they reached the end of the catwalk and Amira twirled around just as Kat had instructed her earlier, Kat caught Zafir's eye where he was sitting in the front row. His grey gaze blazed into hers, and then it dropped explicitly to where the swell of her six-months-pregnant belly was visible under the kaftan she wore.

The baby kicked, and Kat couldn't stop a huge grin breaking across her face as her eyes met Zafir's again. And then she turned and walked serenely back down the catwalk with the little girl.

The following morning the headline on the front page of the *Jahor Times* simply said The Look of Love. And below it was a picture of Kat and Zafir gazing at each other, with her hand protectively cradling the swell of her belly.

Zafir threw down the newspaper and turned to face Kat, where she lay in bed. He splayed a big hand possessively over her naked pregnant belly and Kat rolled her eyes when the baby kicked.

She grumbled good-naturedly, 'It's already two against one...'

Zafir pulled Kat close and smoothed his hand down her body until he found her left thigh. He lifted it up so that the centre of his body came into contact with the centre of hers. She gasped when she felt him, hard and ready.

'No, my love...' he said huskily. 'It'll never be two against one. It's going to be three against the world...' He bent his head and kissed her before lifting his mouth for a second to say, 'And then four...' Another kiss. 'And then five...'

Kat huffed out a chuckle that turned into a moan of pleasure as Zafir angled his body against hers in a very intimate way. She gripped his shoulders and bit her lip, and whispered as he filled her with a smooth thrust, 'I love you, Zafir...'

He kissed her again. 'And I love you...for ever.'

* * * * *

DEDICATION

I'd like to dedicate this story and give huge thanks to Peggy Chenoweth, who runs the website AmputeeMommy.com. I thank her for her kind patience and her answers to my questions. Her website and blog are an invaluable resource for anyone seeking information and/or support around being an amputee. Any inaccuracies relating to Kat's limb loss in this story are purely my own.

PRINCE HAFIZ'S
ONLY VICE

SUSANNA CARR

To Sarah Stubbs, with thanks for her
guidance and encouragement.

CHAPTER ONE

HER LOVER'S PICTURE was on the front page of every paper in the small newsstand.

Lacey adjusted the dark sunglasses that concealed her bright blue eyes and squinted at the newspaper on display. Although the headline was in Arabic, the print was big and bold. She could tell that something important had happened. Something that could explain the jubilant attitude that shimmered in the marketplace. No doubt Prince Hafiz had made his countrymen proud again.

She wondered what he had done this time as she requested the daily English paper in halting Arabic. Did he add a fortune to the royal coffers? Convince another industry to make the Sultanate of Rudaynah their headquarters? Win an award?

She decided it would be best to wait until she got home before she read the paper. Lacey took another glance at the pictures of Hafiz that covered the stall. His expression was solemn, but it didn't stop the secret thrill sweeping across her heated skin. It was unnerving that Hafiz could elicit that kind of response through a photograph.

The photo was an official head shot the palace systematically offered to the press, but while the image was familiar, it always grabbed the reader's notice. No one could look away from Prince Hafiz's mysterious dark eyes and harsh mouth. He was devastatingly handsome from his luxuriant black hair to his sharp bone structure. Women watched him from afar, too awed of his masculine beauty.

Or perhaps they sensed his raw power beneath his sophisticated manners. Lacey had instantly recognized the sexual hunger lurking below his ruthless restraint. His primitive aura was a silent warning that most women heeded. But for Lacey, it drew her closer.

She had found Hafiz's relentless self-discipline fascinating. It had also been a challenge. From the moment they had met, she had been tempted to strip him from his exquisitely tailored pinstripe suit and discover his most sensual secrets.

Just the thought of him made her impatient to get back home. She needed to return before Hafiz got there. His workload would crush a lesser man, but he still managed to visit Lacey at nightfall.

The blazing sun began to dip in the desert sky, and she didn't want to contemplate how Hafiz would respond if she weren't home.

He never asked what she did during the day, Lacey thought with a frown. At first his lack of interest had bothered her. Did he think time stood still for her until he appeared?

There were moments when she wanted to share her plans and ideas, even discuss her day, but she had always held back. She wasn't ready to reveal the work she had done. Not yet. Lacey wanted to show Hafiz what she was capable of. How she could contribute.

She wanted to show that she was ready to make his sultanate her permanent home.

It hadn't been easy. There were days, weeks, when she had been homesick. Lonely and bored. She had missed her wide circle of friends and colorful nightlife, and she craved the basic comforts.

It was aggravating that the newspaper hadn't been delivered today at her penthouse, but that wasn't surprising. After living in the small Arabian country for almost six months, Lacey still hadn't gotten used to sporadic service, frequent power outages and laborers arriving at work anywhere from three hours to three days late.

Her connection to the outside world was just as erratic. The communication services were usually down, like today. When they were running, the content was heavily censored.

Definitely not the lifestyle she had enjoyed in St. Louis. Not that she was complaining, Lacey hurriedly assured herself. She was willing to forego many comforts and conveniences for the one thing she couldn't get back in the States: Hafiz.

Lacey shivered with anticipation and handed the coins to the newspaper boy. She practiced her Arabic and felt a sense of accomplishment when the young man understood her. Lacey shyly tugged at the bright orange scarf wrapped around her head and tucked in a wayward strand of hair.

Maybe she was ready to show Hafiz what she had learned over the past few months. She wasn't fluent and didn't know everything about the culture, but she was getting impatient. It was time to meet his family and friends.

Lacey bit her lip as she imagined making that demand. The idea made her uncomfortable. She had been stalling. Not because his family was royal but because she was worried she would push too soon.

Lacey didn't want to give an ultimatum. The last time she'd taken a stand she had lost everything. She wasn't ready to lose Hafiz. Unlike her parents, who had no problems walking away from her in pursuit of their dreams, Hafiz hadn't been able to bear leaving her and had brought her to his home. Well, not his home, but his home country.

As much as she wanted to be part of Hafiz's life and share her life with him, she needed to be patient. She had to trust that Hafiz knew what he was doing. Lacey sighed deeply. She wasn't used to allowing another to take charge.

But she was in a country that followed different codes of conduct. She was also in love with a prince, and she didn't know much about royal life. Her presence in Hafiz's world required delicacy.

Lacey was amazed that Hafiz could even breathe among all the rules and regulations. But not once did he complain. His strong shoulders never sagged from the burden. The man was driven to attack every challenge and reach a goal he never discussed, but Lacey guessed that world domination was just the beginning. His obligations were never far from his mind. That is, until he was in bed with her. Then the world stopped as they fulfilled every fantasy their bodies craved and every wish their hearts desired.

Pleasure nestled low in her stomach, beneath the stifling black gabardine caftan. Lacey stuffed the English newspaper into her plastic shopping bag that contained the crimson desert flowers. She hoped the article offered good news, although she couldn't imagine the press saying anything less than flattering.

She hurried off the curb, and the blowing horn of a filthy truck had her jumping back to the sidewalk. Reddish clouds billowed from the dirt road and settled into a fine layer on her soft black boots.

She waved her hand in front of her face, blinking away the grit. Lacey wrinkled her nose at the tart smell of animals, car fumes and rotting sewage. She knew the small country just recently came into wealth, but if this was a decade of progress, she was grateful she hadn't seen the unenlightened country.

A memory flickered of Hafiz talking about his country when they had first met. He'd spoken with love and pride about the rich heritage and romance of the desert. Hafiz had described the tribal music and the exotic spices lingering in the starry nights. When he'd told the story of how the sultanate had been named after the first sultana, Lacey had thought Rudaynah had to be a romantic paradise.

Never trust a man's idea of romance, Lacey decided as she determinedly stepped into traffic. The high-pitched ring of bicycle bells shrieked in her ears as she zigzagged her way across the street. She dodged a bored donkey pulling a cart of pungent waste matter. A bus whipped past, her plastic bag swatting against one of the male passengers hanging outside the over-crowded and rusted vehicle.

Lacey hurried to her apartment in earnest. Shadows grew longer and darker as the sun dipped precariously closer to the horizon. She nodded a greeting to the armed guards at the gates of the condominium complex. The men, all in olive green uniforms and sporting bushy mustaches, waved her in without a pause in their conversation.

She scurried across the bare courtyard, pausing only as a big insect with a vicious-sounding buzz flew in front of her. Gritting her teeth as she shuddered with revulsion, Lacey turned the corner to access the private elevator that would lead her straight to the penthouse apartment.

She halted when she saw a man waiting for the elevator. Lacey barely had time to gasp as her mind snatched a flurry of disjointed images. A white flowing robe. A golden chord over the white *kaffiyeh* that covered his hair. She didn't need to see the man's face to sense the impenetrable wall of arrogant masculinity. Of power and privilege. There was only one man who enjoyed a life with no limitations or impossibilities.

"Hafiz?" she whispered.

Prince Hafiz ibn Yusuf Qadi whirled around. "Lacey?" He moved forward and stared at her. He slowly blinked and frowned. His sexy and glamorous mistress was wearing a shapeless caftan and a hideous scarf. There wasn't a hint of makeup on her pale face, but she was still a stunning beauty.

"What are you doing down here?" Prince Hafiz plucked off her sunglasses. He needed to see her eyes. He could always tell what she was thinking and feeling when he met her bright blue gaze.

After he snatched the glasses, Hafiz pushed down the head scarf and was rewarded with a cascade of copper-red curls. His fingers flexed. He wanted to touch her hair. Fan it out and allow the last rays of the sun to catch the fiery color. Sink his fingers into the soft weight as he kissed her hard.

Instead, he slowly, reluctantly, let his hand fall to his side. He gripped her sunglasses until the tips of his fingers whitened. He could not touch her. Not here, not in public. One graze, one brush of skin, and he wouldn't stop.

It didn't help that Lacey wanted to greet him with a kiss. The sight of her closed eyes and parted lips whirled him back to the first time he'd seen her. That fateful night he had entered the luxury hotel near the St. Louis waterfront.

The lobby had bustled with activity and there was a piano bar to the side. The deceptively languorous music had caught his attention, but it was her singing that had made him turn around. Soft and clear like the voice of a well-bred lady, but so rich and velvety that it sparked his wicked imagination.

And when he had seen her, his heart had slammed against his ribs. Lacey was an intriguing mix of contrasts. She had looked like an innocent girl, but her voice held a wealth of experience. Her red hair had flowed past her shoulders like a veil, touching the simple blue evening gown. It should have been a modest dress that covered her from her slender neck to her delicate ankles, yet it had lovingly clung to every curve.

Hafiz had known she was trouble, but that hadn't stopped him from walking toward the piano as she'd coaxed a longing note from the ivory keys.

She hadn't seen his approach as she closed her eyes and raised her flushed face to the sky, swept away from the music. And he had allowed her to take him with her.

Hafiz forced himself to the present and away from the untroubled past. His gaze drifted to the voluminous black gown veiling her body from his eyes. For some reason, that irked him. "What are you wearing?"

She opened her eyes and frowned before she placed her hands on her hips. The movement gave him some indication of where the soft swells and curves were underneath her outfit. "I could ask the same about you," she said as her wide eyes roamed over his appearance. "I have never seen you like this. It's straight out of *Lawrence of Arabia.*"

Lacey's voice was deep and husky as the desire shone in her eyes. When she looked at him like that… His skin flushed and pulled tight. How did this woman make him this hot, this fast, without even touching him?

His body hardened, and he gulped in the hot desert air. He could take Lacey against this hidden corner and capture her cries of ecstasy with his mouth within minutes. All he needed was… Hafiz shook his head slightly. What was he thinking? The last thing he needed was for the sultan to discover he had a mistress living in the shadow of the palace.

"This is a *dishdasha,*" he explained gruffly as he tried to contain the lust that heated his blood. "I wear it for royal functions. Now explain what you are doing outside alone."

She held up her plastic bag and lightly jostled the contents. "I went shopping."

"Shopping," he repeated dully.

"Yes, I wear this whenever I leave the apartment." She glided her hand down the black gabardine with the flair of a game show model demonstrating a prize.

"I know Rudaynah only asks tourists to dress modestly, but I don't know if I fall in that category. I'm not quite a tourist, but I'm not quite a resident, am I? I didn't want to take any chances."

Hafiz barely heard the question. *Whenever she left?* She had done this more than once? Routinely? What did she do? Where did she go? And with whom?

It wouldn't be with a man. He knew he could trust Lacey. She had fallen in love with him that first night and saw no reason to deny it.

But he didn't like the possibility that she had a life apart from him. He was the center of her world, and he didn't want that to end. "Whenever you leave?" he asked as his eyebrows dipped into a ferocious frown. "How often do you go out?"

"You don't need to worry about me." Lacey's smile dropped. "Or are you worried that one of your friends or relatives will meet me?"

Hafiz heard the edge in her tone and felt her impatience. He surrendered to the need to touch her and delve his hands into her hair. He needed to feel the connection that sizzled between them.

Hafiz spanned his fingers along the base of her head and tilted her face up. "I thought you spend your days playing your music," he murmured distractedly.

"And dreaming about you?"

"Of course," he said with a slanted smile.

Her smooth brow wrinkled as she considered what he said. "I can think of you while I'm shopping. I'm talented that way."

"No." His sharp tone stanched any argument. "No more excursions. You don't know the language or the country."

"How else am I going to learn if I don't get out and—"

"You have servants who can shop for you. Yes, yes." He held his hand up as she tried to interrupt. "You've already told me. You're not comfortable with the idea of someone waiting on you. But they are here to take care of you."

"You can't hide me inside all the time," she insisted as she pressed her hand against his chest. His heart thudded from her touch. "I'm not Rapunzel."

"I know," he said resignedly. She often mentioned that European fairy tale. She once told him the basic story line, but someday he needed to read it in case there was more he should know.

Lacey leaned against the wall and sighed. Hafiz flattened his hands next to her head, her sunglasses dangling from his loose grasp. He stared at her mouth, his lips stinging with the need to kiss her.

But this was as close as he would allow himself. If he leaned into her softness, he wouldn't leave.

The tip of her tongue swept along her bottom lip. "Hafiz, we're outside," she reminded him, her voice hitching with scandalized excitement. "You shouldn't be this close."

He knew it, but it didn't stop him. She was his one and only vice, and he was willingly addicted. He had already risked everything to be with her. Each day he made the choice to risk everything for her. But now the choice was taken away from him, and it was all coming to an end.

He bent his head and stopped abruptly. He should pull away. Hafiz remained still as he stared at Lacey's mouth. Their ragged breathing sounded loud to his ears. One kiss could bring him peace or could set him on fire. One kiss would lead to another.

As if he were in a trance, Hafiz grazed his fingertips against her brow. He caressed her cheek, wishing it were his mouth on her. Hafiz swallowed hard as he remembered how her skin tasted.

He shouldn't be with her. No, it was more than that. He shouldn't *want* to be with her. Lacey Maxwell was forbidden.

Wanting Lacey went against everything he had been taught. He should only find honorable and chaste women from his sultanate attractive. Yet the only woman he noticed was Lacey.

She was bold and beautiful. Instead of hiding her curves, she flaunted her body. She showed no shame in her desire for him. And instead of trying to tame him, Lacey encouraged the wild streak inside him that he had tried so hard to suffocate.

The sound of his heartbeat pounded in his ears as he stroked Lacey's jaw. She tilted her head, exposing her slender throat. He wanted to sweep his fingers along the elegant column and dip his hand beneath the caftan. He wanted to hear her shallow breaths turn into groans and whispers.

But that would be reckless. Hafiz dragged his thumb against her lips. He traced the shape of her mouth over and over until her lips clung to his skin.

Lacey turned her face away. Hafiz gripped her chin and held her still. With a growl of surrender, he bent down to claim her mouth with his.

"Hafiz," she whispered fiercely. "We will be seen."

That warning could form ice in his sizzling veins

like no other. His chest rose and fell as he reined in runaway needs. With great reluctance, he drew away.

"We should leave before one of the neighbors spots me," Lacey said shakily as she pulled the scarf over her head.

Disappointment scored his chest as she tucked her glorious hair away. "I don't like seeing you covered up like this." He never thought about how he would feel seeing his woman veiled, but it felt intrinsically wrong to conceal Lacey's captivating beauty and character.

"Believe me, I don't like wearing it." She reached for her sunglasses. "It's like an oven, but it makes me invisible and that's all that matters."

He flashed a disbelieving look. "Lacey, you could never be invisible."

Her smile was dazzling as she blushed with pleasure. It was as if he had given her the ultimate compliment.

"Take off your scarf," he insisted in a rough whisper. "No one will see. Everyone will be at prayer." Hafiz wondered why he resented the scarf and sunglasses so much that he was willing to risk the chance of discovery. He reached for her arm and pulled her close.

"Don't be too sure. Most people acted like they were ready to celebrate tonight. I don't know why—" The plastic bag fell from her wrist. She bent down to retrieve the contents, and he followed her descent. Her sharp cry startled him.

"Lacey?" He looked down at the cracked cement floor and didn't understand what was wrong when he saw the dark red flowers resting unblemished on the floor. He almost missed the English newspaper

with his picture on the front page. The bold headline grabbed him by the throat and hurtled him into
despair.

Prince Hafiz to Marry

CHAPTER TWO

LACEY STARED AT the engagement announcement. Her mind refused to comprehend the words. "Marry?" she whispered. Her wild gaze flew to Hafiz's harsh face. "You're getting married?"

She waited in agony as he rose to his full height. He looked very tall and intimidating. Almost like a stranger.

Lacey didn't realize she was holding her breath until he answered. "Yes."

The single word sent her universe into a spiral. "I don't…I don't…" She stared at the headline again, but the pain was too raw, too intense. She hurriedly stuffed the newspaper and flowers back into the bag.

Her hands shook as the rage and something close to fear swirled inside her. Fear of losing everything. Pure anger at the thought of Hafiz with another woman. The fury threatened to overpower her. She wanted to scream at the injustice and claw at something. Stake her claim. Hafiz belonged to her.

"You have been with another woman." She couldn't believe it. "All this time, you were with someone else."

Hafiz's eyes narrowed at the accusation. "No. You

have been the only woman in my life since I met you in St. Louis a year ago."

She was the only woman, and yet he was going to marry another? Lacey fumbled with her sunglasses and tossed them in the bag. "Then how are you...I don't understand."

He braced his feet a shoulders' width apart and clasped his hands behind his back, preparing for battle. "I met the bride today and she agreed."

Lacey's mouth gaped open. "You just met her?" She snatched the flicker of hope and held on tight. "So, it's an arranged marriage."

Hafiz let out a bark of humorless laughter. "Of course."

"Then, what's the problem?" She moved slowly as she stood. Her arms and legs felt limp and shaky. She lurched as she stepped on the hem of her insufferable caftan. "Say that you won't get married."

He looked away. "I can't." Regret tinged his voice.

Lacey wanted to stamp her foot and demand a better answer, but she knew she wouldn't get it. Not with his shuttered expression and the regal tilt of his stubborn chin. "It's not like you're the crown prince," she argued, "although I don't understand that since you're the oldest son. But this means you have more freedom."

Hafiz's eyes closed wearily for a brief moment. "For the last time, the sultan chooses the next in line for the throne. My father chose my brother. And, no, I don't have any freedom in this matter, even though I will never rule. In my case, I have less."

She didn't want to hear that. Thick emotions already clogged her aching throat. "You should never have agreed to marry this woman," she said as her voice wobbled.

He turned his attention back to her. "I gave my consent," he said gently. "I can't take it back."

What about the promises he made to her? The ones he made first. The ones about how they would be together. Didn't those promises matter? Didn't *she* matter?

"Why did you agree in the first place?" She held the plastic bag to her chest. She would rather hold on to something solid and strong like Hafiz until the emotional storm passed, which would still leave her feeling battered and stinging with pain, but he would prevent her from breaking. "You should have refused."

"I couldn't this time." Hafiz winced the moment he revealed too much. He pressed his lips into a straight line.

Lacey stared at him with open suspicion. "This time?" she echoed. "How long have you been looking for a wife?"

"Could we not discuss this here?" he bit out tersely. "Let's go back to the apartment." He guided her to the elevator, keeping a firm hand on her arm as she still weaved from the unpleasant shock. He pressed the call button, and she watched as if her life depended on it, but her brain couldn't register the simple, everyday action.

"Marry," she repeated and shook her head. "I don't believe this. Why didn't you tell me?"

"I am telling you." He kept his eyes on the descending lighted floor numbers.

"Now. After everything is settled." She couldn't be bothered to hide the accusation in her voice.

He spared a glance at her. "Not quite, but it is official as of this morning. I wanted to tell you before you found out from another source."

That explained the missing newspapers. "How considerate." She felt his start of surprise from her bitter sarcasm, but she didn't care. Hafiz was getting married. To someone else. The knowledge stabbed at her heart. It was a wonder she didn't break from the piercing force. "When is the wedding taking place?"

"After Eid." His answer was almost swallowed by the clank and thump of the arriving elevator.

Eid. That holiday came after the month of Ramadan, if she recalled correctly. She remembered something being mentioned in the paper about that coming soon. "Three months?" she made a guess.

He held the sliding metal doors open for her. "More or less."

Lacey walked into the elevator compartment, her head spinning. Three months. She only had three months with Hafiz.

What was she thinking? She had no more time left. Oh, God. She wasn't strong enough to handle this. She was going to shatter from the pain. Hafiz was an engaged man. Off-limits. And she never had any warning.

Her mouth suddenly felt dry as she instinctively pressed the burgeoning wails and sobs into silence until they were ready to burst from her skin. "You should have told me you were looking for a wife."

"I wasn't. I have no interest in getting married. I held it off for as long as possible."

Lacey reeled back in shock. Hafiz had no interest in marriage? *At all?* Not even to her? If that was the case, then what had the past six months been about?

"My parents were looking for a wife for me," he clarified sternly.

"But you knew they were," she argued. "You knew this was going to happen."

Hafiz said nothing and pressed the top floor button several times as the elevator doors slowly shut.

Winning that point of the argument was a hollow victory. "How long have they been looking?" A part of her wanted to know, the other part wanted to deny that any of this was happening.

He stood silently, his jaw tightly clenched. A muscle twitched in his cheek. Lacey thought for a moment he didn't hear her and was about to repeat the question when he finally answered. "A couple of years."

"A…couple of *years*?" She couldn't possibly have heard that correctly. Lacey folded her arms across her chest. "From the time that you knew me, from the very first time you *propositioned* me, you were also on the marriage market? And not once did you find the chance to tell me?"

Why would he? Lacey thought bitterly. He hadn't considered her to be in the running. She was just a bit of fun on the side. A temporary distraction. Oh, she was a fool.

"Marriage negotiations are delicate and complex," he explained as impatience roughened his words. "It could have taken even longer to find a suitable match."

Suitable. She sneered at the term. It was a code word for the right bloodline and the right upbringing from the right family. Not a blue-eyed American who was also an unemployed nightclub musician.

Oh, and suitable meant someone who was pure and virginal. She mustn't forget that.

The injustice of it all flared to new heights. "Not once did you tell me, and yet I dropped my entire life to be with you." Her voice raised another octave. "I moved to the far-off corners of the earth, to this hell—"

"The Sultanate of Rudaynah is not hell." His low growl was similar to that of a wild cat ready to pounce.

"—And exist solely for you and your pleasure! And you don't have the decency to tell me that you're getting married?" Her eyes narrowed into a withering glare.

He gestured with his hands. "Calm down."

"Calm down?" She thought now was as good a time as any to rant. She was ready to punctuate her tantrum by throwing her shopping bag at his sinfully gorgeous face. "Calm down! No, I will not calm down. The man I love, the man I sacrificed everything for is throwing it all away right back into my face," she hissed, her cheeks hot with fury. "Believe me, this is not a time to calm down."

Hafiz was suddenly in front of her. He made a grab for her, but she raised her hands, warding him off. Lacey fought the urge to burrow her head into his shoulder and weep.

"I am not throwing you away, damn it. How could I?" he asked as his bronze eyes silently pleaded for understanding. "You are the best thing that has ever happened to me."

Lacey looked away and tilted her head against the corner. She needed something to lean against anyway as her knees were incapable of supporting her. A buzzing filled her head. She took short, even breaths of the stifling air and blinked back the dark spots.

As the elevator made its slow, rocky ascent, Lacey realized that Hafiz must be equally unnerved by the turn of the events. He had cursed. Another first for the day. Hafiz never, ever cursed. But then, he always controlled the situation and his environment with the same iron will he used over his temper.

Over himself, really. The man never drank alcohol or gambled. He did not live in excess. His sculpted muscles were that of an athlete in training. He barely slept, too busy working to improve the living conditions of Rudaynah. When he wasn't fulfilling his royal and patriotic duties, he met every family obligation. Even marry his parent's choice.

The only time he went wild, the only time he allowed his control to slip, was when they were in bed. Lacey winced, and the first scalding teardrop fell.

Tears streamed out of her eyes and burned jagged lines down her hot cheeks. Why had she thought Hafiz was considering a future with her? Not once did he mention the possibility of happily-ever-after. Never did the word "marriage" ever cross his lips.

But the dream had been harbored deep in her heart, secretly growing. It had been incredibly naïve and wrong to think all she had to do was be patient. She thought that if she came here and slowly entered the culture, she would eventually stand publicly by Hafiz's side as his wife.

Only that dream died the moment Hafiz pledged himself to another. She gasped as the words plunged into her heart. The surrounding blackness she had been fighting back swiftly invaded her mind.

Pledged to another...

The buzzing grew louder and almost masked Hafiz's shout of alarm.

"Lacey!" Hafiz caught her as she slid down the wall. He plucked off her scarf, and her head lolled to one side. He supported her head with his shoulder and noted that her unnaturally pale face was sticky with sweat. He patted her clammy cheek with his hand. "Lacey," he repeated, trying to rouse her.

Her eyelashes fluttered. "So hot."

He gathered her in his arms. The ill-fitting black gown bunched around her slender figure. "I'll take care of you," he promised, holding her tighter. And he would, he vowed to himself, until his last breath. No matter what she thought, he would never cast her aside.

The elevator finally stopped on the penthouse floor. He searched her features, vaguely aware how her curly long hair hung defiantly like a copper flag and her bare legs dangled from the crook of his elbow, exposing her ivory skin for the world to see. If they were caught in this compromising embrace, so be it. Lacey's safety and comfort were always top priority, but now it was more essential than his next heartbeat, Hafiz decided as he stepped out of the elevator and onto the open-air hallway to the apartment.

The sun was setting. Dark reds and rich purples washed the sky as evening prayers were sung from a nearby loudspeaker. Hafiz kept his eyes out for any potential trouble, but he saw no one strolling the grounds or outside the condominiums across the courtyard. But from the domestic sounds emitting from the neighbors' homes on the other floors, the situation could change in an instant.

Carrying Lacey to her front door at a brisk pace, Hafiz noted he wasn't even breathing hard from lifting her. She weighed barely anything. He glanced down at her face and the fragility struck him like a fist.

Not for the first time did he wonder if moving Lacey to Rudaynah had been the best decision for her. Life in hiding had taken its toll. Why hadn't he seen that before? Or did he not want to see it?

Lacey stirred as if she was acutely aware of his perusal. "I'm fine," she murmured and tentatively ran her tongue over her parched lips.

"No, you're not." He leaned heavily against the doorbell and waited at the iron grille door until the American servant wearing a loose T-shirt and cargo pants came to the door.

"Your Highness! What happened?" Glenn asked as he unlocked the door bolts with economical movements. His craggy face showed no alarm, but his watchful eyes were alert. His body, lean from many years of military training, vibrated with readiness to act on the first command from his employer.

"It's all right. She fainted from the heat." Hafiz kicked off his sandals at the door and moved past the older man. "I'll get her into the shower. Have your wife prepare something very cold and sweet for her to drink."

"I'm sorry, Your Highness." Glenn raked his hand over his bristly gray hair. "She said——"

"It's all right," he repeated, calling over his shoulder as he made way to the master bedroom. "Lacey has always had a problem following directions."

"I'm not dead, you know," Lacey said with her eyes closed. "I can hear every word."

"Good, because I do not want you venturing outside again without Glenn," Hafiz said as he stepped into the large room where he spent many hours exploring Lacey's body and revealing the darkest recesses of his heart. This time the sumptuous silks and oversized pillows didn't stir his hot blood. He wanted to tuck Lacey between the colorful sheets and not let her out of bed until she regained her vibrancy. "He is your bodyguard and—"

"He is to play the role of my next of kin if any questions are asked because single women are not allowed to travel alone in this country," Lacey ended in a monotone. She let out a slow, stuttering sigh that seemed to originate from somewhere deep inside her. "I know."

"Then, don't let it happen again." He pushed the bathroom door open with his bare foot. Slapping the light switch outside the door with the palm of his hand, he entered the windowless room now flooding with light.

"It won't."

The determination in her voice made him hesitate. He cautiously watched her face as he set her down gently, sliding her feminine curves along his length. For once her expression showed nothing. Her eyes veiled her feelings. Usually her eyes would darken with righteous indignation, glow with rapturous delight and twinkle with every emotion in between. The sudden change in her behavior troubled him.

He wanted to hold her close until he could read her thoughts, but Lacey had other ideas as she moved away from him. "Can you stand on your own?" he asked.

"Yes." She took another step back and shucked off her cloth boots. The movements lacked her usual energy.

He kept one hand outstretched in case he had to catch her as he started the shower full blast. Hafiz turned his attention on Lacey and quickly divested her of her black caftan.

"Lacey!" His startled hoarse cry echoed in the small room. The sight of her barely-there peach lingerie was a shocking contrast against the conservative cloth. Hafiz's body reacted immediately. The heavy black material dropped from his fists and flopped on the wet floor.

"What?" She inspected her arms and legs. "What's wrong?"

He cleared his throat, wishing he could also clear the sharp arousal tightening his body. "You're supposed to wear several layers of clothes under the caftan." He unhooked the front closure of her bra, his knuckles grazing her breast. He saw the tremor in his hands. He was acting like a callow youth.

"Are you kidding?" She skimmed the high-cut panties down her legs and kicked them aside. "I would boil alive."

His gaze traveled as the peach satin landed on the black fabric. The searing image branded in his mind. The way he would look at women in the shapeless caftan was forever changed. He swallowed roughly as he controlled his baser instinct. "What if you had gotten caught?"

"No one would have found out. You are the only person who has shown enough nerve to get that close." She arched her eyebrow in disapproval.

And he was going to keep it that way. "Here, get under the water." He pulled her to the showerhead.

"Oh! Ow!" Lacey squealed in dismay as the icy cold spray hit her body. She jumped back and rubbed her hands over her arms. "This is so cold."

"You'll get used to it in just a minute," he replied as he always did to her comments on the lack of heated water. The familiarity calmed him while her beaded nipples made his brain sluggish.

"You can leave now," she said through chattering teeth. She looked away from him and tested the temperature by dipping her foot in the cold water.

He leaned against the door and folded his arms across his chest. "I don't want you passing out in the shower."

"I won't. Now go before your royal gown gets soaked." She shooed him away with her hands.

She had a point. The bathroom, already hot as a sauna, was in the traditional Rudaynahi design, with the exception of a European commode. The concrete floor had a drain and was also to be used as the shower floor. Since there was no plastic curtain or glass shower door, the water was already spraying every inch of the bathroom.

"If you're sure," Hafiz said and flashed a wicked smile. "But I can just as easily take it off."

She glared back at him. "I'm sure."

His smile turned wry at her ungracious rejection.

He shouldn't have made the offer. He knew that but went for it anyway. "I'll be outside," Hafiz said. Lacey didn't respond as she stuck her head fully under the spray.

He stepped out of the bathroom and almost collided with the housekeeper who carried a small tray into the bedroom. The tall frosty glass of juice rattled against a plate of figs and dates.

"How is she doing?" Annette asked as she set the tray on the bedside table. "Do we need to call a doctor?"

"No, she's not sick." The uncertain look of the older woman irritated him. If he truly felt Lacey needed medical care, he would call the American doctor who'd already discovered that cashing in favors from a prince was worth more than any currency in a country that relied heavily on the bartering system.

The physician was brilliant and up to date on medicine. Hafiz had seen that firsthand when Lacey arrived in the country and had drunk water that had not been purified. That week had been torture, and Hafiz was insistent that she was given the best care, no matter what. Hafiz would never place secrecy above Lacey's well-being, and it stung to have someone silently questioning his priorities.

"She's overheated," he explained, keeping the defensiveness out of his voice. "The shower is already doing wonders."

"We threw away the newspapers like you requested, but we never thought Lacey would leave to get one." The woman twisted the pleat of her yellow sundress with nervous hands and slid a worried glance at the closed bathroom door.

"It's no one's fault," he said. No one's but his own. He should have prepared Lacey for the possibility of his wedding, but he'd held on to the hope that his intended bride would have declined the offer. "Please, find something light for her to wear."

"Of course." The housekeeper gratefully accepted the task and opened the doors to the armoire, revealing gossamer-thin cotton in every color of the rainbow.

Hafiz walked into the simply appointed drawing room and tried to recapture the peace he always felt whenever he stepped into this home. Decorated with an eclectic mix of wood tables carved in the severe Rudaynahi style and chunky upholstered sofas from the Western world, Lacey had managed to add her upbeat personality with tribal throw rugs and colorful paintings from local artisans.

The apartment was more than a home. It was a haven. It was the only place he felt both passion and peace. The only place in the world he experienced unconditional love.

Hafiz walked slowly to the grand piano that sat in the middle of the room and under the carefully positioned spotlight. It had been incredibly difficult shipping the instrument into the country. Flying in a piano tuner every couple of months was no easy feat, but seeing Lacey's joy and listening to her soulful music made it all worthwhile.

He fingered the sheet music scattered on the polished black wood. The woman had the talent to become a successful recording artist. Hafiz had told her enough times, but she always shook her head in disagreement. Music was a big part of her, but she didn't want to be consumed with the ladder of success like her parents, who were still striving for their big break. She didn't have the desire.

But she stored up all her passion for him. Did that make him feel less guilty in whisking her to his country? The edges of the sheet music crinkled under his fingertips. Because she had no interest in pursuing a career? Because she didn't have family ties?

Hafiz pondered the question as he walked to the doors leading to the balcony that overlooked the Persian Gulf. He admitted that it made it easier to ask her to drop everything and follow him. To stay in the apartment and wait for him. Not once had she complained or shown resentment until today.

And she had every right. He had risked everything for more time with Lacey. The relationship they had was forbidden. And now, as of today, it was impossible.

Only Hafiz didn't allow that word in his vocabulary, and he wasn't willing to let the idea invade his life with Lacey.

"What are you still doing here?" Lacey asked at the doorway on the other side of the long room.

Hafiz turned around. Lacey's wet hair was slicked back into a copper waterfall. She had changed into a pink cotton caftan that clung to her damp skin. Gold threads were woven into the fabric and sparkled like stars.

"Are you feeling better?" he asked, silently watching the housekeeper duck into the kitchen.

"Much. You're free to go." She walked toward the front door.

"Lacey, we need to talk."

"No kidding, but I don't want to right now." She

gripped the thick door handle. "You have had years to think about this. I have had less than an hour."

"Lacey—" He crossed the room and stood in front of her, prepared to take the brunt of her anger and soak up her tears.

"I want you to go." She flung open the door.

Hafiz's shoulders flexed with tension. Every instinct told him to stay, but he knew what she said made sense. It was strange to have her as the calm one and he filled with impetuous emotions. He didn't like the role reversal.

Hafiz agreed with a sharp nod. "I will be here tomorrow after work." He leaned down to brush her cheek with a gentle kiss.

She turned her head abruptly. "Don't." Her eyes focused on the hallway outside the iron grille.

His heart stopped. Lacey had never rejected his touch. "What are you saying?" he asked in a low voice as his lungs shriveled, unable to take in the next breath.

The muscles in her throat jerked. "You shouldn't touch me." The words were a mere whisper. "The moment you became engaged, the moment you chose another woman, we no longer exist."

Hafiz grasped her chin between his thumb and forefinger. "You don't mean that," he said, staring at her intensely. As if he could change her mind through his sheer willpower.

"Yes, I do."

He swallowed down the rising fear. "Obviously, you are still suffering from your collapse." The tip of his thumb caressed the angry line of her bottom lip.

Lacey yanked away from his touch. "I'm thinking quite clearly. You made your choice." She took a step back behind the door, shielding herself from him. "And this is mine."

"You are going to regret those words. You can't send me away." He stepped toward her, ready to prove it.

Lacey's glare was so cold it could have frozen the desert air seeping into the apartment. "Do you want me to cause a scene in front of this complex to get you to leave?"

Her threat surprised Hafiz. That wasn't like her. She knew his weak spots but had always protected him. Now she was so angry, she was becoming a dangerous woman.

Would she try to hurt him because he was getting married? No, not Lacey. She was loyal to him…but when she thought she didn't have any competition. How could he convince her that this marriage was in name only?

He decided to change his strategy. "I will return," he said, shoving his feet into his sandals. The expensive leather threatened to snap under his angry motions. "And you will be here waiting for me."

Defiance flared in her blue eyes. "Don't tell me what to do. You have no right."

"You still belong to me, Lacey," he announced as he left. "Nothing and no one will change that."

CHAPTER THREE

THE WHITE ROBES slapped angrily against Hafiz's legs as he stormed into his office. He would rather be anywhere else but here. Although the palace's murky shadows descending on the spartan rooms were good companions to his dark mood this evening.

"Your Highness." His private secretary clumsily hung up the phone. The withered old man bowed low, his fragile bones creaking. "His Majesty wishes to speak to you."

Hafiz set his jaw as dread seeped inside him. The day couldn't get any worse. The sultan didn't command appointments from his eldest offspring unless there was or would be an unpleasant event.

"When did he make this request?"

"Ten minutes ago, Your Highness," the elderly man answered, his focus on the threadbare Persian rug. "I called your cell phone and left several messages."

Of course. He had turned off his phone so he wouldn't bend to the overwhelming need to call Lacey. His show of confidence that she would follow his orders was going to cost him in more ways than one. Hafiz wanted to roar with frustration, but he needed to stay calm and focused for the sultan.

Hafiz turned and checked his appearance in the gilt-edged mirror. He didn't see anything Sultan Yusuf would find offensive, but the ruler didn't need to hunt long for something to disapprove about his son. Unable to delay the inevitable, Hafiz set his shoulders back and strode to the palace offices.

When he entered the sultan's suite, Hafiz stood respectfully at the double doors and waited to be announced. As one of the secretaries hurried to the massive wooden desk to convey the message to the sultan, Hafiz grew aware of the sideway glances and growing tension. He coldly met the employees' stares one by one until the gazes skittered down in belated respect.

Sultan Yusuf dismissed his secretaries with the flick of his hand. The men hurried past Hafiz and through the doors. Their expressions of grateful relief concerned him.

The sultan continued to sit behind his desk and read a note on thick white paper. He took his time to deign to acknowledge his son's presence. "Hafiz," Sultan Yusuf finally said.

Hafiz approached the sultan. "Your Majesty." Hafiz gave the briefest deferential nod as defiance flowed through his veins.

The sultan tossed the paper on to his desk. "Be seated."

The lack of mind games made Hafiz suspicious, which it was probably supposed to achieve. Hafiz sat down on the chair across from the desk. Tradition dictated that he should keep his head down and his gaze averted. He was never good at tradition.

The sultan leaned back in his chair, steepled his fingers, and studied Hafiz. Not even a whisper of affection crossed his lined face. "You are very fortunate that the Abdullah daughter agreed to the marriage."

Fortune had nothing to do with it. It didn't matter who his bride was. He was marrying this woman for two reasons. It was his royal duty and it was another step toward redemption.

"This girl knows about your—" the king's fingers splayed apart "—misspent youth, as does her family."

Hafiz clenched his teeth and willed his hands to stay straight on his knees. He would not respond. He would not allow his father to spike his temper.

"They will use that knowledge to their advantage as the wedding preparations draw closer. The dowry is not nearly worthy enough for a prince. We're fortunate they didn't demand a bridal price."

Hafiz still said nothing. His teeth felt as if they would splinter. His fingers itched to curl and dig into his knees.

"Have you anything to say, Hafiz?"

He did, but most of it wasn't wise to say aloud. "I regret that my past mistakes still cost our family." And his regret was as honest as it was strong. Nothing could erase the suffering he'd caused Rudaynah. The simple truth destroyed him, and his life's mission was to prevent any future suffering from his hand.

"As do I." Sultan Yusuf sighed heavily. "The reason I'm telling you this is that I expect many maneuvers from the Abdullah family." He smacked his lips with distaste as he mentioned his future in-laws. "Any male relative could trick you. Talk you down the dowry. Say you made a promise or agreement when there was none."

Annoyance welled up inside Hafiz's chest. From

years of practice, his expression didn't show his feelings. Hafiz negotiated multi-million-dollar deals, bro-
kered delicate international agreements and increased
the wealth of this country ten times over. But his family didn't respect his accomplishments. They only remembered his mistakes.

"You will have no interaction with the Abdullah
family," the sultan commanded. "All inquiries must
be directed to my office. Do you understand, Hafiz?"

"Yes, Your Majesty." He didn't have a problem following that order. If that was the purpose of the meeting, Hafiz wondered why the sultan didn't dictate a
memo so he didn't have to speak to his son.

"After all," the ruler continued, "your mother and
I cannot afford another scandal from you."

Hafiz closed his eyes as the pain washed over him.
He should have seen that coming.

"This marriage must happen." The sultan tapped
an authoritative finger on the desk. The thud echoed
loudly in Hafiz's head. "If the engagement is broken,
it will shame this family."

Shaming the family was his sole specialty. The
statement was left unspoken, but Hafiz could hear
it plainly in his father's manner. It wasn't anything
his conscience hadn't shouted for more years than he
cared to remember.

"You've already lost your right to the throne because of your poor choices," Sultan Yusuf said with
brutal frankness. "If you harm this agreement, I will
make certain you lose everything you hold dear."

Did his father think he would try to sabotage the
wedding agreement? Hafiz was stunned at the pos-

sibility. Hadn't his actions proven he would sacrifice his personal wants for the good of the country?

"But, if you do not cause any delay or scandal—" he paused and sliced a knowing look "—I will give you the one thing you desire."

Hafiz flinched. His mind immediately went to Lacey. A white-hot panic blinded him. Did the sultan know about her?

"Marry the bride I choose, and you will resume your rightful place. You will become the heir to the throne once again."

Lacey's fingers dragged against the ivory keys of her piano, but she didn't play a note. She couldn't. The music inside her had been silenced.

Glenn and Annette had retired hours ago, but she couldn't sleep no matter how hard she tried. Her body felt limp and wrung out, and her mind craved for oblivion.

What was it about her? Why was she so easy to discard? First her parents and now Hafiz. She didn't understand it.

Lacey always held on to the belief that she would have bonded with her parents if they had taken her on the road with them. They would have remembered her birthdays and special occasions. They wouldn't have forgotten her all those times or accidentally left her to fend for herself on school vacations. If they hadn't sent her off to live with distant relatives or family friends, she would have some sort of relationship today with her mother and father.

But now she knew her parents didn't get the full blame. There was something wrong with her. It didn't matter how freely and completely she gave her love; she would not get it in return. She was unlovable.

Lacey stood and walked to the balcony doors and peered outside. No lights glowed against the darkness. Outside appeared silent and empty.

If only her mind would quiet down like the town below her. She leaned her head against the glass pane that was now cool from the desert night. The moment Hafiz had left, fragmented thoughts and fears had bombarded her mind. She'd paced her room as unspoken questions whirled through her head. She'd stared numbly at the walls for hours.

No matter how much the housekeeper had tried to tempt her with food, Lacey refused to eat. Her throat, swollen and achy from crying, would surely choke on the smallest morsel. Sustenance meant nothing and she had curled up on Hafiz's side of the bed. There she had muffled her cries in his pillow when one more minute of living without him became unbearable.

Her mind felt as chaotic as the clothes jumbled inside her suitcase. She packed her belongings, which were pathetically few. It was a mocking symbol of the emptiness of her life before she'd met Hafiz and her barren future without him. Only now she had even less, because she was leaving everything behind along with her heart.

Lacey frowned, trying to hold her emotions together. There were too many things she had to do, like finding a new home.

Lacey pressed the heels of her hands against her puffy eyes. The business of breaking up was beyond her. She needed a fresh start. Somewhere that held no memories. A place where Hafiz couldn't find her.

Not that he would follow her across the world. He'd made his choice. And it wasn't her. It was never going to be her.

She didn't want to know anything about the woman who got to share Hafiz's life. The one who would wear his ring, bear his name and carry his children in her womb. Lacey blinked as her eyes stung, but she'd already used up her tears.

Lacey twisted around when she heard the key in the lock. Hope stuttered through her exhausted body as Hafiz entered. He halted when he saw her across the room.

"Hafiz." She instinctively moved toward him like a moth to a flame. "What are you doing here?"

She stared at him, memorizing every detail. He was dressed like a laborer. While the outfit was an unusual choice for a member of the royal family, Hafiz lent a sophisticated elegance to the rough work clothes.

The simple tunic was as black as his short hair. The cotton sluiced down his muscular chest and skimmed past his knees. His jeans strained against his powerful legs as he slid his feet out of scuffed sandals. His high-tech watch was nowhere to be found, but the royal ring gleamed proudly on his hand.

"I wasn't sure you would be here." His hands clenched and unclenched the keys.

Lacey guiltily flashed a look in the direction of the bedroom where her bags were packed and stowed away under the bed. "And you're checking up on me?" she asked as her eyebrows arched with disbelief. "You could have called."

"No. I came here to say goodbye." He set down the key with hypnotic slowness. "Tonight."

She froze as the words pummeled her bruised heart.
Tonight? Her chest heaved, and she struggled for her
next breath. "Now?"

Hafiz nodded. "I had a meeting with the sultan earlier this evening." He stared at the keys as though he
wanted to snatch them back. "If any of my actions prevent the forthcoming marriage, I will lose everything."

"Your father threatened you?" she whispered in
horror.

"The sultan warned me," he corrected. "And I can't
help but wonder if he knows about you. Maybe not
your name or where you live, but that I have someone
like you in my life."

Someone like you... The phrase scratched at her.
What did that mean? More importantly, what did it
mean to Hafiz?

She stood in front of him, and placed her hand on
his arm, offering him comfort. Not that he needed it.
Hafiz had the strength to stand alone. "You shouldn't
be forced to marry someone you don't love."

Her words seemed to startle him. "Lacey," Hafiz
said in a groan as he cupped her cheek with his hand.
"A royal marriage never has anything to do with love.
It has always been that way."

She closed her eyes as she leaned into his hand,
knowing it would be the last time he would caress
her. She gathered the last of her self-discipline and
withdrew from his touch. Energy arced and flared
between them.

"I will miss you, Hafiz," she said brokenly as her
throat closed up. The tears she thought couldn't happen beaded on her eyelashes.

Hafiz let out a shuddering breath. He swept his fingertip against the corner of her eye, taking her tears with him. The moisture clung to his knuckle, and he rubbed it into his skin with his thumb, silently sharing her agony.

The image took a chink out of her hard-earned resolve. Lacey wrapped her arms around her stomach before she crumbled altogether. "I had so many questions to ask you, and now I can't remember what they were." All except for one that danced on her tongue. "Did you ever love me?"

Silence throbbed in the air.

Lacey blinked at the question that had tumbled from her mouth. *Of all the things to ask,* her mind screamed.

Hafiz went unnaturally still.

"I don't know why I asked." She shrugged as her pain intensified. "Please, don't answer that."

The words were ripped from deep within her. She desperately wanted to know the answer. She never questioned it before, but she had been living in a fantasy.

Lacey had always felt Hafiz loved her. It was in his touch, in his eyes, and in his smile. But he never said the words, even when she chanted her declaration of love in the height of ecstasy.

It was too late to find out. If he didn't love her, she would never recover. If he did love her, then she would never let go. Even if he was married, even if he kept her hidden. And she couldn't let that happen.

Hafiz frowned. "Lacey…"

"Ssh." She silenced him by pressing her fingers against his parted lips. *"Please."*

He covered her hand with his and placed soft kisses

in the heart of her palm. "I don't want you to leave," he said against her skin.

"Then, come away with me!" She impulsively tangled her fingers with his and pulled him away from the door. His torn expression shamed her. She drew back and let go of his hand. "I'm sorry. That was wrong."

He moved swiftly and crushed her against him. "I can't leave Rudaynah," he whispered, his breath ruffling her hair. "And you can't stay. I don't know what I'm going to do without you. I'm only half alive when you are not around."

He didn't want to give her up, but he had the strength to do it when she wanted to ignore the inevitable. Hafiz would flourish without her while she wilted into a slow death. "In time, you'll forget all about me."

He tightened their embrace. "How can you say that?"

"You will," she predicted with a sigh. It happened to her before, and nothing she did would stop it from happening again. "You need to leave." Now, before it became impossible. Before she threw herself at his feet and begged him to stay.

"Yes." He gradually relaxed his hold but didn't let go. "This was already a risk."

She looked up into his face. The scent of the desert night clung to his warm skin. The steady and strong beat of his heart pounded under her hand. The passion he felt for her shone in his eyes. This was how she wanted to remember him. "Goodbye, Hafiz."

He lowered his face and gently brushed his mouth against hers. Like Lacey, he kept his eyes open, needing to commit this last kiss to memory. The unshed tears in her eyes blurred his image. Lacey's lips clung to his. The craving to deepen the kiss radiated between them. She felt his need to carry her away and the struggle to leave her behind.

"I have to go," he murmured against her mouth.

"I know." The world tilted as he withdrew, and his arms dropped away from her. She felt exposed and weak. A single tear spilled down her cheek. "I wish…" She stopped and bit her lip.

"You wish what?" When she didn't answer, he grabbed her upper arms with his large hands. "Tell me," he pleaded, his fingers biting into her flesh.

"No." She shook her head. She had to be strong and ignore her wants. For both of them. "I wish you… happiness."

Hafiz shook her slightly until tendrils of her hair fell in front of her face. "That was not what you were going to say. Don't end this on a lie," he ordered, agony threading his voice. "Don't leave me with a half-spoken wish, so that I will go mad trying to figure out what you wanted to say."

Lacey looked away. She'd ruined the moment, all because she couldn't let him go. "I can't."

"Tell me what you wish," he said against her ear, teasing her willpower with his husky voice full of promise. "I will make it come true if it's in my power."

"I wish we…" She swallowed. Damn her weakness! "I wish we had at least one more night."

She saw the gleam in Hafiz's bronze eyes. Her request unleashed something dark and primitive inside him. He wanted to claim her, possess her so completely that she would never forget him. As if she could.

"I can grant you that wish," he promised as his features sharpened with lust. "Tonight."

"No." Lacey shook her head. They had to stop now. If she went to bed with him tonight, she would do everything in her power to keep him there. "We can't. You are an engaged man. The sultan has warned you—"

"This is my wish, too." He gathered her close and lifted her in his arms before he strode to the bedroom. "Don't deny me one more night."

CHAPTER FOUR

LACEY CLUNG TO Hafiz as they entered her bedroom. The bedside lamp offered a faint glow in the large room, casting shadows on the unmade bed. Hafiz barely broke his stride when he kicked the door shut.

She wasn't sure why he wasn't rushing to the bed. Lacey felt the urgency pulsating between them. This was the last time they would be together. They had to get a lifetime into one night.

The unfairness of it all hit Lacey, and she tried to push it away. She didn't want to focus on that. She wasn't going to waste her last moments with Hafiz on something she couldn't control.

The only thing she could do was make one beautiful and lasting memory. Have something that could ease the pain when she thought about the love she lost.

Hafiz stood by the edge of the bed, and Lacey knelt on the mattress before him. She pressed her hands against his cheeks and looked deep into his eyes.

She bit the inside of her lip to prevent from speaking when she saw Hafiz's sadness. It wasn't like him to show it, but the emotion was too strong; he couldn't contain it. Lacey closed her eyes and rested her head against his chest. She wanted to ease his pain. Take it away from him.

She was hurting, too. It hurt knowing that after tonight she wouldn't see him, and she couldn't touch him. She wouldn't be allowed anywhere near him.

Her shaky breath echoed in the room.

"Lacey?" Hafiz's voice was tender as he smoothed his hand against the crown of her head.

She tilted her face up and sought his mouth. She poured everything she felt into the kiss. She held nothing back. The pain and the anger. The love and the unfulfilled dreams.

The heat between them wasn't a slow burn. It flared hot and wild. Lacey sensed the dangerous power behind it, but this time she didn't care. In the past they danced around it, knowing it could rage out of control. This time she welcomed it. Encouraged it.

Hafiz bunched her caftan in his fists. She knew it was a silent warning. He needed to leash his sexual hunger, or it could become destructive.

She didn't think that was possible. There was nothing left to destroy. She wanted to climb the heights with Hafiz and disregard the possibility of plunging into the depths.

Lacey wrenched her mouth away from Hafiz. Her breath was uneven as her chest rose and fell. She watched him as she tore off her caftan, revealing that she wore nothing underneath.

As she tossed her clothes on to the floor, a part of her warned her to slow down. This was not what she wanted their last night to be like. She wanted it soft and romantic. This was primal and elemental. And she couldn't stop. She didn't *want* to slow down.

Hafiz shucked off his tunic, exposing his muscular chest. She reached out with the intention to trail her hand down his warm, golden skin. Instead she hooked her hand over the low-slung waistband of his jeans and pulled him close. She gasped as the tips of her breasts rubbed against his coarse chest hair.

Hafiz stretched his arms and wrapped his hands around the bedposts. His move surprised her. He didn't gather her close or take over. He was giving the control to her.

It was a rare gift. Hafiz was always in control. She watched him as she boldly cupped his arousal. A muscle bunched in his jaw, but he said nothing. He didn't move as she teased him with her hands. She lowered the zipper and pushed his clothes down his legs.

She wasn't gentle as she stroked him. She felt the tension rise inside him and felt the bedposts rattle under his grip. But even a man like Hafiz had his limits. He suddenly growled and grabbed Lacey's arms.

His kiss was hard and possessive. Her heart raced as the anticipation built deep inside her.

Hafiz tore his mouth away, and she tumbled down on to her back. She was sprawled naked before him. The ferocious hunger in his eyes made her shiver as the excitement clawed at her. She needed Hafiz, and she would go mad if she had to wait.

"Now," she demanded. She almost couldn't say the word, her chest aching as her heart pounded against her ribs. She rocked her hips as the desire coiled low in her pelvis.

Hafiz didn't argue. He grabbed the back of her legs and dragged her closer. Her stomach gave a nervous flip when she saw his harsh and intense expression.

After he wrapped her legs around his waist, Hafiz ruthlessly tilted her hips. She felt exposed. Wild and beautiful. Vulnerable and yet powerful.

Her heart stopped as he drove into her. Lacey moaned as she yielded, arching her body to accept him. There was no finesse or sophistication. Her hips bucked to an ancient rhythm as she met his thrusts.

She wanted to hold on to this moment and make it last, but she couldn't tame the white heat that threatened to overpower her. Lacey closed her eyes and allowed the sensations to claim her as she cried out Hafiz's name.

Hours later, they lay together. Lacey's back was tucked against Hafiz's chest. Her long hair, tangled and damp with sweat, was pushed to the side as he placed a soft kiss on her neck. The blanket and sheets were in disarray on the floor, but Lacey didn't feel the need to warm their naked bodies. Hafiz's body heat was all she needed.

Lacey deliberately took an even breath and slowly exhaled. She wasn't going to cry. Not yet. She didn't want Hafiz's last memory of her to include that.

She focused her attention on their joined hands, barely visible in the darkened room. She idly played with his hand, rubbing his palm and stroking the length of his fingers. Hafiz did the same, as if silently memorizing every inch of her hand.

They were so different, Lacey decided. Hafiz's hand was large and strong. Hers was more delicate. Her job as a pianist relied on her hands while Hafiz never used his for physical labor. His skin was golden and hers was ivory.

Her fingers clenched his. She stared at their clasped hands, noticing the soft shine of Hafiz's royal ring. She glanced at the window, her heart aching with knowing, when she saw the light filtering through the gap in the curtains.

The night had ended. Their time was over.

Lacey was reluctant to point it out. If Hafiz wasn't going to comment on it, why should she? After all, they didn't define when night ended. The people of Rudaynah didn't start the day until close to noon.

She knew she was grasping for more time. Lacey bit her lip as she watched Hafiz twist his fingers around hers. She wanted to grab his hands and hold them tight.

She was in danger of never letting him go.

Lacey glanced at the window again. They had not squeezed out every minute of their night together. How long had they spent gazing in each other's eyes, holding each other, not saying a word? But she wouldn't regret those quiet moments. They meant something to her. It made her feel connected to Hafiz.

Lacey swept the tip of her tongue along her bottom lip before she spoke. "It's morning."

Her voice shattered the peaceful silence. She felt the tension in Hafiz's muscles before his fingers gripped hers.

"No, it's not," Hafiz replied in his deep, rumbling voice as his warm breath wafted against her ear.

She frowned and motioned at the window. "It's sunrise."

"I disagree." Hafiz gently turned her so she lay on her back. "The sun is still rising. It isn't morning yet. We still have time."

He wasn't ready to end this, either. Lacey gazed lovingly at his face above hers. She brushed her fingertips along his jaw, the dark stubble rough against her skin.

"I love you, Hafiz."

A dark and bittersweet emotion she couldn't define flashed in his eyes. Hafiz slowly lowered his head and bestowed a gentle kiss on her lips.

She didn't move as he placed another soft kiss on her cheek and yet another on her brow. It was more than saying goodbye. He touched her with reverence.

She closed her eyes, desperate to hide her tears, as Hafiz cupped her face with care. He tipped her head back against the pillows and kissed her again. His mouth barely grazed hers.

Lacey wanted to capture his lips and deepen the kiss. But Hafiz slid his mouth to her chin before leaving a trail of kisses along her throat.

She swallowed hard as Hafiz darted his tongue at the dip of her collarbone before pressing his mouth against the pulse point at the base of her throat. She gasped as he suckled her skin between his sharp teeth and left his mark on her.

He didn't need to brand her. She was already his, and nothing—not time, not distance—would change that.

"Hafiz…" she said in a moan as she reached for him. He stopped her and wrapped his hands around her wrists before lowering her arms on the mattress.

"Shh," he whispered as he settled between her legs. He continued his path and kissed the slope of her breast. Lacey arched her spine as he teased her with his mouth.

Hafiz knew how to touch her, how to draw out the pleasure until it became torment. She hissed between her teeth as he laved his tongue against her tight nipple before drawing it into his hot mouth.

She fought against his hold, wanting to grab the back of his head, needing to hold him against her chest, but Hafiz didn't let go.

As sweat formed on her skin while she trembled with need, Hafiz silently continued his descent down her abdomen. Lust, hot and thick, flooded her pelvis. She rocked her hips insistently as Hafiz licked and nibbled and kissed her.

His path was slow, lazy and thorough. She glanced at the window. The sunlight was getting brighter and stronger.

Hafiz bent his head and pressed his mouth on her sex. Lacey moaned as she bucked against his tongue. He released her wrists to spread her legs wider. Lacey grabbed his head, bunching his short hair in her fists as he pleasured her.

She tried to hold back, wanting to make this last, but her climax was swift and sharp. She cried out as it consumed her. Her hips bucked wildly as she rode the sensations.

Her stomach clenched with anticipation as Hafiz slid his hands under her hips. His touch was urgent. She opened her eyes to see him tower over her. There was a primitive look in his eyes as he knelt between her legs.

She felt the rounded tip of his erection pressing against her. Hafiz entered her fully, and she groaned with deep satisfaction. She watched as he closed his eyes and tipped his head back as he struggled for the last of his control.

Lacey's flesh gripped him hard as she felt her body climbing fast toward another climax. She bucked against Hafiz, and he braced his arms next to her. He recaptured her hands and curled his fingers around hers.

"Hafiz…" she whimpered as he rested his forehead against hers. She went silent as he met her gaze. She allowed him to watch her every emotion and response flicker in her eyes. She hid nothing as she climaxed again, harder and longer.

And when her release triggered his, she didn't look away. Lacey let Hafiz know how much pleasure she received from watching him. She heard his hoarse cry before she closed her eyes, allowing exhaustion to claim her.

Lacey's eyes bolted open. The first thing she heard was the drone of the high-speed ceiling fan. Then she noticed the sheets tucked neatly around her body.

Panic crumbled on top of her. She jackknifed into a sitting position and looked at Hafiz's side of the bed. It was empty.

"No," she whispered. "Noooo." She pushed the sheets away as if he would suddenly appear.

She wildly looked around the room. She knew she'd asked for this night only, but she wished she had asked for more. Much more. Even if she knew it wasn't possible, she would have thrown her pride to the wind and begged for more time.

Lacey stumbled out of bed and grabbed for her

robe. Hafiz's side of the bed was warm. There was a chance that he was still there.

"Hafiz?" she called out with a nervous tremble as she tied the sash of her robe. The silence taunted her. Biting down on her bottom lip, she opened the bedroom door. Hope leached from her bones as she stared into the empty drawing room.

Lacey slammed the door shut and ran to the window, her bare feet slapping against the floor. She ripped the curtains to the side and searched the quiet streets.

Her heart lodged in her throat as she saw the familiar figure walking across the street.

For a brief moment, Lacey thought she was mistaken. The man didn't stride through the streets with regal arrogance. Hafiz walked slowly. Hesitantly. His head was bowed, his shoulder hunched.

She raised her fists, ready to beat at the glass and call for him to turn around.

Instinct stopped her. She knew it was hard for him to walk away. Probably just as difficult as it was to let him leave. She had to be strong. For him, if not for herself.

She pressed her forehead against the window, letting her fingers streak against the glass. "Hafiz…" she cried weakly.

Her eyes widened as she watched him slow to a halt. It was impossible for him to have heard her whimper. Hafiz turned slightly to the side and caught himself before glancing at her window.

Her heart pounded until she thought her ears would burst from the sound. She needed one more look. Just one more so she could carry it with her to ease her loneliness. She needed another look to remember that she was loved once.

But she also didn't want him to turn around. She needed him to be strong. She needed to see his strength and know that he was going to be okay. That he was going to stand alone as he had before he met her.

Lacey pressed her lips together, her breath suspended as Hafiz paused. Tears cascaded down her cheeks as she felt her future clinging to this moment.

Hafiz straightened his shoulders and resolutely turned away. Lacey felt shell-shocked. Her future took a free fall into the dark and desolate abyss.

It was a bittersweet sight for her to see Hafiz stride away. She stared at him, sobbing noisily until he turned the corner. Her gaze didn't move from the empty spot just in case he changed his mind. Her vision blurred and her eyes stung as she kept watch for the possibility that he needed to steal one more glance.

But it wasn't going to happen. He was strong enough for the both of them. The knowledge chipped away at her as she sank against the wall into an untidy heap.

It was over. They were no longer together.

Lacey felt as if she was going to splinter and die. And she had no idea how she was going to prevent falling apart without Hafiz holding her tight and giving a piece of his strength to her.

CHAPTER FIVE

HAFIZ REALIZED HE must have looked quite fierce by the way the office workers cowered when he strode in. *Too bad,* he thought as he cast a cold look at a young businessman who had the misfortune of being in his eyesight. Hafiz didn't feel like altering his expression.

Usually he looked forward to coming into his downtown office in the afternoon once he had met all of his royal duties for the day. It felt good to get out of the palace that was as quiet as a mausoleum. Although it had been built by his ancestors, the historical site—or the people inside it—didn't reflect who he was. The royal viziers were too concerned with protocol and tradition. They didn't like any new idea. Or any idea *he* had.

The royal court seemed to have forgotten that he was brought up to serve and look after the sultanate. His education and experience had been focused on international relations and business. He had so many plans and initiatives to improve the lives of his countrymen, but no one wanted to listen to the prince who had fallen out of favor. That would change once he married the sultan's choice.

He strode to his desk and noted that, unlike his

troubled mind, everything in his office was in order. The modern building, complete with state-of-the-art equipment, usually crackled with energy from dawn to dusk. The sultan and the palace had no say in what went on in these offices. Here Hafiz had the freedom to explore and take risks.

The young men he employed outside of the palace were unquestionably loyal, efficient and brilliant. They were men who were educated outside of Rudaynah, but returned home so they could make a difference. They spoke Arabic and English fluently, usually within the same sentence. They were comfortable in business suits and traditional Rudaynahi robes. Men very much like him, except for a few drops of royal blood and a few years in the world that had stripped away any idealism.

From the corner of his eye, Hafiz saw his executive secretary hurry toward him. One of the office assistants was already at his desk, trying to look invisible while carefully setting down a mug of coffee. The bitter scent was welcoming since he hadn't slept for days. Hafiz walked around his desk, determined to lose himself in his work.

"Good afternoon, Your Highness," the secretary said cautiously as he tugged at his silk tie. The man eyed him like he would a cobra ready to strike. "The changes in your schedule have been entered—"

Hafiz's attention immediately began to fade, which was unlike him. He was known for his focus and attention to detail, but he had been distracted for the past few days. Perhaps he was coming down with something. It had nothing to do with Lacey. He did not wallow in the past. He didn't focus on the things he couldn't change. He had moved on from Lacey.

Lacey. He refused to look at the window, but the pull was too great. Hafiz reluctantly looked outside, his gaze automatically seeking Lacey's penthouse apartment. A few months ago, he had picked the office building specifically for the view. He had found himself staring out of the window throughout the workdays, even though he knew he wouldn't catch a glimpse of Lacey. The knowledge that she was there always brought him peace. Until now.

The buzzing of his cell phone shattered his reverie. His gut twisted with anticipation and dread. Only a few people had this number. He grabbed the phone and looked at the caller ID. Disappointment crashed when he saw it wasn't Lacey. Hafiz dismissed his secretary with the wave of his hand and took the call.

"Your Highness? This is Glenn," Lacey's body-guard quickly said to identify himself. "I'm sorry to call you, but we've hit a setback. Our exit visas have been delayed."

"Nothing works on time in Rudaynah." Hafiz rubbed his hand over his forehead and gave a short sigh of frustration. A sense of unease trickled down his spine. Was the palace behind this? Did they know about Lacey?

Hafiz discarded that thought. The palace wouldn't be concerned about an American nightclub singer. "Did they say why?"

"No. I bribed the right government officials, sat down and had tea at the chief of police's office, but I'm not getting any information."

Hafiz glanced out the window again. He had to

get Lacey out before her presence could ruin everything he had worked toward. "Ordinarily I would have
someone from the palace make a special request with
the right official, but that would bring unwanted attention. We will have to wait it out. They should be
ready in another day or two."

"Yes, sir."

"Would you please put Lacey on the phone, and I'll
explain it to her." He shouldn't talk to Lacey. After
all, they had said their goodbyes. He wanted that night
to be their last memory, but he also didn't want her
to think he had abandoned her when she needed as-
sistance.

There was a beat of silence, and Glenn cleared his
throat. "Miss Maxwell is not here, sir."

"What?" Hafiz stared at Lacey's apartment. She
had promised that she wouldn't venture out again.
"Where is she?"

"She is at the Scimitar having tea with friends."

Hafiz's muscles jerked with surprise. *Friends?*
What friends?

His gaze darted across the skyline to the luxurious
hotel. The tall building was like a glass and metal spiral reaching out to the sun, reflecting the rays against
the dark windows. "I don't understand."

"I apologize, sir. I would have accompanied her,
but I was dealing with the exit visas. She had left before I got back."

Lacey had friends? Hafiz felt his frown deepen.
Lacey had a world outside of the apartment. A world
that didn't include him. He wasn't sure why he was
so surprised. Lacey had a large group of friends in
St. Louis.

But she never talked about these friends. That was strange. Lacey told him everything. Or he thought she did. Why had she been hiding this information?

"Who are these friends?" Hafiz asked tersely, interrupting Glenn's excuse. If one of them had a male name… Hafiz gritted his teeth and clenched his hand into a fist.

"No need to be concerned, sir," Glenn replied. "These women are above reproach. They are the wives of ambassadors and government ministers."

Hafiz went cold as he remained perfectly still. His ex-mistress was socializing with the most influential and powerful women of Rudaynah? The very mistress he broke up with so he could marry another? Hafiz slowly closed his eyes as the tension wrapped around his chest and squeezed. Glenn was incorrect. He had every reason to worry.

Lacey always thought the tearoom at the Scimitar was an unlikely mix of cultures. She stared at the plate that offered scones and slices of cinnamon date cake. A copper *cezve* for Turkish coffee sat next to an ornate silver teapot. A golden table runner with an intricate geometric design lay on top of the white linen tablecloth.

"You look so different in Western clothes," Inas told Lacey as she nibbled on a fried pastry ball that was dipped in a thick syrup. "I hardly recognized you."

"I feel different," Lacey admitted as she self-consciously tucked her hair behind her ear. She felt undressed wearing a simple green dress with long sleeves and a high neckline. Her makeup was minimal, and her shoes had a low heel. She was covered, but it didn't feel as if it was enough. "It's strange not wearing a caftan."

"Why the sudden change?" Janet, an ambassador's wife, asked as she patted a linen napkin to her bright red lips. Tall, blond and willowy, Janet had lived in the sultanate for years but chose not to wear the native clothes, no matter how warm the weather turned. "We're still in Rudaynah."

"I'm trying to get used to my old clothes," Lacey explained, but it wasn't the whole truth. When she'd first moved here, Lacey had originally chosen to wear the scarves and caftans, believing it was the first step to enter this world. Now she realized it had been a waste of time. "Although I really didn't fit in here."

"Nonsense." Inas flipped her long black braid over her shoulder. "You were one of my hardest-working students. So determined. If you had stayed here a little longer, I'm sure you would have become proficient in Arabic."

"Thank you." She had wanted to surprise Hafiz with her grasp of the language. One of her goals had been to watch his face soften when she declared her love in his native tongue.

"I don't know what our charity is going to do without you," Janet said with a sigh. "We made great strides once you joined. Are you sure you have to leave right away?"

"Yes, we need to move. It's urgent for my…uncle to get to his next work project." Part of her wished she could have left on the first flight out, but she was finding the idea of permanently leaving Hafiz very difficult. "We're just waiting for the exit visas."

"Those are just a formality," Inas insisted. "But if

you're still going to be here this weekend, you must attend my daughter's wedding reception. The marriage contract ceremony is for family only, but the reception is going to be here for all of our friends. Oh, and you should see the dancers we hired for the *zaffa* procession!"

"I would like that." She had heard every detail about the upcoming wedding and wanted to be there to share her friend's special moment. But her moments with Hafiz had come first, and she had reluctantly declined because it would have interfered with her time with him.

What had Hafiz given up to spend time with her? Lacey frowned as the thought whispered into her mind. She shouldn't compare. Hafiz was a busy and important man.

"Most of the royal court will be there because my husband and the groom's father are government ministers. I know you couldn't attend before because your aunt and uncle had a previous engagement, but this will be the last time we see each other. Extend the invitation to them and…" Inas frowned when the quiet buzz of conversation suddenly died. She set down her teacup, her gold bracelets tinkling, as she looked over her shoulder. "What's happening?"

"I'm not sure," Janet murmured as she craned her neck. "Everyone is looking at the door to the lobby."

"Oh, my goodness," Inas whispered and turned to face her friends. Her eyes were wide with delight. "It's the prince."

Lacey flinched at her friend's announcement. Her heartbeat stuttered over the possibility of seeing Hafiz again. "Which one? Which prince?"

"The oldest. Hafiz."

Lacey struggled for her next breath when she saw Hafiz being escorted through the tearoom. He effortlessly commanded attention. It wasn't because the aggressive lines of his dark business suit emphasized his muscular body, or the haughty jut of his chin. It wasn't because he walked like a conqueror or because of his royal status. It was because he exuded a power that indicated that he was a valuable ally or a dangerous opponent. This was someone who could ruin a man's life with the snap of his fingers or steal a woman's heart with a smile.

Hafiz strode past her, never meeting her startled gaze. His face was rigid, as if it had been hewn from stone.

He didn't see her. Lacey's lips parted as she stared after him. How was that possible? She would always capture his gaze the moment she walked into the room.

A thousand petty emotions burst and crawled under her skin. She wouldn't give in to them. She shouldn't care that she was invisible three days after he left her. She expected it. That would have always been her status in public had she stayed with Hafiz.

And she didn't want a life like that, Lacey reminded herself, closing her eyes and drawing the last of her composure. She didn't want to come in second, even if it meant a life without Hafiz. She refused to be on the side. She wouldn't be an afterthought again.

"He's gorgeous," Janet said in a low voice as they watched Hafiz stride out of the tearoom to what she suspected was the private dining areas.

"So is his fiancée," Inas informed them. "I know the Abdullah family."

Lacey winced. She wished she hadn't heard that. She didn't want to know anything about the woman who got to marry Hafiz. It was easier for her that way.

Janet leaned forward. "What is she like?"

"Nabeela is the perfect Rudaynahi woman."

Lacey's muscles locked. Now she had a name to go with the woman. Somehow that made it worse. She didn't want to put a name or a face to the person who got the man she loved.

"She has been groomed for life at the palace. Her parents were hoping she would marry a royal adviser or minister. They never thought the sultan and his wife would choose her to become a princess. She'll make a good wife for Hafiz."

No, she won't. He's mine. The thought savagely swiped at her like a claw. It tore at the thin façade she'd carefully constructed after finding out about Hafiz's wedding, exposing the truth that bled underneath. It punctured the festering pain she tried to ignore.

She knew Hafiz was going to be married, but she didn't allow herself to think past the wedding. She thought of Nabeela as the bride. She'd never thought of them as a couple. As partners. As husband and wife.

Lacey looked down hurriedly, the table weaving and buckling before her eyes. The knowledge made her physically ill. She knew it wasn't a love match, but it didn't stop the bilious green ribbons of jealousy snaking around her heart.

Her poisonous emotions ate away at her until she felt like a brittle, hollowed-out shell. A series of primal responses, each sharper than the previous one, battered her mind, her heart and her pride.

"Well, I heard it's not Nabeela's beauty that made Prince Hafiz accept," Janet said in a sly tone.

Lacey wanted to change the topic immediately. But she was scared to open her mouth, not sure if her secrets or a scream of howling pain would spill out. She stared at her teacup and forced herself to reach for it. She didn't like how her hands trembled.

"Rumor has it that the sultan and the prince made an agreement," Janet whispered fiercely. "If he marries this Nabeela without incident, Hafiz will become the crown prince."

Lacey's breath hitched in her throat. She set the cup down before it snapped in her hands. So that was the reason. It made sense, and she didn't question it.

Lacey sank back in her plush chair and tilted her head up. She stared at the mosaic ceiling made of lapis lazuli as the low murmur of different languages faded into a hum. The clink of fine china blurred into nothing as her thoughts spun wildly.

She always knew Hafiz was ambitious. Driven and determined. A man like Hafiz couldn't give up the chance of the throne. Even if it meant discarding his mistress. Although now she wondered if it had been a difficult decision for him. She couldn't compete with a crown.

She should have seen the signs. After all, she had been in this position before. Her parents had been just as driven, just as single-minded with their dreams to become rich and famous. Once they decided having a child was holding them back, they had abandoned her with a swiftness that still took her breath away.

But this time she hadn't looked for signs because she thought they were in love. She had wanted to believe that this time she wasn't the burden. That she was not only welcomed into Hafiz's life, but that he would move heaven and earth to be with her.

When was she going to learn? She did not inspire that kind of devotion. No one would ever love her like that.

"What about his brother?" Lacey's voice sounded rough to her ears. She pushed her plate away with tense fingers. "I thought he was the crown prince."

"Ashraf?" Janet asked. "Yes, I wonder how he feels about this new development. He's been the heir to the throne for a decade."

"A decade?" Lacey repeated slowly. "How old is he?"

"Just a few years younger than Prince Hafiz," Janet said, glancing at Inas for confirmation. "He became the heir to the throne when Hafiz lost his birthright."

Lacey blinked slowly as a buzzing sound grew in her ears. "Hafiz lost—?" She gripped the edge of the table as her heart fluttered against her rib cage. "I mean...*Prince* Hafiz? What do you mean by birthright?"

"He was in line to be the next sultan," Janet explained.

Lacey tilted her head sharply. Her arms went lax as she slumped in her chair. She felt as if she was missing a vital piece of information. "He was *supposed* to inherit the throne? When did this happen?"

"How do you not know this?" Inas's eyes widened as she leaned over the table. "I thought we covered this during your history lessons."

Lacey slowly shook her head. "How can a prince be displaced in the line of succession?" She was hesitant to even ask. Did he renounce his right? Did he commit a heinous crime? Neither sounded like something Hafiz would do. "You have to do something really bad, right?"

"I don't have all the details on that, but I can tell you this." Inas gave a cautious glance at the tables surrounding them before she went on. "It had something to do with a woman."

Lacey felt her lungs shrivel up as the bitter taste of despair filled her mouth. Hafiz lost everything over a woman? Numbness invaded her bones, protecting her before she doubled over from the intense pain.

"What woman?" Lacey asked dully. She must have been extraordinary for Hafiz to take such a risk. It didn't make sense. The man would do anything to protect and serve his country. He did not put anyone before his duty. Hafiz did not put *himself* before Rudaynah.

"I heard it was a mistress," Janet said quietly. "A series of mistresses."

Inas shrugged. "One woman is all that it would take to lose the throne."

A mistress. No, *mistresses*. She shouldn't be surprised. Hafiz was incredibly sophisticated and knowledgeable in the bedroom. Yet for some reason she felt as if her role in his life was different from all the other women. That she was somehow special.

Maybe she was special. Maybe... Lacey clenched her hands together under the table. She should stop trying to make her relationship with Hafiz into a fairy tale.

But why had he risked everything again by bringing her to his sultanate? By starting the relationship in the first place? What provoked him to flaunt authority and break the rules again?

Again? There was no indication that he went without a mistress after he lost his right to the throne. Lacey went cold. Was bringing his mistress to the sultanate something he did often? Did he get a new model every year? Lacey slowly closed her eyes. Her jaw trembled as the hot tears stung her eyes.

She needed to figure out what was going on. She wanted to go home, lock herself in her room and curl up in a ball to ward off the anguish that was crashing against her in waves. But first she had to leave the tearoom before she embarrassed herself.

Lacey opened her eyes and kept her head down before anyone saw her distress. "Oh, look at the time!" she said as she barely glanced at her wristwatch. "I didn't realize it was so late."

Her movements felt awkward as she rose from the table and said goodbye to her friends. The flurry of hugs and promises did nothing to calm her. Her heart pumped fast as she struggled with the information about Hafiz's past.

She turned and saw one of the hotel bellmen standing in front of her. His blue uniform was the same color as the mosaic ceiling. "Miss Maxwell? Are you leaving?" the young man asked. "A Mr. Glenn called for you. He says it's urgent."

"Oh!" She clumsily patted her purse and realized she didn't bring her cell phone because it hadn't been charged due to another power outage. "Is there a phone I can use?"

"Please follow me to one of the conference rooms, and you may contact him in private."

"Thank you." She hurried after the bellman, her legs unsteady after the surprise she had received. She felt dizzy, as if her world had been knocked off its axis. Lacey was out of breath by the time she reached the conference room. She managed to give the man a simple nod as he opened the door with a flourish.

She stepped inside the long room and felt the door close behind her. The conference room was intimidating with its heavy furniture and arched ceilings. The thick blue curtains were pulled shut, and the silence was oppressive.

Lacey frowned when she noticed there was no phone on the oversized conference table. She inhaled the familiar scent of sandalwood that never failed to stir a deep craving inside her.

Hafiz.

It was her only warning before her spine was pressed up against the wall.

Strong arms bracketed her head. Hafiz's broad shoulders were encased in an expensive suit jacket. She wanted to cling on to them. She looked up and saw that Hafiz's face loomed above hers.

He was just a kiss away. After convincing herself that she would never be able to touch him, having him so close was overwhelming. She leaned forward as her eyelashes drifted shut.

"What the hell are you up to, Lacey?" Hafiz asked through clenched teeth.

CHAPTER SIX

SHE STIFFENED AND her lashes fluttered. Hafiz's brown eyes shone with cold anger. Lacey's stomach quavered at his ferocious look. It was not the kind of greeting one lover gave to another.

But then, they weren't lovers anymore. Any momentary fantasy she harbored broke like crackling ice. They might have been alone in the room, but they were not together. They were acquaintances. Their past was erased as if it never existed. She needed to remember that.

She rested heavily against the wall as if it was the only thing in the room that seemed to be able to support her. She tilted her chin and looked directly at Hafiz. "Good afternoon to you, too, Your Highness," she replied as tears pushed against the backs of her eyes.

"Lacey," he bit out. "I want an answer."

She pressed her lips together and dug her fingers against her purse. Lacey wished she could turn off her emotions with the same effortlessness as Hafiz. She wished his cool treatment didn't feel like a slap in the face.

She looked away and wrapped her arms around her middle. She couldn't handle the lack of intimacy in his dark eyes. She already missed the aura of shared secrets that cocooned them for a year.

She felt as if she was being tugged into a sandstorm and had nothing to hold on to. She could only rely on herself. It had always been that way. When she first met Hafiz, she thought she wouldn't be so alone in the world. Now she understood that it had been an illusion.

"I was having tea with a couple of my friends," she said, hating how her voice cracked.

"Why is this the first I've heard about these so-called friends?"

"You never asked." Lacey felt the flare of anger. "You never asked about my day or how I was coping living in this country." The anger burned hotter, and she ducked under his arm and walked away. "You just assumed I spent every waking moment in my apartment. Did you think I powered down until you returned?"

"If you wanted to share something, there was nothing and no one holding you back." Hafiz's eyes narrowed as he watched her move to one end of the table. "Why am I hearing about this now?"

She shrugged. Some of it was her fault. She was reacting in the same way as when she had felt her parents' interest slipping. She'd known if she wanted to retain Hafiz's attention, have him keep coming back, she needed to be positive. She had to be entertaining, and put all of the focus on him. If she had been too needy, he would start to distance himself.

"How is someone like you friends with an ambassador's wife? Or the wife of a deputy minister?"

Lacey raised her eyebrow and met his gaze. She

would not show how much those words hurt. "Someone like me?"

"You know what I mean." Hafiz rubbed the back of his neck with impatience. "You don't share the same status or have the same interests."

"So, what you're really asking is how a mistress became friends with respectable women?" she asked in a cool tone.

"Yes." Hafiz crossed his arms. "That's exactly what I'm saying."

The room tilted sickeningly for a moment. Did he know what he was saying? Did he care? She closed her eyes and swallowed. "You do realize that you're the one who made me a mistress."

"And you accepted the offer."

His indifference cut like a knife. A sarcastic rejoinder danced on her tongue like a hot pepper.

"Why are you friends with these women," he asked, "and why did you meet with them today?"

"Do you know why I play the piano?" Lacey asked as she pulled out a chair and sat down at the head of the table.

Hafiz gave her an incredulous look and spread his arms out wide. "What does this have to do with the women you were with?"

"A lot of people think I play piano because I grew up in a musical environment," Lacey continued as if he hadn't spoken. "My parents are musicians, so, therefore, I must have their interests rub off on me."

Hafiz leaned his shoulder against the wall. "Get to the point, Lacey."

"My parents didn't care if I took up a musical instrument or not. I thought that if I learned how to play the piano, and played exceptionally well, I could be part of their lives. They would take me on the road with them and I wouldn't be left behind all the time."

"And?"

The corner of her mouth twitched as she remembered her parents' harsh and immediate rejection to that plan. How her father had declared that one of the benefits of the road trips was taking a break from being parents. "It didn't work. But for some reason, I thought it would work this time."

Hafiz frowned. "This time?"

"When you invited me to live here, I thought we were building toward a future. A life together." She hastily looked away. She was embarrassed by her ignorance, her belief that they would live happily ever after. "And I worked to make this my new home. Inas is very proud of her heritage and she used to be a teacher. She's been my Arabic and history tutor."

"You've been learning Arabic? I've never heard you speak it."

She saw the deep suspicion in his eyes and a dull ache of disappointment spread through her chest. "I wasn't ready to show off my language skills just yet. I'm nowhere near fluent."

His mouth twisted, and she knew he didn't believe her. "And the ambassador's wife?"

"I met Janet at her charity against hunger. We've been working together for the past six months." Her voice trailed off when she noticed that she was following the same pattern and getting the same results.

Both times she had placed all of her energy into another person's interest. Both times she had thought the commitment would pay off. That they would see how she fit seamlessly into their world and welcome her with open arms. At the very least, appreciate her efforts.

It shouldn't be this hard to keep her loved ones in her life. She had to stop giving her all to people who didn't want it. Didn't want her.

"And you just happen to become friends." Hafiz's voice broke through her thoughts. "With the two women who could destroy everything I've worked for if they mention a rumor to one of their powerful friends or husbands."

"Is that what you're worried about?" Lacey began to tap her fingers on the table. "In all our time together, I've never done anything to hurt you. Why would you think I'd do that now?"

"Because you thought I would marry you one day, and instead I'm marrying someone else. You want revenge."

"Wait a minute! Are you saying—" She sat up straight and pressed her hands against her chest. "Do you think I'm trying to—"

He speared her with an icy cold glare. "Hell hath no fury like a woman scorned."

"Scorned woman? You've scorned me? No, you've sacrificed me, but—"

"And you needed to hit me back." He widened his arms as if offering her another shot.

"You think I have the power to hurt you?" she asked through barely parted lips. She realized that she did have that power, temporarily. "That's why you didn't tell me. I never thought you were a coward. And you aren't. You just don't give information unless it's in your interest."

She bit the inside of her lip as he walked to her, his stride reminding her of a stalking panther.

"Explain yourself, Lacey," he said softly with just a bite of warning.

"The agreement between you and the sultan," she said hurriedly. "The one about you becoming the crown prince if you marry his choice of bride."

Surprise flashed in his dark eyes before he placed his fists on his lean hips. "How do you know about that?"

Lacey dipped her head as the last glimmer of hope faded. So it was true. He gave her up for a chance to become the next sultan. "Everyone knows."

"The agreement came after I was engaged," he said stiffly before he turned around. "I don't know why I'm explaining this to you."

You mean, to someone like you, Lacey silently added. "Do you want to be the sultan?"

Hafiz's shoulders grew rigid as he turned around. "Of course. I know I can do the job. For the past ten years, I've worked hard to prove it to others."

"Don't you want to do something different?" she asked.

"Why would I give up this opportunity?"

Why would he, other than to have a life that would include her? It wasn't worth the sacrifice. And he supposedly made the decision to end their relationship *before* the sultan's offer.

"Look at the impact you've made on your own," she pointed out. "Think of what else you could do without the interference of the palace."

"You don't understand, Lacey," he said wearily as

he thrust his fingers in his dark hair. "I was born for this. It's my destiny."

"I know. It's why you push yourself." Her toe tapped a nervous staccato beat before she dove into uncharted territory. "It's not out of ambition, is it? You're looking for redemption."

He tilted his head as if he was scenting danger. As if she was getting too close to his secret. Too close to the truth.

"You lost your birthright ten years ago. That's why your brother was chosen over you. And you've been trying to get it back."

She knew the truth. Shame swept through Hafiz. It burned through his veins, and he instinctively hunched his shoulders to ward it off.

He looked at the floor, unable to meet her eyes, even though she had the right to judge him. "How do you know about that?" he asked hoarsely.

The tapping of her toe halted. The silence vibrated around him. "I wish I had heard it from you."

Hafiz said nothing. He wished he could have denied it, but he'd withstood the disgrace for nearly a decade. It should be no different now.

But it was. He didn't want Lacey to know about his mistakes. About the person he used to be.

Lacey was the first to break the silence. "Why didn't you tell me?"

Because he was a better person when he was with Lacey. He could be the man he wanted to be, the prince he strived to become for his country. She believed he could do the impossible, and he knew he could with her by his side. Had she known about his past, would she still have believed? He knew she wouldn't.

But Lacey knew now. And her opinion meant the most to him. He didn't know how he would stand up against her disillusionment. "It's not something I'm proud of."

"So you hid it from me?" she asked. He heard the anger wobbling in her voice. "You only showed me one side of you? I thought we had been closer than that."

Hafiz pulled open a curtain and let the bright sunlight stream in the dark room. The image of his beloved country didn't soothe the twinge inside him. He was drowning in regret and there was no hope of escape.

He bunched his hands into tight fist, imagining the relief if he punched through the glass. He could hear the shattering window in his mind, but he wouldn't act on the impulse. But, oh, what he wouldn't do to get out of this room…away from Lacey's steady gaze.

"You were just a teenager when you lost your title as crown prince?"

"No, I was an adult. I was twenty-one." Hafiz had a feeling that was the easiest question he would be facing from Lacey.

"Really?" She made a sympathetic cluck with her tongue. "That's harsh. Being twenty-one is all about pushing the limits. Pushing boundaries."

He shook his head. It should have warmed his heart that Lacey automatically defended him, but he knew it wasn't going to last. "It's different for me."

"Because you're a prince? The heir to the throne?"

"Because my country came into a great deal of

wealth when I was eighteen. I was sent to the States to get an education. To learn how to protect and grow the wealth." He took a deep breath and turned to face her. "Instead I spent it."

Her eyes widened as her mouth open and shut. "All of it?" she croaked out.

"No. It doesn't matter how many millions I spent." The amount was branded into his soul for eternity, but the numbers could never convey the suffering of others. "I spent it. I stole it." He still flinched at the stripped-down version of his action. "I stole the money from the people of Rudaynah for my own pleasure. I was the playboy prince the tabloids love to hate."

Lacey stared at him as if he was a stranger to her. It was better than looking at him with the disgust he felt for himself. "That doesn't sound like you at all."

"It was me," he said brutally. "Look it up. The sultan tried to hide the story, but you can find it if you look hard enough. My spending habits had been legendary," he said, humility threading his voice.

"What stopped it?"

"The sultan received reports and called me home. The moment I returned I saw how Rudaynah had yet to see any progress. It humbled me. Shamed me more than any lecture or punishment."

Lacey frowned. "And your punishment for spending the money was losing your right to the throne?"

"No. I was stripped of any responsibility or authority. Of any rights or privileges. I was spared getting lashes because of my royal status. I didn't leave Rudaynah until I could regain my father's trust. And

I still didn't leave the borders until I felt it was necessary."

"But that doesn't explain to me how you lost your birthright."

The punishment he'd received was paltry considering his crime, but the sultan didn't want people to know the whole story. "One of the reports the sultan received had to do with my mistress at the time."

"I see," she said stiffly.

"You don't see." He looked directly in her blue eyes and braced himself. "My mistress became pregnant."

Lacey turned pale, but she regained her composure. "Is it yours?" she asked brusquely.

"I found out too late that she had an abortion," Hafiz said, the bitterness corroding inside him. "I've often wondered if the sultan campaigned for and funded it. Not directly, of course," he added cynically.

"I still don't understand—"

"Don't you get it, Lacey?" he barked out. "I couldn't uphold the expectations placed on me. I proved I wasn't leadership material." The list of his sins bore down on him. "I used the money for my own pleasure. I couldn't make my country proud. I couldn't provide the security of giving a rightful heir to the throne. But most of all, I couldn't protect my unborn child."

"Hafiz," Lacey said grimly as she walked toward him. He braced himself for her to launch into a tirade. For a stinging slap. It wouldn't hurt nearly as much as her disappointment.

She surprised him by placing a gentle hand on his arm. He looked down at her, bemused by the sincerity gleaming in her eyes. "Don't let your mistakes define you. You are a good man."

He drew back. She still believed in him. How could she? Wasn't she listening? "You're biased, but thanks."

"Give me some credit. I wouldn't give up everything familiar for a playboy prince. I certainly wouldn't follow any man to the ends of the earth."

"I believe the term you're looking for is 'this hell'," he reminded her.

Lacey looked chagrined but wouldn't be deterred. "And Rudaynah needs you. The mistake you made will serve you well." She paused, obviously searching for the right words. "You have risen from your past like…a phoenix from the ashes. You're stronger and smarter. You have worked hard all these years to take care of your countrymen."

But he would never regain the trust of the people. His brother kept his distance, as if poor judgment was contagious. His own parents couldn't stand the sight of him.

"I am not the kind of man you're trying to make me out to be." But he wanted to be. He wanted to deserve her admiration.

"You're good for Rudaynah. This sultanate needs you," Lacey insisted and cupped his face with her hand. "If I thought otherwise, I would take you away with me."

Hafiz leaned into her touch just as his cell phone rang. They both jumped as the harsh sound echoed in the cavernous room.

"Don't answer it," Lacey whispered.

"It would be Glenn. He would only call if it was important." He reached for the phone and answered it. "Yes?"

"Our exit visas have been denied," Glenn said.

A coldness settled inside Hafiz as he considered what that could mean. "Did they give a reason?"

"No, but they were acting strange. As if it hasn't happened before. What do you want me to do next, Your Highness?"

"Let me get back to you." Hafiz ended the call and pressed the phone against his chin as he stared out the window. He quickly analyzed the sultan's latest move and what it represented. He didn't like any of the answers.

"Is something wrong?" Lacey asked.

"Your exit visas have been denied," he murmured as he considered his next move.

"I thought the process was just a formality." Lacey gasped, and she clapped her hand over her mouth. "Your father knows about me. He knows I'm your mistress."

"Let's not jump to conclusions. It could be a clerical error." Hafiz wanted to calm Lacey, but he knew his answer wouldn't soothe her.

"This doesn't make sense. Why can't I leave the country? Wouldn't your father give me the red carpet treatment to the first car out of here?"

"Not necessarily," Hafiz replied grimly.

Lacey pressed her lips together. "What's going on?"

"There's a possibility," he said, emphasizing the word, "that the sultan sees your presence as an advantage to him. It would make me the most agreeable groom."

"I don't like the sounds of that," Lacey said. "Am I in trouble? Is he going to use me to get to you?"

"I should have predicted it," Hafiz muttered. "The sultan had done this before."

"When? Ten years ago?" Lacey took a deep breath. "Hafiz, I need to know. What happened to your last mistress? The one who got pregnant?"

CHAPTER SEVEN

HAFIZ LEANED AGAINST the windowpane and closed his eyes as the guilt swamped him. He never forgot that time in his life, and he refused to forgive himself. The actions he took, the mistakes he made were part of him and had influenced his decisions to this day. And yet, he tried not to look too closely and inspect his flaws.

"Her name was Elizabeth," he said quietly. "I had already earned my reputation as the playboy prince when I met her in Monte Carlo."

"What was she like?" Lacey asked.

"Beautiful. Professional. Ambitious."

Lacey frowned. "You make her sound cold and un-feeling."

What he had shared with Elizabeth had nothing to do with warmth and affection. "She made her way through life as a mistress. Our relationship had been purely physical, and we both wanted it that way."

Because he hadn't been interested in romance or commitment. He had been too busy partying, gambling and exploring the world outside of Rudaynah and royal life.

Hafiz forced himself to continue. He knew Lacey needed to hear this. "We had only been together for a few months when I found out she was pregnant." Hafiz looked away. "I didn't handle the news well. I wish I could take back that moment and react differently."

"What did you do?" Lacey asked.

He didn't want to give a voice to the memories that haunted him. The moments that had demonstrated what kind of man he had been. Only he hadn't acted like a man.

"I was furious. Scared," he admitted with a sigh. "I knew that a baby was going to change everything. I swore the baby couldn't possibly be mine. I didn't *want* it to be mine."

Lacey rested her hand against his shoulder. "I can't imagine you acting like that, Hafiz."

"It was me. A spoiled and selfish prince who knew his freedom was about to be taken away from him. I accused Elizabeth of being unfaithful. I wasn't going to let her trap me or extort money from me." Hafiz raked his hand through his hair. "I hate the way I treated her."

"That may have been your first reaction, but I'm sure you saw reason once you calmed down."

Hafiz shook his head. Lacey thought too highly of him. He slowly turned around and faced her. "I left Elizabeth," he said, watching the surprise in Lacey's eyes. He hunched his shoulders as the remorse weighed heavily on him. "My father had demanded that I return home, and I used that as a way to hide from my responsibilities."

Lacey stared at him in disbelief. "You wouldn't do that."

"That was the lowest time of my life. I was trying to hide what I had done and conceal the person I was.

Hide everything from the sultan and my countrymen. At times, I tried to hide the truth from myself."

"Impossible."

"It wasn't that hard to do. I wanted to convince myself that Elizabeth was the villain. I believed she tried to trick me and that she got what she deserved for attempting to get her claws into a prince."

"When did you decide she was not the villain?"

"It wasn't just one event. I started seeing how I treated everyone during that time. I should have treated her better. I had cut off all contact. And somehow I had convinced myself that I did the right thing."

"Did you try to find her after that and make it right?"

He nodded. "I wasn't able to travel, but I wasn't going to let it stop me. I was done making excuses. I had one of my representatives track her down." Hafiz took a deep breath. "But I was too late. Elizabeth had gotten an abortion."

The silence permeated the room as Hafiz remembered getting that call. He had shattered from the grief. He had never been the same man after knowing he hadn't protected and provided for his unborn son.

"I was furious at myself," Hafiz said quietly. "If I had shown Elizabeth any concern or any sign that she could depend on me, she wouldn't have taken extreme measures."

"And you think your father was behind that?"

"I'm sure of it. Elizabeth had hinted it to my representative, but I think she was too afraid to speak plainly. She was afraid to cross the sultan, with good reason."

"Should I be afraid?"

"No," Hafiz said. "You can depend on me. I will not abandon you."

Lacey moved closer to him until her hip brushed against his. "I'm sorry. I'm sorry that my presence in your life is causing so many problems." The air around them pulsed with energy, but Hafiz didn't reach out for her. His fingers flexed, but his hands stayed by his side.

"You're not a burden," he said gruffly. Having Lacey in his life had been a gift.

Lacey leaned forward and pressed her forehead against his shoulder. Hafiz tensed and remained where he stood. It was still a risk. If someone walked into this room and saw him alone with Lacey…he didn't want to think about the consequences.

Hafiz cleared his throat and took a step away from her. "I have to go. I know how to fix this."

"What are you going to do?" she called after him as he strode to the door.

He set his mouth into a grim line. "Whatever it takes."

"This wedding reception is one of the most lavish I've seen. I don't know how Inas and her husband paid for it," Janet said a few days later as they slowly made their way through the crowded ballroom to the buffet. "I can't wait to eat."

"Where are the men?" Lacey asked. The ballroom was packed with women. Bright, garish colors swirled around Lacey and her friend Janet as the conversations swelled to an earsplitting decibel. Heavy perfumes of every imaginable flower clashed against one another.

"They are in the ballroom across the hall having

their party," Janet informed her. "The men and women in Rudaynah don't celebrate together. This way the women can literally let their hair down and dance."

Lacey glanced at the stage where the bride sat. It seemed strange to Lacey that the newlywed couple would spend their wedding reception apart. Did it signify what was yet to come? That the marriage meant separate paths, separate lives, for the couple? Was this what all marriages were like in this country?

She studied the group of relatives on the stage surrounding the bride. "I still don't see Inas."

"We'll find her. By the way, I love what you're wearing. I thought you had given up wearing the traditional caftan."

"Thank you." Lacey glanced down at her pale blue caftan. She hadn't been certain about the transparent sleeves or the modest neckline. The skirt flared out gently, and the intricate embroidery design that ran down the front of the caftan matched her slippers. "I wanted one chance to wear it before I leave."

"Did you get your exit visas sorted out?"

"Uh…yes," she lied. "I'll be leaving very soon." As in tonight. But she couldn't let anyone know that.

She glanced at her jeweled watch and winced. The wedding reception had started late, and she should have returned home by now and gathered her things.

"Janet, why don't you go on ahead to the buffet? I have to leave."

"Already?" She shook her head. "You're going to miss the professional dancers and the wedding march. Not to mention the food!"

"I know, but I'm glad I had a chance to be here. I just hope leaving early doesn't offend Inas."

"She'll understand," Janet said as she hugged Lacey goodbye. "You'll probably find her near the door greeting all the guests."

Lacey fought her way through the cluster of women. She couldn't help but wonder if Hafiz's wedding reception would be like this. She pushed the thought aside. She wasn't going to torture herself imagining what Hafiz's wedding to another woman was going to be like.

Lacey saw her friend near the entrance. "Inas!" She waved and hurried to greet the mother of the bride. "Inas, this wedding is beautiful. And your daughter!" She glanced at the woman on stage in the back of the ballroom. The young woman wore an embroidered red gown and veil. Heavy gold jewelry hung from her wrists and throat. "She looks like a princess."

"Lacey, I'm so happy to see you." Inas gave her a kiss on each cheek. "And you wouldn't believe who is here!"

The woman almost squealed. Lacey couldn't imagine who would cause this level of excitement. "Who?"

"Inas?" An older woman's voice wafted over them. Inas's demeanor changed rapidly. Her smile widened, and she trembled with exhilaration. Inas struggled to lower her eyes as she gave a curtsey to the woman. She folded her hands neatly in front of her as she spoke respectfully in Arabic.

Lacey took a step back. Her instincts told her to melt into the crowd and disappear.

"Allow me to introduce you," Inas said as she grasped Lacey's elbow and brought her forward. Lacey stared at the older woman who wore a white scarf over her gray hair and a brocade caftan that concealed her body.

"Your Majesty, this is Lacey Maxwell. I tutored her in Arabic while she was visiting our sultanate. Lacey, this is the Sultana Zafirah of Rudaynah."

And Hafiz's mother. Lacey's knees buckled, and she quickly covered it up with a shaky curtsey.

She glanced at the sultana through her lashes and found the older woman inspecting her like a mangled insect carcass. It took every ounce of willpower for Lacey not to meet the woman's gaze. *This was probably why Hafiz didn't want you to meet his family.*

Lacey covertly looked at the exit and wondered how she was going to extract herself from this situation. Her mind went blank as panic congealed in her throat. "I understand one of your sons will be married soon," Lacey said in what she hoped was a respectful tone. "Congratulations."

The sultana stiffened, and Lacey wondered if she had broken some protocol. "Thank you," Sultana Zafirah said with a sniff.

Lacey hesitated, uncertain how to proceed. "I'm sure Miss Abdullah will be a worthy addition to your family."

The sultana gave a careless shrug. "More worthy than my son."

A startled gasp quickly evaporated in Lacey's throat as indignation mushroomed inside her chest. How dare the sultana say that about Hafiz? Lacey was stunned that the woman would say it to a stranger. There was no telling what was said in private.

Lacey looked away and fought back her words. Didn't Sultana Zafirah see how much her son worked and sacrificed to correct his mistakes? Didn't she care that he strove to become worthy, all the while knowing he would never reach his goal? Or was the sultana unwilling to recognize what her son has already achieved?

Tears smarted Lacey's eyes as hope shriveled up inside her. Why did Hafiz want to be with his family instead of her? The idea alone was like a knife sliding between her ribs before it gave a vicious twist. Was this what he really wanted?

How could she leave Hafiz here to face this alone? But deep down, she knew she wasn't an ally. She was a liability. She was going to leave so Hafiz could become the man he wanted to be. She wanted Rudaynah to benefit from his ideas and leadership, and she wanted the people to recognize his worth and abilities.

On a purely selfish level, she wanted her sacrifice to mean something. She wanted it be worth the pain, if that was possible.

The ballroom suddenly plunged into darkness. The initial squeals from the crowd turned into groans of people who were used to power outages. Lacey blinked wildly as the darkness shrouded her. She could already feel the difference in temperature as the air conditioner silenced.

"Nothing to worry about, Miss Maxwell." Sultana Zafirah said. The royal entourage bumped Lacey as they quickly surrounded the sultana. "The generator will turn on soon."

"Yes, Your Majesty."

The emergency lights gradually came on, casting an eerie green over the wedding guests. Just as everyone cheered, the lights blinked and flared before shutting off.

"No, no, no." Inas said. "This cannot happen at my daughter's wedding."

"I'll go see if there are any lights on in the hotel," Lacey offered. Sensing she only had a few minutes before the lights and power returned, she slowly retreated.

Using the flurry of activity to her advantage, Lacey turned around and made her way to the exit. Her hands brushed against the heavy metal door. She wrenched the handle, opening the door a crack, and found the hallway was just as dark as the ballroom. The moment she passed the threshold, she breathed a sigh of relief.

As much as she wanted to celebrate her friend's special moment, she found the business of marriage in Rudaynah too depressing. It wasn't a union of two hearts as much as it was a business alliance. The combining of two families and two properties.

The lights came back on, and she heard the murmurs of delight from the ballroom. Lacey hurried down the steps to the main lobby when she saw a familiar figure in a gray pinstripe suit waiting at the bottom of the stairs.

"Where have you been?" Hafiz asked, glancing at his wristwatch. "We were supposed to meet at your apartment."

"Hafiz?" She remembered that the sultana and the most influential people in the country were in the next room. He was placing himself at risk. "You can't be here. It's too dangerous. Your—"

"I'm fully aware of it," Hafiz said as he fell into

step with her. "If you want to get to Abu Dhabi to-night, we must leave now."

"I'm sorry I'm late. I'm never late."

Hafiz set his mouth in a grim line. "My limousine is waiting right outside the entrance. Once we leave, then we will discuss what you were doing with my mother."

Lacey stiffened as she heard the accusation in his tone. How did he find out about that? She didn't have to see Hafiz's face to know he was angry. But why was he blaming her?

"I didn't know the sultana was going to make an appearance. How would I?"

Hafiz muttered something succinct as he ushered her out the hotel. Guilt slammed through her. She didn't want to be a hindrance. She hated being the cause of his troubles.

Lacey paused. She wasn't a hindrance. She wasn't a liability. The only thing she was guilty of was loving a man who didn't think she was good enough to marry.

CHAPTER EIGHT

HAFIZ KEPT HIS anger in check as he got into the waiting limousine. Tonight he had to send away the one person who mattered the most to him. He wanted to rage against the world, destroy everything around him and allow the fury to consume him. Instead he closed the car door with deliberate care.

The car jerked into full speed. He barely glanced at Lacey sitting regally on the other side of the back seat. He didn't trust himself to speak or look at her.

What was it about this woman? Did she trigger a self-destructive tendency in him? Why had he been willing to risk everything for Lacey? What made him lower his guard when they had been in danger of discovery? Why couldn't he have fallen for someone who would make his life easier?

"I have nothing to say." Lacey stared straight ahead. "I did nothing wrong."

He sliced his hand in the air. "Yes, you did," he replied in a low growl. In the past Lacey's hurt would have destroyed him until he did everything in his power to make her happy, but at the moment he wished she would see the world through his eyes.

"I don't have to explain myself," Lacey continued.

"My friend introduced me to your mother. She thought I was worthy enough to meet the sultana. Why don't you?"

"Does your friend know everything about you?" The words were dragged from his mouth. "Is she aware that you are the prince's mistress?"

"Of course not." Lacey said and rolled her eyes.

He speared a hard look at Lacey. She had spent half a year in his country but still didn't have a basic understanding how the Sultanate of Rudaynah worked. He risked everything to help her tonight. It would be scandalous if he were found alone with a woman. If it were discovered that she was his mistress, the results would be cataclysmic.

"I'm sorry if my meeting the sultana made you uncomfortable," she said angrily.

Was she? Had she not suggested a few days ago how he was better off without that title? Lacey had to be furious that her dream life ended abruptly while he was offered the one thing he had relentlessly worked toward. It wouldn't take much to crush his chances, but Hafiz didn't want to believe Lacey could be that diabolical.

"No, you're not. You want me to be uncomfortable and worry. You're enjoying it." Hafiz grabbed a hold of the door as the limousine took a sharp, fast turn. "I want to know the whole truth. How long have you known my mother?"

"I just met her," Lacey insisted. "It's not like we had an in-depth conversation."

Hafiz shook his head. Her eyes shone with innocence, and yet he didn't trust that the meeting was happenstance. She could have arranged to meet the sultana and dropped a few bombshells. He didn't want to think of how many times those blue eyes possibly duped him in the past.

"I swear, I didn't tell her anything."

And yet, despite careful planning of keeping his family and private life separate, his mother managed to meet his mistress. "This is not happening," he muttered. Being introduced to a mistress or concubine was considered a deep offense to the sultana. If the truth came out, he would pay the penalty for it. "You planned this, didn't you?"

"Planned what? An introduction with your mother?" Lacey asked listlessly, as if the fight had evaporated from her. She looked out the window at the dusty city streets whizzing past them.

"You hinted at it when you first arrived here. How you wanted to meet my family. Then it turned into a bold request and finally a demand."

Lacey rubbed her hands over her face and gave a deep sigh. "That was before I understood our relationship was completely forbidden. That I was somehow beneath you and not good enough to meet your family."

Beneath him? Where did she get that idea? "I told you that it was complicated."

"But you didn't tell me that it was impossible." She returned her attention to the window as if she couldn't bear to look at him. "I should have known something was up when you didn't introduce me to your friends. I was so naïve."

"I have nothing to apologize for."

She shook her head. "You brought me over here

under false pretenses. I thought we were going to live together."

Hafiz's mouth dropped open in surprise. "I never made that offer. Us, together in the palace?" He shuddered at the thought. "We would have been cast out in seconds."

"Obviously you and I had different ideas about being together. I didn't think you would hide my existence from your family."

"And when you realized that meeting them wasn't going to happen, you decided to take matters into your own hands."

"Like my introduction to your mother? What would be the point?" She turned to face him. "What do you think I did? Just walk up to her and say, 'Hi, I'm Lacey. I'm Hafiz's mistress and I hope to continue even after he's married?' Do you really think I'm capable of that?"

He stared at her with disbelieving horror as something close to panic clenched his stomach. "You would if you thought it would help."

"Help?" She watched him with growing suspicion. "Help what?"

"To stop me from getting married." She would eventually realize that he wasn't going to stop it. He accepted that his future wasn't going to be happy or loving. He had known that for the past decade.

"For the last time," she said, her voice rising, "I was not trying to wreck your wedding. I am going against every instinct I have by not fighting for you." She tilted her head back and rested it against the seat. "Is that what makes you so suspicious? You gave me up and thought I would fight for you. For us. Because I immediately backed off, I must be up to something?"

"You think I gave you up easily? That there was no thought involved, no hesitation? I had put off my marriage for as long as possible so I could be with you."

"You put off your marriage so you could get a better deal," Lacey said through clenched teeth. "Like getting another shot at becoming the crown prince. Then you couldn't get rid of me fast enough."

"Lacey, I am not your parents. Try not to compare me with them. I didn't discard you to pursue my life's ambition."

Lacey's eyes narrowed into slits. "Don't bring my parents into this."

"You think I'm abandoning you out of ambition just like your parents. You act as if my life is going to overflow with happiness and abundance once you're out of my life. Do you think your parents had a better life without you?"

"Yes!" she bit out.

Hafiz drew his head back and stared at her. "You're wrong, Lacey. They missed out on so much."

"No, you are wrong. I held them back from what they really wanted in life. Once I was gone, they pursued their passion. They are happier than they've ever been."

Did she think he wouldn't look back at their time together? That he wouldn't feel the regret of letting her go? "Why do you act like I'm giving you up for something better? I am entering a marriage with a stranger," he reminded her.

"You made a choice, Hafiz. And it wasn't me. It was never going to be me."

A thought suddenly occurred to him. *She had been waiting for this to happen.* "You're not fighting for me because deep down you knew I was going to have to make a choice one day. And you knew it wasn't going to be in your favor."

"I'm not fighting for you because I know we have run our course." She gave a sharp intake of breath and tossed her hands in the air. "I should have just kept our relationship to a one-night stand and be done with you."

"Excuse me?" Anger flashed hot and swift inside him. What he and Lacey shared could not have been contained in one night.

"I knew you were trouble, but that didn't stop me. No, quite the opposite." She shook her head in self-disgust. "And, let's face it, you weren't thinking about forever after one night with me."

Hafiz wearily rubbed his hands over his eyes. "All I knew is that I couldn't stay away."

"And you kept coming back. I would count the days until we could see each other again. I thought you felt the same way, too."

"I did." The anticipation that burned in his veins, the excitement pressing against his chest had never waned.

"No, it's only been recently when I realized we had approached this affair very differently. I was so happy in love that I wanted to share it with the whole world. You wanted to keep this relationship secret because you were ashamed."

"For the last time, Lacey, I am not ashamed—"

"No, not of me." Her jaw trembled as she tried to hold her emotions in check. "You were ashamed that you couldn't stay away. After all those years of resisting temptation, of demonstrating your willpower, your strength, you couldn't stay away. An ordinary woman, a nobody, was your weakness."

He closed his eyes, momentarily overwhelmed. She was right. He didn't like how Lacey saw right through him. Understood him better than he understood himself.

"I am Prince Hafiz ibn Yusuf Qadi," he said quietly. "I have spent the last ten years proving that I am worthy of that name. I had purged every wild impulse, and nothing could tempt me off the straight and narrow path. And then I met you."

"You make me sound like I'm a vice. Something you need to give up to be a better person."

Hafiz was too deep into the memory to reply. "And then I see you at the piano in a hotel lobby. I didn't even stop to think. I was drawn to your singing as if I was a sailor listening to the sirens."

"Being attracted to me does not show weakness of character. Falling for me is not a sin."

"It is if you are a prince from the Sultanate of Rudaynah."

She crossed her arms and stared at him. "And yet, you asked me to live here. I thought it was because you loved me. No, it's because you see me as some kind of bad habit that you couldn't give up."

Fury flashed through him, and he held it in check. "You don't have that kind of power over me. No one does."

"Especially a young woman who doesn't understand the royal court politics or influential people. That's why you felt safe to bring me over here."

He scoffed at her statement. "Having you here was never safe."

"I thought you trusted me. I thought that made me different from everyone you knew. It made me special to you. But that's not it at all, is it? It's that you contained the situation. You made sure I wasn't in a position to break your trust."

"Not a lot of good it did me," he muttered.

Lacey's fingers fluttered against her cheeks as if she was brushing something away. "I wish I didn't know any of this. I wish I could have left Rudaynah the night I found out about your engagement."

Hafiz remained silent. He knew he should feel the same way. She was his weakness, his vulnerability, but he didn't want her to go.

"That night had been magical," she said softly. There was a faraway look in her eyes. "It was the right way to say goodbye. I would have left here believing that…what we had was special. That I had been special."

Hafiz clenched his hands. He wanted to tell Lacey how special she was to him. But what purpose would it serve? What they had was over. It could not continue.

"You think I'm bad for you," Lacey said. "That I'm proof of your bad judgment, or that I symbolize all of those wild impulses you couldn't get rid of. One of these days you're going to realize that I was the best thing that had ever happened to you." She pointed her finger at him. "Someday you'll realize that everything I've done was to protect you."

"I don't need your protection, Lacey." He shook his head. "It was my job to protect you."

Lacey blinked rapidly as if she was preventing

more tears from falling. "I wanted to be your confidante. Your partner. My goal was to help you be the best prince you could be."

"And in return, you would become a princess." Hafiz grimaced. Even as he said it, he knew that wasn't her true motivation.

"If you believe that, you don't know me at all." Her shoulders drooped as if she didn't have the energy to fight anymore. "I thought you knew everything about me," Lacey announced dully as she pulled her hair away from her face.

"And you know everything about me," Hafiz said. "I confided in you when I shouldn't have."

Lacey jerked at his harsh tone and slowly turned to meet his gaze. "Why do you continue to believe that I would betray you?"

Her question was carried out with a wispy puff of air. The wounded look in her eyes threatened to shatter him inside. He drew from the dark edges that hovered around him, knowing he had to be callous, and knowing he was going to regret it.

"Because you are a mistress. A fallen woman. Betrayal is your only power against me." Hafiz knew what he said hurt her where she was most vulnerable, but it was his only guarantee. That cold response would prevent Lacey from trying to hold on to him and what might have been. He had to protect her even if it meant tearing down the love she felt for him.

The darkness surged through Hafiz, and he struggled against the cold bitterness invading his body. He'd battled it before, only this time he had to do it alone. In the past, Lacey was the only person he knew who could stem the flow.

"If I'm a fallen women, you shouldn't be seen with me. So, why are you still here?" Lacey asked in a withering tone. She folded her arms more tightly and crossed her legs. Hafiz wondered if it was an attempt to get as far away from him as possible. "Stop the car and I'll get out."

"That's enough." Hafiz's tone held a steely edge. "I'm making sure you get on that helicopter."

She gave a haughty tilt of her chin. "I'm perfectly capable of finding my way."

"I'm sure you could, but you don't have access to the palace."

"Palace?" Hafiz saw her tense as a sound of panic rumbled in the back of her throat; she turned abruptly to her window. When she didn't see anything on her side of the limousine, she frantically searched out his window.

He knew the minute she saw the towering mud brick walls that surrounded the palace. The historical site was constructed as more of a fortress than the home of a sultan. It wasn't opulent or majestic. The curved buildings, domed roofs and large archways were made out of clay. The buildings were functional and cool against the desert heat.

It was also designed to intimidate the enemy. Lacey had a look of unease as they passed through the guarded gates, and she got the first good look of the palace. Hafiz held back his assurances. He needed her to focus on leaving without looking back.

"I can't see you again," he began.

Her eyes dulled with pain. "I don't want you to."

Hafiz scowled at her statement. "I mean it, Lacey."

"I do, too. I'm not really big on sharing." Her chin

wobbled, and she blinked back the moisture from her eyes. "Don't contact me unless you've changed your mind and only want me."

That wasn't going to happen, Hafiz thought. It couldn't.

The limousine lurched to a stop next to the helicopter pad. Hafiz immediately stepped out of the car and reached for Lacey's hand. When she hesitated, he grasped her wrist. Fierce sensations scorched his skin from the touch. He grimly ignored the way his pulse tripped and assisted her outside.

Her long hair blew in the desert wind, and he escorted her to the pilot who was waiting by the helicopter. After Hafiz yelled instructions over the noise, Lacey climbed in. He tried to assist her, but she batted him away. He flashed a warning look at her.

The warning dissipated as he looked into her eyes. Even after what had happened, after everything they'd said, he wished for one more kiss. He was desperate for it and felt the pull. His mouth craved her taste and her softness. The yearning pierced at him like swift jabs of a knife, because he knew after this moment, circumstances would snatch Lacey away from him.

He looked away. The darkness inside him eclipsed the pain of knowing this was the last time he would see her. Their paths would never cross, and he could never contact her again. He wouldn't know where she lived or if she was safe. She would disappear but linger in his mind as he worried and wondered.

"Your Highness," the pilot shouted, breaking through Hafiz's thoughts. "We need to leave now."

Hafiz hesitated. He couldn't make a clean break

from Lacey, no matter how much he wanted to. How much he needed to, for both their sakes.

He glanced at her and met her gaze. No tears escaped her eyes. She didn't speak. Didn't move, but he knew she struggled for composure. He knew her poise was for his benefit. It was her way to prove that she would be fine.

She looked so beautiful and elegant. Regal. Hafiz thought his heart was going to blast through the wall of his chest. Lacey was more beautiful than when he first saw her. He was fortunate to have known and loved her, and she would never know. His throat closed shut as his strength seeped out of his bones.

He had to tell her. He had thought it would be kinder not to say anything. Not to give her the answer because it would have given her hope. Something to fight for. But he could not let her go with the belief that she didn't matter.

"I love you, Lacey."

Her lips parted, and she stared at his mouth. She frowned as if she had heard incorrectly. As if she had heard what she wanted to hear.

"You may think I hate you or I'm ashamed of you," he said over the whine of the helicopter, "but it isn't true. I took all of these risks because I love you. I will always love you."

She began to reach out as the helicopter started to lift off. Hafiz wanted to grab her hand, but he forced himself to back away.

He watched her, unblinking, as the helicopter rose into the sky and turned, taking his love, his last chance of happiness, away from him.

But he didn't deserve happiness. He didn't deserve a life with Lacey.

Hafiz remained where he stood when every instinct screamed for him to run after Lacey. A ragged gasp escaped his raw throat as he watched the helicopter fly off until it was no longer a speck in the air. The silence sliced deep into his dreams and wishes until they lay tattered at his feet and darkness descended in his heart.

CHAPTER NINE

"LACEY, MY WORK shift is about to start," Priya shouted over the music. "Are you going to be okay? I feel weird leaving you alone."

"That's sweet of you, but you don't have to worry." Lacey smiled at her roommate. She felt bad that Priya felt the need to mother her. And drag her to this party so she would get out of the apartment. "I'm going to be fine. It's been a while since I've been to a party, but it's all coming back to me."

"Good," Priya said with a nod. "I know you've been mending a broken heart, but you are too young to spend all your time working at the hotel and staying in bed."

"You're right," she said as her roommate walked away. Taking a small sip from the beer bottle she had been nursing for an hour, Lacey stood at the sidelines and watched her coworkers mill around the pool room located in their housing complex. It was an eclectic mix of young people in swimwear and colorful sundresses. While some splashed around in the pool and others danced to the blaring music, most of the guests nibbled on the spicy snacks and drank the boldly colored concoctions.

Once Priya left the party, Lacey closed her eyes and exhaled. She would stay another five minutes and then leave.

She still wasn't sure why she'd chosen to stay in Abu Dhabi, but it had proven to be a good decision. The rich nightlife had allowed her to find a job performing at the hotel lounge. She'd also managed to make a few friends within the month she arrived. She was determined to get out and meet more people. Forget the past and make up for lost time.

Sometimes determination wasn't enough. Her time in Rudaynah had changed her. Marked her in ways she hadn't considered. Lacey glanced down at the purple bikini she wore and the wispy sarong around her hips. These days she wasn't comfortable showing too much skin. She preferred the modest dress code she had to follow once she was outside the housing complex.

"Lacey!" Cody, another American who worked in the hotel, was at her side. His wide smile, unbuttoned shirt and bright red swim trunks conveyed his casual attitude toward life. He liked to flirt with her, and while she knew it didn't mean anything, she tried to discourage it.

"You haven't danced once the whole time you've been here." He held out his hand. "We need to fix that."

She hesitated for a second. She knew the invitation wasn't going to jump-start her love life, but the idea of dancing with another man—touching another man—felt wrong.

It's just a dance. It's no big deal. But she knew Cody would try for more. How could she explain to him that she didn't feel whole or intact? That she was definitely not strong enough to even expose herself to a lighthearted fling or a one-night stand?

Looking into Cody's face lined by the sun rather than by hardship, Lacey realized falling in love again was impossible. She felt the corners of her mouth quirk as she considered her foolishness. What was she worried about? She was safe with Cody and every other man. No one could measure up to Hafiz.

"Okay, sure. Why not?" She set down her beer and took his hand. Lacey didn't feel any thrill of anticipation when he placed his other hand on the curve of her hip or when her fingers grazed his bare skin. She felt no excitement, no awareness. Nothing.

But, quite honestly, she hadn't felt a thing since the helicopter touched down in Abu Dhabi a month ago. She went through the motions of living, but she felt dead inside. She had a feeling it was going to be like that forever. And still she didn't worry over the possibility.

As Lacey danced in Cody's arms, she wondered how long the song would last. She knew that if Hafiz had been her dance partner, she would have wanted the music to go on forever.

Hafiz. She had to stop thinking about him. Lacey abruptly pulled away just as the song changed into something harsh and angry.

Cody motioned for her to keep dancing, but she wanted to go home. No, that wasn't true. She wanted to find Hafiz.

But that was not going to happen, Lacey reminded herself. He didn't want her near him. She was a vice. A sin. Hafiz's words ricocheted through her head.

Nothing had changed. Nothing ever would. She had to move on.

"Don't hold back, Lacey!" Cody yelled as he jumped up and down to the drumbeat.

Move on. Start now. Fake it until you make it. Lacey swayed to the music. She wished it had the power to make her forget everything. But the music didn't reach her heart or fill her soul like it used to.

She needed to feel it again. Music was part of who she was. It was more than her livelihood; it was how she expressed herself and how she found solace. She couldn't let Hafiz take that away from her, too.

Lacey pushed harder as she danced. She moved her shoulders and swished her hips to the beat of the drums. The music still didn't reach her.

She pulled and pushed her body to move as far as it would go, wishing that the numbness that held everything back would break. That the music would grow louder until it seeped inside her. If that didn't work, then she hoped the dancing would exhaust her so she could sleep without dreaming.

From the corner of her eyes, Lacey saw that someone wore all black. A jacket…no, a suit. The formality was at odds with the party. The darkness was out of place among the bright rainbow colors. But there was something familiar about the person's movement. What was it that… Her heart lurched, and she went still.

Hafiz. She froze as the wild hope and surprise ripped through her. Hafiz was here? No, that was impossible. She blinked, and he was suddenly gone. Lacey rubbed her eyes. Was she now having hallucinations about him along with her dreams?

Her pulse skipped hard as she quickly scanned the crowd. Why did he seem so real? Shouldn't her memory become hazier as time went on?

She frowned as she resumed her dancing. Her memory was definitely playing tricks. Lacey didn't understand why she envisioned him in a black linen jacket, collarless shirt and black trousers. Usually she remembered him in a pinstripe suit, in traditional robes, or in nothing at all.

Lacey squeezed her eyes shut as she tried to discard the images of Hafiz in various stages of undress flickering through her mind. *Forget about him,* she decided as she forced herself to dance. *It's time to start living again.*

Hafiz watched Lacey dance, her body moving with the same earthiness as when they shared a bed. It had been four weeks since he'd seen Lacey. Since he had declared his love. It felt like an eternity. He shouldn't be here, and yet he couldn't stay away.

Now he wished he hadn't given in to the impulse. Anger and indignation swirled inside him, ready to explode. From what he could see, Lacey was the center of the party. She wasn't laughing or smiling, but her intense expression suggested that nothing mattered more than exploring the music.

He glared at the bikini and sarong she wore. It flaunted her curves instead of hiding them. The bikini top lovingly clung to her breasts. Her nipples pressed against the fragile fabric. The sarong hung low, emphasizing her tiny waist and the gentle swell of her hips.

His gaze traveled down her taut stomach. The ivory

skin was sun-kissed, but she had lost weight. Pining for him? Hafiz glanced around the party and scoffed at the idea as he crossed his arms. He wished. More like too much partying.

The brightly colored sarong teased his senses, and he couldn't drag his gaze away from her bare legs. He remembered how they felt wrapped around his waist as he drove into her.

When Lacey rolled her hips, Hafiz's restraint threatened to shatter. Where was a voluminous caftan when you needed one? He was beginning to see the advantages.

Lacey was surrounded by cheering men, and she unknowingly taunted them with the thrust of her hips. Hafiz swore she was more sensual than any belly dancer without even trying. Did she know that these men would do anything to get her into bed? They couldn't hide the desperation to take his place in her life.

Had they already?

The possibility fueled his bitter jealousy. He could not hold back any longer. He stepped through the circle of the men posturing for Lacey's attention and reached for her. Hafiz grasped her wrist and was painfully aware of the heat coursing through him from the simple touch.

Lacey opened her eyes just as he slid her against him. Blood sang through his veins as her soft breasts pressed against his hard chest. He shuddered as his control slipped. After a month without her, every primal instinct told him to pounce and never let her go.

"Miss me, Lacey?" he murmured in her ear.

He watched as she blinked at him. His chest ached

as he waited, wondering how she would greet him. Would she push him away? Would she welcome him with the same cool friendliness she'd welcome an old acquaintance? Or would she treat him with indifference?

"Hafiz?"

He drew her closer as the people and the noise faded around them. He had eyes only for Lacey. She pressed her hands to his face. "I can't believe you're here," she whispered.

He held her hand and pressed his mouth against her palm. "You did miss me," he said, purring with satisfaction.

"Of course I did." She wrapped her arms around his neck and held him fiercely. "How can you ask?" she asked against his chest.

"Let's get out of here," he insisted as he drew her away. He was too impatient to taste Lacey's mouth on his. He needed her more than his next breath. "I want you all to myself."

Hafiz held her hand tightly as he guided her out of the party as if he couldn't risk losing her. As if she might break away. He was striding to the elevators that would whisk them to her apartment when he abruptly turned and pulled her into a shadowy corner.

It had been too long. He wasn't going to wait anymore. He pressed her back against the corner and braced his arms against the walls, trapping her. "Show me how much you missed me."

Lacey didn't hesitate and claimed Hafiz's mouth with hers. The one touch, one kiss, was all it took for the numbness to disappear. Her skin tingled, her heart pounded against her chest, and blood roared in her ears as she violently came back to life.

She still couldn't believe it. Hafiz had come for her. He chose her over his fiancée and his duty. Over his country. He chose *her*.

Lacey pulled away and stared at Hafiz. She searched his face, noticing how much he had changed in a month. His features were harsher, the lines and angles more pronounced. The sexual hunger in his eyes was ferocious.

She trembled with anticipation and grabbed his jacket lapels. Hafiz wrapped his hands around her waist and ripped off her sarong. He tossed it on the ground with an impatience she'd never seen in him.

She knew Hafiz was almost out of his mind with lust. He was desperate to touch her. To taste her. She understood this driving need, but the intensity was almost painful. She felt as if she could explode from it.

Hafiz pushed the bikini top away and exposed her breasts. They felt heavy under his hot gaze. Lacey almost wept as Hafiz captured one tight nipple in his mouth. She raked her fingers through his hair, encouraging him closer.

Lacey gasped at the primal, almost savage way he stripped her bikini bottoms from her hips. She could tell that his control was slipping. He couldn't hold back. This reunion was going to be hard, fast and furious.

She couldn't believe she had this power over him. That they had this power over each other. Lacey liked how his fingers shook as he tore the flimsy piece of fabric from her trembling legs. She bit her lip when he roughly cupped her sex.

"Now," she muttered. "I need you in me now."

Hafiz didn't follow her demands. Instead he dipped his fingers into her wet heat. Lacey panted hard as her flesh gripped him tight and drew him in deeper.

As Hafiz stroked her with his fingers, Lacey pressed her mouth shut to prevent a throaty moan from escaping. They were hidden as the party continued around them. No one could hear them, no one could see, but old habits died hard. She couldn't risk being discovered, but she couldn't bear the idea of stopping.

Lacey dove her hands under his shirt and slid her fingers along his hot, flushed skin. She wanted to rip his clothes off his perfect body, but that would take too much time. She smiled when his breath hitched in his throat as his muscles bunched under her touch. He countered with the flick of his finger inside her. She shuddered as the fiery sensations swept through her body.

"Now, Hafiz. I can't wait any longer." She heard the metallic sound of his zipper and rocked her hips with impatience. She gulped for air and inhaled the musky scent of his arousal. Her chest ached with excitement as he lifted her up and hooked her legs over his hips.

He entered her with one smooth thrust. Hafiz's long groan rumbled from his chest, and he didn't move as if he was savoring this moment. His penis stretched and filled her, but Lacey couldn't stay still. She wanted more—needed everything Hafiz had to give her. She rolled her pelvis slowly and was rewarded with a warning growl before he clenched his fingers into her hips. Hafiz withdrew and plunged into her again and again.

She eagerly accepted each wild thrust. Lacey held on to Hafiz tightly and closed her eyes as her cli-

max forked through her. Her heart faltered as the fury
rushed through, taking the last of her strength. Her
mind grasped on the only thing that mattered—he had
chosen her above all else.

"This bed is too small," Hafiz complained in a murmur as he held Lacey in his arms. She lay on top of
him, naked and warm. She rested her head against his
chest, and he threaded his fingers through her long hair.

He was right where he wanted to be.

"It's fine," she said sleepily.

Fine? He shook his head at the thought. His feet
dangled off the edge, and his shoulders were almost
too wide for the bed. The mattress was as thin and
cheap as the sheets.

It was too dark to see all of Lacey's bedroom, but he
could tell that it was tiny with just a few furnishings. It
was nothing like the apartment she had in Rudaynah.

"We should go to my hotel suite," Hafiz suggested.
"It's more comfortable. Bigger." *Better.* He felt Lacey
deserved more. How did she wind up here?

"Mmm-hmm." Lacey made no move to get up.

He slid his hand down and caressed her spine. He
felt her shiver of pleasure under his palm. "Do you
like Abu Dhabi?" he asked.

"Mmm-hmm."

"Why did you choose to live here?" He had been as-
tounded when he discovered she was still in the UAE.
He thought she had gone home. Back to St. Louis.
"Did you know someone? Had business contacts?"

"I didn't know anyone," she said with a yawn. "But
I applied for some jobs, did the necessary paperwork,
and I got this one at the hotel."

"Adventurous of you," Hafiz said as he cupped the base of her head and held her close. He didn't like the idea that she was all alone in the world. That there was no one looking out for her. Protecting her.

"You sound surprised," Lacey said. "May I remind you, I moved to Rudaynah sight unseen? Some people consider that adventurous. My friends thought it was crazy."

"That was different. You had me to take care of you."

"I've been looking after myself for as long as I can remember."

"You let me take care of you," Hafiz said. The words echoed in his mind. She *let* him. She had given her trust in so many ways, and he took it for granted.

"It wasn't easy for me," Lacey admitted as she pressed her mouth against his chest and gave him a kiss. "I didn't want to be dependent on you."

Lacey Maxwell wasn't cut out to be a mistress, Hafiz decided. Most women took the role because they wanted to be taken care of.

"What's wrong with depending on me?" he asked. "On anyone?"

"I remember what it was like when I had to rely on my parents. They really didn't want to deal with me."

His fingers tightened against her. Anger flared inside him as he imagined a young Lacey, ignored and neglected. "You don't know that."

"I do." There was no sadness in her voice. She spoke as if she was giving the facts. "They have not reached out to me once I've been on my own. It's better this way. I know I made the right decision to cut them out of my life."

A cold chill swept through Hafiz. *"You're* the one that walked away?"

"I tried for years to be the daughter they wanted and needed. But I couldn't earn their love or attention. I walked away and didn't look back."

His heart started to race. He had always thought Lacey was tenacious. It was one of her most admirable traits. He had seen her practice a piece of music until she got it right or talk him through a work problem even if it took all night. But even she had limits. "But…they're your parents."

"And that's why it took me so long to walk away. I kept thinking circumstances would change. But they didn't see any need to change. They weren't being malicious. They were extremely selfish. It took me years to forgive them, but I'm not trying to make them love me anymore."

Hafiz couldn't shake the fear that gripped his chest. He had always felt that Lacey's love was unconditional. It was the one thing he could count on. Yet Lacey had walked away from the strongest bond a person could have. He thought that once Lacey loved someone, it was forever.

This changed everything.

"Lacey." She felt a large hand cupping her shoulder, rousing her out of the best sleep she'd had in a long, long time. "Lacey, wake up."

She peered through bleary eyes. A whisper of a smile formed on her lips when she saw Hafiz looking down at her. Last night hadn't been a dream. "Come back to bed," she mumbled drowsily and patted the mattress next to her.

"It's time to get up, Sleeping Beauty," he said with a smile.

She looked at him and noticed for the first time that he was already dressed in his black T-shirt and trousers. His hair gleamed with dampness from a recent shower.

Lacey sighed and stretched, murmuring in protest at the twinges in her muscles. "Sleeping Beauty isn't my favorite fairytale princess," she said as she rubbed the sleep from her eyes.

"You prefer Rapunzel?" he asked. "I finally read that fairy tale you kept talking about."

"Really?" She slowly sat up in bed and pushed her hair away from her face. "What did you think of it?"

Hafiz's mouth set in a grim line. She suspected he was going to ask something but wasn't sure if he would like the answer. "Did you see me as the prince who saved the day, or did you see me as the witch who trapped Rapunzel in the tower?"

Lacey blinked, startled by the question. The corners of her lips tilted into a sad smile as she wrapped the bed sheet around her nude body. "It took me a while before I realized that you were the Rapunzel in the story."

Hafiz jerked his head back. "That's not funny."

"I'm serious. Think about it," she said. She knew she should have kept her opinion to herself. What man would want to be compared to Rapunzel? But it was too late, and she needed to explain her way of thinking. "Rudaynah was your tower and you were trapped."

"I am not trapped," he said stiffly. "I have duties and obligations, but that is not the same thing."

"Those expectations were holding you back. The sultan was more interested in how you acted than what you accomplished."

"I don't want to talk about that right now." The flash of annoyance in Hafiz's eyes indicated that the topic would be discussed at length later.

"It doesn't matter. It's the past. You're free now," she said with a wide smile. "You escaped the tower. Although I'm sure you would want to visit the sultanate every once in a while. It is your homeland."

Hafiz tilted his head and stared at her with incomprehension. "Lacey, what are you talking about?"

"You left Rudaynah. Didn't you?" she asked slowly. "We agreed that we wouldn't see each other unless you chose me and only me."

"I never agreed to that."

She tried to remember what had been said that night. Hafiz had said he loved her. It was the one thing that held her together when she wondered what it all had been for.

"You love me. You found me," she said softly. "But you're not staying?"

Hafiz sighed. "No."

She flinched as his answer clawed at her. It tore her to shreds before she had a chance to ward off the pain. "And you're still…"

"Getting married. Yes."

Those three words ripped away the last fragment of hope. She closed her eyes and hunched her shoulders. Hafiz hadn't chosen her. He hadn't chased her across the world to get her back.

CHAPTER TEN

HE WAS STILL getting married to Nabeela. The stark truth sliced through her. He'd failed to mention that important piece of information before he possessed her body and soul throughout the night. The rat. The snake.

She couldn't believe he would do this to her. Again. How many times would she fall for this routine? "Get out," she ordered hoarsely, clutching the sheet against her.

"What?" Arrogant disbelief tinged his voice.

"I thought you chose me. I'm such a fool," she whispered, gently rocking back and forth. It felt as if she was bleeding inside. She was going to drown in it.

Hafiz exhaled sharply. "I am choosing to be with you."

"Temporarily," she said. "You came here for sex." She stiffened and looked at the bed before scrambling off of the mattress. She gave a fierce yank to the bed sheets that covered her body. Her body, which she'd freely given to him with her love hours before.

He splayed his hands in the air. "I didn't plan it."

"Right." This from a man who was in control of everything and everyone around him. "You didn't plan to travel to Abu Dhabi. You didn't plan to search for me. You didn't plan to take me against a wall minutes after you found me."

He rolled his shoulders back as if he was bracing himself for a direct hit. "I traveled here for a meeting. I'm staying at this hotel, and I didn't know you were still in Abu Dhabi until I saw the poster at the hotel lounge about your performance."

Just when she thought she couldn't feel any worse. He hadn't come here just to find her. He didn't go out of his way to seek her. She stared at Hafiz, not sure if she was going to burst into tears or start laughing maniacally at the unfairness of it all.

She needed to cover herself. Protect herself. Lacey grabbed her robe that had fallen on the floor. "You needed to scratch an itch. Why? Your fiancée won't sleep with you until the wedding night?"

His eyes darkened. "I have no contact with my future bride because it is an arranged marriage. It is not a love match."

As if that was supposed to make her feel better. The muscle in her cheek twitched with fury. "It's probably best that way. You don't want her to find out how rotten to the core you are until after the vows are exchanged."

"Lacey, I apologize for the misunderstanding."

"Misunderstanding? There was no misunderstanding. You withheld that information because if I knew you were still engaged, I wouldn't have welcomed you with open arms."

"Don't be too sure. We have a connection that is too—"

"Connection?" She gave a harsh laugh. "No, we have

a past. That is it. You severed that connection when you got me out of your life as quickly as possible."

"We still have something," he argued. "That's why I came to check up on you and—"

"You came to have sex because you're not used to going without." Lacey thrust her arms through the sleeves of her robe. The fiery orange silk felt like needles across her sensitive skin. "And you knew I wouldn't deny you. Especially since you had lied to me and said you loved me."

Hafiz drew back. "That wasn't a lie."

She glared at him, fighting the urge to strike out with her nails unsheathed. "Your timing was suspicious."

He placed his hands on his hips. "Suspicious?"

"You tell me that you love me the moment before I was out of your life forever. Was it a way to keep me dangling on your hook? That way, when you looked me up, you didn't have to work too hard to get back into my bed."

"I told you in a moment of weakness," he said in a low growl. "I didn't want you to look back and think the year we spent together meant nothing."

Their time had meant everything to her. It had been the one time when she felt safe and wanted. She had honestly believed during the months in Rudaynah that they had been growing closer and that their relationship could weather anything.

"You could have told me you loved me at any time, but you didn't. Why?" She took a step closer and pointed her finger accusingly at him. "Because saying those words at the last minute meant you didn't have to do anything about it."

He raked his fingers through his hair. Lacey had the feeling he wanted to grab her by the shoulders and shake her. She took a prudent step back.

"If you don't believe me," Hafiz said in a clipped tone, "that is your problem."

Lacey glared at him. Wouldn't a man in love want to express his emotions? Wouldn't he show it with grand gestures and small, intimate moments?

But not this man. No, not Prince Hafiz. He wasn't going to lower himself and try to convince her. He wasn't going to waste his energy on proving something that didn't exist.

"You want to forget everything I did for you? For us? Go right ahead," Hafiz said. "I love you and nothing is going to change that."

"What am I supposed to think? You say you love me when you are engaged to another woman." She tied the sash of her robe with enough force that it could have ripped.

Hafiz ground the heels of his palms against his eyes. "I'm not replacing you."

"Of course not," Lacey said as she walked out of the bedroom. "I would have had to be part of your life for Nabeela to replace my role."

Hafiz followed her into the main room with long, brisk strides. His presence made the apartment feel smaller, as if it couldn't contain him. Lacey wished Priya had not had the night shift. She wanted him to leave and could have used some backup right now. Knowing what kind of man he was, Hafiz wouldn't leave until he got what he was after.

"You made sure I wasn't part of your world," Lacey continued. "I thought I needed to earn that privilege because I was a foreigner and a nobody. Now I real-ize that nothing I did would have made a difference. It just wasn't going to happen."

She was done trying to earn love. It didn't work. She had twisted and bent herself into knots, deter-mined to give her all and make her relationships work. She had made Hafiz the most important part of her life, and he could not do the same. He had accepted her love as if it was his due, but he did not see her as a priority in life.

No more. Hafiz did not value her role in his life, and he wasn't going to. From now on, she would put herself first because no one else would. She would not settle or compromise.

She heard Hafiz's cell phone ring. Lacey whirled around and saw him retrieve it from his pocket. "Don't you dare."

He frowned as he glanced up from the touch screen. "I'm just—"

"No, you are not answering that phone. I don't care if Rudaynah suddenly disappeared from the face of the earth. It can't be as important as what's going on here."

"Lacey, don't be—"

"I'm serious, Hafiz. For once, I am your top prior-ity. The most important person in your life is right in front of you, so put the phone away."

Hafiz's austere face tightened, clearly holding his anger in check.

"If you'd rather take the call," she said coldly, "then leave and don't come back."

Her heart was pounding as the phone continued to

ring. Hafiz silently turned off the ringer and returned the phone to his pocket as he held her gaze.

Lacey tried to hide her surprise. She had never given him an ultimatum like that. She had always been reluctant, always knowing that he held the power in the relationship. She'd believed that if she made any demands, placed any expectations on him, he would exchange her for another woman.

It turned out that he'd done it anyway.

"I am marrying Nabeela, but the marriage is in name only," Hafiz assured her.

"What exactly does that mean?"

"It means that we will not live in the same suite of rooms in the palace. It means that we will see each other on official occasions, and, even then, we won't stand next to each other."

Lacey's eyes narrowed as she listened to his explanation. "And this is what you want?"

"It's not about what I want to do. It's about meeting my obligations. Meeting the expectations of my country and my family."

"Will you consummate the marriage?"

His nostrils flared as he reined in his patience. "It is required by law."

The idea of him in bed with another woman made her sick to her stomach. How would he feel if she chose to sleep with another man? Claimed it was required? Hafiz would do everything in his power to prevent that from happening. Why did he think she wouldn't respond in the same way? Because she was a woman? Because as a mistress she had no claim on him?

"Will you have children?" she asked.

The muscle in his jaw twitched. "As the second in line to the throne, I am not required to have an heir."

She noticed he didn't answer her question. "But you won't be second in line," she reminded him. "You will be the crown prince if you marry Nabeela."

"That is the sultan's promise, but I don't know if or when it will happen. I need to be the crown prince," Hafiz admitted. "I didn't expect to get a second chance, and I have to take it."

"It's what you want most," she said in a matter-of-fact tone. He wanted it more than he wanted her. "It's what you strove for all these years."

"I had abused that power ten years ago. If I get the title back, I can make amends. I can show that I'm different. That I am the leader that they need."

Power. It was all about the power. "But the sultan has the ultimate power. And he can strip your title whenever he sees fit."

"That is true, but I won't let that happen. I know how to protect what is mine. This time no one will intimidate or harm those who are important to me. This time I have the power to fight back."

Lacey shook her head with resignation. That sounded like the Hafiz she knew and loved. "You already have that power," she pointed out. "You don't need to be a prince to use it."

He reared his head back as if she had said something blasphemous. "I disagree. Taking care of Rudaynah is my purpose in life. I can't do that if I'm not their prince."

Lacey tried to imagine what Hafiz would be like without a royal title. He would still be arrogant and influential. People would continue to clamor for his attention and advice. But would his countrymen allow him to represent the sultanate if he wasn't a prince, or would they treat him as a celebrity? She didn't know.

"I may not agree with you every time, Lacey, but I always listened. You made me look at the world differently. I missed the way we used to talk," Hafiz said.

Lacey looked away. "We didn't talk. I was your mistress, not your girlfriend. We had sex. Lots and lots of sex."

"Don't," Hafiz said harshly. "Stop rewriting our history."

Was she guilty of that? Lacey sank her teeth into her bottom lip. She had felt loved and adored when she was with Hafiz. He had been generous and caring. Maybe it wasn't just about sex.

"Think about the times you listened to the troubles I had on a project or my concerns for the sultanate," Hafiz said quietly. "You gave me advice and ideas. I knew I could count on you to give me honest feedback. Your opinion always mattered to me."

"And now you have Nabeela for that."

"Nabeela won't look after my best interest. She can't drive me wild. She can't love me the way you do."

"Then break the engagement," she whispered.

He froze and turned his head away. "No, Lacey," Hafiz said as he took a step back.

"You don't have to do this to redeem yourself. You have made up for your mistakes years ago."

"I don't deserve forgiveness."

"You don't deserve a loveless marriage," she insisted. "I know what it's like to be unloved. To be surrounded by indifference. It chips away at you until you become a shadow of yourself."

"I can't break the engagement. It's too late."

Lacey closed her eyes as the pain flashed through her. "And you can't walk away from me. So, what do you plan to do?" She slowly opened her eyes as it occurred to her. "You plan to have both of us?" she asked in a scandalized whisper.

Hafiz remained silent as he watched her closely.

She felt the blood drain from her face. "You need to leave right now. I can't believe you would insult me this way."

"I told you, my marriage would be in name only. It's not a real marriage. It's not even a relationship."

She thrust her finger at the door. "Get out," she said, her voice trembling with outrage.

Hafiz sighed and went to collect his jacket. "Give me one good reason why this won't work."

"I don't want to be your mistress." At one time in her life, she gladly accepted the role. It had been the only way she could be in his life. She'd gratefully accepted the crumbs he offered, but now she knew she deserved more.

"But you can't be my wife," he murmured.

"You made sure that couldn't happen. Even if you didn't accept Nabeela as your bride, I still wouldn't be your wife. Because I was a mistress. *Your* mistress."

"That's not the only reason."

"Because you don't think I'm worthy of the title."

"That's not true," he said, grabbing her wrists with his large hands, forcing her to stand still as he towered over her. "I love you and I want to spend the rest of my life with you. This is the best compromise I can make."

"Compromise." Her lips curled with disgust as she said the word. "I'm done compromising."

"There are rules," he said in an impatient growl.

"Break them," she suggested wildly. "You've done it before."

"And I regret it every day. This is different."

"Here's a thought. Stop hiding me from the world and present me to your family with pride. Show them that it's not a sin to love me. Tell them that I am everything you need and that I'm the one you will marry."

"That isn't going to happen. Ever."

Lacey looked down at her bare feet. She had gone too far. She had made an ultimatum that showed the limit of his love for her. She should have known, should have been happy with what he offered, but she couldn't. She wasn't going to take a smaller and demeaning role just to stay in his life. That wasn't love. That was the first step on the path to her destruction.

She had to protect herself. She suddenly felt weak, so much so she couldn't raise her head to meet his gaze. Lacey took a deep breath, the air hurting her raw throat and tight chest.

"And this, what we had together, isn't going to happen again," she said in a low rush. It took all of her strength to raise her head and meet his gaze. "I need you to leave now."

She saw the calculating gleam in his eye just as she heard a key fumbling in the lock of the front door. Lacey turned just as her roommate rushed in.

"Lacey! Why haven't you been answering your texts?" Priya asked as she slammed the door closed.

Priya looked flustered. Her topknot threatened to collapse, and her name tag was crookedly pinned on her black blazer. She appeared out of breath, and her face gleamed with sweat.

"Are you all right?" Lacey asked as her roommate openly studied Hafiz. "Priya, this is—"

Priya raised her hand. "Prince Hafiz, the guy who broke her heart."

Lacey straightened her spine and clutched the lapels of her robe. "How do you know that? I never told you his name."

"No need." Priya swiped her finger against the screen of her phone. "It's all right here in full color."

"What are you talking about?" The lethal tone in Hafiz's low voice made Priya hesitate.

"This." She turned the phone around to show a picture of Hafiz and Lacey in a hot embrace at the party. It was a good quality picture from someone's phone. There was no denying that Prince Hafiz was the man in the picture. Lacey's face was partially hidden, but her identity didn't matter. The fact that her bikini-clad body was plastered against Hafiz was damning enough.

The sharp twist of dread in Lacey's stomach almost made her sick. She clapped a shaky hand against her mouth.

"How many pictures are there?" Hafiz asked.

Lacey's gaze clashed with his. Her eyes widened as she remembered those stolen moments in the corridor outside the party. They hadn't been aware of their surroundings as they made love. What if their recklessness had been caught on camera?

Oh, God. What had they done? It had been madness. Lacey watched Hafiz's gaze harden, no doubt considering the repercussions.

"I've only seen this one so far."

So far. Lacey wanted to sit down before she tumbled to the floor. Hafiz was right. She was his vice. No, she was his poison. She was going to ruin everything for him.

"Who sent it to you?" Lacey asked. "Maybe we can get them to delete it from their camera." Maybe they would luck out. Maybe one of their friends had no idea who Hafiz was and sent it to Priya because she was in the picture.

"I don't know," Priya said as she pressed the screen. "One of our friends was sharing pictures of the party. But it's only a matter of time before someone finds out Hafiz is the playboy prince. Once that happens, there's no containing this."

CHAPTER ELEVEN

Hafiz stared at the image on the small screen. The picture revealed everything. He had greeted Lacey with an intensity that indicated they were more than acquaintances. The passion, the love, the desperate yearning was evident in his expression.

Why? Why hadn't he been more careful? He knew the risks. Did he think the rules only applied when he was home?

He hadn't been thinking. The moment he had seen Lacey's picture in the hotel lounge he had been on the hunt for her. He should have resisted the urge. He had not contacted Lacey for a month and managed to get through each day. But that didn't mean he hadn't thought of her constantly.

"Hafiz?"

He jerked at the sound of Lacey's voice. His gaze slammed into hers. He saw the concern and the tears. But it was the defeat in her eyes that slayed him. Lacey always looked at him as if he was invincible. That he could achieve the impossible.

Now she wasn't so sure. Not when it looked as if he would lose everything over a damning photo.

Priya cleared her throat and only then did Hafiz remember she was in the room. He was always like this when he was around Lacey. Nothing else mattered. It was becoming a major problem.

"I'm going to give you guys some privacy," the roommate said as she started to back away. "Lacey, text me when the prince is ready to return to his hotel suite."

"Why?" Lacey asked.

"If this picture gets out, other photographers will try to find me. A picture of me is worth a lot of money, especially if it includes you," Hafiz explained.

He remembered how this worked. It was humbling that he was in the same predicament that he'd found himself in ten years ago. It didn't matter how much he had tried to control his wilder impulses, he had not changed at all.

Priya nodded. "I can get you to your room unseen."

"Thank you." He returned his attention to Lacey. She crossed her arms tightly against her body and began to pace.

The moment Priya closed the door, Lacey whirled around to face him. "I had nothing to do with this."

Hafiz narrowed his eyes. He wasn't sure what Lacey was talking about, but he often found being silent was the best way to get information.

"I did not set you up," Lacey said. "I know you think that I'm out to sabotage your wedding, but I wouldn't do that."

"You wouldn't?" he asked softly. The thought hadn't crossed his mind. He knew his appearance had been unexpected, and Lacey's attention had been focused on him from the moment they had reconnected. He knew he could trust Lacey about this.

The fact that she immediately leaped to the conclusion that he would suspect her bothered him. He didn't trust easily, and yet he trusted Lacey more than anyone. But since his trust wasn't blind or absolute, Lacey thought he didn't trust her at all.

"Of course, I wouldn't. Do you think all mistresses are manipulative schemers who would do anything to maintain their lifestyles?"

"You aren't like any other mistress." Lacey hadn't been motivated by money, status or power.

"I wouldn't know. I have nothing to compare," Lacey said as she continued to pace. "But, believe me, I am not interested in returning to Rudaynah and maintaining the lifestyle of secrets and hiding."

"Hate Rudaynah that much?"

"I don't *hate* it," she corrected him. "There were parts of it that I found intolerable, but I also saw the beauty and wonder."

Hafiz doubted she could list what she found beautiful. "No, you hated it."

"I hated that I was separated from you," she said. "I hated that we had to hide our relationship."

"Our relationship is about to be brought out into the open," he murmured. He would have to deny it, but no one would believe him. It was clear in the photo that he was intimate with Lacey. And if they had photos of what happened immediately after that embrace... He would protect Lacey from the embarrassment, no matter the cost or the consequences.

"Do you think I forced your hand?" Lacey stopped pacing and stood directly in front of him. "I didn't. I don't know how to convince you that I have nothing to do with this picture. I don't have any proof. But once I find the person who is responsible…"

Hafiz was momentarily fascinated as he watched her shake her fist in the air. He hadn't seen her like this. She was in full protective mode. Of *him*. He took care of Lacey, not the other way around.

"I know you don't have anything to do with it," Hafiz said.

She lowered her fist and gave him a sidelong glance. "You do?" She said the words in a slow drawl.

Hafiz nodded. "It's not your nature." He knew that, but it hadn't stopped him from accusing her in the past. He had let his past experiences with women cloud his judgment.

"Just like that?" She snapped her fingers. "A month ago I couldn't have lunch with a few friends without you accusing me of betrayal."

"I had jumped to conclusions," he admitted. "I thought…"

"That I would retaliate because I was kicked out of your life with little ceremony?"

He felt his mouth twitch with displeasure at her description. Their relationship ended abruptly, but he did not kick her out.

"Something like that," he admitted. "I'm sorry I considered that was a possibility. I know you're not that kind of person. You are loyal and sweet. Innocent about the world, really."

"That's an unusual choice of words for a mistress."

He raked his fingers through his hair and exhaled. "Stop calling yourself a mistress."

She looked at him with surprise. "Why? That was my role in your life. We weren't a couple. We weren't partners. We led separate lives during the day and spent the nights together. Only you didn't stay all night."

"No, I didn't." It had been a test of willpower every night to get out of Lacey's bed and return to the palace.

"Where is this coming from?" Lacey asked as she planted her hands on her hips. "You don't have to pretty up the past, Hafiz."

"I don't want people to think the worst about you." He should have considered that before he brought her over to Rudaynah, but all he had cared about was having her near.

"You don't want them to know that I was a mistress?" She tilted her head as she studied his expression. "Or is it that you don't want people to know about your role?"

Those words were like a punch in the stomach. Was that the real reason he didn't want Lacey to wear that label? He was a prince, was held to a higher standard, but he had brought Lacey to his world by any means necessary.

"Because deep down that goes against what you believe in, doesn't it, Hafiz? You don't want to be the playboy prince, but you had a kept woman. Instead of making a commitment or having a relationship based on mutual feelings, you made arrangements with a woman so you could have exclusive access to her body."

"Our relationship was more than just sex," Hafiz said in a growl. Not that anyone would see it that way.

"The palace may have some questions about that if they see that picture." Lacey dragged her hands down her face. "What are we going to do about it?"

Hafiz went still. "*We?* No, you aren't getting involved with this."

Lacey rolled her eyes. "We're in this together, and we're going to get out of it together."

He was conflicted. Hafiz had always appreciated it when Lacey was ready to fight alongside him, but he didn't want to drag her into this battle.

"No one can see your face in the picture," Hafiz insisted. "You can't be identified. Let's keep it that way."

"It's only a matter of time," Lacey said. "Someone at the party is going to remember what I wore and how you dragged me out of the party."

"It was late, and people had been drinking. No one can be too sure what happened."

"Anyway," she continued, "I don't care if people know it's me."

Why didn't Lacey care about her reputation? A public scandal never died. He hadn't thought much about his until he destroyed his reputation and took the slow, hard road to repair it. He knew it would be much worse for a woman.

"I care." Hafiz knew his voice sounded harsh, but he had to get Lacey to understand. "If you get caught up in a scandal with me, it will cling to you for the rest of your life. You will always be known as the woman who slept with the playboy prince."

Lacey lifted her chin. "I've done nothing to be ashamed about."

"Nothing?" he asked with a tinge of incredulity. "We lost control. We made compromises and excuses even when it went against everything we've been taught. Everything we believe in." He turned away from Lacey. "And even though we swear that we won't meet again, that we won't think about what might have been, we break our promises. The moment we see each other, we destroy everything we tried to create."

The silence pulsed between them.

She made him dream about a life he had no right to pursue. Hafiz winced as resentment shot through his chest. He took in a deep sigh, and he realized nothing had changed. No, that wasn't true. When he was with Lacey, everything he felt was sharper and stronger. Life after Lacey was going to be excruciating.

He needed to be strong and not give in to his wants. He had done that for years until he met Lacey. After disappointing a nation, he had sacrificed his happiness to make amends. He could do it again, but he had to stop teasing himself with the fantasy of life with Lacey.

"Hafiz," Lacey said in a husky voice, "there are many reasons why I love you. You have worked hard to make up for your mistakes. You try to be a good man, a good son and a good prince. I have always admired your willpower and your strength. But your one weakness is me."

Hafiz wanted to deny it.

She slowly shook her head. "All this time I've hated the idea that I'm your one and only vice. Your weakness. But it's true. I am making you into the man you don't want to be."

"That's not true. I like who I am when I'm with you."

"You like sneaking around?" she asked. "Breaking

promises? Feeling guilty because you shouldn't love a woman like me?"

"No," he admitted gruffly.

"Would you have acted this way with another woman? Would you make love to her in public?"

Hafiz wanted to lie and say yes. But even when he was known as the playboy prince, he had always been aware of his surroundings. But when he was with Lacey, nothing else mattered. It wasn't just a weakness. It was a sickness.

"You know what kind of woman I want to be?" she asked.

He knew. She never said it out loud, but he knew of her plans and dreams. Lacey wanted to be a woman surrounded by love and family.

"I can tell you that I didn't grow up thinking I wanted to be a femme fatale. I didn't want to be the kind of woman who ruined lives."

"You're not ruining my life. My—" He stopped. He wasn't going to think it. Voice it. His royal status was part of his identity and the one true constant in his life. It was not an obstacle that kept him from being with Lacey.

"I'm a problem for you, Hafiz. What do you think is going to happen if this photo gets out? What will the sultan do?"

Hafiz gritted his teeth. He wasn't going to tell Lacey. She would try to protect him and keep him in Abu Dhabi. "I can take care of myself."

"No, that's the wrong way to go around it," Lacey said. "That's expected. You'll probably use the words that every powerful man has used when denying an affair. I will take care of this."

Hafiz's shoulders went rigid. "No, you will not."

"Why not?" Lacey's eyes lit up, and she held up her hands. Hafiz knew that look. Lacey had a plan. "This is what we're going to do. If the picture gets published, I'll take the blame."

"Not a chance."

"Listen to me, Hafiz." She placed her hand on his arm as she pleaded. "It's so simple. I'll tell people that I saw you at this party, and I came onto you. You rejected my advances."

He wasn't going to let anyone think that his woman was an indiscriminate seductress. "The picture says otherwise."

"Pictures lie." She dismissed his words with the wave of her hand. "No one knows what happened before or after. It's very possible that I propositioned you. It's just as possible that you declined my offer."

Hafiz gave her a disbelieving look. He couldn't remember a time when he refused Lacey. "No."

She squeezed his arm. "It will work."

He placed his hand over hers. "No, it won't. I am not hiding behind a woman."

She jerked her hand away. "Excuse me?"

He leaned closer. "And no one is going to believe you."

"Yes, they will."

"Not when every gossip site is going to drag up my playboy past and follows up with my former lovers."

He felt the weight of his past on his shoulders. Why had he thought he could erase those moments? And why did it all have to be dug up now?

"Lacey, there is a very real chance that someone

took a picture of us after the party." He was furious at himself that he'd put her in this position.

She blushed a bright red. "If they had a picture, they would have already used it, right?"

"No, they would hint that something even more scandalizing is coming out," Hafiz said. "Stir up interest and sell it to the highest bidder."

"Hafiz, I'm sure there aren't any more pictures," she said in a shaky voice. "We would have seen someone."

He wasn't so sure. They had been lost in their own world. "I need to call a few people and find out if someone is shopping the pictures," he said as he turned on his cell phone and walked to the door.

"Good. And I—"

He halted and turned around, stopping her with one warning look. "You will stay here."

She glared at him. "You have no say in the matter. Anyway, I have to go to work in a couple of hours."

"Promise me that you won't try to fix this," Hafiz said in a low tone. "I need you to trust me on this. Let me handle it."

"But—"

"I won't let you down."

She hesitated, and Hafiz knew what she was thinking. He had let his former mistress down. Back then, he had abandoned his woman when she was vulnerable and in need. At that time, he didn't have the power to protect what was his from the sultan. Now he did, and he wasn't going to let anything happen to Lacey.

"Fine," she said through clenched teeth. "I will hang back...for now. But if I see that you are in trouble, I am—"

"No, you won't." He didn't care what she was planning to do. He wasn't going to let it happen. Hafiz grabbed the door handle and was about to cross the threshold when he turned around. "And, Lacey, one of these days you will realize that I don't need saving."

CHAPTER TWELVE

LACEY LOOKED OUT on the audience and gave a warm smile as she played the last note on the piano.

Why am I wasting my life doing this? she wondered. *Why do I still feel as if my life is on hold?*

Her smile tightened. The spotlight above her felt extraordinarily hot as sweat trickled down her spine. There were only a few people in the hotel lounge on the weekday afternoon.

That was not unusual, Lacey decided as she rose from the bench and bowed to the smattering of applause. It was common to see a few businessmen sitting in the audience at this time of day. They all had a dazed look from back-to-back meetings or constant travel.

She knew they weren't really listening to the music. If asked, they wouldn't remember her or describe her hair in a tight bun or her black lace dress. They were here because they didn't want to return to their quiet hotel rooms. They didn't want to be alone.

Lacey knew how they felt. She had struggled with loneliness before she had met Hafiz. It permeated her life and had been the theme in all the songs she had performed.

And when she met Hafiz, she had felt a connection between them. It had excited and frightened her. She didn't want to lose it. She didn't want it to end.

She glanced around the lounge and noticed Hafiz was not there. He knew when she was going to perform but he didn't stop by. Hafiz had always claimed that he enjoyed listening to her music, but now she wondered if that was just an empty compliment. Or perhaps he enjoyed it when she performed only for him.

She knew he wouldn't be there, but yet she still couldn't stop the disappointment dragging her down. Did he not show up because he was too busy or because he didn't want to be seen in the same room with her?

It shouldn't hurt. She was used to Hafiz not being part of her life. If he had shown up, she would have been unreasonably happy. Thrilled that he graced her with his presence.

And even with the decision that she wasn't going to let him treat her this way anymore, Lacey knew she would weaken her stance. She wanted him in her life no matter how little time she got with him.

Her dreams were not as grand as Hafiz's goals. Her plans for her life wouldn't lead her on the road to glory. At times what she wanted in life seemed impossible. But that didn't mean her dreams were less important than Hafiz's dreams. She needed to remember that.

What she wanted in life was to be with Hafiz. Build a life together and have a family. Create a home that was filled with love, laughter and music.

Lacey quickly got off the stage and glided between the empty tables. There was no use yearning for that kind of life. She wasn't going to get it. Not while she was on this path, waiting, hoping for Hafiz to change his mind.

Maybe she was Rapunzel. Lacey's footsteps slowed as the thought crashed through her. Oh, hell. She *was* the one who was stuck. She kept following the same pattern, waiting for a different outcome.

This was why she felt like her life was on hold. She was waiting for Prince Hafiz to reach out, take her away from her tower, and carry her away with him.

Not anymore. As much as she loved Hafiz and would greedily accept whatever he could spare, she didn't want a part-time love. She couldn't agree to sharing him.

She wanted a love that was exclusive and one that would last. She was willing to work for it, willing to give up a lot to make it happen. But she would not be his mistress or long-distance lover. She deserved more than that.

Lacey hurried through the hotel and headed for the staff housing. An enclosed garden separated the employee residences from the hotel. She usually found it peaceful walking past the fountains and ponds, inhaling the fragrance of the brightly colored flowers. Today the formal garden seemed too big.

"Lacey?"

Her pulse gave a hard kick when she heard the familiar masculine voice. She whirled around and saw Hafiz. Her heart started to pound as she stared at him. He was devastatingly handsome in his black suit. The severe lines of his jacket emphasized his broad shoulders and lean torso. He looked powerful and sophisticated. She was very aware of her cheap lace dress and secondhand shoes.

"Hafiz?" she whispered and frantically looked around the garden. "What are you doing here?"

"What do you mean?" he asked as he approached her. "I'm staying at this hotel."

"I mean you shouldn't be seen speaking to me. The last thing you need are more pictures of us together."

"The picture has been deleted," he said.

"Oh." Lacey knew that it was the wisest course of action, but getting rid of the picture bothered her. She realized it was because she had no pictures of them together. It was as if all evidence of them together had been erased.

"Why do you look upset?" Hafiz asked. "I took care of it just like I said I would."

"I had no doubt that you would be successful." Hafiz always got what he wanted. Except her. It made her wonder just how much he really wanted her in his life.

"You don't have to worry about it being released."

"I wasn't worried," she said, crossing her arms as a gentle breeze brushed against her skin. "I don't care if people know I'm with you."

Hafiz frowned. "You don't care if people know that you were a mistress?"

Did she care that people knew she didn't hold out for a wedding ring? That she accepted whatever Hafiz offered so she could be with him? No, she didn't regret those choices, but she knew she couldn't make them again.

In the past she'd thought accepting his offer to live in Rudaynah was one step toward a future together. Now she understood the rules. She either got to be his mistress, or she didn't get to be with him at all.

If he asked her to be his mistress now, she would decline. Even if he was unattached, even if he moved out of Rudaynah. It would be hard to say no, but these days she placed more value on herself and her dreams.

"I just finished working," Lacey said as she took a few steps away.

"I know," he said as he moved closer.

"I didn't see you in the lounge." Lacey bit down on her lip, preventing herself from saying anything more.

He frowned at her sharp tone as if he sensed an emotional minefield. "I wanted to be there."

"Something more important came along?" she asked with false brightness. "Something better?"

"You know why I couldn't be there."

"No, I really don't." She had automatically accepted the belief that they couldn't be seen together, and yet, here they were alone in a garden, deep in conversation. It felt as if he chose when he could and could not see her. "Explain it to me. Why were you not there to support me?"

"Did you need my support?" he asked.

"Yes." She never asked because she didn't want to set herself up for rejection. Her parents had not taken the time to see her perform while she was in school or early in her career. Hafiz had only seen her a few times early in their relationship.

"You have performed on stage countless times," he pointed out.

"Doesn't matter. I was always there for you, behind the scenes and in the shadows. I didn't stand next to you during ceremonies and events, but I supported your work. Why don't you support mine?"

His eyes narrowed. "Where is this coming from?"

"You wouldn't understand," she said as she closed her eyes. She realized she surprised him with her demand. It was rare to demand anything from him. She had spent so much energy trying to be part of his life that she didn't expect him to take part in hers.

"Lacey, the next time I'm here, I will sit in the front row and watch your entire performance," he promised.

She went still. "The next time you're here?"

"I'm leaving Abu Dhabi in a few hours," he said. "It's time for me to home."

He was going back. Lacey shouldn't be surprised, but she was struggling not to show it. "You are returning to Rudaynah?"

"I have to go back." His tone suggested that there had never been a question. "I'm still the prince. I have obligations."

"And a wedding?" she bit out.

Hafiz tilted his head back and sighed. "Yes, I am getting married."

"Why?" Lacey asked as the hopelessness squeezed her chest. "I've seen what kind of marriage you're entering. It's bleak and lonely. There is no happiness, no partnership and no love. Why are you doing this?"

"Because this is what I deserve!" he said in a harsh tone.

She gulped in air as she stared at Hafiz. "You're still punishing yourself for something you did over ten years ago," she said in a daze. "Hafiz, your countrymen have forgiven you. In fact, they adore you."

"It's not about my country. Yes, I accepted an arranged marriage because it is my duty. But I don't deserve a love marriage. Not because I'm a prince. It's because of what I did to Elizabeth."

"Your mistress who had become pregnant?" she asked. "I don't understand."

"I discarded her and I denied my son. I had a chance to take care of them, but instead I abandoned them. I treated them worse than how your parents treated you."

"Don't say that," Lacey whispered. "You are nothing like my parents. You value family. Your children will be your highest priority."

"I don't deserve to become a father after what I did. I neglected my responsibilities because I had been selfish. One day my brother will have a son, and he will become the heir to the throne."

She was stunned by his words. Lacey had always known that Hafiz would make a good father. He would be attentive but allow his children to forge their own paths and make their own mistakes.

"All this time," Lacey said, "you've been avoiding a love marriage and creating a family because of the way you treated Elizabeth?"

"Yes," he said. "It's only right."

"No, it's not. I'm sure Elizabeth has moved on."

"That doesn't matter," Hafiz replied. "My suffering doesn't end because she can accept what happened in the past. What I did was unforgivable."

"You have suffered enough," Lacey declared. "You have sacrificed your happiness for years while you've taken care of Rudaynah. You did everything you could to be the dutiful son and the perfect prince. When is it going to stop?"

"I don't know. What if the selfish and spoiled prince

is the real me? What if the playboy prince is underneath the surface, ready to break free?"

"It's not," Lacey insisted. "What I see before me is the real you. Caring and loving. Strong and protective. This is the man you're supposed to be."

"I want that to be true, but I can't take that risk. I am going back to Rudaynah and marry Nabeela, who understands that this marriage is nothing more than a business arrangement."

"This is crazy!"

"But I promise, Lacey, I will be back one day."

"How? When?" She frowned. "Why?"

"Why? Because I'm not giving up on us."

Her eyes widened. "Are you saying that you want a long-distance relationship?"

"Yes," he said as he reached for her. "We did it before when you lived in St. Louis."

She snatched her hands back. "That wasn't what it was. You kept visiting me because you couldn't stay away."

"It started out that way."

"And then you visited more frequently. Your trips were longer. But you never made the commitment."

"I was faithful to you." His eyes flashed with anger. "I haven't been interested in another woman since I met you."

"We weren't living together. Your main residence was somewhere else. And it was the same in Rudaynah. We were in the same country, the same city, but we lived separately."

"So what?"

Lacey crossed her arms and hesitated. She wasn't asking for marriage, and she wasn't asking for forever, but she knew she might be asking for too much. "If you want to be with me, then you have to make the commitment. You have to live with me."

"We can't." His answer was automatic.

"You mean, *you* can't."

"I just explained why I can't," Hafiz said. "If you expect a commitment from me, you are setting yourself up for disappointment."

"And I don't mean living in the same town or in the same hemisphere," she continued. "We will share a home and live as a couple."

"You can't return to Rudaynah."

"I know." She rolled her shoulders back and met his gaze. "You will live elsewhere."

"You mean leave the sultanate?" He angrily barked out the word, but she could see the fear in his eyes. The fear of losing her again. "Do you understand what you are asking of me?" He splayed his hands in the air.

"Yes, I'm asking to you to make a choice." And she had a feeling that she was setting herself up for rejection. "You asked me to make the same choice when I moved to Rudaynah."

"That is different. You didn't have obligations that tied you down to one place."

"It's not different. I made a choice of staying home or being with you. I chose you."

Hafiz took a deep breath. "Lacey," he said quietly, "I wish I could live with you. You are the only woman I've ever loved."

"But you don't want anyone to know it." She felt the first tear drip from her eyelashes, and she dashed it away with the side of her hand. "You love me as long as nothing is expected of you."

"That is not true." Hafiz's voice was gruff. "I want to take care of you. I want to be with you. Share a life together."

"You mean share *part* of your life," Lacey said. "You want to give me the occasional day or weekend. That's not good enough. I want it all."

He splayed his hands in the air. "You are asking me to do the impossible."

"Then there is nothing you can do but—" her breath hitched in her throat "—walk away."

Hafiz stared at her with incredulity. "I tried to do that, but I can't. I won't!"

"You have to," she pleaded, her tears falling unchecked. "If you really love me, if you really want the best for me, you will."

"What's best?" He flinched as if she slapped him. "Suddenly I'm not good for you?"

"You have to set me free." She didn't realize how hard it would be to say those words. Hafiz's devastated look made her want to snatch them back. It took all of her courage to continue. "Let me find a life where my needs are equal to everyone else's."

"What do you—" Hafiz's eyes lit with brutal understanding, and he recoiled from her. "You mean you want to find another man," he spat out.

"If it comes to that." Lacey knew it wasn't possible, but she couldn't let Hafiz know that, or he would continue to pursue her. "I need someone in my life who will put me first, just like I place him first. I can't have that kind of life with you."

"I have always put you first," he said in an angry hiss. "I took care of you the best way I knew how.

I—" He covered his face with his hands. "I would die for you."

Lacey believed him, and it bruised her heart. She didn't want him to die for her. She wanted to share her life with him. The thought speared her chaotic mind. Everything became clear.

She swept her tongue across her lips as her jittery heart pounded against her chest. "If it was between living with me or dying for the good of Rudaynah, which would you choose? The ultimate shame of loving me or the highest honor of serving your country?"

Hafiz was frozen in silence. She held her breath in anticipation as Hafiz dragged his hands from his face. She saw all of the emotions flickering in his ashen face. Shock. Pain. Hesitation.

"That's what I thought." She dragged the words out of her aching throat as hope shriveled up and died inside her. Hafiz might have loved her and he might have trusted her, but he couldn't be proud of her. He couldn't respect himself for loving her.

Nothing she could do would change that. She wasn't going to make the mistake of trying to earn her way. She wasn't going to think that being patient and uncomplaining would be rewarded.

"You need to leave and never come back," she said as she marched away. "Right now."

He shook his head. "I am not leaving. Not until you listen."

"I've listened, and I know nothing is going to change. I need to leave to protect myself. Goodbye, Hafiz," she said, her voice breaking as she fled.

CHAPTER THIRTEEN

SHE HAD TO protect herself. Hafiz silently leaned back in his chair and listened to the business presentation given in his conference room, but he turned Lacey's words over and over in his head. *I need to leave to protect myself.*

From him. Hafiz clenched his jaw as the hurt stung through his chest. It was that thought that had kept him up at night for the past week. Why did she think he was harmful to her? He would never touch her in anger or deny her anything. Everything he did for Lacey was to support her. Protect her.

Hadn't he proved it in Abu Dhabi when he'd kept the pictures from being released? Hadn't he spent lavishly on her throughout their affair? How did her life get worse because of him?

He was the one who needed to protect himself. He could have lost everything if their relationship had been revealed. He was addicted to Lacey Maxwell and risked everything for her. Why didn't she see that?

But instead she cut off all contact. She gave up on them. She abandoned *him.*

Hafiz wanted to believe it was for the best. She was a distraction he couldn't afford. He had almost everything he worked for just within his grasp. His work to improve the lives in the sultanate was making progress. He had made Rudaynah a wealthy country. He would regain the title of crown prince that had been stripped from him.

So why did he feel as if he had failed Lacey?

I need someone who will place me first.

Lacey's words echoed in his head. He was a prince. He could not make a person more of a priority than his country.

Because he was a prince, he was not the man she needed. The knowledge devastated him. Most women would have accepted that. Most women would have been thrilled with the arrangement he offered Lacey.

But not Lacey. She wanted the one thing he couldn't give her. No, *wouldn't* give her. His duty to the sultanate may have sounded noble, but she understood him too well. All this time he thought he was trying to make up for his past sins, but he was just as driven hiding the fact that he was a man who couldn't meet the high standards placed on him.

All he managed to prove was that he was not worthy of Lacey Maxell.

He had worked hard to make up for his mistakes, and he was a prince who was respected and admired. But was he the man he wanted to be? No. He was making the same mistakes.

Despite the punishment he had received for having a kept woman in the past, Hafiz had made Lacey his mistress. Not his girlfriend or wife. He hadn't thought she needed that status. He had treated her as a sexual convenience instead of the woman he loved.

Hafiz had known about Lacey's upbringing, but he

had done nothing to make her feel safe in the relationship. She had been neglected and abandoned. Marginalized in her family. Instead of showing how grateful he was that she was in his life, he had kept her on the sidelines of his life.

Hafiz frowned as he gave a good look at his affair with Lacey. He thought their relationship had been perfect. A dream. A fantasy. He thought he had been generous and good to Lacey, but he had failed her.

He had to fix this. Somehow he would show Lacey that she was the most important person in his life. She thought it could only be demonstrated by marriage, but that was wrong. Marriage was about alliances and property. It was about lineage and power.

He would prove to Lacey that marriage had nothing to do with love.

Lacey sighed as she tiredly unlocked the door to her apartment. The stupor that had encased her almost a week ago when she left Hafiz now felt cracked and brittle. Exhaustion had seeped in. She couldn't wait to tumble into bed, regardless of the fact that it would be cold and lonely.

She pushed the door open and stumbled to a halt as she was greeted by Damask roses everywhere. Lacey inhaled the heavy fragrance with her gasp of surprise. The front room looked like a garden with red and pink flowers.

An image splintered through her mind. St. Louis, in the hotel's penthouse suite. Hafiz dragging a rose bud along her naked body. Longing swept through her as a flush of red crept under her pale skin.

"Lacey, I have to know," her roommate Priya said

as she strolled into the room, wearing wrinkled pajamas. "What have you done to deserve all these flowers?"

"They're for me?" Her stomach clenched. She'd sensed they were. Only one person would send her flowers. Only one man would make such a grand gesture. Trust Hafiz to disregard her demands and to this extent. Suddenly she was a challenge that he had to overcome. "Uh...nothing."

Priya cast a disbelieving look. "No guy goes through all this trouble without a reason," she said as she walked over to one oversized bouquet and stroked the fragile petals. "And this one is very sure he has no competition. He didn't sign the cards."

Lacey felt her mouth twist into a bittersweet smile. Hafiz didn't need to say anything because the flowers said it all. He wanted to remind her of the passion between them, the love they shared and of what she was turning her back on.

As if she was in a trance, Lacey walked from one bouquet to the next. The shades of pink and red thawed the coldness inside her. She felt the vibrant flowers questioning her choice to exist without Hafiz. Lacey sighed, knowing she should have ignored the bouquets and gone straight to bed.

"Prince Hafiz doesn't want you to forget him," Priya said with a sigh and placed her hands on her hips. "As if you could."

"I'm not getting back together with him."

"If you say so," her roommate said softly.

She bent her head and brushed her cheek against the soft petals. "I've learned that being with him wasn't worth the tears," she lied.

"No guy is," Priya muttered.

Lacey pressed her lips together. Hafiz was worth it. What she had really learned was that he didn't think *she* was worth the sacrifice or the struggle. Hafiz desired her, he may even believe that he loved her, but he didn't love her enough.

"I should call...and tell him to stop," Lacey said. She needed to let him know that she couldn't be wooed like the first time. She understood the rules now. Another affair with him would destroy her.

"Uh-huh." Priya rolled her eyes. "Right."

Was she kidding herself? Lacey wondered as she grabbed her cell phone from her purse and headed for her bedroom. Maybe those flowers stirred up a longing she didn't feel strong enough to deny. Maybe she was desperate to hear from Hafiz, and she was jumping on to this weak excuse. Lacey knew she should talk herself out of it, but instead she paced the floor as she called, wondering why she hadn't deleted his number. She held the phone to her ear with shaky fingers.

"Hello, Lacey."

She halted in the middle of her room. "Hafiz." She closed her eyes, tears instantly welling. Her heartbeats stuttered as a shiver swept through her. He sounded so close to her, as if his mouth was pressed against her ear, ready to whisper sweet nothings. Lacey curled her head into her shoulders, wanting to hold on to the feeling, wanting it to be real. "Thank you for the flowers, but I don't think you should be sending me presents," she said huskily. She gritted her teeth. She needed to be firm.

"Why?" His voice was silky and smooth, heating her body from the inside out.

Lacey frowned. Why? Was he kidding? Wasn't it obvious? "Because it's not—" she resumed pacing as she searched for the word "—appropriate."

"When have we ever been appropriate?" Hafiz's sexy chuckle weakened her knees.

She had to follow through and tell him to stop. She had to be strong. "I mean it," she said sternly, hoping he didn't catch the slight waver. "I don't want anything from you."

"That's not true."

She closed her eyes as his low voice made her skin tingle. It wasn't true. She wanted everything from him. But why would he give it to her? After a year of eagerly accepting whatever he offered, she knew Hafiz thought he could wear her down. That this was some sort of negotiation.

She couldn't live that way anymore. She deserved more. She deserved everything. She refused to settle.

"I've already told you that I'm not interested in married men."

Hafiz was quiet for a moment. "What if I broke the engagement?" he asked.

Her breath hitched in her throat. "Would you?" Her knees started to wobble. Was it because of her? Was he going to give the palace an ultimatum? "Could you?"

"I'm not interested in marriage."

"Oh." She sank on the bed. So many emotions fought inside her, struggling to surface, that they felt as if they would burst through her skin. Hope soared through her, and realization pulled her down. He may no longer be the playboy prince, but he also had no interest in marriage. With her, with anyone.

As much as she didn't want him to get married, she

also wanted to weep because she couldn't be with him and never would. "But it's only a matter of time before the palace can prove why marriage is necessary."

"I don't need a wife to be a good prince."

"Now, there you are wrong," Lacey said as she lay down on the bed and drew her knees to her stomach. "You need a woman at your side. A family of your own."

"I had that with you," he reminded her, his voice filled with such tenderness that she ached. "But Rudaynah wouldn't recognize it like that. The palace would never accept it."

And the ties that bound him to Rudaynah were too powerful for her to cut. Hafiz might withstand the burdens placed on him, but not if he held on to her. Lacey winced with pain as she had to make a decision, her face already wet with tears. She had to be the strong one, or they both were headed for destruction.

She took a deep breath. She could do this. She had to do this and take the brunt of the fall. Even if it meant she would wither and die, she would do it, as long as Hafiz thrived and flourished. "What we had was good." She choked out the words. "But we can never recapture it."

"Lacey?" Hafiz asked in an urgent tone.

"No more presents." She thought she was going to gag on her tears. "No more trying to… No more…." She disconnected the call and turned off the phone.

Lacey curled up into a ball as her spirit howled with agony. She clutched the phone, the last tangible connection she had with Hafiz, to her chest. Her weary body convulsed as she cried.

She wished she could disintegrate. But she knew

the ramifications of her decision were just beginning. She had to live without Hafiz, and she had to
be ruthless about it. Starting now. It meant leaving
Abu Dhabi. Tonight. Without a trace. Without hope.

Hafiz stood at the arched window and watched the
laborers set up the decorations along the route to the
palace. The colorful flags and banners celebrated his
upcoming nuptials while street vendors displayed wedding souvenirs.

He wished he could be as excited about the week-
long ceremony. Maybe, if it had been a different bride.
A woman with copper hair and a smile that warmed
his heart. A woman he loved and who fiercely loved
him in return.

"Having second thoughts?"

He turned to the sound of his brother's voice. From
the concern lining the crown prince's face, Hafiz knew
he must look like hell.

Ashraf strode down the open hallway, the desert
morning wind tugging his white robe. His younger
brother looked how a crown prince should. Hafiz felt
scruffy and tarnished in comparison in his tunic and
jeans.

That was no surprise. Ashraf was the perfect son.
The perfect prince. And did it all effortlessly when
Hafiz failed spectacularly.

While Ashraf embraced tradition, Hafiz always
questioned it. Hafiz was tempted by the world outside of Rudaynah, and Ashraf preferred to stay home.
Hafiz couldn't resist the charms of an inappropriate
woman. From all accounts, his brother lived like a
monk, nothing distracting him as he fulfilled the role

of the heir apparent. One day he would be the benevolent sultan this country needed. Rudaynah would be in good hands with Ashraf on the throne.

"I was thinking about something else," Hafiz said.

"Someone else. A woman," Ashraf guessed. "And from the look in your eyes, not the woman you are about to marry."

Hafiz nodded. "Her name is Lacey Maxwell."

No recognition flickered in his brother's eyes. "Who is she?"

"She's my…" Mistress? The term bothered Hafiz. It had been Lacey's status, but the word minimized her place in his life. She was not a sexual plaything. The label of mistress didn't describe her generous spirit or inquisitive mind. It didn't explain how important she had been in his life.

"She's yours," Ashraf said simply.

"She should be my bride." It hurt to say it. He hadn't said it to Lacey, and now it was too late. He gave voice to the idea, even though he knew it couldn't happen. And yet…Hafiz pushed away from the window.

"I know that look," Ashraf said. "Whatever you're thinking, just forget about it."

"You don't know what's going through my mind," Hafiz said with a scowl.

Ashraf grabbed Hafiz's arm. "Back out of this wedding and you could lose everything."

Okay, so his brother was a mind reader. "I've already lost everything," Hafiz replied.

"Not quite. This is just wedding nerves," Ashraf said, his fingers biting into Hafiz's arm. "Marry the sultan's choice and keep this Lacey Maxwell on the side."

"No, she deserves better. She should be the one who should have my family name. I don't want to hide how I feel about her anymore."

"Listen to me, Hafiz. I'm giving you advice even though it's against my best interest," Ashraf said. "I understand you will be made crown prince once you marry."

The pause between them sat uncomfortably on Hafiz. "Does everyone know about that agreement?" he finally asked. "Don't worry, Ashraf. Knowing the sultan, he will find a loophole to prevent that from happening."

"Typical Hafiz," Ashraf muttered. "You always think someone is going to betray you. That they are destined to fail you."

"I'm cautious," Hafiz corrected. "The more I know of this world and the more I understand people, I become more cautious."

"That shouldn't include your family." The shadows darkened on his face. "Despite what you may think, I didn't betray you when I became crown prince. I had to preserve the line of succession."

Hafiz drew back, astounded by the guilt stamped on his brother's face. "I don't blame you. I blame myself. I'm sorry you were dragged into this. In fact—" Hafiz tilted his head as a thought occurred to him "—you were affected most of all by what happened."

"You have the chance to redeem yourself and reclaim the title of crown prince."

"Maybe I don't want it anymore," Hafiz said. "Maybe I found something better."

"Like the title of Lacey's husband?" Ashraf asked in disbelief.

He wasn't worthy of that title. He had disappointed Lacey too many times. But he was willing to spend the rest of his life earning the right to be with her.

"You are very close to regaining your birthright," his brother said. "Don't ruin it now."

He was very aware of completing his ten-year quest, and yet he didn't think it was going to happen. He didn't believe it should happen. "Sometimes I think ruling Rudaynah was never my destiny."

"What has gotten into you?" Ashraf asked. "This isn't you talking. This is Lacey."

Lacey made him look at his life differently. She showed him what really mattered. "Perhaps I was only supposed to hold on to the crown prince title temporarily."

Ashraf gave him a suspicious look. "Do you really believe this, or are you trying to talk yourself into giving it up again?"

"I was holding on to the title until you were ready."

"You were born a crown prince," Ashraf said, his voice rising with anger. "You were destined to take care of this country, just like you were destined to marry for duty."

"I marry tomorrow," Hafiz said, grimacing.

His brother studied him carefully. "If you don't marry, you will be exiled. For life."

Hafiz flinched. He lifted his head and allowed the cool breeze to glide across his skin. Inhaling the scent of palm trees and sand warmed from the sun, he felt the land beckon his Bedouin blood. He opened his eyes and stared at the dunes in the distance, feeling the depth of his connection to his ancestors.

"Marry their choice of bride." Ashraf gave him a

firm shake. "You were going to before. What could possibly have changed?"

"I found out what life was like without Lacey." Life without any contact with his woman was slowly destroying him. Hafiz returned his attention to the horizon, wondering where she could be. She'd vanished, sending her message loud and clear. *Don't follow me. Don't find me. Get on with your life.*

"Do you have any idea what life will be like without Rudaynah?" Ashraf asked.

Living away from the land he loved was a misery all of its own. No matter where he had been and how much he enjoyed his travels, his heart always heard the call from the land of his people. Sometimes the ancient call brushed against him like a haunting song. Other times, it crashed against him with the beat of tribal drums. "I've lived elsewhere," Hafiz finally said.

"But always knowing that you could return in an instant," Ashraf pointed out.

Hafiz closed his eyes, and his shoulders sagged. Was he wrong to consider life with Lacey when she'd made it clear she'd moved on without him? Was it foolish to hope for the impossible or was his faith in his love being tested?

"No matter what happens, you are my brother, and that will never change."

Hafiz inhaled sharply as the emotion welled in his chest. Ashraf would never know how important it was to hear those words. He stepped forward and embraced his brother.

Ashraf returned the embrace. "And when I reign," he promised fiercely, "you will be invited back to Rudaynah with open arms."

"Thank you." His words were muffled into his brother's shoulders.

Ashraf stepped away and met his brother's gaze. "But our father could reign for years. Decades. Are you willing to risk exile for that long?"

Hafiz realized he couldn't answer that. What did that say about him and the strength of his love for Lacey? "I don't know."

"Rudaynah is a part of you," his brother reminded him. "You can't deny that."

"But Lacey is a part of me, as well." To deny that was to refuse the man he was. The man he could potentially be.

"Then for the next twenty-four hours you need to decide which one you can live without." Ashraf pressed his lips together as his stark face tightened with apprehension. "Because this time, my brother, there's no second chance."

CHAPTER FOURTEEN

THE ELEGANT SURROUNDINGS in the lounge seemed a world away from the trendy nightclubs and blues bars of her past. She *was* a world away, Lacey decided as her fingers flew over the piano keys. Istanbul was a culturally diverse city, but it wasn't home.

Home. Lacey gave a slight shake of her head. A simple word but a complicated idea. Home wasn't St. Louis. She had no family or connection there. Nor was it Abu Dhabi. While she had friends in the beautiful city, she didn't feel as if she had belonged.

She chose to move to Istanbul because it felt like a bridge between Hafiz's world and hers. She tried to take the changes in stride, but she felt the loss of everything familiar. Of everything she'd left behind.

The only time she had felt at peace was in the penthouse apartment in Rudaynah. Lacey didn't know why she missed that place so much. She had been hidden and isolated. She couldn't count on the basic necessities. She'd had difficulty living in the sultanate, but that apartment had been the one place where she and Hafiz could be together.

She wondered what had happened to the apartment. Hafiz undoubtedly got rid of it. He no longer needed a hideaway, since he would live in the palace with his wife.

Lacey's fingers paused on the piano keys for a moment as the pain ripped through her. She continued to play, her touch a little harder, as she imagined Hafiz as a newlywed.

The last news she read about Rudaynah was about the preparations for his wedding. After that, she stopped searching for information about the sultanate. It didn't matter if his marriage was arranged or if his bride was incompatible. Hafiz would do whatever it took to make the marriage work. Even give up the woman he loved.

When the audience applauded while the last mournful note clung to the air, a uniformed waiter approached the piano. "A request." He presented his silver serving tray with a flourish.

The Damask rose lying on the cream card caught her attention. The sight of the pale pink flower was like a punch in the stomach. They were just like the roses Hafiz used to send her.

Lacey swallowed and hesitated before she took it from the waiter. Her hands trembled as she nestled the fragrant flower between her fingers before picking up the card.

She stared at bold slashes in black ink. Lacey blinked, scrunching her eyes closed before opening them wide. She stared incomprehensively at Hafiz's handwriting.

It couldn't be. It looked like Hafiz's scrawl only because she was thinking of him. She was always thinking of him. But the request was for the song Hafiz always wanted her play. It had been their song.

The clink of stemware clashed in her ears. The murmur of different languages boomed in her head. She wet her suddenly dry lips with the tip of her tongue. "Where did you get this?" she asked huskily. She felt as if she was paralyzed with shock.

"That man." Lacey's heart leaped into her throat as the blood roared in her ears. From the corner of her eyes, she saw the waiter pointed in the direction of a window that offered a breathtaking view of the Bosphorus strait. "Well, the man who had been over there," he said with a shrug and left.

Lacey's shoulders tightened, and her pulse continued to pound a staccato beat. Had it been Hafiz? If so, then why did he leave once he found her? Had he given into temptation to see her one more time and thought better of it? She couldn't stop the pang of betrayal even when she wanted him to stay away.

Lacey cast a furtive glance around the lounge, ignoring the disappointment that flooded her bones. She didn't understand how Hafiz had found her. She thought she had made it impossible for him to follow, but then the prince never gave up on a challenge. The more difficult the test, the more determined he was to conquer.

She returned her attention to the rose in her hands. She thought she would never hear from Hafiz again. She had been his vice and the one thing in the way of his goals. No matter what she did, she could never give him what he needed.

This time he had stayed away longer. She knew it was because of his upcoming wedding. It had been ridiculously easy to avoid all news sources after that tidbit of information. She wouldn't have been able to look at his wedding pictures or cope with comparing herself and his chosen bride. But why did he seek her out? Was the pull just too strong to deny?

Rubbing the rose petals with short, agitated strokes, Lacey gave into temptation and brought the exquisite flower to her nose. Inhaling the delicate fragrance, she relived everything from the instant Hafiz invaded her life to the moment she'd retreated from his.

Regret seized her heart until the last of her strength oozed out. With clumsy fingers, Lacey set the pink flower aside on the grand piano. She couldn't cope with the sweet ache of remembering.

Her gaze fell upon the card again, wincing at the song title. The lyrics had captured how she felt about Hafiz. About them. She'd had so much faith in their love. She had believed anything was possible.

Now she knew better. Lacey wanted to crumple the card in her fists and toss it away. She knew the song by heart, had sung it to Hafiz countless times, but she no longer had the resilience to play the song. It held a glimpse of her innocent, carefree days. It was a testament of her naïve love.

And she still loved Hafiz. That was how naïve she truly was. Even though he was forbidden, married and out of reach, she still loved him.

Her love was actually stronger than when she first played the song. It might be as battered and bruised as her heart, but her feelings reached a depth she couldn't have even imagined a year ago.

Lacey paused at the thought, her fingers curved over the ivory keys. She couldn't play it. Not now, not here. This was a song just for him, not for a roomful of strangers. She would only bare her soul for Hafiz.

She *wouldn't* play it, Lacey decided, despite his request. Even if he were here, she wouldn't cave. If he were watching over her, she would play him a different song, one that offered another message but still held a poignant memory. The song she played when they first met.

Her determination wavered as the first few chords twanged deep in her heart. She would have stopped altogether, but an inner need overrode her misery, guiding her through the song. Her smoky voice was coaxed out of her raw throat, occasionally hitching and breaking with emotion. She closed her eyes, fighting back the tears as the last note was wrung out of her, depleting her remaining strength.

The enthusiastic applause sounded far away when she felt a shadow fall over her. Lacey froze, instinctively ducking her chin. She knew who was standing next to her before she inhaled a trace of the familiar scent of sandalwood.

Lacey was reluctant to look up. She wasn't strong enough to see Hafiz and let go of him again. But she also wasn't strong enough to deny herself one more glance.

Cautiously opening her eyes, Lacey saw the expensive leather shoe on the traditional Persian rug. Her chest tightened as her gaze traveled along the black pinstripe trousers. She remembered every inch of Hafiz. The crimson red tie lay flat against his muscular chest, and the suit jacket stretched against his powerful shoulders.

Her pulse skipped hard as she looked at Hafiz's face. Her skin flushed as she stared at his harsh, lean features. When she looked into his eyes, Lacey felt the full force of his magnetic power crash over her.

Hope and devastation escaped her fractured heart. *Hafiz.*

She couldn't turn away. "What are you doing here?" Her voice croaked.

"Why didn't you play my request?" he asked softly. His voice skittered across her skin, blanketing it with goose bumps.

Lacey gnawed her bottom lip. She didn't expect the gentleness. His reticence was surprising. In fact, it bothered her. Where was the primal man who made a fierce claim on her?

She cringed as she remembered how she'd misunderstood his motives the last time he sought her out. She wasn't going to repeat that mistake. "That's not an answer," she said as she reached for the flower.

Hafiz's watchful eyes made her feel awkward. Her simple black dress suddenly felt tight against her chest and hips. The silky fabric grazed against her sensitive skin.

"When are you taking your break?" he asked.

"Now." She covered the keys and stood up abruptly. How could she work when he was nearby? At the moment, she didn't care if she received a reprimand for her boss or got docked in pay. "What are you doing here?" she repeated as she stepped away from the piano.

He arched his eyebrow in warning. "I'm here for you."

Lacey's brisk stride faltered when she heard the words she craved. But she knew better. There had to be a catch, a dark side to her deepest wish. She kept walking and sensed him following her.

"Hafiz, we've been through this," she said, grateful for her firm tone that came out of nowhere. "I am not available every time you're in town. I'm not a one-night stand. And I don't sleep with married men."

"I'm not married."

Lacey whirled around and stared at Hafiz. "What? How is the possible?"

"Is that why you didn't play my request?" his voice rumbled.

The rose threatened to snap, and she relaxed her grip. "No. Why are you not married? You were supposed to have your wedding after Eid."

"I refused." A shadow flickered in his dark eyes. Lacey had a feeling his refusal wasn't as easy as he made it sound.

"When? Why? I don't understand. You had to. There was no way out of it."

"I found a way." Hafiz dipped his head next to hers. "Why didn't you play my request?" He was so close, sending a burst of sensations spraying through her veins. "Because you thought I was married?"

Lacey stopped in front of the lounge's entrance and folded her arms across her chest. He wasn't married. The relief swirled inside her, only to be pulled down by a heavy sadness. One day Hafiz would have to marry, and she wouldn't be the bride.

"Did you forget the words to the song?" he asked softly. "Like you tried to forget us?"

She didn't know if it would be wise to explain anything. To encourage a love that was impossible. "You wouldn't understand," she finally said.

"You don't know that," he said as he placed his large hand against the gentle swell of her hip. The contact nearly undid her. Lacey stiffened, fighting the urge to sway into his body and melt against his heat.

She needed to calm down before her heart splintered. Lacey cleared her throat. "I don't play that song anymore. It reminds me of our time together."

His fingers flexed against her spine. "And you regret what we had?" Hafiz's penetrating eyes made her feel vulnerable and exposed. "Do you regret loving me?"

Lacey exhaled wearily. Nothing could be further from the truth. In a way, her life would be so much easier if she regretted her love. "I told you that you wouldn't understand," she said as she strode away.

She didn't get very far. Before she knew it, her back was pressed against one of the alabaster columns. The Damask rose fluttered to the champagne-colored carpet as Hafiz barricaded her with his strong arms. Her eyes widened anxiously as he leaned into her. "Make me understand," he growled.

The anguish deepened the lines of his stark face, and she struggled with the wrenching need to erase it from him altogether. Lacey tilted her head in the direction of the piano. "I don't play that song because it's about you. How you changed my life, how you changed me. How much you mean to me and what I would do to keep you." She pressed her clammy palms against the column, but they streaked against the cool, slick surface. "And that is why it belongs *only* to you."

Comprehension flashed through his bronze eyes. "Ah." Hafiz straightened and removed his hands from the alabaster.

Lacey frowned at his sudden retreat. She'd revealed more than she was comfortable with, and this was how he responded. "Ah, what?" she asked defensively, doing her best not to feel slighted. Why was he pulling away? "I knew you wouldn't understand."

"No, I do." The corner of mouth slowly slanted up. "It's how I feel when I give you this."

She watched with growing alarm as he removed his royal ring from his finger. The gold caught the light. Lacey stared at it, transfixed, unable to move until Hafiz grasped her wrist.

Lacey bunched her hand up into a fist. "What are you doing?" she asked in a scandalized whisper. She struggled to keep her arm flat against the column.

"I'm giving you my ring." He easily plucked her hand and moved it closer to him.

Her knuckles whitened as her tension grew. There was no way she was going to let him. She knew the rules, but she could only imagine the consequences of breaking them. "But, but—it's a royal ring." She gestured wildly at it. "Only someone born into royalty is allowed to wear it."

"And," Hafiz added as he leisurely caressed her fingers, enticing them to unfurl, "I'm allowed to give it to the woman I want to marry."

Lacey's hand tightened, her short fingernails digging into her palm. Her mouth gaped open as the remainder of her argument dissolved on her tongue. "Marry?"

"Yes." His gaze ensnared her. The depths challenged. Tempted. Pleaded. "Marry me, Lacey."

"I—I—" she spluttered, unable to connect two words together. Her heartbeat drummed painfully against her breastbone. "I…can't."

"Why not?" Hafiz didn't sound crestfallen. His

taunting tone indicated that he was primed and ready to argue. And win.

Her gaze clung on to the ring. It looked big and heavy. It belonged on Hafiz's hand, not hers.

"I'm not from the right family," she blurted out. She knew her shortcomings.

"I disagree," Hafiz said confidently. "You are the only family I need. Together we will create the home we always wanted."

And he would give it to her. He would be loving and protective. Hafiz would do everything in his power to make her feel safe and secure.

She felt herself weakening, but she couldn't let that happen. She had to be strong. Strong enough for the both of them. Lacey struggled to voice another reason. "I'm your mistress."

"You are my heart," he corrected in a husky voice. "Marry me."

"I can't marry you." Her firm statement trailed off in a whimper. She frowned ferociously and tried again. "I can't return to Rudaynah."

His hand stilled against hers. "Neither can I," he confessed.

His words froze her racing thoughts. Hafiz couldn't return to Rudaynah? What was he saying? "What?" The startled question tore past her lips as she stared at him with horror.

"I've been exiled." He broke eye contact, the frown lines burrowing into his forehead. "Banished for life."

Her hand fell from his. "Why?" she cried out, but instinctively she knew. "Because of me?" She sagged against the column as tears burned her throat and eyes.

Her body threatened to collapse into a broken heap on to the floor.

"Because I refuse to give you up again," Hafiz said, his voice rough with emotion. "I was given the choice to remain in my homeland or be with you. I chose you."

Hafiz chose her. He gave up everything he wanted for her. It didn't make her feel triumphant. The news destroyed her. Lacey struggled to contain the sob rising in her throat. "You shouldn't have done that."

"I don't want to stay in Rudaynah if I can't have you at my side."

She wanted to be at his side, but not if it cost him his world. "You say that now, but one day you're…"

"I refuse to hide how I feel about you, Lacey," Hafiz said in a low voice as his eyes flashed with determination. "I have nothing to be ashamed about."

"How can you say that? After all you did, you didn't get the respect you deserve. Your father exiled you." Lacey cringed as she said those words. She knew how important his status was to Hafiz.

She'd sacrificed everything, but she wasn't able to give Hafiz the one thing he needed. He hadn't redeemed himself in the eyes of his family. He would never gain the recognition that belonged to him.

Lacey covered her face with her hands. She didn't want this to happen. She had done everything in her power to prevent Hafiz from losing the world he fought so hard to keep.

"Hafiz, you can't give up being a prince," she begged. "Not for me. Not for anyone. It's who you are."

"No, it's not." His voice was clear and steady. "I am myself, I am who I want to be, when I am with you."

"No… No…"

"I'm not fully alive unless I'm with you," he said as he wrapped his fingers around her wrists and lowered her hands. "I'm not myself when you are not around. I love you, Lacey."

Tears dampened her eyelashes. "That can't be," she whispered. "It's impossible."

He cupped his hand against her cheek. The gentle touch contrasted with the demand in his eyes. "All I know is that this ring belongs only to you. *I* belong only to you." He held the glittering royal ring in front of her.

She slowly shook her head. "Hafiz…" Her eyes widened when he bent down on one knee in front of her.

"Lacey Maxwell, will you do me the honor of marrying me?"

EPILOGUE

"LACEY, WHERE ARE you?" Hafiz looked over the assembly of dignitaries that crowded the throne room and spotted his wife lurking in the shadows. As she turned, the diamonds in her hair shimmered under the chandelier lights.

Pride swelled in his chest as she made her way through the sea of evening gowns and military uniforms. Hafiz watched statesmen and socialites respectfully lower their heads when she passed, but his attention was focused on his woman.

It amazed him how Lacey's regal image concealed her passionate nature. Just thinking about it, he was tempted to sink his fingers in her copper red hair and pull down the sophisticated chignon. The rose taffeta caftan encrusted with iridescent pearls teased his senses as it skimmed her curves with each step she took.

When Lacey drew close, he captured her hand. "The coronation is about to start," Hafiz informed her and entwined his fingers with hers.

Lacey's uncertain smile tugged at his heart. He swore it gleamed more brightly than any jewel or medal in the room. "I'm sure the vizier said I'm not supposed to be here."

"You are right where you belong." He made a mental note to give the adviser a more explicit explanation of the new protocol. No one was going to hide his woman. No one was going to separate him from his wife.

The first few notes of the procession march filtered through the throne room. Exhilaration pressed against his chest. Soon Ashraf would be crowned sultan, and then he and his brother would bring Rudaynah to its full glory. The revitalizing plans that Hafiz dreamt for years could now be realized.

Lacey cast a troubled glance at the empty throne. "Do you regret—"

He shook his head. "No, I have everything I want," he replied truthfully. Most importantly, he had Lacey. He shared a life with the woman he loved and trusted.

She also helped him realize that he didn't need a royal title to take care of his countrymen. In fact, he was more successful without the restraint of royal protocols and rituals. For the past few years they'd traveled worldwide while promoting the Sultanate of Rudaynah's resources to other countries and international businesses.

And now with the passing of his father, Hafiz could return to Rudaynah any time he wanted.

It had been a bittersweet homecoming. Hafiz had felt like a stranger in his own country until Lacey lured him to the dunes. She knew that once he visited the desert, he would reconnect with the land.

The corner of his mouth kicked up in a wicked smile as he remembered how he and Lacey had spent those cold desert nights. His mind buzzed with anticipation as he rested his hand on her stomach. It was fate to have his first child conceived in Rudaynah.

Lacey's eyes widened from his possessive touch. "Stop that!" she whispered fiercely as she tried to dislodge his hand with a subtle push. "The formal announcement isn't until the end of the month. People will speculate."

Hafiz lowered his head and brushed his mouth against hers. "Let them talk."

* * * * *

MAJESTY, MISTRESS...
MISSING HEIR

CAITLIN CREWS

CHAPTER ONE

JESSA glanced up from her desk automatically when the door to the letting agency was shoved open, and then froze solid in her chair.

It was like a dream—a dream she had had many times. He strode inside, the wet and the cold of the Yorkshire evening swirling around him like a great black cape.

She found herself on her feet without knowing she meant to move, her hands splayed out in front of her as if she could ward him off—keep him from stepping even further into the small office. Into her life, where she could not—would not—allow him to be, ever again.

"There you are," he said in a deep, commanding voice, as if he had satisfied himself simply by laying cold eyes upon her—as if, unaccountably, he had been looking for her.

Jessa's heart thudded against her ribs as her head spun. Was he an apparition, five years later? Was she dreaming?

"Tariq," she said, dazed, as if naming the dream could dispel it.

But Tariq bin Khaled Al-Nur did not look like a dream. He was nothing so insubstantial, or easily forgotten in the light of day. When she had known him he had claimed to be no more than a wealthy, overindulged member of his country's elite class; she knew that he was now its ruler. She hated that she knew—as if that knowledge was written across her face and might suggest to him that she had followed his every move across the years when the truth was, she had wanted only to forget him.

But she could not seem to pull her gaze from his.

Jessa found that all these years later she could remember every detail about Tariq with perfect, shocking clarity, even as the evidence before her made it clear that he was far better—far much *more*—than she had allowed herself to recall. His features were harder, more impenetrable. He was more of a *man,* somehow. It seemed impossible, but her memories had diminished him. The reality of Tariq was powerful, alive—dazzling.

Dangerous.

Jessa tried to concentrate on the danger. It didn't matter that her heart leaped when she saw him, even now. What mattered was the secret she knew she must keep from him. She had foolishly begun to hope that this particular day of reckoning would never come. She looked at him now, clear-eyed thanks to her shock, though that was not the improvement she might have hoped for.

He was hard-packed muscle in a deceptively lean form, all whipcord strength and leashed, impossible power beneath skin the color of nutmeg. Time seemed to stop as Jessa stood in place, cataloging the harsh lines of his face. They were more pronounced than she remembered—the dark slash of his brows beneath his thick black hair, the masculine jut of his nose, and the high cheekbones that announced his royal blood as surely as the supremely confident, regal way he held himself. How could she have overlooked these clues five years ago? How could she have believed him when he'd claimed to be no one of any particular importance?

Those deep green eyes of his, mysterious and nearly black in the early-evening light, connected hard with a part of her she thought she'd buried years before. The part that had believed every lie he'd told her. The part that had missed, somehow, that she was being toyed with by a master manipulator. The part that had loved him heedlessly, recklessly. The part that she feared always would, despite everything.

When he was near her, she forgot herself.

He closed the door behind him, the catch clicking softly on the doorjamb. It sounded to Jessa as loud as a gunshot, and she almost flinched away from it. She could not allow herself to be weak. Not with so much at stake! Because he must know what had happened. There could be no other reason for an appearance like this, here in the forgotten back streets of York at an office that was surely far beneath his imperial notice.

He must know.

With the door closed, the noise of the evening rush in York's pedestrian center disappeared, leaving them enclosed in a tense, uncomfortable silence. The office was too small, and felt tinier by the moment. Jessa's heart hammered against her chest. Panic dug sharp claws into her sides. Tariq seemed to loom over her, to surround her, simply by standing inside the door.

He did not move, nor speak again. He held her gaze with his, daring her to look away. Challenging her. He was effortlessly commanding even in silence. Arrogant. Fierce.

He was not the easygoing playboy she remembered. Gone was his quick smile, his lazy charm. This man was not to be trifled with. This man was the king who had always lurked within the Tariq she'd known, who she'd but glimpsed in passing here and there. A shiver traced cold fingers down her spine and uncurled in her belly.

He must know.

Her pulse sounded too loud in her ears. She could feel their tangled history and her secrets all around her, dragging at her, forcibly reminding her of the darkness she'd fought so hard to escape back then. But she had more to protect now than just herself. She had to think of Jeremy, and what was best for him. Wasn't that what she had always done, no matter the cost to herself?

She let her eyes travel over Tariq, reminding herself that he was just a man, no matter how fierce. And for all his regal bearing now, back then he had disappeared without so much as a word or a backward glance or a forwarding address. He was as treacherous and formidable as the exotic desert that was his home. The exquisitely tailored clothes he wore, silk and cashmere that clung to the bold, male lines of his body, did nothing to disguise the truth of him. He was a warrior. Untamed and wild, like a shock of brilliant color in the midst of grays and browns. He was a predator. She had known it then, on some deep, feminine level, though he had smiled and joked and concealed it. Her body knew it now, and horrified her by thrilling to it even as she fought for control. Her lungs felt tight, as if he sucked up all the air in the room.

She had never thought she would see him again.

She didn't know how to react now that he was in front of her.

"No," she said, astonished to hear that her voice sounded calm even when the world around her seemed to shimmer and shake. It gave her the courage to continue. It didn't matter how compelling he was. His being so compelling had been the problem in the first place! She squared her shoulders. "No. You cannot be here."

His dark brows rose, haughty and proud. His hair, thick

and black and a touch too long for civility, seemed to sparkle with the autumn rain from outside. He kept his impossible, haunting eyes trained on her face. How she had once loved those eyes, which had seemed so sad, so guarded. Tonight they seemed to see right through her. His expression was unreadable.

"And yet here I am." His voice was low, husky, and held the barest hint of the foreign lands he'd come from, wrapped in something both chocolate and smooth. *Dangerous.* And once more—a blatant, unmistakable challenge. It hit Jessa like a fist to the midsection.

"Without invitation," she pointed out, pleased her tone was just this side of curt. Anything to seem stronger than she felt. Anything to look tougher than she was. *Anything to protect Jeremy.*

"Do I require an invitation to enter a letting agent's?" he asked, unperturbed. "You must excuse me if I have forgotten British customs. I was under the impression places such as these encourage walk-in clientele."

"Do you have an appointment?" Jessa asked, forcing her jaw to stop clenching. It was what she would ask any other person who appeared off the street, wasn't it? And really, why should Tariq bin Khaled Al-Nur be any different?

"In a manner of speaking," he said, his tone hinting at some significance that was lost on Jessa, though she sensed he expected her to understand his meaning. "Yes."

His eyes traveled over her, no doubt comparing her to his memories. Jessa felt her cheeks flame, in some combination of distress and fury. She had the sudden worry that she fell short, and then could have kicked herself. Or, preferably, him. Why should she care about such things? Nothing would change the fact that she was an ordinary girl from Yorkshire and he was a king.

"It is nice to see you again, Jessa," Tariq said with a dangerous politeness that did not conceal the ruthlessness beneath. She wished he would not say her name. It was like a caress. It teased at the back of her neck, swirled through her blood, and traced phantom patterns across her skin.

"I'm afraid I can't say the same," she replied coolly. Because she had a spine. Because she needed to get rid of him, and make certain he never returned. Because their past was far too complicated to ever be brought out into the present. "You are the very last person I would ever wish to see again. If you go away quickly, we can pretend it never happened."

Tariq's dark jade eyes seemed to sharpen. He thrust his long, elegant hands into the pockets of his trousers with a casualness Jessa could not quite believe. The Tariq she'd known had been nonchalant, at ease, but that man had never existed, had he? And this man in front of her was nothing like the man Tariq had pretended to be. He was too hard, too fierce.

"I see the years have sharpened your tongue." He considered her. "What else has changed, I wonder?"

There was one specific way she had changed that she could not possibly share with him. Did he already know it? Was he baiting her?

"*I* have changed," Jessa said, glaring at him, deciding that an offense was better than any defense she might try to throw up against this strangely familiar man, who was much more like steel than the lover she remembered. "It's called growing up." She lifted her chin in defiance, and could feel her hands ball into fists at her sides. "I am no longer likely to beg for anyone's attention. Not anymore."

She did not see him move but she had the sense that he tensed, as if readying himself for battle. She braced herself, but he only watched her. Something too ruthless to be a smile curled in the corner of his hard mouth.

"I do not recall a single instance of you begging," Tariq replied, an edge in his dark voice. "Unless you mean in my bed." He let that hang there, as if daring her to remember. Mute, Jessa stared back at him. "But if you wish to reenact some such scene, by all means, do so."

"I think not," she gritted out from between her teeth. She would not think about his bed, or what she had done in it. *She would not.* "My days of clinging to pathetic international playboys are long past."

She felt the air tighten between them. His dark green eyes narrowed, and once again she was reminded that he was not a regular man. He was not even the man she had once known. He was too wild, too unmanageable, and she was a fool to underestimate him—or overestimate herself. Her weakness where he was concerned was legendary, and humiliating, and should have left her when he had.

But she could feel it—feel him—throughout her body, like nothing had changed, even though everything had. Like he still owned and controlled her as effortlessly and carelessly as he had years before. Her breasts felt tight against her blouse, her skin was flushed, and she felt a familiar, sweet, hot ache low in her belly. She bit her lip against the heat that threatened to spill over from behind her eyes and show him all the things she wanted to hide.

She knew she could not let this happen, whatever *this* was. She wanted nothing to do with him. There were secrets she would do anything in her power to keep from him. Chemistry was simply that: a chemical, physical reaction. It meant nothing.

But she did not look away.

* * *

She had haunted him, and Tariq bin Khaled Al-Nur was not a man who believed in ghosts.

He stared at the woman who had tortured him for years, no matter where he went or with whom, and who now had the audacity to challenge him with no thought for her own danger. Tariq considered himself a modern sheikh, a modern king, but he understood in this moment that if he had one of his horses at his disposal he would have no qualm whatsoever about tossing Jessa Heath across the saddle and carrying her away to a tent far off in the desert that comprised most of his homeland on the Arabian Peninsula.

In fact, he would enjoy it.

He was right to have come here. To have faced this woman, finally. Even as she called him names, and continued to defy him. Just as she had done so long before. His mouth twisted in a hard smile.

He knew that he should be furious that she wished to keep him at arm's length, that she dared to poke at him as if he was some insipid weakling. He knew that he should feel shame that he, Sheikh Tariq bin Khaled Al-Nur, King of Nur, had come crawling back to the only woman who had ever dared abandon him. The only woman he had ever missed. Who stood before him now in an ugly suit that did not become her or flatter her lushness, unwelcoming and cold instead of pleased to see him again. He should be enraged at the insult.

But instead, he wanted her.

It was that simple. That consuming. He had finally stopped fighting it.

One look at the curvy body he still reached for in his sleep, her wide eyes the color of cinnamon, her sinful, lickable mouth, and he was hard, ready—alive with need. He could taste her skin, feel the heat of her desire. Or he remembered it. Either way, he needed to be deep inside her once again.

Then, perhaps, they could see how defiant she really was.

"A pathetic playboy, am I?" he asked, keeping his tone light, though he could not disguise the intent beneath. This woman reminded him so strongly of his other, wasted life—yet he still wanted her. He would have her. "An intriguing accusation."

Temper rose in her cheeks, turning ivory to peach. "I can't imagine what that means," she snapped. "It is not an accusation, it's the truth. It is who you are."

Tariq watched her for a long moment. She had no idea how deep his shame for his profligate former existence ran within him. Nor how closely he associated her with all he had been forced to put behind him, and now found so disgusting. He had fought against her hold on him for years, told himself that he only remembered her because she had left him, that he would have left her himself if she'd given him the opportunity, as he had left countless other women in his time.

Still, here he was.

"It means that if I am a playboy, you by definition become one of my playthings, do you not?" he asked. He enjoyed the flash of temper he saw in her face much more than he should have. The warrior inside him was fully roused and ready to take on his opponent. "Does the description distress you?"

"I am not at all surprised to hear you call me a *plaything*." Her mouth twisted. "But I was never yours."

"A fact you made abundantly clear five years ago," he said drily, though he doubted she would mistake the edge beneath. Indeed, she stiffened. "But is this any way for old friends to greet each other after such a long time?" He crossed the room until only the flimsy barrier of her desk stood between them.

"Friends?" she echoed, shaking her head slightly. "Is that what we are?"

Only a few feet separated them, not even the length of his arm. She swallowed, nervously. Tariq smiled. It was as he remembered. She still looked the same—copper curls and cinnamon eyes, freckles across her nose and a wicked, suggestive mouth made entirely for sin. And she was still susceptible to him, even from across a desk. Would she still burn them both alive when he touched her? He couldn't wait to find out.

"What do you suggest?" she asked. Her delicate eyebrows arched up, and that sensual mouth firmed. "Shall we nip out for a coffee? Talk about old times? I think I'll pass."

"I am devastated," he said, watching her closely. "My former lovers are generally far more receptive."

She didn't like that. The flush in her cheeks deepened, and her cinnamon eyes darkened. She stood straighter.

"Why are you here, Tariq?" she asked, in a crisp, no-nonsense voice that both irritated and aroused him. She crossed her arms over her chest. "Are you looking to let a flat in the York area? If so, you'll want to return when the agents are in, so they might help you. I'm afraid they're both out with clients, and I'm only the office manager."

"Why do you think I'm here, Jessa?"

He studied her face, letting the question hang there between them. He wanted to see her reaction. To catalog it. Her fingers crept to her throat, as if she wanted to soothe the beat of her own pulse.

"I cannot imagine any reason at all for you to be here," she told him now, but her voice was high and reedy. She coughed to cover it, and then threw her shoulders back, as if she fancied herself a match for him. "You should go. Now."

And now she ordered him out? Like a servant? Tariq

shifted his weight, balancing on the balls of his feet as if readying himself for combat, and idly imagined how he would make her pay for that slight. He was a king. She should learn how to address him properly. Perhaps on her knees, with that sinfully decadent mouth of hers wrapped around him, hot and wet. It would make a good start.

"If you won't tell me what you want—" she began, frowning.

"You," he said. He smiled. "I want you."

CHAPTER TWO

"ME?" Jessa was taken aback. She would have stepped back, too, but she'd locked her knees into place and couldn't move. "You've come here for *me?*"

She did not believe him. She couldn't, not when his dark eyes still seemed laced with danger and that smile seemed to cut right through her. But there was a tiny, dismaying leap in the vicinity of her heart.

She could face the unwelcome possibility that she might still be a fool where this man was concerned, on a purely physical level. But she had absolutely no intention of giving in to it!

"Of course I am here for you," he said, his eyes hot. One black eyebrow arched. "Did you imagine I happened by a letting agent's in York by accident?"

"Five years ago you couldn't get away from me fast enough," Jessa pointed out. "Now, apparently, you have scoured the countryside to find me. You'll forgive me if I can't quite get my head around the dramatic change in your behavior."

"You must have me confused with someone else," Tariq said silkily. "You are the one who disappeared, Jessa. Not I."

Jessa blinked at him. For a moment she had no idea

what he was talking about, but then, of course, the past came rushing back. She had gone to the doctor's for a routine physical, only to discover that she had been pregnant. Pregnant! She had had no illusions that Tariq would have welcomed the news. She had known he would not. She had needed to get away from him for a few days to pull herself together, to think what she might do while not under the spell his presence seemed to cast around her.

Perhaps she hadn't phoned him. But she hadn't left him.

"What are you talking about?" she asked now. "I was not the one who fled the country!"

His mouth tightened. "You said you were going to the doctor, and then you disappeared. You were gone for days, and then, yes, I left the country. If that is what you want to call it."

"I came back," Jessa said, her voice a low throb, rich with a pain she would have said was long forgotten. "You didn't."

There was an odd, arrested silence.

"You will have heard of my uncle's passing, of course," Tariq said, his gaze hooded. His tone was light, conversational. At odds with the tension that held Jessa in a viselike grip.

"Yes," she said, struggling to match his tone. "It was in all the papers right after you left. It was such a terrible accident." She took care to keep her voice level. "Imagine my surprise when I discovered that the man I'd known as simply the son of a doctor was, as it happened, a member of the royal family and the new king of Nur."

"My father *was* a doctor." His brows rose. "Or do you think I impugned his honor after his death merely for my own amusement?"

"I think you deliberately misled me," she replied evenly, trying not to let her temper get the best of her. "Yes, your father was a doctor. But he was also the younger brother of a king!"

"You will forgive me," Tariq said with great hauteur, "if your feelings did not supercede legitimate safety concerns at the time."

How could he do that? How could he make her feel as if she had wronged him when *he* was the one who had lied and then abandoned her? What was the matter with her?

"Safety concerns?" she asked with a little laugh, as if none of this mattered to her. Because none of it *should* have mattered to her. She had come to terms with her relationship with Tariq years ago. "Is that what you call it? You invented a man who did not exist. Who never existed. And then you pretended to be that man."

He smiled. Jessa thought of wolves. And she was suddenly certain that she did not wish to hear whatever he might say next.

"I'm sorry about your uncle," she murmured instead, her voice soft. Softer than it should have been, when she wanted only to be strong.

"My uncle, his wife, and both of their sons were killed," Tariq said coolly, brushing off her words of condolence. The wolf smile was gone. "And so I am not just King of Nur now, but the very last of its ancient, founding bloodline. Do you know what that means?"

She was suddenly terrified that she knew exactly what that meant, and, more terrifying, what *he* would think it meant. She could not allow it.

"I imagine it means that you have great responsibilities," Jessa said. She couldn't think of any reason he would drop by her office in Yorkshire to discuss the line of succession in his far-off desert kingdom, save one. But surely, if he knew the truth, he would not be wasting his time here with her, would he? Perhaps he only suspected. Either way, she wanted him gone. "Though what would I know about it?" She spread her hands out, to encompass the letting office. "I am an office manager, not a king."

"Indeed." He watched her and yet he made no move. He only kept that dark green gaze trained upon her while the rest of his big, lean body seemed too still, too much raw power unnaturally leashed. As if he was poised and ready to pounce. "I am responsible to my people, to my country, in a way that I was not before. It means that I must think about the future." His voice, his expression, was mocking, but did he mock her, or him? "I must marry and produce heirs. The sooner the better."

All the breath left Jessa's body in a sudden rush. She felt light-headed. Surely he could not mean…? But there was a secret, hidden part of her that desperately hoped he did and yearned for him to say so—to make sense of these past lonely, bittersweet years by claiming her, finally, as his. To fulfill the foolish dream she'd always held close to her heart, and fervently denied. *His wife. Tariq's wife.*

"Don't be absurd," she chided him—and herself. She was nothing. A no one. He was the King of Nur. And even if he had been a regular, accessible man, he was also the only one with whom she had so much tangled history. It was impossible. It had always been impossible. "You cannot marry *me!*"

"First you mock me," Tariq said gently, almost conversationally. And yet the nape of Jessa's neck prickled in warning. "You call me a pathetic playboy. Then you order me to leave this place, like some insignificant insect, and now you scold me like a child." His lips curved into a smile that did not reach his eyes. "Perhaps you forget who I am."

She knew exactly who he was. She knew too well what

he could do to her. What he had done already. She was much more afraid of what he might do now.

"I have not forgotten anything, Tariq," she said, glad that her voice was calm yet strong, as it ought to be. Glad that she sounded capable and unmoved, as she should. "Which is why I must ask you to leave. Again."

Tariq shrugged with apparent ease, but his eyes were hot.

"In any case, you misunderstand me," he said. He smiled slightly. "I am not in the habit of proposing marriage to ex-lovers who harbor such disdain for me, I assure you."

It took a moment for his words to fully sink in. Humiliation followed quickly, thick and hot. It was a dizzying reminder of how she had felt when his mobile phone had come up disconnected, his London flat vacated, one after the other, with her none the wiser. Mortification clawed at her throat and cramped her stomach. Had she really imagined that he had appeared out of nowhere because he wished to *marry* her? She was unbearably foolish, again, as if the past five years had never happened.

But they had happened, she reminded herself. And she had been through far worse than a few moments of embarrassment. It was the memory of what she'd survived, and the hard choices she'd made, that had her pushing the humiliation aside and meeting his gaze. There were more important things in the world than Tariq bin Khaled Al-Nur, and her own mortification. Her cheeks might still be red, but her head was high.

"Then what is it you want?" she asked coolly. "I have no interest in playing games with you."

"I have already told you what I want," he said smoothly, but there was still that hard edge beneath. "Must I repeat myself? I do not recall you being so slow on the uptake, Jessa."

Once again, the way he said her name nearly made her shiver. She shook it off and tried to make sense of what he was saying but then, abruptly, gave up. Why was she allowing this to happen? He had waltzed in after all this time, and cornered her behind her desk? Who did he think he was?

With a burst of irritation, at herself and at him, Jessa propelled herself around the side of her desk and headed for the door of the office. She didn't have to stand there and let him talk to her this way. She didn't have to listen to him. He was the one who had had all the choices years ago, because she hadn't known any better and hadn't *wanted* to know any better, but she wasn't that besotted girl any longer. That girl had died years ago, thanks to him. He had no idea what she'd been through, and she didn't owe him anything, including explanations.

"Where do you imagine you can go?" he asked, in an idle, detached tone, as if he could not possibly have cared less. She knew better than to believe that, somehow. "That you believe I cannot follow?"

"I have some ideas about where you can go," Jessa began without turning back toward him, temper searing through her as she stalked toward the door.

But then he touched her, and she had not heard him move. No warning, no time to prepare—

He touched her, and her brain shorted out.

His long fingers wrapped around her arm just above the elbow. Even through the material of her suit jacket, Jessa could feel the heat emanating from him—fire and strength and his hard palm against her arm, like a brand. Like history repeating itself. Like a white-hot electricity that blazed through her and rendered her little more than ash and need.

He closed the distance between them, pulling her up hard against the unyielding expanse of his chest. She gasped, even as his other hand came around to her opposite hip, anchoring her against him, her back to his front, their two bodies coming together like missing puzzle pieces.

She could feel him everywhere. The sweet burn where his powerful body connected with hers, and even where he did not touch her at all. Her toes curled in her shoes. Her lungs ached. Deep in her belly she felt an intoxicating pulse, while between her legs she felt herself grow damp and ready. For him. All for him, as always.

How could her body betray her like this? How could it be so quick to forget?

"Take your hands off me," she demanded, her voice hoarse with an emotion she refused to name. At once, he stepped back, released her, and all that fire was gone. She told herself she did not feel a hollowness, did not feel bereft. She turned slowly to face him, as if she could not still feel the length of his chest pressed against her.

She thought of Jeremy. Of what she must hide.

Of what Tariq would do if he knew.

"Is this what you think of me?" she asked, her voice low, her temper a hot drumbeat inside her chest. She raised her chin. The hoarseness was gone as if it had never been. "You think you can simply turn up after all this time, after vanishing into thin air and leaving me with nothing but your lies, and I'll leap back into your arms?"

"Once again, you seem to be confused," Tariq said, his voice hushed, his gaze intent. Almost demanding. But there was something else there that made a shiver of silent warning slide along her spine. "I am not the one who ran away. I am the one who has reappeared, despite all the time that has passed."

"You are also the one who lied about who he was," Jessa pointed out. "Hardly the moral high ground."

"You have yet to mention where you disappeared to all those years ago," Tariq said, his voice sliding over her, through her, and making her body hum with an awareness she didn't want to accept. "Exactly what moral high ground are you claiming?"

And, of course, she could not tell him that she had found out she was pregnant. She could not tell him that she had suspected, even though she had loved him to distraction, that he would react badly. She could not tell him that after days of soul-searching, she had come back to London to share the news with him, only to find him gone as if he had never been. As if she had made him up.

And she certainly could not tell him that he was a father now. There was absolutely no doubt in her mind that Tariq's reaction to the news would be brutal. She sucked in a breath and forced a serene expression onto her face.

"The truth is, I have no interest in digging up the past," Jessa said. She shrugged. "I got over you a long time ago."

His eyes were like jade, and glittered with something darker.

"Is that so?" he asked in the same quiet voice, as if they were in the presence of something larger. She shoved the notion away, and had to restrain herself from reaching out and shoving *him* away, too. She knew better than to touch him.

"I'm sorry if you expected me to be sitting in an attic somewhere, weeping over your picture," Jessa said, trying to inject a little laughter into her voice, as if that might ease the tension in the room and in her own body. Tariq's eyes narrowed. "But I've moved on. I suggest you do the same. Aren't you a sheikh? Can't you snap your fingers and create a harem to amuse yourself?"

She thought for a tense, long moment that she had gone too far. He was, after all, a king now. And far more unnerving. But he looked away for a moment, and his mouth curved in something very nearly a smile.

"I must marry," Tariq said. Then he turned his head and captured her gaze with his. "But before I can do that particular duty, it seems I must deal with you."

"Deal with me?" She shook her head, not understanding. Not wanting to try to understand him. "Why should you wish to deal with me now, when you have had no interest in me for all these years?"

"You and I have unfinished business." It was a statement of fact. His eyebrows rose, daring her to disagree.

Jessa thought for a moment she might faint. But then something else kicked in, some deep protective streak that would not allow her to fall before this man so easily. He was formidable, yes. But she was stronger. She'd had to be.

Maybe, on some level, she had always known she would have to face him someday.

"We do not have unfinished business, or anything else," she declared, throwing down the gauntlet. She raised her chin and looked him in the eye. "Anything we had died five years ago, in London."

"That is a lie." His tone brooked no argument. He was the king, handing down his judgment. She ignored it.

"Let me tell you what happened to me after you left the country," Jessa continued in the same tone, daring him to interrupt her. His nostrils flared slightly, but he was silent. She took a step closer, no longer afraid of his nearness. "Did you ever think about it? Did it cross your mind at all?"

How proud she had been of that internship, straight out of university that long-ago summer. How certain she had been that she was taking the first, crucial steps to a glittering, high-powered career in the city. Instead, she had met

Tariq in her first, breathless week in London, and her dreams had been forever altered.

"You were the one who left—" he began, frowning.

"I left for two and half days," she said, cutting him off. "It's not quite on a par with what you did, is it? It wasn't enough that you left the country, disconnected your mobile phone, and put your flat up for sale," she continued, keeping her gaze steady on his. "Actually telling me you no longer wished to see me was beneath you, I suppose. But you also withdrew your investments."

His frown deepened, and his body tensed. Did he expect a blow? When he had been the one to deliver all of them five years ago, and with such cold-blooded, ruthless efficiency? Jessa almost laughed.

"What did you think would happen?" she asked him, an old anger she had thought she'd forgotten coloring her voice. She searched the dark green eyes she had once artlessly compared to primeval forests, and saw no poetry there any longer. Only his carelessness. "I was the intern who was foolish enough to have an affair with one of the firm's biggest clients. I had no idea you were *the* biggest client. And it was smiled upon as long as I kept you happy, of course."

Jessa could picture the buttoned-up, hypocritical investment bankers she had worked for back then. She could see once more the knowing way they had looked at her when they thought she was just one more fringe benefit the firm could provide for Tariq's pleasure. Just another perk. A bottle of the finest champagne, the witless intern, whatever he liked. But then he had severed his relationships—not only with Jessa, but with the firm that handled his speculative investments, all in the span of three quick days following the September Bank Holiday.

"I thought it best to make a clean break," he said, and there was strain in his voice, as if he fought against some strong emotion, but Jessa knew from experience that his emotions were anything but strong, no matter how they might appear.

"Yes, well, you succeeded in breaking something," she told him, the anger gone as quickly as it had come, leaving only a certain sadness for the girl she had been. "My career. Into tiny little pieces. They sacked me, of course. And once they did, who do you think wanted to hire the promiscuous intern who'd lost her previous firm so much money along with such a high-profile client?"

His mouth flattened and his eyes flashed that dark jade fire. But Jessa remembered the look of disgust on the senior partner's face when he'd called her into his office. She remembered the harsh words he'd used to describe her behavior, the same behavior that had received no more than a wink and a smile the week before. She'd stood there, pale and trembling, unable to process what was happening. She was pregnant. And Tariq had not only left her so brutally, he had left England altogether, to become a king. On top of all that, he had never been the person he'd claimed to be, the person she'd loved. It was all a lie.

"And that was the end of my brilliant career in London," Jessa said in a quiet, matter-of-fact manner. She tilted her head slightly to one side as she considered him. "I suppose I should thank you. It takes some people a lifetime to figure out that they're not cut out for that world. Thanks to you, it took me only a few short months."

"My uncle was killed," Tariq said in a low, furious voice, his body seeming to expand as he stood in the middle of the office floor, taking over the entire space. "I was suddenly thrust upon the throne, and I had to secure my position. I did not have time to soothe hurt feelings half the world away."

"They don't have notepaper or pens where you come from, then," Jessa said sarcastically, pretending she was unaffected by his magnetism, his power. "Much less telephones. Perhaps you communicate using nothing save the force of your royal will?"

He looked away then, muttering something harsh in a language she was just as happy she didn't know. In profile, he was all hard edges except for his surprisingly mobile mouth. He looked like the king he was. Noble features, royal bones. The sort of profile that would end up stamped on coins.

When she thought about it that way, the absurdity of the situation was almost too much for her. They should never have met in the first place—it was all too fantastical. It was one thing to dream of fairy-tale princes when one was fresh out of university and still under the impression that the world was waiting only to be bent to one's will. Tariq bin Khaled Al-Nur had always been too sophisticated, too dangerous, *too much* for the likes of Jessa Heath, and that was long before he became a king. She was a simple person, with a simple life and, once, a few big dreams, but she'd quickly learned the folly of dreams. She knew better now.

"Never fear," she said, folding her arms over her chest. "I'm a survivor. I picked myself up, dusted myself off, and made myself a life. It might not be the life I wanted when I was twenty-two, but it's mine." She lifted her chin and fixed her eyes on him, unafraid. "And I like it."

There was another silence. A muscle worked in Tariq's jaw, though he was otherwise motionless. Jessa had said things she had once only dreamed about saying, and that had to count for something, didn't it?

"There is no apology I can make that will suffice," Tariq said then, lifting his head to catch her gaze, startling her with his seeming sincerity. "I was thoughtless. Callous."

For a moment Jessa stared back at him, while something seemed to ease inside of her. Almost as if it was enough, somehow, that he had heard her. That he offered no excuses for what he had done. And perhaps it might have been enough, if that had been the end of what his abandonment had cost her. But it had only been the beginning. It had been the easy part, in retrospect.

"Congratulations," she said sarcastically, thinking of everything she'd suffered. The impossible decision she'd made. The daily pain of living with that decision ever since, no matter how much she might know that it was the right one. "You have managed to avoid apologizing with such elegance, I nearly thanked you for it."

"It is obvious that I owe you a great debt," he said then. If she hadn't been staring straight at him, she might have missed the flash of temper that came and went in his eyes. And she couldn't shake the strange notion that he meant to say something else entirely.

"There is no debt," she told him, stiffening. If he owed her something, that meant he might stay in the area, and she couldn't have that! He had to go, back to his own world, where he belonged. Far away from hers.

"I cannot make up for the loss of your prospects," Tariq continued as if she hadn't spoken. His voice was both formal and seductive. An odd mix, yet something inside her melted. "And perhaps there is nothing you wish for that I can provide."

"I've just told you I don't want anything," she said, more forcefully. "Not from you."

"Not even dinner?" He didn't quite smile. He inclined

his head toward her. "It is getting late. And I have wronged you. I think perhaps there is more to it, and the very least I can do is listen to you."

She didn't trust him for a second, much less his sudden gallantry and concern. She knew exactly how manipulative he could be. He'd lied to her for months and she'd bought it, hook, line, and sinker! And she had not forgotten that he'd said they had unfinished business between them. She should refuse him outright, demand he leave her alone.

But she didn't do it.

She was still buzzing from the unexpected rush she'd gotten when she'd told him exactly what he'd done to her. When she'd laid it out, piece by piece, and he'd had no defense. She had no intention of sharing the rest of it with him, but she'd be lying if she didn't admit that she liked being the one in charge. Perhaps she wasn't quite ready to dismiss him. Not quite yet. Was it that she felt powerful, or was it that melting within?

It was by far the most terrifying moment of the day.

"I'm afraid that's impossible," she told him stiffly, appalled at what she had nearly done. Was she mad? "I already have plans."

"Of course." Something passed through his eyes and made her catch her breath. "I understand. Another time, perhaps."

"Perhaps." She was noncommittal. Surely there could be no other time? Surely he would simply vanish back into the ether as he had before?

"Until then," he murmured, and then he turned and let himself back out of the office door. Jessa had the sense of his body moving like liquid into the night, and then she was alone.

He was gone as abruptly as he had come.

Jessa let out a breath, and sagged where she stood,

finding herself on her knees in the center of the industrial blue carpet. She pressed her hands against her face, then let them drop.

The room was again just a room. Just an office. Without Tariq crowding into it, it was not even small.

Jessa stayed where she was until her breathing returned to normal. She had to think. She was not foolish enough to believe that he was gone for good, that he might have hunted her down in York for a simple conversation most regular people would have on the telephone, or via the Internet, or not at all. The crazy part of her that still yearned for him swelled in the knowledge that he would, inevitably, return, and she felt something like a sob catch in her throat. She had come to terms with having loved and lost Tariq years ago. She had had no other option. But she had never expected that he would swing back into her life like this. She had never dreamed she would see him again, unless it was on the television.

She excused herself for being so uncharacteristically overwhelmed. He was an overwhelming man, to say the least! Jessa climbed to her feet and smoothed her hands over her skirt, straightening her ill-fitting suit jacket with a quick tug. If only she could set her world to rights as easily. It was one thing to mourn the man she had loved so much she'd let him change the course of her whole life while she was on her own these past years. It was something else again when he was in front of her. But she couldn't allow any of that to distract her from the main point.

Because all that mattered now was Jeremy.

The child she had fiercely and devotedly cared for while she'd carried him inside of her for nine long months. The baby she had kissed and adored when he'd finally decided to greet the world after so many hard, lonely hours of painful labor, his face red and his tiny fists waving furiously in front of him.

The son she had loved so desperately that she'd given him up for adoption when he had been four months old despite how agonizing that decision had been—and how hard it continued to be—for her. The son she still loved enough to fight with everything she had to maintain his privacy, his happiness, no matter the cost.

No matter what she might have to do.

CHAPTER THREE

JESSA was not surprised to find Tariq at her front door the following morning. If anything, she was surprised he had waited the whole of the night before reappearing. It might have lured her into a false sense of security had she not known better.

Perhaps she did still know him after all.

She opened the door to his peremptory knock because she knew that simply ignoring him would not only fail to deter him, it might also rouse her neighbors' interest and Jessa didn't want that. She didn't want someone noticing that the King of Nur was lounging about outside her otherwise unremarkable terraced house on a quiet Fulford side street just outside York's medieval walls. What good could come of drawing attention to the fact they knew each other? She needed to get him to go back to his own country, his own world, as quickly as possible.

She cracked the door as little as she could, and stood in the wedge, as if she was capable of keeping him out with her body if he wanted to come in.

Their eyes caught and held. Time seemed to halt in its tracks. Jessa felt her heart quicken its pace to thud heavily against her ribs, and her breath caught in her throat.

She was aware on some level that the morning was gray and wet, but the weather faded from her notice, because *he* was all she could see. And he was distressingly, inarguably real. Not the figment of her imagination she had half convinced herself he had been, conjured from the depths of her memory to torture herself with the night before. Not a dream, not even a nightmare.

"Good morning, Jessa," he said, as casually as if he spent all of his Saturday mornings fetched up on her doorstep, looking impossibly handsome and as inaccessible as ever.

He was no hallucination. He was flesh, blood, and all male, packed into one deceptively lean and powerful body. Today he wore black jeans and a tight black jersey that hugged the muscular planes of his chest and announced that whatever else the King of Nur might do while enjoying his luxurious lifestyle, he kept himself in top physical condition. His jade eyes burned into hers, nearly black in the morning gloom.

"I didn't make you up, then," Jessa said in as even a tone as she could manage. She wanted to order him to leave her alone, but she suspected he would pounce on that and use it against her, somehow. Best not to hand the warrior any weapons. "You're really here."

"How could I stay away?" he asked, with one of those predatory smiles that managed to distract her even as it unnerved her. She did not believe that he was here simply for her, no matter what he claimed. What was the likelihood that the lover who had had no qualm discarding her so completely would have a sudden drastic change of heart five years later, apropos of nothing? *Slim,* she had decided sometime in the early morning hours, long after she'd given up on sleeping. *Slim to none and bordering on less than zero.*

He had to know about Jeremy. Didn't he?

"You do not believe me," he murmured. He leaned in closer, taking up far too much space, blocking out the world behind him. "Perhaps I can convince you."

The good part about this situation, Jessa thought as he moved closer, close enough that she could smell the familiar, haunting scent of sandalwood and spice and his own warm skin, was that it made her choices very simple. There was only one: ease his fears and suspicions however she could, and send him on his way.

She told herself she could do this. Her head felt too light, her knees too weak. But she would do what she must, for her son's sake. She could handle Tariq. She could. She stepped back and opened the door wider.

"You'd better come in."

Tariq let Jessa lead him inside the house, which felt dark and close as all English dwellings felt to him. This whole country of low clouds and relentless rain made him crave the impossibly blue skies of Nur, the horizon stretching beyond imagining, the desert wide and open and bright. The fact that he was not where he was supposed to be, where he needed to be—that he was still in England when he should be at the palace in Azhar handling the latest threat of a rebel uprising near the disputed border— reminded him too much of his playboy past. Yet he had still come to find her.

He had no time for this. He had no patience for ghosts or trips through the past. It was finished. He was no longer that self-indulgent, wasteful creature, and had no wish to revisit him now. Yet she had haunted him across the years, as no other woman ever had. He could recall her smile, the arch of her back, the scent of her skin, in perfect detail. He had

had no choice but to find her. He had to exorcize her once and for all, so he might finally get on with his life as he should have done five years ago. Marriage, heirs. His duty.

Jessa walked before him into her sitting room, and came to a stop beside the mantel. Slowly, she turned to face him, her tension evident in the way she held herself, the way she swallowed nervously and pulled at her clothes with her hands. He liked that she was not at ease. It made his own uncertainty less jarring, somehow. She could deny it all she liked, but he could feel the awareness swell between them.

Tariq's eyes swept the room, looking for clues about this simple woman who made him feel such complicated things, so complicated he had tracked her down after all this time, like a besotted fool. The sitting room was furnished simply, with an eye toward comfort rather than glamour. The sofa seemed well used and neat rather than stylish. A half-drunk cup of tea sat on the coffee table, with the remnants of what he assumed to be toast. There were a few photographs in frames beside her on the mantelpiece—a family of three with a mother he took to be Jessa's sister. Others of the sisters together, as small children, then with Jessa as a gawky teenager.

Her eyes were wide and cautious, and she watched him apprehensively as he finally turned his attention to her. If she thought to hide her responses from him, it was much too late. He was as attuned to her body as to his own.

Tariq reminded himself that he could not simply order her to his bed, though that would be far simpler than this dance. He did not know why she resisted him. But he was not an untried boy. He could play any games she needed to play. He picked up the nearest photograph and frowned down at it.

"You resemble your sister," he said, without meaning to comment. "Though you are far more beautiful."

Jessa's cheeks colored, and not with pleasure. She reached over and jerked the photograph from his hand, leaving him with only a blurred impression of her less attractive sister, a fair-haired husband, and their infant held between them.

"I won't ask what you think you're doing here," she said in a low, controlled voice. But he could see the spark of interest in her eyes.

"By all means, ask." He dared her, arching his brows and leaning closer, crowding her. He liked the lick of fire that scraped across his skin when he was near her. He wanted more. "I am more than happy to explain it to you. I can even demonstrate, if you prefer." She did not step away, though her color deepened.

"I don't want to know how you justify your behavior," she retorted. She tilted her chin into the air. "We have nothing to discuss."

"You could have told me this on the doorstep," he pointed out softly. "Why did you invite me into your home if we have nothing to discuss?"

She looked incredulous. "Had I refused to answer the door, or to let you in, what would you have done?"

Tariq only smiled. Did she realize she'd conceded a weakness?

"This game will not last long if you already know I will win it," he said. His smile deepened. "Or perhaps you do not wish for it to last very long?"

"The only person playing a game here is you," Jessa retorted.

She put the photograph back on the mantel and then crossed her arms over her chest as she faced him. He moved closer. He stretched one arm out along the mantel and shifted so that they were nearly pressed together, held back only by this breath, or the next. She stood her ground, though he could see it cost her in the pink of her cheeks, hear it in the rasp of her breath. He was close enough to touch her, but he refrained. Barely. He could see her pulse hammer against the side of her neck. It was almost unfair, he thought with a primal surge of very male satisfaction, that he could use her body against her in this way. Almost.

"You keep testing me, Jessa," he whispered. "What if I am no match for it? Who knows what might happen if I lose control?"

"Very funny," she threw back at him, her spine straight though Tariq could tell she wanted to bolt. Instead, she scoffed at him. "When is the last time that happened? Has it *ever* happened?"

Unbidden, memories teased at him, of Jessa sprawled across the bed in his long-ago Mayfair flat, her naked limbs flushed and abandoned beneath him. He remembered the rich, sweet scent of her perfume, her unrestrained smile. The low roll of her delighted laughter, the kind that started in her belly and radiated outward, encompassing them both. The lush swell of her breasts in his hands, her woman's heat against his tongue. And the near-violent need in him for her, like claws in his gut, that nothing could satiate.

He didn't understand all the ways he wanted her. He only knew that she had burrowed into him, and he had never been able to escape her, waking or sleeping. She was his own personal ghost. She haunted him even now, standing so close to him and yet still so far away.

He looked away from her for a moment, fighting for control. She took that as a response.

"Exactly," she said as if she'd uncovered a salient truth. "You are not capable of losing control. No doubt, that serves you well as a king."

Tariq turned his head and found her watching him, color high on her cheeks and her cinnamon-brown eyes bright. Did she mean to insult him? Tariq did not know. But he did know that he was more than a match for her. There was one arena where he held all the power, and both of them knew it.

"You misunderstand me," he murmured. He reached over and slid his hand around the back of her neck, cupping the delicate flesh against his hard palm and feeling the weight of her thick, copper curls. She jumped, then struggled to conceal it, but it was too late. He could feel her pulse wild and insistent against his fingers, and he could see the way her mouth fell open, as if she was dazed.

He did not doubt that she did not *want* to want him. He had not forgotten the days she had disappeared, which had been shockingly unusual for a girl who had always before been at his beck and call, just as he had not forgotten his own panicked response to her unexpected unavailability, something he might have investigated further had history and tragedy not intervened. But there was no point digging into such murky waters, especially when he did not know what he would find there. What mattered was that she still wanted him. He could feel it with his hands, see it in the flush of her skin and the heat in her gaze.

"Tariq—" she began.

"Please," he murmured, astounded to hear his own voice. Astonished that he, Sheikh Tariq bin Khaled Al-Nur, would beg. For anything, or any reason. And yet he continued. "I just want to talk."

Was he so toothless, neutered and tame? But he could not seem to stop himself. He had to see this through, and then, finally, be rid of her once and for all. If there was another way, he would have tried it already. He *had* tried it already!

"About us."

* * *

Us. He'd actually said the word *us.*

The word ricocheted through Jessa's mind, leaving marks, much like she suspected his hand might do if he didn't take it off her—if she didn't burst into flame and burn alive from the slight contact.

As if there had ever been an *us* in the first place!

"You have to get on with your life," her sister Sharon had told her, not unkindly, about two weeks after everything had come to such a messy, horrible end in London and Jessa had retreated to York. Crawled back, more like, still holding the secret of her pregnancy close to her chest, unable to voice the terrifying truth to anyone, even her sister. And all while Tariq's face was on every television set as the tragedy in Nur unfolded before the world. The sisters had sat together in Jessa's small bedroom while Sharon delivered her version of comfort. It was brisk and unsentimental, as Sharon had always been herself.

"I don't know what that means," Jessa had said from the narrow bed that had been hers as a girl, when Sharon had taken the reins after their parents died within eighteen months of each other. Eight years older, Sharon and her husband Barry had taken over the house and, to some extent, the parenting of Jessa, while they tried and failed to start their own family.

"It means you need to get your head out of the clouds," Sharon had said matter-of-factly. "You've had an adventure, Jessa, and that's more than some people ever get. But you can't lie about wallowing in the past forever."

Tariq hadn't felt like the *past* to Jessa. Or even an *adventure.* Even after everything that had happened—after losing her job, her *career*, her self-respect; after finding herself pregnant and her lover an unreachable liar, however little she might have come to terms with that—she still yearned for him. He'd felt like a heart that beat with hers, louder and more vibrant inside her chest than her own, and the thought of the gray, barren life she was expected to live without him was almost more than she could bear. She had choked back a sob.

"Men like him are fantasies," Sharon had said, with no little pity. "They're not meant for the likes of you or me. Did you imagine he'd sweep you off to his castle and make you his queen? You, little Jessa Heath of Fulford? You always did fancy yourself something special. But you've had your bit of fun and now it's time to be realistic, isn't it?"

Jessa had had no choice but to be realistic, she thought now. But Tariq was back and there was far too much at stake, and she still couldn't think straight while he touched her. And he wanted to talk about *us,* of all things.

"There is no *us*," she said crisply, as if she was not melting, as if she was still in control. She met his gaze squarely. "I'm not sure there ever was. I've no idea what game you thought you were playing."

"I have a proposition for you," he said calmly, as if what she'd said was of no matter. He lounged back against the mantelpiece, letting his hand move from her skin slowly. He was every inch the indolent monarch.

"It is barely half-nine and here you are propositioning me," Jessa replied, determined to get her balance back. She kept her voice dry, amused. Sophisticated, the way she imagined the glamorous women he was used to would speak to him when he propositioned them. "Why am I not surprised?"

If her heart beat faster and her skin felt overheated, and

she could still feel his hand on her like a tattoo, she ignored it.

"Am I so predictable?" His hard face looked cast in iron in the low gloom from the front windows. And yet Jessa sensed that the real shadows came from within him.

She stood ramrod straight because she could not allow herself to move, to back away from him. She thought it would show too much, be too much of a concession. She laced her fingers together in front of her as tightly as possible.

"It is not a question of whether or not you are—or were—predictable," she said coolly. She raised her eyebrows in unmistakable challenge. "Perhaps you were simply like any other man when things got too serious. Afraid."

He stilled. The temperature in the room seemed to plunge. Jessa's heart stuttered to a halt. She knew, suddenly, that she was in greater danger from him in that moment than ever before. Something dark moved across his face, and then he bared his teeth in something far too wild to be a smile.

"Proceed with care, Jessa," he advised her in a soft voice that sent a chill snaking down her spine. "Not many people would dare call a king a coward to his face."

"I am merely calling a spade a spade," Jessa replied, as if she did not have a knot of trepidation in her stomach, as if she was not aware that she was throwing pebbles at a lion. She shook the loose tendrils of her hair back from her face, wishing her curls did not take every opportunity to defy her. "You were not yet a king when you ran away, were you?"

"Ran away?" he echoed, enunciating each word as if he could not quite comprehend her meaning.

"What would you call it?" she asked coolly. Calmly. She even smiled, as if they shared a joke. "Adults typically have conversations with each other when an affair is ending, don't they? It's called common courtesy, at the very least."

"Again," he said, too quietly, "you have forgotten the sequence of events. You were the one who disappeared into thin air." He stood so still, yet reminded Jessa not of a statue, but of a coiled snake ready to strike. Yet she couldn't seem to back down.

"I merely failed to answer my mobile for two days," Jessa replied lightly. "That's not quite the same thing as quitting the country altogether, is it?"

"It is not as if I was on holiday, sunning myself on the Amalfi Coast!" Tariq retorted.

Jessa shook her head at him. "It hardly matters now," she said carelessly, as if her heart hadn't been broken once upon a time. "I'm only suggesting that perhaps it was a convenient excuse, that's all. An easy way out."

Tariq was so still it was as if he'd turned to stone. He studied her as if he had never seen her before. She had the sudden, uncomfortable notion that he was assessing her as he might an enemy combatant on the field of battle, and was coldly scanning her for her weaknesses. Her soft points.

And all the while that awareness swirled around them, making everything seem sharper, brighter.

"I will not explode into some dramatic temper tantrum, if that is your goal with these attacks," Tariq said finally, never looking away from her. She felt her cheeks heat, whether in relief or some stronger emotion, she didn't know. "I will not rage and carry on, though you question my honor and insult my character." His hard mouth hinted at a curve, flirted with it. "There are better ways to make my feelings known."

She refused to feel the heat that washed through her. She would not accept it. The tightness in her belly was agitation, worry, nothing more. But the desperate, purely feminine part of her that still wanted him, that thirsted for his touch in ways she could not allow herself to picture, knew better.

"What, then?" she demanded, unable to pull her gaze from his. What was this intoxicating fire that burned between them, making her ask questions she knew she did not want the answers to? "What is your damned proposition?"

"One night." He said it so easily, yet with that unmistakably sensual edge underneath.

Somewhere deep inside, she shuddered, and the banked fire she wanted to deny existed flared into a blaze.

His gaze seemed to see into her, to burn through her.

"That is all, Jessa. That is what I want from you."

CHAPTER FOUR

TARIQ'S words echoed in the space between them, bald and
naked and challenging. Jessa swallowed. He saw her hands
tremble, and a kind of triumph moved through him. She
could not control what would happen. Perhaps she even
knew it. But she did not back down. She still thought she
could fight him. It made him want her all the more.

He knew, even if she did not, that she was going to end
this confrontation in his bed. Beneath him, astride him,
on her knees before him—he didn't care. He only knew
that he would win, and not only because he always won.
But because he would accept no other outcome, not with
this woman. Not when she had been in his head for all
these years.

Because he already knew how this would end, he could
be patient. He could wait. He could even let her fight him,
if she wished it. What would it matter? It would only make
it that much better in the end.

"I don't want to misunderstand you again," she said
after a long moment. She searched his face, her own carefully blank.

He realized that he liked this grown-up, self-assured
version of Jessa. He liked that she stood up to him, that she

was mysterious, that she was neither easily read nor easily intimidated. When was the last time anyone had defied him?

"One night of what?" she asked.

"Of whatever I want," he said softly, pouring seduction into every syllable. "Whatever I ask."

"Be specific, Tariq," she said, an edge to her voice. He interpreted it as desire she would have preferred not to feel.

"As you wish," he murmured. He leaned toward her, pleased with the way she jerked back, startled, and the way her breath came too quickly. "I want you in my bed. Or on the floor. Or up against the wall. Or all of the above. Is that specific enough?"

"No!" She threw one hand into the air as if to hold him back, but it was too late for that. Tariq moved closer and leaned toward her, until her outstretched palm pressed up against his chest. Her hand was the only point of contact between them, her fingers trembling in the hollow between the hard planes of his pectoral muscles.

She did not drop her hand. He did not lean back.

"No, what?" he asked with soft, sensual menace. "No, you do not wish to give me that night? Or no, you do not want to hear how I will sink inside you, making you clench and moan and—"

"Don't be ridiculous!" She whispered the words, but her eyes glazed with heat and something else, and the hand she held between them had softened into a caress, touching him rather than holding him off.

"It is many things," Tariq said in a low voice, "but it is not ridiculous."

He took her hand in his and, never looking away from her, raised her wrist to his lips. He tasted her, her skin like the finest silk, and her pulse beneath it, fluttering out her excitement, her distress. It was like wine and it went to his head, knocking into him with dizzying force.

She made some sound, as if she meant to speak. Perhaps she did, and he could not hear her over the roaring in his ears, his blood, his sudden hardness. He had not expected the surge of lust so sharp and consuming. It barreled through his body from their single point of contact, making him burn. Making him *want*.

It was worse now that he touched her, now that he was before her, than it had been when he only remembered. Much worse.

"I want you out of my system," he told her, his voice urgent and deep. Commanding, because he meant it more than he had just moments before. Because he was desperate. He needed a queen and he needed heirs, and she was what kept him from doing that duty. He had to erase the hold she had on him! "Once and for all. I want one night."

One night.

Jessa stared at Tariq in shock for a moment, as the impossible words shimmered between them like heat. The breathtaking strength of his hard chest against her palm made her whole arm ache, and the ache radiated through her, kicking up brushfires everywhere it touched. Her mind could not seem to process what he'd said, but her body had no such difficulty. She felt her breasts swell in reaction, her nipples hardening into tight, nearly painful points that she was grateful he couldn't possibly see beneath the wool sweater she'd thrown on earlier. Between her legs, she ached, even as her body readied itself for him. Awareness, thick and heavy and intoxicating, thrummed through her. She was electric.

And he was watching her.

Jessa could no longer bear his proximity. And why was she still touching him? Why had she let the moment draw out? No longer caring that he might see it as a victory—only needing space between them—she snatched her hand away from the heat of his body and moved to the other side of the room. There was only her coffee table between them when she stopped, but it was something. It made her feel slightly less hysterical, slightly less likely to pretend the past five years had never happened and fling herself into his arms. How had she lost control of herself so quickly?

"I beg your pardon," she began in her stiffest, most formal tone.

"Do you?" he interrupted her, leaning so nonchalantly against her mantel, so big and dark and terrifying, with all of that disconcerting, green-eyed attention focused intently upon her. He was like her own personal fallen angel, come to take her even further into the abyss. She had to remember why she could not let him. "Do not beg my pardon when there are so many more interesting things you could beg me for."

He was so seductive even when she knew better. Or perhaps it was only that she was so susceptible and weak where he was concerned. She could feel his hands on her, though he had not moved. Her palm itched with the need to soothe itself against the steellike muscles of his chest once more. How could her body want him, still? She had been so sure she was over him, finally. She had been certain of it. She had even, recently, begun to imagine a future in which Tariq was not the shadow over her life, but a bittersweet memory.

"You must be joking," she said, because that was what she might say if her body wasn't staging a full-scale revolt—if, in fact, she felt as she ought to feel toward this man. It had taken her five years to get over him once. What would it be like a second time? It didn't bear considering.

"I assure you, I have no sense of humor at all where you are concerned," he said.

Somehow, she believed him. And yet there was a certain gleam in his dark eyes that convinced her she was better off not knowing exactly what he meant by that remark.

"Then you are insane," she declared. "I would no more spend one night with you then I would prance naked down Parliament Street!"

As she heard it echo around her lounge, it occurred to her that a wise woman might not have used the word *naked* in front of this man, in defiance of this man. Tariq did not seem to move, and yet at the same time he seemed to grow larger. Taller, darker, *more*. As if he blocked all the exits and kept her chained where she stood, all because he willed it. How did he do such a thing? Had he always been so effortlessly irresistible? In her memories, he had taken over every room he had ever entered with the sheer force of his magnetism, but she had supposed that to be her own infatuation at play, not anything he did himself.

"What I mean," she said when he simply studied her in that hawkish, blood-stirring way that made her mouth go dry and made her wonder if she might be more his prey than she knew, than she wanted to know. "What I mean is that of course I will not spend a night with you. There is far too much water under the bridge. I'm surprised you would ask."

"Are you?" He looked supremely unconcerned. Imperial. A brow arched. "I did not ask."

Of course he had not actually asked. Because he was the King of Nur. He did not need to ask. He needed only to incline his head and whatever he desired was flung at his feet, begging for the chance to serve him. Hadn't she done the same five years ago?

He had no more than glanced at her across the busy office that fateful day and Jessa had been his. Just like that. It had been that immediate and all-consuming. She had not even waited for him to approach her. As if she was a moth drawn inexplicably and inexorably to the flame that would be the death of her, she had risen to her feet and then walked toward him without so much as a thought, without even excusing herself from the conversation she was taking part in. She had no memory of moving, or choosing to go to him. He had merely looked at her with his dark sorcerer's eyes and she had all but thrown herself at him.

And that had been while he was playing his game of pretending to be a doctor's son with some family money, but otherwise of interest to no one. Now he was no longer hiding—now he was a king. No wonder he seemed so much more powerful, so much more alluring, so much more devastating.

"Then you have saved me the trouble of refusing you," Jessa said, fighting to keep her voice calm, with all the tension ratcheting through her. "Good thing you did not bother to ask."

"Why do you refuse?" Tariq asked quietly, straightening from the mantel. It was as if he stepped directly into her personal space, crowding her, though he was still all the way across the room. Jessa eased away from him, from the powerful energy he seemed to exude like some kind of force field, but she had to stop when the backs of her knees hit the couch.

You cannot run, she warned herself. *He would only chase you. And you must think of Jeremy. You must!*

"Why do you want one night?" Jessa retorted. She

shoved her hands into the pockets of her trousers, trying to look calm even if she didn't feel it. "And why now? Five years is a bit too long for me to believe you've been carrying a torch." She laughed at the very idea, the sound dying off when he only looked at her, a truth shimmering in his dark gaze that she refused to accept.

"I told you that I must marry." He shrugged, as if a lifelong commitment was no more interesting to him than a speck of dust. Perhaps it was not. "But first I wanted to make sure you were no longer a factor. You can understand this, can't you?"

"I would have thought I ceased being any kind of factor some time ago," Jessa said. Was her tone the dry, sophisticated sort of tone she'd aimed for? She feared it was rather more bitter than that, and bit her lower lip slightly, wishing she could take it back.

Tariq rubbed at his chin with one hand, still watching her closely, intently, as if he could see directly into her.

"Who can say why certain things haunt a man?" He dropped his eyes. "After my uncle died, my life was no longer my own. My every breath and every thought was of necessity about my country. It was not enough simply to accept the crown. I had to learn how to wear it." He shook his head slightly, as if he had not meant to say something so revealing. He frowned. "But as it became clear that I could not delay my own marriage further, I knew I could not marry with this history hanging over me. And so I resolved to find you. It is not a complicated story."

This time, when he looked at her, his dark green eyes were even more unreadable than before.

"You expect me to believe that you..." She couldn't bring herself to say it, it was too absurd. "There is no history hanging over us!"

"You are the only woman who has ever left me," he told her. His tone was soft, but there was a hard, watchful gleam in his gaze. "You left an impression."

"I did not leave you!" she gritted out. There was no way to explain why she had gone incommunicado for those days—she who had rarely been out of his sight for the wild, desperate weeks of their affair.

"So you say." He shrugged, but his attention never left her face. "Call it what you wish. You were the only one to do it."

"And this has led you to track me down all these years later," Jessa said softly. She shook her head. "I cannot quite believe it."

The air around them changed. Tightened.

"Can you not?" he asked, and there was something new in his voice—something she could not recognize though she knew in a sudden panic that she should. That her failure to recognize it was a serious misstep.

Satisfaction, she thought with abrupt insight, but it was too late.

He crossed the room, rounded the coffee table in a single step and pulled her into his arms.

"Tariq—" she began, panicked, but she had no idea what she meant to say. All she could feel were his arms like steel bands around her, his chest like a wall of fire against hers. And all she could see was his hard face, lit with an emotion she could not name, serious as he looked down at her for a long, breathless moment.

"Believe this," he said, and fitted his mouth to hers.

CHAPTER FIVE

JESSA'S world spun, until she no longer knew if she stood or if she fell, and the mad thing was that she didn't much care either way.

Not as she wanted to. Not as she should.

Tariq's hard, hot mouth moved on hers and she forgot everything. She forgot all the reasons she should not touch him or go near him at all. She forgot why she needed to get rid of him as quickly as possible, so that he could never find out her secrets. So that he could not hurt her again as easily as he'd done before.

None of that seemed to matter any longer. All she cared about was his mouth. All she wanted was *more*.

He knew exactly how to kiss her, how best to make her head spin in dizzy circles. Long, drugging strokes as he tasted her, sampling her mouth with his, angling his head for a better, sweeter fit.

"Yes," she murmured, barely recognizing her own voice.

Sensation chased sensation, almost too much to bear. His strong hands moved over her, one flexed into the thick mass of her hair at the nape of her neck while the other splayed across the small of her back, pressing her hips against his. His clever, arousing mouth moved slick and hot against hers. Fire. Heat. Awe. The potent mix of vibrant memory and new, stunning sensation. Touching him was the same, and yet so very different. He tasted like some heady mix of spices, strong and not quite sweet, and she was drunk on it, on him, in seconds.

She could feel him everywhere, pumping through her veins, wrapped around each beat of her heart as it pounded a hectic rhythm against her chest. How had she lived without this for so long? She could not get close enough to him. She could not breathe without breathing him in. She could not stop touching him.

She let her hands explore him, trailing down the length of his impossibly carved torso, like something sculpted in marble, though his skin seemed to blaze with heat beneath her hands. He was nothing as cold as stone. He was so big, bigger than she remembered, and huskier. His strong shoulders were far wider than his narrow hips, his muscles hard from some kind of daily use. She traced patterns across the breadth of his lean back, feeling his strength and his power in her palms.

Tariq muttered something she could not understand. His hands stroked down the length of her back to cup her bottom, urging her closer until she was pressed tight against his thighs and the rock-hard maleness between them. She gasped. She felt her core melt and tremble against him. He sighed slightly, as if in relief. Jessa heard a distant crooning sound and realized, only dimly, that it came from her.

And still, he kissed her. Again and again. As if he could not stop. As if he, too, remembered that it had always been this way between them—this dizzying, terrifying rush of lust and need and *now*. Jessa could not seem to shake the memories that scrolled through her mind, each more sensual than the last, or the shocking fact that this was real, that they were doing this, all these years later.

She could not think. She could not imagine why she *should* think.

She twined her arms around his neck, arching her back to press her swollen, tender breasts against the hard planes of his chest, tilting her head back to give him better access. He did not disappoint. He broke from her mouth, his breathing harsh, and kissed his way down her cheek, her neck. His mouth was like a hot brand against her skin.

"More," he whispered, and his hands went to the hem of her sweater, pulling it up past her hips, then pausing when he uncovered her breasts. He looked at them for a long moment, as if drinking them in. Then he caressed each puckered nipple and tight globe in turn, shaping them through the camisole she wore, while Jessa moaned in mindless, helpless pleasure. Her sex ached, and she could feel an answering heat behind her eyes. She felt burned alive, eaten whole. She wanted more than his hands. She *wanted*.

Muttering a curse, Tariq stripped the sweater from her body, guiding her head through the opening with his strong, sure hands. He tossed it aside without glancing at it, and then paused for a moment to look down at her, his hard eyes gleaming in the gray morning light. The expression she read there made her belly clench, and pulse to a low, wild drum within.

Jessa's nipples stood at attention, tight and begging for his mouth. She could feel the hungry, restless heat in her core, begging for his mouth, his hand, his sex. Even her mouth was open slightly and softened, swollen from his kisses, begging for more of the same.

Could actual begging be far behind? How soon before she was right where she swore she'd never be again—literally on her knees, perhaps? Clutching desperately at him as he walked away once more?

The thought was like cold water. A slap. Jessa blinked, and sanity returned with an unwelcome thump, jarring her.

She staggered backward, away from him, out of reach of his dangerous hands. How could she have let this happen? How could she have allowed him to touch her like this?

Again, she thought wildly. *How can he do this* again?

"Stop," she managed to say, pushing the word out through the hectic frenzy that still seized her. He had broken her heart five years ago. What would he do this time? What else could he break? It had taken all these years to come to a place of peace about everything that happened, and here she was, tumbling right back into his arms again, just like before.

She hadn't believed that he could want her then, and she didn't believe it now, not deep inside of herself. She had never known what game he had been playing and what had led a man like him to notice someone like her. And here she was, much older and wiser, about to make the same mistake all over again! Just like last time, he would leave her when he was finished with her. And he *would* finish with her, of that she had no doubt. The only question was how much of herself she would turn over to him in the meantime, and how far she would have to go to get herself back when he left her, shattered once more.

No. She could not do this again. She would not.

"You do not want to stop," he said in that dark, rich voice that sent her nerve endings into a joyful dance and made her that much more resolute. "You only think that you do. Why think?"

"Why, indeed?" she asked ruefully, trying to pull herself together. She stood up straight, and smoothed her palms over the mess of her hair. She was afraid to look into the

mirror on the far wall. She felt certain she didn't wish to
know how she looked just now. Wanton and on the brink
of disaster, no doubt.

"Whatever else passed between us, there is still this,"
Tariq continued, just short of adamant. "How can we
ignore it?"

His voice tugged at her, as if it was something more than
sex for him. As if it could ever be anything more than that,
with this man! Why hadn't she learned her lesson?

"I won't deny that I'm still attracted to you," Jessa said
carefully, determined that her inner turmoil should not
come out in her voice. That she should somehow transmit
a calmness she did not feel. "But we are adults, Tariq. We
are not required to act on every last feeling."

"We are not *required* to, no," Tariq replied smoothly, a
perfect echo of the easy, tempting lover he had been before,
always willing to pursue passion above all else. It was
how he had lived his life. He even smiled now, as if he was
still that man. "But perhaps we should."

Jessa took a moment to reach over and draw her sweater
toward her, trying to take deep, calming breaths. She pulled
it back over her head as if it were armor and might protect
her. She smoothed the scratchy wool material down over
her hips, and then adjusted the heavy copper spill of her
hair, pushing it back over her shoulders. Then she realized
she was fidgeting. He would read far too much into it, and
so she stilled herself.

How could she want him, as if it were no more than a
chemical decision, outside of her control? Yes, of course,
he was a devastatingly handsome man. There was no
denying it. If he were a stranger and she saw him on the
street, Jessa would no doubt find him enthralling.
Captivating. But he was not a stranger. He was Tariq bin

Khaled Al-Nur. She knew him too well, and she had every reason in the world to be effectively allergic to him. Instead, she melted all over him and had to bite the inside of her cheek to keep from asking for more.

Begging for more, even.

She wanted to be furious with herself. But what she was, instead, was terrified. Of her own responses, her own reaction to him. Not even of Tariq himself.

"I thought perhaps you wished to talk about something of import," she said, sounding merely prim to her own ears, when she wanted to sound tough. She cleared her throat and then indicated the two of them with her hand. "*This* is not something I want. It's not something I need in my life, do you understand?"

"Is your life so full, then?" His dark eyes bored into her. His mouth was serious, flat and firm. "You never think of the past?"

"My life is full enough that the past has no place." She raised her chin, a bolt of pride streaking through her as she thought about how she had changed since he had known her. In ways both seen and unseen, but she knew the difference. She wondered if he could see those differences, but then told herself it hardly mattered. "It would not seem so to a king, I imagine, but I am proud of my life. It's simple and it's mine. I built it from scratch, literally."

"And you think I cannot understand this? That I cannot grasp what it is to build a life from nothing?" He shifted his weight, reminding Jessa that they were standing far too close to the sofa, and that it would be much too easy to simply fall backward and take him with her, letting him crush her so deliciously against the sofa cushions with his—

Enough! she ordered herself. *You cannot allow yourself to get carried away with him!*

"I know you cannot possibly understand," she replied. She moved then, rounding the coffee table and putting more space between them. She had always thought her sitting room was reasonably sized, a bit roomy, even. Now it felt like the inside of a closet. Or a small box. She felt there was nowhere she could go that he could not reach her, should he wish to. She felt trapped, hemmed in. *Hunted.* So why did something in her rejoice in it? "Just as I do not pretend to understand the daily life of the ruler of a country. How could I? It is beyond imagination."

"Tell me, then," he said, tracking her as she moved toward the window, then changed direction. "Tell me what it is like to be Jessa Heath."

"How could I possibly interest you?" she demanded, stopping in her tracks. She threw him an incredulous look. "Why would you want to know anything so mundane?"

"You would be surprised at the things I want to know." He slid his hands into the pockets of his dark jeans and considered her for a moment. Once more, Jessa was certain there was more going on than met the eye. As if, beneath those smooth words he hid sharp edges that she could only sense but not quite hear. "I have told you that you have haunted me across the years, yet you do not believe it. Perhaps if you told me more about yourself, I would find you less fascinating."

"I am a simple woman, with a simple life," she told him, her voice crackling with a kick of temper that she did not entirely understand. She didn't believe that he was mocking her. But neither did she believe that she could have fascinated him. With what? Her utter spinelessness? Or had he truly believed that she had left him and was one of those men who only wanted what he thought out of reach?

"If you are as proud of this life as you claim, why should

you conceal it?" he asked, too reasonably. Too seductively. "Why not seek to sing it from the rooftops instead?"

Frustrated, Jessa looked away for a moment, and felt goose bumps rise along her arms. She crossed them in front of her and tried to rub at her shoulders surreptitiously. She just wanted him to leave. Surely once he did, everything would settle back into place, as if he had never been.

"I would think you as likely to be interested in watching paint dry as in the life and times of an ordinary Yorkshire woman," she said in a low voice.

"It is possible, I think, that you do not know me as well as you believe you do," Tariq said in a haughty, aristocratic voice. No doubt he used this exact tone when ordering his subjects about. No doubt they all genuflected at the sound of it. But Jessa was not one of his subjects.

"My life is not a great story," she threw at him, daring him to judge her and find her lacking, yet knowing he could not fail to do so. "I wake up in the morning and I go to work. I like my job and I'm good at it. My boss is kind. I have friends, neighbors. I like where I live. I am happy." She could feel the heat in her eyes, and hoped he would think it was nothing more than vehemence. She wished she could convince herself of it. "What did you expect? That my life would be nothing but torment and disaster without you?"

His mouth moved, though he did not speak. It was tempting to tell him exactly how much she had suffered, and why—but she knew better. If he did not know too much already, then he could not know about Jeremy, ever. What was done was done. Tariq might think she did not know him, but she knew enough to be certain that he would handle that news in only one, disastrous way. And if he was only going to disappear again—and she knew without a single doubt that he was—she knew she couldn't risk telling him about Jeremy.

"Please go," she said quietly. She couldn't look at him. "I don't know why you came to find me, Tariq, but it's enough now. We did not require a reunion. You must leave."

"I leave tonight," he said after a moment, and her gaze snapped to his, startled. "You seem skeptical," he taunted her softly. "I am devastated that you find me so untrustworthy. Or is it that you did not expect me to go?"

"I hope you found what you were looking for here," she said, unable to process the various emotions that buffeted her. Intense, all-encompassing relief. Suspicion. And a pang of something she refused to call loss. "It was not necessary to dredge up ancient history, however."

"I am not so sure I agree," Tariq mused. His mouth looked so hard and incapable of the drugging kisses she knew he could wield with it. "Have dinner with me, tonight." He paused. Then, as an afterthought, as if he was unused to the word, he added, "Please."

Jessa realized she was holding her breath, and let it out.

"I don't think that's a good idea," she said, frowning, but more at herself than at him. Why did something in her want to have dinner with him—to prolong the agony? What could she possibly have to gain? Especially when there was so much to lose—namely, her head and her heart?

"If it is a good idea or a bad one, what does it matter?" Tariq shrugged. "I have told you I am leaving. One dinner, that is all. Is that too much to ask? For old time's sake?"

Jessa knew she should refuse him, but then what would he do? Show up here again when she least expected it? Somehow, the idea of him in her house at night seemed far more dangerous—and look what had happened already in broad daylight! She could not let him come back here. And if that meant one more uncomfortable interaction, maybe it was worth it. She was a grown woman who had told herself for years now that she had been an infatuated child when she'd met Tariq, and that the agony of losing him had been amplified by the baby she had carried. It had never occurred to her that seeing him again might stir up such strong feelings. It had never crossed her mind that she could still harbor any feelings for him! Maybe it was all for the best that she finally faced them.

And anyway, it was in public. How dangerous could even Tariq be in a roomful of other people?

In the back of her mind, something whispered a warning, but it was too late. Her mouth was already open.

"Fine," she said. It was for the right reasons, she told herself. It would bring closure, no more and no less than that. "I will have dinner with you, but that is all. Only dinner."

But she was not certain she believed herself. Maybe she could not be trusted any more than he could.

Satisfaction flashed across his face, and his mouth curved slightly.

Jessa knew she'd made a terrible mistake.

"Excellent." He inclined his head slightly. "I will send a car for you at six o'clock."

CHAPTER SIX

IT WAS only when Jessa found herself seated at a romantic table out on the fifth-story terrace of one of the finest houses she had ever seen, improbably located though it was in Paris, France, not far from the Arc de Triomphe, that she accepted the truth she had known on some level from the moment she'd so thoughtlessly agreed to this dinner: she was outmatched.

"I am pleased you could make it," Tariq said, watching her closely for her reaction. Jessa ordered herself not to give him one, but she could feel her mouth flatten. Had he had any doubt she would come?

"I was hardly given any choice, was I?" she asked. He had played her like the proverbial fiddle, and here she was, out of the country and entirely within his power.

Tariq only smiled arrogantly and waved at the hovering servant to pour the wine.

They sat outside on the terrace that circled the top floor of the elegant home, surrounded by carved stone statuary and wrought iron, the Paris night alive around them with lights and sounds. Yet Jessa could not take in the stunning view laid out before her, much less the beautiful table set with fine linen and heavy silver. Her head still whirled until she feared she might faint. She stared at Tariq from her place across from him while conflicting emotions crashed through her, but he only smiled slightly indulgently and toyed with the delicate crystal stem of his wineglass. And why should he do anything else?

She had taken care to wear her best dress, there was no pretending otherwise. If it was within the realm of possibility for someone like her to impress him, she'd wanted to do it—and now the royal-blue sheath dress she'd felt so pretty in earlier felt like sackcloth and ash against her skin, outclassed as it was by the splendor of Paris and what she knew was simply *one* of the homes Tariq must own.

How had she ever dreamed she could compete with this man, much less fascinate him in any way, no matter what lies he told? And the most important question was *why* had she wanted to do so in the first place? What did she hope to win here? She knew that he desired her, but she had already learned exactly how much stock he put in such things, hadn't she? As her sister had told her years before, *at the end of the day you're not the type a man like that will marry, are you?*

Whatever happened tonight, Jessa could never tell herself she hadn't known better.

Of her own free will she had stepped into the car he'd sent. She hadn't complained when, instead of delivering her to some appropriately luxurious hotel in the York area that might live up to the expectations of a king, whatever those might be, it had taken her instead to the Leeds Bradford Airport. She hadn't uttered a sound when she was handed aboard the impressive private jet by his ever-courteous, ever-solicitous staff. She'd told herself some story about Tariq's self-importance and had imagined she would make cutting remarks to him about his having to fly down to London for dinner. She had even practiced the sort of urbane, witty things she might say as she relaxed against the deep, plush leather seats and accepted a glass of wine from the friendly and smiling air hostess.

But then one hour had turned to two, and she had found herself emerging not in London at all, but in Paris. France.

To whom, exactly, should she complain? Tariq hadn't even been aboard the plane to compel her to come here. The scary thing was that Jessa knew full well that she had compelled herself.

"You cannot be angry with me," Tariq said softly, his voice low but no less intense. Jessa could feel the rich, slightly exotic sound of it roll through her, as if he'd hit some kind of tuning fork and her body was springing to attention. He nodded toward the view of stately buildings and glittering monuments in the cool night air, then returned his dark gaze to hers. "Such beauty forbids it."

"Can I not?" Jessa folded her hands in her lap and resolved to keep the hysteria at bay no matter what else happened. And if she was honest, what she felt when she looked at him was not hysteria, or anger. It was far more complicated than that.

"You agreed to dinner," Tariq said with a supremely arrogant shrug. A smile played with the corner of his mouth but did not quite take root there. "You did not specify where."

"Silly me," Jessa said. She met his eyes calmly, though it cost her something. "It never occurred to me that one was required to designate a preferred country when one agreed to a meal." *Under duress,* she wanted to say but did not. It wasn't entirely true, was it?

"There are many things that have not occurred to you, it seems," Tariq replied. Jessa did not care to explore the layers or possible meanings in that remark.

"You mean because of your vast wealth and resources," she said instead, as if she was used to discussing such things with various members of assorted royal families. "It is only to be expected when one is a king, isn't it? Surely these things would be much more impressive if they were the result of your own hard work and sweat."

"Perhaps," he said, a dark, affronted edge in his voice, though he did not alter his position. He continued to lounge in his chair like the pasha she supposed he really was. Only his gaze sharpened, piercing her, reminding her that she insulted him at her peril—and only because he allowed it.

"Do you find royalty offensive, Jessa?" he asked in a drawl. His brows rose, mocking her. "You English have a monarch of your own, I believe."

"The Queen has yet to whisk me off to a foreign country for a dinner that would have been uncomfortable enough in the local chip shop," Jessa retorted.

"It will only be uncomfortable if you wish it so," Tariq replied with infuriating patience, as if he knew something she did not. This time he really did smile, and it was not reassuring. "I am perfectly at ease."

"Somehow, that is not soothing," Jessa said, with the closest thing to a real laugh that she had uttered yet in his presence. It surprised them both. He looked startled as their eyes met and held. The moment seemed to stretch out and hover, locking Jessa in the green depths of his eyes with the glorious shine and sparkle of Paris stretching out behind him.

Her gaze drifted to his mouth, that hard, almost cruel mouth that could smile so breathtakingly and could do things to her that made her feel feverish to imagine. She felt her own lips part on a breath, or perhaps it was a sigh, and the world seemed to narrow and brighten all at the same time. She felt the now familiar coiling of tension in her belly, and the corresponding melting in her core. She felt the arch of her back and the matching curve of her toes inside her shoes. She began to *feel* each breath she took, as her heart kicked into a heavy, drugging rhythm that reminded her too well of his mouth upon her own, his hands on her skin.

Suddenly, brutally, the veil lifted. And Jessa realized in a sudden jolt, with an almost nauseating mixture of self-awareness and deep, feminine certainty, that this was exactly why she had come so docilely, so easily. Across borders, onto private planes, with nary a whisper of protest. This was why she had taken such pains in her bath earlier, dabbed scent behind her ears and between her breasts. She had told herself she was putting together her feminine armor. She had told herself she would dress the same way for any person she wished to appear strong in front of, that it was not romantic in the least to want to look her best or pin her hair up into a French twist or wear her most flattering and most lethal shoes. She had lied to herself, even as something within her knew the truth and had cried out for the wicked royal-blue dress that exposed her shoulders, kissed her curves and whispered erotically over her legs.

She had come here for him. For Tariq. For this raging passion that coursed through her veins and intoxicated her, this all-consuming desire that the intervening years and her own sacrifices had failed to douse in any way.

With a muttered oath that even she wasn't sure was a cry of desperation or a simple curse, Jessa rocked forward and to her feet. Restlessly—agitation making her body feel jerky and clumsy—she pushed herself away from the table and blindly headed toward the wrought-iron railing that seemed to frame the Paris street five stories below her feet as much as protect her from falling into it.

The truth seemed as cold as the autumn night, now that she had moved away from the brazier that hovered near the table—and the far more consuming fire that Tariq seemed to light in her.

She wanted him. Arguing with herself did nothing to stop it. She had spent the whole day determined to simply not be at home when he sent his car for her, and yet she had found herself immersed in the bath by half past four. She had ordered herself not to answer the door when the driver rang, but she had had the door open and her wrap around her shoulders before he could press the button a second time.

"Surely this should not distress you," Tariq said from behind her. Too close behind her, and once more she had not heard him move. Jessa closed her eyes. If she pretended, it was almost as if he was the magical, trustworthy lover she had believed him to be so long ago, and she the same starry-eyed, besotted girl. "It is a simple dinner, in a lovely place. What is there to upset you here?"

What, indeed? Only her own betrayal of all she'd thought she believed, all she thought she had gained in the years since his departure. What was that next to a luxurious meal on a Paris rooftop with the man she should avoid above all others?

"Perhaps you do not know me as well as you think," she replied, her voice ragged with all the emotion she fought to keep hidden. Or perhaps she did not know herself.

"Not for lack of trying," Tariq murmured. "But you will keep your mysteries, won't you?"

It was no surprise when his warm, strong hands cupped her shoulders, then stretched wide to test her flesh against his fingers, sending inevitable currents of desire tingling down her arms. She let out a sigh and bowed her head.

Perhaps this was inevitable. Perhaps this had always been meant to happen, somehow. She had never had the chance to say her goodbyes to Tariq, her fantasy lover, had she? She had run away to a friend's flat in Brighton to get her head together. The man she had loved had disappeared, and she learned soon after that he had never existed. But there had been no warning, no opportunity to express her feelings with the knowledge that it was their last time together.

A rebellious, outrageous thought wormed its way through her then, making her catch her breath.

What if she took, instead of lost? What if she claimed, instead of letting herself be deprived? What if she was the one in control, and no longer so passive, so submissive? What if she was the one who needed to get him out of her system, and not the other way around?

She turned in his loose grip, and leaned against the railing, tipping her head back so she could look him in the eye. What if she made this about what *she* wanted?

And what she wanted was the one last night she'd never had. She wanted to say her goodbyes—and it didn't hurt that in giving him one night, in taking it for herself, she was acknowledging that it could never be more than that between them. This was a memory, nothing more.

"I will give you one night," she said, before she lost her nerve. And then it was said, and there was no taking it back.

He froze. His face lost all expression, though his dark eyes glittered with jade fire. She had surprised him. *Good.*

"I beg your pardon?" he asked, enunciating each word very carefully, as if he thought he had misheard her, somehow. It made Jessa feel bolder. "What do you mean?"

"Must I repeat myself?" she asked, taking too much pleasure in tossing his own words back at him. She felt the power of this choice surge through her. She was the one in charge. She was the one who decided whether or not she would burn on this particular fire. And then she would walk away and finally be done with him. It would be like being reborn. "I don't recall you being so slow—"

"You must forgive me," he interrupted her with precious little civility, his teeth bared in something not at all as mild as a smile. "But why would you change your mind so suddenly?"

"Maybe I've considered things in a different light," Jessa said. Did she have to explain this to him, when she could hardly explain it to herself? She raised her brows. "Maybe I'm interested in the same things that you're interested in. Putting the past behind us, once and for all."

"For old time's sake?" he asked. He moved closer, his big body seeming to block out the City of Lights. Tension radiated from every part of him, and she knew she should be afraid of what he could do to her, what he could make her feel. She knew she should feel intimidated, outmatched once again.

But this was the one place where it didn't matter if he was a king and she a commoner. He wanted her with the same unwelcome intensity that she wanted him. In this, at least, they were equals. They matched.

She felt her mouth curve slightly into a smile that was as old as time, and spoke of a knowledge she had never put into words before, never felt so completely, down into her bones.

"What do you care?" she taunted him softly, daring him, challenging him.

His eyes went darker, his mouth almost grim with the passion she could feel surging through her veins.

"You are right," he said, his voice hoarse, and rough against her, though she welcomed it. Exulted in it. "I do not care at all."

His mouth came down on hers in something like fury, though it was much sweeter. Once again, he tasted her and went wild, and yet he merely kissed her, angling his head to better plumb the depths of her mouth, to intoxicate himself with her, with the feel of her soft body pressed against his. Her softness to his hardness. Her moan against his lips.

He had been prepared to seduce her if he had to. He had not been prepared for her to be the aggressor, and the surprise of it had desire raging through him.

"Be certain this is what you want," he growled, lifting his head and scanning her expression with fierce intensity. Her eyes were glazed with passion, her lips swollen from his kisses. Surely this would put an end to all the madness, all the nights he'd woken and reached for the phantom woman who was never there.

"Have I asked you to stop?" she asked, her breath uneven, her tone pure bravado. She tilted her stubborn chin into the air. "If you've changed your mind—"

"I am not the one who required so many games to achieve this goal," he reminded her, passion making his voice harsh. "I made my proposal from the start, hiding nothing."

"It is up to you," she said, her eyes narrowing in a maddening, challenging manner, her words infused with a certain strength he didn't understand. Who did Jessa Heath think she was that she so consistently, so foolishly, stood up to him, all the while refusing to tell him anything about her life, claiming she could only bore him? He could not recall the last person who had defied, much less taunted, him. Only Jessa dared.

A warning bell rang somewhere deep inside of him, but he ignored it.

"You will find that most things are, in fact, up to me," he replied, reminding them both that he, not she, was the one in charge, no matter how conciliatory he might act when it suited him.

He was a king. He might not have been born to the position, and he might have spent the better part of his life as an embarrassment to the man who had been, but he'd spent the past five years of his life atoning. He was in every way the monarch his uncle would have wished him to be, the nephew he should have been while his uncle lived. No imprudent and foolish woman could change that, not even this one, whom he realized he regarded as a kind of specter from his wastrel past. He would never fully put that past behind him until he put her there, too.

Jessa reached out her hand and placed it against his cheek. Tariq's mind went suddenly, scorchingly, blank as electricity surged between them.

"We can talk, if that is what you want," she said, as calmly as if discussing the evening's dinner menu. As unaffected, though he could feel the slight tremor in her delicate palm that belied her tone. "But it is not what I want."

"And what is it you want?"

"I do not want to talk," she said distinctly, purposefully, holding his gaze, her own rich with suggestion and the desire he was certain was written all over him. "And I don't think you want to, either. Do you?"

"Ah, Jessa," he said on a sigh, while a kind of moody triumph pumped through him and pulsed hard and long into his sex. She thought she was a match for him, did she? She would learn. And soon enough he would have her exactly where he wanted her. "You should not challenge me."

She cocked her head to one side, not cowed in the least, with the light of battle in her cinnamon eyes, and smiled.

It went directly to his head, his groin. He reached for her without thought, without anything at all but need, and pulled her into his arms.

CHAPTER SEVEN

IT WAS not enough. Her taste, her scent, her mouth beneath his and her hands tracing beguiling patterns down his chest. He wanted more.

"I want to taste you," he whispered in Arabic, and she shuddered as if she could understand him.

He wanted everything. Her surrender. Her artless, unstudied passion. The past back where it belonged, and left there.

But most of all, he wanted her naked.

Tariq raked his fingers into her hair, never lifting his mouth from hers, sending her hairpins flying and clattering against the heavy stones at their feet. Her heavy mass of copper curls tumbled from the sophisticated twist at the back of her head and fell in a jasmine-scented curtain around her, wild and untamed, just as he wanted her. Just as he would have her.

He lifted his mouth from hers and took a moment to study her face. Why should he spend even an hour obsessing over this woman? She was no great beauty, like some of the women he had been linked with in the past. Her face would never grace the covers of magazines nor appear on twelve-foot-high cinema screens. Yet even so, he found he could not look away. The spray of freckles across her nose, the sooty lashes that framed her spice-colored eyes—combined with her courtesan's mouth, she was something more unsettling than beautiful. She was… viral. She got into the blood and stayed there, changing and growing, and could not be cured using any of the usual methods.

Tariq had no idea where that appallingly fanciful notion had come from. He would not even be near her now were it not for the mornings he had woken in the palace in Nur, overcome by the feverish need to claim this woman once more. He scowled down at her, and then scowled harder when she only smiled that mysterious smile again in return, unfazed by him.

"Come," he ordered her, at his most autocratic, and took her arm. Not roughly, but not brooking any argument, either, he led her across the terrace and ushered her into the quiet house.

His staff had discreetly lit a few lamps indoors. They cast soft beams of light across the marble floors and against the high, graceful ceilings. He led her through the maze of galleries filled with priceless art and reception rooms crowded with extravagant antiques that comprised a large portion of the highest floor of the house, all of them boasting stellar views of nighttime Paris from the soaring windows. He barely noticed.

"Where are we going?" she asked, but there was a lack of curiosity in her voice. As if she was as cool and as unaffected as she claimed to be, which he could not countenance. Surely it shouldn't matter—surely she could pretend anything she wished and he should not care in the slightest—but Tariq fought to keep himself from growling at her. He could not accept that she was so calm while he felt so wild. Even if her calmness was, as he suspected and wanted to believe, an act.

None of this matters, he reminded himself, coldly. *As long as you get her out of your system, once and for all.*

After all, despite his obsessive concentration on a single woman for far too long, the truth was that Tariq did not have time for this. He had a country to run. Nur was poised on the brink of great change, but change did not come easily, especially in his part of the world. There was always a price. There were always those who preferred to stick to the old ways, out of fear or faith or sheer stubbornness. There were those who wanted only to see the old regime, of which Tariq was the last surviving member, crumble and disappear, and no matter that such a thing would cause even more chaos and bloodshed.

There were border disputes to settle, and tribal councils to oversee. Tariq loved his beautiful, harsh, deeply complicated and often conflicted country more than he had ever loved a human being, including himself. It felt like the worst kind of disloyalty to be tangled up with this woman, especially since she was the last one he had been with in his previous incarnation. Perhaps he judged her more severely because she was the other face he saw when he revisited his old disgraceful behavior in his mind.

Tariq led Jessa into the sumptuous master suite that sprawled across the back of the house, and only released her arm when he had closed the door behind them, shutting them in. Would she still be so brave now that the games were quickly coming to an end? Would she dare to continue this foolishness?

She took a few steps into the room ahead of him, her head slightly bent and her hands clasped in front of her as if she was listening for second thoughts or offering up a prayer. *Too late,* he thought with no little satisfaction. He let his gaze follow the soft indentation of her spine down to the flare of her hips, as the royal-blue dress shimmied in the low lights and seemed to grow brighter in the reflection of the gilt-edged opulence that surrounded them. Tariq was no particular fan of French furniture—he found it too fussy, too liable to collapse beneath his large frame—but he could appreciate the way so much Continental splendor seemed to enhance her natural glow. She turned her head then, looking at him over her shoulder.

It was as if the room smoldered. Tariq thought only of flame, of heat, of burying himself so deeply inside of her that the only thing he'd care about would be the way she gasped his name.

She did not speak. She only watched him, her eyes wide but without apprehension as he closed the distance between them with a few short strides. He reached out and used his hands to trace the parts of her body that his eyes had so recently touched: the soft nape of her neck, the sinuous length of her spine, the mesmerizing place where her hips curved gently into her bottom. He reached down and drew the silky dress up over her legs, slowly, letting the fabric caress her. The room was silent, only the sounds of their breathing and the faint, seductive whisper of fabric moving against flesh. He prolonged the moment, enjoying the way the dress felt in his hands, enjoying more the way her flushed skin felt as he touched her in passing, and then he drew the filmy dress over her head and cast it aside.

She turned to face him then, a flush rising in her cheeks, and he saw her arms move as if she wanted to cover herself or hide from him. She stopped herself, her expression betraying nothing more than a quick blink of her eyes, and dropped her arms back down to her sides.

She stood before him, clad only in a black lace bra that

pushed her breasts toward him, the swell of all that creamy flesh calling his name, begging for his tongue, his hands. Below, she wore nothing save a pair of sheer panties and her wickedly high shoes. She looked like something she was not, or had not been when he knew her, when he had claimed her innocence as his right. She looked decadent. Delicious.

Mine.

"It appears I will have my dessert before my dinner," Tariq said, pushing aside the possessive urge that roared through him. He traced the delicate ridge of her collarbone, dipping into the hollow where her pulse beat hard against her throat. She was like his own private banquet. Just because he had ulterior motives it didn't mean he wasn't prepared to thoroughly enjoy himself.

"Perhaps I want dessert as well," Jessa replied, only the slightest tremor in her voice, as if she was not flushed with color and practically naked before him.

She wanted to be tough. Tariq smiled, released her.

"Then by all means, help yourself."

She swayed toward him, rocking slightly on her feet. It could be the precarious shoes in the deep carpet, though Tariq rather thought it was the same strange hunger that gripped him and made him feel curiously close to unsteady himself. Then her hands were on him, sweeping across the hard planes of his chest, testing the hardy muscles he'd built up after five years of intensive training with his royal guard. A king must be prepared to fight the battles he expected his subjects to fight, Tariq's uncle had always believed. And so Tariq had transformed himself from an idle playboy who visited a fancy spa-like gym merely to maintain a certain trouser size that photographed well, to a warrior capable of lethal combat. He shrugged off his jacket and let it drop to the floor. The expertly tailored concoction barely made a sound as it hit the ground. Jessa did not spare it so much as a glance.

Tariq's eyes narrowed against his own pounding hunger as he let Jessa explore this new, fierce body of his, sliding her palms from his shoulders to his waist to yank his shirt-tails free from his trousers. He watched her pull her seductive lower lip between her teeth as she worried the buttons out of their holes one by one and slowly, torturously, exposed his skin to the slightly cooler air of the suite around them. When she had unbuttoned every button and unhooked his cuff links, she pushed the shirt back on his shoulders so it hung there, exposing his chest to her view.

She let out a long hiss of breath. He could feel it tickle across his skin, arrowing straight to his arousal, making him thicken. He made no move to hide it, only continued to wait, to watch, to see what she would do.

She looked up then, and their gazes clashed together in a manner that seemed as intimate and passionate as the kisses they'd shared before. Tariq moved to speak, but no words came.

He did not expect her to move, her expression taking on a look of intense feminine satisfaction. He reached for her, but she shocked him by leaning forward and placing her hot, open mouth, that wicked courtesan's mouth that had featured prominently in his fantasies since he'd tasted it again this morning, in the valley between his pectoral muscles.

When he swore, he swore in Arabic, Jessa discovered in a distant kind of amusement, and he still sounded every inch a king.

Not that she cared. She could not seem to stop tasting him. She trailed kisses across one hard pectoral plane, then moved to the other, worrying the hard male nipple she found with the tip of her tongue, laughing softly when she heard him groan.

Jessa moved even closer and pushed the soft linen shirt from Tariq's broad shoulders, letting it fall to the floor behind him. His strong, muscled arms came around her, crushing her breasts against his chest and drawing her into the cradle of his thighs. Just like that, they were pressed together, bare skin against bare skin, so that the intrusion of her lacy, delectable bra seemed almost criminal. Heat coiled in her groin and shot through her, making her head spin. She fought to breathe, and wasn't sure she much cared if she could not. She felt his bare skin against hers like an exultation, like memory and fantasy come to life.

She had not felt like this in five long years. She had missed his skin, the addictive heat of him that sizzled through her and left her feeling branded and desperate for more. Her head dropped back of its own volition, and she heard him muttering words she could not understand against the soft flesh of her neck. He used his tongue, his lips, his teeth. He surrounded her, held her, his hands finding her curves and testing them against his palms, stroking and teasing and driving her hunger to fever pitch. And all the while his exciting, overwhelming hardness pressed against the juncture of her thighs, driving her ever closer to senseless capitulation.

This was how it had always been, this rush to madness, to pleasure, to the addictive ecstasy that only Tariq could bring her. She could not get close enough. She could not think straight, and she could not imagine why she would want to. This was how she remembered him, so hard, so male, dominating her so easily, so completely—

Careful! a voice in the back of her mind whispered, panicked. Jessa pulled herself back from the brink of total surrender, blinking to clear the haze of passion from her eyes. It was so easy to lose herself in him. It was much too easy to forget. She raised her head and searched Tariq's expression. His features were hard, fierce and uncompromising as he stared back at her. She felt herself tremble deep inside—warning or *wanting*, she wasn't sure. But it didn't matter. She had been the one to make this decision. She was not weak, malleable, *senseless*. She could call the shots. She would.

"Second thoughts?" His voice was a rasp, thick with passion, and her hips moved against his in unconscious response. His eyes glittered dangerously, nearly black now in the center of the opulent gold-and-blue room.

"None whatsoever," she replied. She eased back from him, aware that he let her do it, let her move slightly in the circle of his embrace.

Holding his gaze with all the defiance she could muster—*I am strong, not weak; I am in charge*—she dropped her hands to his trousers. His hard mouth curved, and he shifted his weight, giving her easier access.

Jessa remembered her horror at exactly this image earlier this same day—her fear that she would far too easily find herself doing what she was about to do. But it was different now, because he was not compelling her to do it. She was not begging him for anything—she was taking what she wanted. He was not orchestrating anything. He was hers to experience as she wished, to make up for all those lonely nights when she would have done anything at all for the chance to touch him again.

She pulled his belt free of its buckle and unbuttoned the top button of his whisper-soft trousers, letting the backs of her fingers revel in the blazing heat of his taut abdomen and the scrape of the coarse hair that surrounded his manhood.

She moved the zipper down slowly, careful to ease it over the hard ridge of his jutting sex, and then she freed him entirely, reaching between them to cup him in her hands.

He muttered something too low to catch, though she thought it was her name.

She could not recall him ever allowing her this kind of unhurried exploration before. Their passion back then had always been too explosive, too all-encompassing. She had never thought to ask for anything. She had been too awash in sensation, too overcome and swept off her feet. She had surrendered to him entirely, body and soul.

But that was the past. Here, now, she caressed his impressive length. He let out a sound too fierce to be a moan. He reached for her, his hands diving once again into the thick mass of her hair and holding her loosely, encouraging her, not correcting her. Jessa ignored him, and concentrated on this most male part of him instead. He was softer here than anywhere else on his rugged warrior's form, like the softest satin stretched across steel. And so much hotter, so hot that she felt an answering heat flood her own sex, and an ache begin to build inside her.

She raised her head up to meet his gaze, while his hands moved to frame her face. She frowned slightly when he bent his head toward hers. He paused, his mouth a scant breath away. Jessa felt her heart pound and could feel him stir in her hands.

"No?" he asked softly. He did not quite frown in return. "Is this another game, Jessa?"

"This is my night." She felt his hands flex slightly, but she felt too powerful to allow him to cow her. "My game."

"Is that so?" His eyes mocked her, though his expression otherwise remained the same. He did not believe she could take control, perhaps. Or he knew how close she came to losing herself, her head, when he touched her. Jessa told herself it didn't matter.

"Perhaps you should tell me the rules of this game, before you begin it." His voice and his eyes were more distant, suddenly, but his hands against the delicate skin of her cheekbones were still warm, still exciting.

"There is only one rule," Jessa said evenly. Deliberately, so there could be no misunderstanding. "And it is that I am in charge."

Something ignited in his gaze then, and sent an answering shudder down along her spine to weaken her knees. He pulled himself up without seeming to move, arrogant and imperial, and looked at her as if he could not comprehend what she had said. Jessa held her breath.

"And what does that entail, exactly?" he asked, his voice lower and laced with warning. "Will I wake to find myself bound naked from the chandelier, to be tittered over and eventually cut down by the housekeeper?"

Jessa tested out the image of Tariq so completely at her mercy and smiled slightly, even as a hectic kind of restlessness washed through her, urging her to continue what her hands had already started. She tested his length against her palm once again and watched his arrogant focus shatter.

"If that is what I want, then yes," she said recklessly. "Don't pretend you won't enjoy it."

"And what about what I want?" he asked. Idly, he wrapped a single long, copper curl around his finger and tugged. Jessa did not mistake the sensual menace underlying his tone. She shrugged.

"What about it?" she asked.

"Jessa—"

But he cut himself off, because Jessa sank down in front of him, onto her knees, in a single smooth motion. She heard his breath leave him in a rush. She watched his eyes darken even further, becoming like night.

She did not feel diminished. She did not feel mindless or senseless, or under his power. Quite the opposite.

She felt like a goddess.

"Jessa," he said again, but this time her name was a prayer. A wish.

She smiled. And then she took him deep into her mouth.

CHAPTER EIGHT

JESSA heard him sigh, or maybe he said her name once more, too low to be heard.

It was thrilling. Jessa felt her own sex throb and melt in time to his slow, careful thrusts, and felt him grow harder. He moaned and she felt potent. Alive. Powerful beyond imagining.

"Enough," he said suddenly, abruptly disengaging from her.

Jessa sat back on her heels, stunned.

"I'm the one who will decide when it's enough," she retorted, glaring up at him. "Not you. Or have you already forgotten that I'm to be in charge?"

"I have not forgotten anything," Tariq replied, his voice clipped, rough, impatient with need. "But perhaps you have forgotten that I did not agree."

"But you—"

"Later," Tariq said, interrupting her. He sank to his knees on the carpet in front of her, making her heart stutter in her chest before kicking into a frenetic beat. This close, Jessa could see the wildness in his eyes, and the passion stamped across his features, giving him a certain breath-taking ferocity.

She started to argue, but instead he leaned closer and claimed her mouth with his. He held her head between his hands, held her captive, and she didn't think to fight it. He moved her to the angle that best suited him, plundering her mouth with his, taking control. Claiming her. Proving his mastery, and it made her ache and swell and melt against him. Again. Then again, and again.

Heat like liquid washed over her, through her. She felt hectic, frantic, alive with need, shaky from the inside out. She buried her hands in his thick, black hair, exulting in the way it felt like rough silk against her palms, in such contrast to the punishing, glorious demands of his mouth.

It occurred to Jessa that she should protest, wrench back the control she refused to accept he'd only allowed her, indulged her.

Tariq took one strong, capable hand from her head and slid it down her back, leaving trails of sensation in his wake, causing her to arch against him at the wonder of his touch. Then he moved around to her front and pulled once, twice, against the band of her panties. By the time Jessa registered the fact that he was using both of his hands, and that he seemed to be tugging, there was a rip and he was done. He tossed her torn panties aside, and the look he slanted her way dared her to comment on it.

She didn't say a word. She wasn't sure she could speak. She was having trouble breathing, much less thinking, as they knelt together in the center of the thick Aubusson carpet.

Tariq's long, elegant fingers slipped between her thighs, tracing the contours of her sex, then the honeyed heat within. His green eyes held her still, imprisoned her, even as he tested her tight sheath with one strong finger, then another. Jessa felt herself clench around him, and shuddered.

"Forgive me, but I cannot wait for you to finish playing

your games with me," he said then, but there was absolutely no apology in the way he looked at her. He was all arrogant male, every inch a king, and he did not wait for her to respond. Instead, he slid his hands back up the length of her torso and then picked her up as if she weighed no more than a pound coin. He shifted her across the space between them and settled her astride him.

"Tariq—" But she didn't know what she wanted to say, or how to say it, and he merely twisted his hips and thrust deep inside her.

So deep. So full. Finally.

"Yes," he said, need pulling his face taut, his eyes black and wild for her. "Finally."

Only then did Jessa realize she'd spoken aloud. Her breasts seemed to swell even more against their prison of lace, and she rubbed herself helplessly against the wall of his chest, unable to stop, unable to get enough of the feel of him. Again. *Finally.*

The perfection of it, of him, of their bodies fused together, overwhelmed her. She had no memory of looping her arms around his neck, and yet she held him. Other memories, older ones, of the many times they'd tested the feverish joy of this slick, matchless, breathtaking union, threatened to spill from her eyes.

Now she remembered why she had thrown away her life so heedlessly because of this man. Now she remembered why she had let Tariq twist her into knots and cast her aside like a rag doll—why she hadn't even recognized what was happening until it was done. For the glory of this moment, this connection, this addictive, electrifying link.

And then he moved, one long, sure stroke, and Jessa came apart. He thrust once, twice. She sobbed against him while her body exploded into pieces, as she shook and shook and shook. She panted, her face in the crook of his neck. The world disappeared and there was nothing but the singular scent and taste of Tariq's skin at her mouth, and his hard length still buried deep in her sex.

"Come back to me." His voice was rough, intimate. "Now." It was no less an order for the sensual tone in which it was delivered. Still, it made her shiver.

"I am finished," she managed to say, her eyes still closed, her head still cradled between his throat and his wide shoulder. She meant, *I am dead*. She was not sure she would have minded were that true.

"But I am not." Tariq shifted position, holding her bottom in one large hand and keeping her hips flush with his. "Hold on to me," he demanded, and she was too dazed, too drunk on the sensations still firing through her to do anything but what he asked. She wrapped her arms around his shoulders and then everything whirled around and she was on her back on the plush carpet and he was between her legs and still so deep inside her, so hard and so big, she thought she might weep from the sheer pleasure of it.

Tariq bent his head and took a stiff nipple into his mouth, sucking on it through the lace barrier. Jessa moaned as a new fire seared through her, the slight abrasion of the lace and the hot, wet heat of his mouth together almost too much to bear.

He laughed softly, and began to move his hips, guiding himself in and out of her with consummate, devastating skill. He turned his attention to her other breast, making Jessa arch into him again and raise her hips to meet his every stroke. Their hips moved in perfect harmony. Once again, she ached. Once again, the fire grew and raged and consumed her. Jessa felt the storm growing within her, taking her to fever pitch, though she fought against it.

"Let go," he said, his voice fierce, his gaze intense.

"But you—and I—" But how could she concentrate on what she wanted to say when every slide of his body against hers turned her molten, incandescent?

"I command it," he said.

Her eyes flew wide. Tariq smiled. And then he reached between their bodies and touched her, and she flew over the edge again.

This time, he did not stop. He did not wait. He continued to thrust into her, slow and steady, until her sobs became ragged breaths and her eyes focused once more on his face.

"One more time," he ordered her, his eyes gleaming.

"I cannot possibly!"

"You can." He bent toward her, pulling the lace cup away from one breast to tease the flesh beneath with his lips. His tongue. His teeth. Jessa shuddered in response. Tariq slanted a look at her. "You will."

And when she did, he went with her.

It took a long time for Jessa to return to earth, and when she did, he was still stretched out over her, still pressing her into the floor. She was afraid to think too much about what had just happened. She was afraid to allow herself to face it. She wasn't certain she would like what she might find.

That much pleasure could only be trouble. She could not assign it too much meaning, decide it was something it could never be. She could not allow herself to forget that this was her idea. That she was here to take some of this pleasure for herself and hoard it. This was her long-overdue goodbye, that was all. She didn't know why she felt so fragile, so vulnerable.

Tariq stirred and rolled off her, sitting up as he yanked his trousers back into place. As he fastened them, Jessa struggled to sit up herself. Was this it, then? She hadn't thought much beyond the actual pleasure part of the *one night of pleasure* idea. How was one expected to negotiate such moments? The last time she had been with him, she had been openly and happily in love with him. There had been no awkwardness. Jessa pulled her bra back into position, and swallowed when her eyes fell on the torn scraps of what used to be her panties. She looked down and saw, with some amazement, that she still wore her impractical shoes.

Beside her, Tariq rose to his feet in a single, lithe movement that reminded her that he was a warrior now, in ways she could only pretend to understand. He turned and looked down at her, his expression unreadable.

Jessa was suddenly painfully aware of her surroundings, the majestic grandeur of the well-appointed room, from its carved moldings to the graceful furniture that looked more like works of art than places to sit or to store belongings. It was not even the bedroom, merely the first in what she could see now was a series of rooms. A suite, complete with floor-to-ceiling windows that showed off the lights of Paris shooting off in all directions. Tariq stood before her, half-naked, his thick hair tangled and hanging around his face, making him look untamed and remote but no less regal. He belonged in such a place, surrounded by such things. And here she was, half-naked on a priceless rug, Jessa Heath from Fulford with nothing to show for herself, not even her panties.

It occurred to her that he had only said he wanted to get her out of his system. He had never elaborated what might happen when he had.

The moment stretched between them, long past awkward. Jessa could still feel him between her legs, and yet it was as if a perfect stranger stood before her, carved from stone. Some avenging angel prepared to hand down judgment.

But she had been through worse, she reminded herself,

and no matter what happened, no matter how unpleasant the moment, she had chosen this. That was the key point. She had *chosen* this.

Jessa sat up straighter and pushed her hair back from her face. It hardly mattered if she looked disheveled at this point, after all. He must have had his mouth or his hands on every inch of her body. And what could he possibly do or say to her? Would he leave her cruelly, perhaps? She had already survived that once, relatively unscathed. She met his gaze proudly.

"Thank you," she said in her most polite tone. It was the one she used in fancy restaurants and to bank managers. "That was exactly what I wanted."

"I am delighted to hear it." His tone was sardonic. "I live to serve." Now he openly mocked her. She pretended she could not hear the edge in his voice.

"Yes, well." She got to her feet with rather less grace than he had displayed, and looked around for her dress. She saw it in a crumpled heap a few feet away. "If only that were true. You would be a different man, wouldn't you?" She moved toward the dress.

"Jessa." Her name was another command, and she looked at him even though she knew she should ignore him, pick up her things and walk out. "What are you doing?"

"My dress..." She gestured at it but couldn't seem to turn away from him, not when he was looking at her that way, so brooding and dark and something else, something she might have called possessive on another man.

"You won't need it."

"I won't?"

He didn't move, he only watched her, but his eyes were hot. Jessa was shocked to feel her body respond to him. Anew. Again. Her nipples hardened, her sex pulsed.

It was absurd. She had gotten what she'd wanted, hadn't she? What was the point of drawing it out? No matter how ravenous she seemed to be for him.

"We are not done here," he said quietly. His gaze was hard, yet she softened. "We have hardly begun."

CHAPTER NINE

TARIQ stood at the window that rose high above the bedroom, looking out over the city. Dawn snuck in with long pink fingers, teasing the famous rooftops of Paris before him, yet he barely saw it. Behind him, Jessa slept in the great bed that stood in the center of the ornate room, the heavy white-and-gold-brocade coverlet long since discarded, her naked limbs curled beneath her, rose and pink from the exertions of the long night. He did not need to confirm this with his own eyes again; he would hear it if her breathing altered, if she turned over, if she awoke.

It was as if he could feel her body as an extension of his own. Perhaps this was inevitable after such a night, he told himself, but he knew better. He had lived a life of excess for more years than he cared to recall, and he had had many nights that would qualify as extreme, and yet he had never felt this kind of connection to a woman. He didn't care for it. It reminded him of all the things he had worked so hard to forget.

"You make me feel alive," he had told her once, years ago, recklessly, and she had laughed as she rose above him, naked and beautiful, her face open and filled with light.

"You *are* alive," she had whispered in his ear, holding him close. She had then proceeded to prove it to them both.

Tariq had lost count of the times he had reached for her last night, or her for him. He knew he had slept but little, far more interested in tasting her, teasing her, sinking into her one more time. He had reacquainted himself with every nook and cranny of her body, all of its changes, all of its secrets—the pleasure so intense, so astounding, that he could not bring himself to let it end.

Because he knew that once he stopped, he would have to face the truths he was even now avoiding. And as the night wore on, Tariq had found himself less and less interested in doing so.

"This is a feast," Jessa had said at some point, while they sat in the sitting room and ate some of the rich food they'd ignored earlier, wearing very little in the way of clothes. She had smiled at him, unselfconscious and at ease with her legs folded beneath her and her hair tumbled down around her bare shoulders. She had looked free. Just as she had always been with him.

"Indeed it is," he had replied, but he had not been talking about the meal.

Memories chased through him now, hurtling him back to a time he wanted to forget—had worked to forget, in fact, for years. Touching her, tasting her, breathing in her scent. These things had unlocked something in him that he had worked hard to keep hidden, even from himself.

His parents had died in a car accident when he was too young to remember more than fleeting images of his father's rare smile, his mother's dark curtain of hair. He had been taken into the palace by his only remaining relative, his uncle the king, and raised with his cousins, the princes of Nur. His uncle was the only parent Tariq had ever known, and yet Tariq had always been keenly aware that he was not his uncle's son. Just as he had always known that his cousins were the future rulers of the country, and had been trained from birth as such.

"Your cousins have responsibilities to our people," his uncle had told Tariq when they were all still young.

"And what are my responsibilities?" Tariq had asked guilelessly.

His uncle had only smiled at him and patted him on the head.

Tariq had understood. He was not important, not in the way his cousins were.

And so he did as he pleased. Though his uncle periodically suggested that Tariq had more to offer the world than a life full of expensive cars and equally costly European models, Tariq had never seen the point in discovering what that was. He had played with the stock market because it amused him and he was good at it, but it had been no more to him than another kind of high-stakes poker game like the ones he played in private back rooms in Monte Carlo.

He had long since buried the feelings that had haunted him as a child—that he was an outcast in his own family, tolerated by them yet never of them. He believed they cared for him, but he knew he was their charity case. Their duty. Never simply theirs.

Tariq heard Jessa move in the bed behind him. He turned to see if she had awoken and if it was time at last to have a conversation he had no wish to pursue. But she only settled herself into a different position, letting out a small, contented sigh.

He turned back around to face the window, heedless of the cool air on his bare skin, still caught up in the past. The summer he had met Jessa was the summer his uncle had finally put his foot down. He could not threaten Tariq with the loss of his income or possessions, of course, for Tariq had quadrupled his own personal fortune by that point, and then some. But that did not mean the old man had been without weapons.

"You must change your life," the old king had said, frowning at Tariq across the table set out for them on the balcony high on the cliffs. He had summoned his nephew to the family villa on their private island in the Mediterranean, off the coast of Turkey, for this conversation. Tariq had not expected it to be pleasant, though he had always managed to talk his uncle out of his tempers in the past. He had assumed he would do the same that day.

"Into what?" Tariq had asked, shrugging, watching the waves rise and fall far below them, deep and blue. He had been thirty-four then and so world-weary. So profoundly bored. "My life is the envy of millions."

"Your life is empty," his uncle had retorted. "Meaningless." He waved his hand in disgust, taking in Tariq's polished, too fashionable appearance. "What are you but one more playboy sheikh, looked down upon by the entire world, confirming all their worst suspicions about our people?"

"Until they want my money," Tariq had replied coolly. "At which point it is amazing how quickly they become respectful. Even obsequious."

"And this is enough for you? This is all you aspire to? You, who carry the royal blood of the kingdom of Nur in your veins?"

"What would you have me do, Uncle?" Tariq had asked, impatient though he dared not show it. They had had this conversation, or some version of it, every year since Tariq had gone to university where, to his uncle's dismay, he had not approached his studies with the same level of commitment he had shown when approaching the women in his classes.

"You do nothing," his uncle had said matter-of-factly, in a more serious tone than Tariq had ever heard from him, at least when directed at Tariq personally. "You play games with money and call it a career, but it is a joke. You win, you lose, it is all a game to you. You are an entirely selfish creature. I would tell you to marry, to do your duty to your family and your bloodline as your cousins must do, but what would you have to offer your sons? You are barely a man."

Tariq had gritted his teeth. This was not just his uncle talking, not just the only version of a parent he had ever known—this was his king. He had no choice but to tolerate it.

"Again," he had managed to say eventually, fighting to keep his tone appropriately respectful, "what is it you want me to do?"

"It is not about what I want," his uncle had said, disappointment dripping from every hard word. "It is about who you are. I cannot force you to do anything. You are not my son. You are not my heir."

He could not have known, Tariq had supposed then, how deeply his words cut, how close to the bone. No matter that they were no more than the truth.

"But you will no longer be welcome in my family unless you contribute to it in some way," his uncle had continued. He had stared at Tariq for a moment, his eyes grim. "You have six months to prove this to me. If you have not changed your ways by then, I will wash my hands of you." He had shaken his head. "And I must tell you, nephew, I am not hopeful."

Tariq had left the villa that same night, determined to put distance between himself and his uncle and the words his uncle had said, at last vocalizing Tariq's worst fears.

He was not a son, an heir. He was disposable. He was no more than a duty, dictated by tradition and law. But he was not family in a way that mattered. He shared nothing with them but blood. Whatever that meant.

Tariq had never been so angry, so at sea, in all of his life. He had never felt so alienated and alone, and he was not a man who had ever formed deep attachments, so he had not known how to handle what was, he thought in retrospect, grief.

And then he had met Jessa, and she had loved him.

He knew that she had loved him, instantly and thoroughly. She had charmed him with the force of her adoration and her artlessness—her inability to conceal it, or play sophisticated games. Other women had fallen in love with him before, or so they had claimed, but had they loved Tariq or his bank balance? He had never cared before. He had lied about who he was, angrily attempting to distance himself from his reputation as if that might appease his uncle, but she had not noticed.

"You trust too easily," he had told her one night, when they lay stretched out before the fire, unable to stop touching each other.

"I do not!" she had protested, laughing at him, her face tilted toward him, her eyes warm and soft, like cinnamon sugar. "I am quite savvy!"

"If you say so," he had murmured, playing with her curls, coiling them around his fingers. At first he had waited for her to change, as they all did once they learned who he was. He had waited for those knowing looks, or the clever feminine ways of asking for money, or a new car, or an apartment in a posh neighborhood. But Jessa had never changed. She had simply loved him.

"I trust *you*, Tariq," she had whispered then, still smiling. She had even kissed him, with all the innocence and passion she had in her young body.

When she looked at him with those wide cinnamon eyes that reminded him of the home he wasn't sure he would ever be permitted to see again, he felt like the man he should have been.

But then she had disappeared abruptly and completely, which had bothered him far more than it should have. And before he could make sense of what he felt, his uncle and cousins had died, all at once, and Tariq had been forced to face reality. What was the love of one besotted girl when there were wars to prevent and a country to run and those last, terrible words from his uncle that he could never disprove? He could never show his uncle that he was, in fact, a man. That he, too, could uphold the family honor and do his duty. That he had only ever wanted to be treated as a part of the family in the first place.

He turned then, letting his gaze fall upon the sinuous curves of her body as she lay on her side, facing away from him, the curve of her hip and the dip of her waist even more enticing now, after he had had her in every way he could imagine. He had meant only to slake his desire, to have her and be done with her at last. He had spent years convincing himself that she was no more than an itch that needed to be scratched. He had not expected to feel anything but lust.

He had convinced himself he would *feel* nothing at all.

"You are a fool," he whispered to himself.

But Jessa Heath still managed to cast a spell around him. It was the way she gave herself over with total abandon, he thought, studying her form in the morning light. To her anger, to her passion.

Even now that she knew exactly who he was, she still

wanted nothing from him. If anything, his real identity made her like him less. And yet she still fell to pieces in his arms, shattered at the slightest touch. It was as if she had been made specifically for him. As if she could still make him that man she'd seen in him five years ago, as if he was that man, finally, when he was with her.

Which was why he let her sleep, why he crossed the room and sat beside her, drinking her in, knowing that once she woke, the spell would be broken. Reality would intrude once again and remind him that he needed a queen, and she was the girl who had become the emblem of his disappointing former life.

And this night would become one more fever dream, one more memory, that he would lock away and soon enough, he knew, forget.

Jessa woke slowly.

The morning sun poured in from the tall windows, illuminating the bed and making her feel as if she was lit from within. She tugged the tangled length of her hair out from beneath her, knowing it had to be wild after such a night. Knowing she was wild and raw inside as well, though she couldn't think about it. Not yet. Not quite yet.

Not while he was still so near.

She knew he was there before she saw him, as if she had an internal radar that told her Tariq's specific whereabouts. She turned her head and there he was, just where she had sensed him. He sat on the edge of the bed, still gloriously naked, his body like something that ought to be carved in the finest marble and displayed in museums. He was not looking at her for the moment, so Jessa let herself drink her fill of him.

Something in the way he held himself, the way he stared

broodingly toward the window, made her frown. He looked almost sad. She wanted to reach over and soothe him, to kiss away whatever darkness had come upon him while she slept. She might not know *why* he wanted her as he had told her he did from the first, but she had come to accept that it was true, over and over again in the night. The wonder was, she wanted him too. Still. Even now.

But then he turned his head. His expression was unreadable, his dark green eyes solemn, his dark hair the kind of tousled mess that begged to be touched. Though she did not dare.

It was only to be expected that things should feel strained, Jessa reflected, staring back at him for a moment. One night, they had both said. And now it was morning, and the sun was too bright, and it was best to put all of this behind them.

She would not think about what they had done or the ways they had done it. She would not think about how she had sobbed and cried out for him and screamed his name. Again and again and again. It was only sex, she told herself sternly. Just sex. No need to torture herself about it. No need to give her emotions free rein, no matter how much her heart wanted her to do otherwise. She could be more like a man and compartmentalize. Why not? Sex was simply sex. It had nothing to do with feelings unless one wished otherwise. And she did not wish it. End of story.

Now he could go his way and she hers. Just as they had planned. There was no need to dig any further into their past and haul all of that pain back into the light of day. It could be boxed up and locked away, forever.

She remembered that she was supposed to feel empowered, not suddenly shy, no matter how exposed she felt.

"So," she said, trying to sound matter-of-fact. "It is finally morning."

"So it is." Tariq did not move, he only watched her. It was unnerving. Her heart began to pick up speed, though she was not sure why.

"I can't help but notice that I am in France," Jessa said, looking beyond him to the graceful Paris streets outside the window. She had always meant to visit Paris. She wasn't certain this counted. "Rather farther away from York than I expected to be. I hope you will not mind—"

"Jessa."

She flushed, suddenly furious, or that was what she called the emotion that flashed through her, hot and dangerous. She made a fist and struck the soft bedding beside her.

"I hate it when you do that," she threw at him. "You do not have to interrupt me all the time. I don't care if you're a king. You are not *my* king. It's just rude."

"And, of course, I would not wish to appear rude," Tariq replied, an edge in his voice that made the fine hairs on the back of her neck stand up straight. "I have made you come more times than you can possibly count, and you wish to lecture me on—"

"How do you like it?" she demanded, interrupting him. "It's frustrating, isn't it? Because, obviously, the person interrupting believes that whatever he has to say is of far more importance, that *he* is of far more importance—"

"Or perhaps the person talking is overwrought and hysterical." His voice was cool. Jessa bit her lip and looked away. She became uncomfortably aware of her own nudity, and of the fact that the frustrated heat in her cheeks was no doubt evident all over her exposed body.

She knew what she was doing. She was drawing this out, deliberately avoiding any number of elephants in the room. Another way to do that was simply to leave. The agreed-upon night was over and done. There was no more reason for them to be talking about anything. He had claimed what he wanted, as had she, and her secrets remained safe. It was time instead to return to her life and finally put Tariq where he belonged—in the past.

It was long past time to move on.

She swung her legs to the edge of the bed and stood, not looking at him.

"I think I'll take a bath," she said. She had never sounded so chipper, so polite. "Then I need to return to York."

She felt awkward. Tense. Perhaps that was just how she would continue to feel until she was safely back in her own life. She tried to shake it off. But when she started to move toward the bathroom, a luxurious palace all its own, she had to walk in front of him, and he held up a hand.

"Come here," he said quietly.

She hesitated, but then reminded herself that she had already handled him. She had already made it through the night intact. What could he do now? She had made love to him so many times that she'd forgotten anything existed outside of him, and yet she had still woken up herself. Whole, complete. Not lost in him as she had been before. So why was she this nervous?

She moved toward him, wary. It was something about the look in his eyes, something she couldn't place. Not that dark passion he seemed to fight against as much as she did. Not lust. She was more than familiar with those. He beckoned for her to come closer, inside the vee of his powerful legs. Cautiously, she complied.

He did not look up at her. He raised his hands and placed them on her hips, lightly encircling them. His fingers smoothed against her skin, tracing patterns from her hipbone to her navel, then back. Bemused, and not un-affected by his touch, even now, Jessa blinked down at him.

He looked up then and, as their gazes met, Jessa suddenly knew with searing, gut-wrenching certainty exactly what he was doing.

Her breath deserted her in a rush.

Tariq was not touching her randomly. He was not caressing her. He was tracing the faint white lines that scored her belly—the stretch marks she had tried to rub away with lotions and creams, the lines more visible now in the bright morning light than she remembered them ever being before. They were the unmistakable evidence that she had been pregnant—enormously pregnant.

The world stopped turning. Her heart stopped beating. His eyes bored into her as his hands tightened. She heard only white noise, a rushing in her ears, and everything else went blank as if she had lost consciousness for a moment, though she was not so lucky.

He only waited.

And then, when he had stared at her so long she was convinced he had ripped every last secret from her very soul, his mouth twisted.

She wanted to speak—to yell, to defend herself, to deny everything—but it was as if she were paralyzed. Frozen solid, watching her world end in his dark green gaze, colder now than she had ever seen it. He held her still, his captive, and when he spoke, his voice held so much suspicion, so much accusation, she flinched.

"I have only one question for you," he said, every word like a knife. "Where is the child?"

CHAPTER TEN

EVERY instinct screamed at Jessa to run, to escape, to do anything in her power to put space between herself and the knowledge she saw dawning in his eyes.

But she could not bring herself to move.

"Well?" he asked, his voice like a gunshot. "Have you had a child, Jessa?" His voice dropped to the barest whisper of sound as he searched her face. He actually paled, his eyes widening as he read her expression. "Have you had *my* child?"

Her mind whirled as panic flooded through her, cramping her stomach and making little black spots appear before her eyes. She could feel herself waver as she stood before him. *Think!* she ordered herself. She had never planned to see him again, and once he had appeared, had had no plan to tell him about Jeremy. Why should she? She had expected him to disappear again. What good could come of dredging up a past neither one of them could change?

She hadn't expected to be confronted with that past in so dramatic a manner. She was completely unprepared!

Tariq might suspect that Jeremy existed. But he didn't know who Jeremy was, or *where* he was. Only Jessa could protect Jeremy from Tariq and the devastation that would inevitably rain down on Jeremy's world—because Jessa knew without a shadow of a doubt that if Tariq knew where Jeremy was, Tariq would do everything in his considerable power to take him back. And so she would do what she had to do, no matter what it cost her. She would protect Jeremy, even from Tariq.

"I asked you a question," Tariq said, his harsh tone slicing into her, making her jump again. "Do not make me repeat it."

Jessa sucked in a breath. His fingers were like vises, clamped on to her hips and chaining her in place, though he had not increased the pressure of his hands against her flesh. She didn't know how she managed to keep from collapsing, as her heart galloped inside her chest. *Think of Jeremy,* she told herself. *You must be brave for him.*

"I heard you," she said, fear making her voice sound clipped. It was better than terrified. "I just don't have any idea what you're talking about."

His lips pressed together, and he released her suddenly, surging to his feet. Jessa scrambled away from him, determined to put as much space as she could between them. She moved around the end of the huge bed, pulling the decadently soft top sheet from the mattress and wrapping it around herself. She could not bear to remain naked in front of him, not for one second more. She could have kicked herself for failing to remember that her own body could betray her in this way. But she hadn't paid attention to her stretch marks in ages. They were simply there, a part of her personal landscape she noticed as much as she noticed her knees or her ankles. She was such a fool! But then, she had also thought that she could seduce and control Tariq. What had she been thinking?

He did not have to follow her—he loomed over her

from the other side of the bed, his arms crossed over his powerful chest, his anger making him seem even larger than before. He did not seem to care that he, too, was naked. He was as intimidating now as he was when fully dressed. More, perhaps.

"Is that how you want to play this?" he asked, his eyes dark with outrage. As if he had never whispered her name in passion or cradled her against that hard chest as they each fought for breath. "Do you think it will work?"

"I think you're insane!" she threw at him. She had to get over the shock of this change, this about-face from lover to accuser, and she had to do it immediately, no matter her feelings. Or he would roll right over her and take what he wanted. Of that, she had no doubt.

"Do you think I am a fool?" He shook his head slightly, every muscle in his body tensed. His fury was a palpable thing, another presence in the room, a syrupy cloud between them. "I can see the changes in your body with my own eyes. How do you explain them?"

"It's called *five years!*" she cried, throwing up the hand that did not hold the sheet, letting it show her exasperation, hoping he could not see her terror, her desperation. "I have not pointed out the numerous ways *your* body is not the same as it was when you were five years younger—"

Cold and hard, his gaze slammed into her with the force of a blow, and cut her off that effectively.

"I can tell that you are lying," Tariq said, each word distinct and clear. Like separate bullets fired from the same weapon. "Do you doubt it? Your whole face has changed. You look like a stranger! Where is the child? I saw no sign of one in your home."

Still reeling, Jessa clung to the part that mattered most—he could not know anything about Jeremy specifically. He only knew that Jeremy *could* exist. He had not known about Jeremy before he'd come to York. This was all an accident, her fault.

"You will not even answer the question?" he asked, as if he could not quite believe it. "Your body makes you a liar, Jessa. The time for hiding is over." He was not her lover now. Not the charming, easygoing one she knew now had never been more than a convenient costume for him, and not the intensely sensual one who had taken her to erotic heights last night. His voice was crisp. Relentless. Sure. He was a king with absolute power, and he was not afraid to use it.

"Have you seen me with a child?" she asked coolly, praying he could not see how her hands clenched to white knuckles, or hear the tremor in her voice.

"I will rip your life apart, piece by piece, until I find the truth," Tariq bit out, the supreme monarch handing down his judgment, his eyes blazing. "There is no place you can hide, no part of your life you can keep from me. Is that what you want?"

"Why even ask me what I want?" she said, fear and determination a cold knot in her gut, forcing her to play the part of someone far more brave, far more courageous, than she could ever be. For Jeremy, she could keep from falling apart, falling to pieces, as was no doubt Tariq's goal. For Jeremy, she could fight back. "You did not ask me what I wanted when you abandoned me and ruined my life five years ago. You did not ask me what I wanted when you reappeared in my life. Why pretend you have any interest in what I want now?" She shrugged, meeting his eyes with a brazen courage she did not feel. "If you want to dig around in my life, go right ahead. What could I do to stop you?"

His scowl deepened. "Do you think I am still playing games with you?" he demanded, his voice getting louder, his accent growing more pronounced as his temper grew. "You have no right to keep my child from me! The heir to my kingdom!"

Jessa reminded herself that he did not know. He only suspected. *He did not know.*

"You have no right to speak to me this way!" she retorted.

"Where is the child?" he thundered.

But she couldn't back down, though her knees felt like jelly and her lungs constricted painfully. She wouldn't tell him anything.

The truth was, she hardly knew where to start.

She shook her head, too many emotions fighting for space inside of her, and all of them too messy, too complicated, too heavy.

"Jessa." This time the anger was gone, and something far more like desperation colored his voice. "You must tell me what happened. You must."

But she could not speak another word, and she could not bring herself to look at him. She had the sense that she had finally stopped running a very long, very arduous race, and the wind was knocked out of her.

She didn't have the slightest idea what to do now. She had never so much as considered the possibility that Tariq might discover that he had fathered a child. The time for telling him had long since passed, and she knew that she had tried then, to no avail. She had never anticipated that he might return. She had stopped dreaming such foolish dreams long ago.

And now he stared at her in anguish, which she would give anything to fix and couldn't. It wasn't simply that she couldn't bring herself to tell him what he wanted to know. She physically could not seem to form the words. She could not even think them. She could only lie and avoid and deflect. She could only make it worse.

"I will stop at nothing to locate a child of my blood," Tariq said softly. There was a chilling finality to his words then, as if he was making a vow. He took a step toward her, and it took everything she had to stand her ground before him. "I have believed I am the last of my blood, my family, for five years, Jessa. The very last. If that is not so…"

He didn't finish. But then, he did not have to finish.

Jessa still could not speak. It was as if everything inside her had shut down, turned off.

"You can only remain silent for so long," he said. His voice was like a whip, cracking through the room hard enough to leave welts against her skin. "But do not doubt that there is only one outcome to this situation. I *will* find out. The only question is how much of your life I will destroy in the process."

"Do not bully me!" she cried, surprising herself as well as him, the words ripping from her as if she had torn them from her heart.

"You think I am bullying you?" He was incredulous, pronouncing *bullying* as if he had never heard the term before.

"Threats, intimidation." Jessa pressed one hand against her temple. "Is there another word for it?"

"I am not threatening you, Jessa," he said matter-of-factly, with that ruthlessness underneath. "I am telling you exactly what will happen to you if you continue this. You have no right to keep the truth from me. These are promises."

"What kind of man are you?" she whispered. She wasn't sure why she said it. She wanted to sob, to scream, to somehow release the tension that felt as if it swelled up from inside her.

Their eyes locked across the few feet that separated them. He looked as if he had never seen her before, as if she was a perfect stranger who had wounded him. She realized in that moment that she never wanted to be responsible for his pain. That it hurt her, too. But understanding only made the riot inside swirl faster, swell harder, cause more damage. Jessa made herself hold his gaze, though it cost her.

Tariq looked away from her then, as if he had to collect himself before he did something he would regret.

"I suggest you rethink your position," he said quietly.

Suddenly her tongue was loose. And foolish. "I suggest you—"

"Silence!" He slashed a hand through the air, and said something in what she assumed was Arabic. "I am done listening to you."

He did not look at her again, but strode toward the bedroom door. Jessa could not believe it. Relief flooded through her. He was *leaving?* That was it? Could she really be that lucky?

And what was the part of her that yearned, despite everything, for him to stay?

"Where are you going?" she asked, because she wanted to confirm it.

"Shocking as it might seem to you, I have matters of state to attend to," he growled at her. "Or do you think my kingdom should grind to a halt while you spin your little lies? You can consider this conversation postponed."

"I am not going to sit around and calmly wait for you to come back and be even more horrible to me," she told him fiercely. "I am going home."

He turned when he reached the door to the rest of the suite, his eyes narrow and his mouth hard.

"By all means," he said, his voice as dark as his gaze, and his warning clear, "go wherever you like. See what happens when you do." Then he turned his back on her, seemingly still unconcerned with his nudity, and strode from the room.

His sudden absence left a black hole in the room that Jessa feared might suck her in, for a dizzy, irrational beat or two of her heart. For long moments, Jessa could not move. She told herself she was waiting to see if Tariq would return. She told herself she was merely being cautious. But the truth was that she could not have moved so much as an inch if her life depended upon it.

Eventually, when he did not come back, Jessa moved to the edge of the bed and sat down gingerly, carefully, unable to process what had just occurred. Unable to track the course of the past two days. She remembered going to work in the letting agency that morning, having no idea that her whole world would be turned on its ear. That normal, everyday morning felt as far away to her now as if it belonged to someone else, as if it were a part of some other woman's life. She felt as if she'd just been tipped from a roller coaster at its height and sent tumbling to the earth. She raised a hand to her mouth, surprised to find her hand shook.

She almost let out a sob, but choked it back. She could not break down. She was not safe from Tariq or his questions simply because he had left her alone for the moment. He would be back. She knew that as surely as she knew the earth still turned beneath her feet. He was an implacable force, and she did not know how she had failed to recognize that five years ago. Hadn't she known this would happen? Wasn't this why she'd set upon this course in the first place, to divert his attention?

That is not the only reason… a traitorous voice whispered, but she couldn't allow herself to listen to it. Nor could she savor the heated images of the night before. None of that mattered now.

Jeremy is his child too, the same treacherous voice

whispered, and Jessa felt a wave of old grief rock through her then, nearly knocking her over with all the strength of what might have been. If he had been who he'd said he was. If she had been less infatuated and less silly. If his uncle had not died. If she had been able to care for her newborn child as he deserved to be cared for. *If.*

She balled her hands into fists and stood, ignoring her trembling knees, her shallow breaths, the insistent dampness in her eyes that she refused to let flow free. Tariq would be back, and she did not want to imagine what new ammunition he would bring with him. She was not at all sure she could survive another encounter like this one. In truth, she was not even certain she *had* survived. Not intact, anyway.

But she couldn't think of that, of what more she might have lost. She told herself she had to think of Jeremy. She could take care of herself later.

She had to make certain that whenever Tariq returned, she was long gone.

CHAPTER ELEVEN

IT WAS not until Jessa arrived at the Gare de Lyon railway station with every intention of escaping Tariq—and France—that she realized, with a shock, that she did not have any money with her.

Getting out of Tariq's Parisian home had been, in retrospect, suspiciously easy. She had forced herself into action knowing that the alternative involved the fetal position and a very long cry, neither of which she could allow herself. So after she had taken a shower in the luxurious bathroom suite, scrubbing herself nearly raw in water almost too hot to bear, as if that would remove the feel of him from her skin, Jessa had pulled on one of the seductively comfortable robes set out by the unseen staff and tried to see if she could find something to wear. Her blue sheath dress from the night before had been a crumpled mess, and, in any case, she'd been unable to bring herself to wear it again—she couldn't bear to remember how he had removed it. How she had *wanted* him to remove it.

She'd snuck down to the lower levels of the house, looking for the guest suites that she knew must be somewhere, because how could there fail to be guest rooms in such a house? The house was, as she had only noticed in passing awe the night before, magnificent. Glorious works of art by identifiably famous artists graced the walls, a Vermeer here, a Picasso there, though Jessa had not spared them more than a glance. A sculpture she was almost positive she'd seen a copy of in a London museum occupied an entire atrium all its own.

She'd wondered where Tariq's offices were—purely because she'd wanted to avoid him, she told herself—and had frozen in place each time she'd heard a footfall or a low voice, or had eased open a new door to peer behind it. She'd finally found what she was looking for in a set of rooms hidden away in a closed-off wing on the second floor: a closet filled with women's clothes in a variety of sizes.

She'd pulled on a pair of black wool trousers that were slightly too big, and the softest charcoal-gray linen button-down blouse she had ever worn, that was a bit tighter across the chest than she would have chosen on her own. Then she'd found a pair of black-and-brown ballet-style flats, only the tiniest bit too big for her feet. A black wool jacket completed the outfit and, once she smoothed her hair into some kind of order, had made Jessa look like someone far wealthier and much calmer.

It was remarkable, she'd thought, peering into the standing mirror in the corner of the dressing room, that she could look so pulled-together on the outside when she was still too afraid to look at the raw mess on the inside.

She had felt it, though. The sob that might take her at any moment, might suck her down into the heaving mass of emotion she could feel swirling inside, ready to spill over at the slightest provocation…

But there had been no time to think about such things. She had shaken the feelings off, reminding herself that there was only Jeremy to think about, only his welfare and nothing else. She had to get out of Tariq's house, and as far away from him as possible, before she was tempted to share with him things she had never shared, not in their entirety, with anyone.

Jessa had expected it to be difficult to find her way out of the house—had expected, in fact, to be apprehended by Tariq or his staff or *someone*—and had found herself a curious mixture of disappointed and elated when she'd simply walked down the impressive marble stair and let herself out onto the elegant Paris street beyond.

It had been chillier outside than she'd expected, and wet. She hadn't made it to the first corner before it had started to rain in earnest, and the clothes she'd liberated from the closet were little help. Her mind had raced with every step she took. She couldn't go home to York, could she? It would be the obvious place for Tariq to look, and if he was as serious as she worried he must be about tearing into her life, he was much more likely to stumble upon something there than anywhere else. Jessa had walked until she hit a major boulevard, and then had looked at a map at one of the kiosks. She could hardly take in the fact that she was in Paris, one of the most celebrated cities in the world. She had been much too focused on Tariq and what he might do, and how he might do it.

While she walked, the perfect solution had come to her. Friends of hers from home had gone on a holiday last year, and had taken the train from Paris to Rome. Rome was even farther away from Jeremy. Should Tariq come after her as he'd threatened to do, she would be leading him away from his true quarry. So she'd found the train station on the map, happily located not too far away, and had walked.

She walked and walked, down streets she had only ever seen in photographs, the borrowed shoes rubbing at her cold toes and slapping the pavement beneath her feet. She walked past the soaring glory of the Arc de Triomphe and down the Champs-Elysées, the wide boulevard glistening in the rain, achingly beautiful despite the overcast skies above. She walked in and out of puddles in the Jardin des Tuileries, still crowded with tourists under bright umbrellas, toward the iconic glass pyramid that heralded the entrance to the Louvre. She took shelter from the rain in the famed arcades that stretched beneath the great buildings along the Rue de Rivoli, filled with brightly lit shops and the bustling energy of city life.

And if tears fell from her eyes and rolled down her cheeks as she walked, tears for Tariq and for herself and for all the things she'd lost, they were indistinguishable from the rain.

It was only when she'd finally made her way into the impressive rail station with the huge clock tower that reminded her of Big Ben back home in the UK that the reality of her situation had hit her.

She had no money. And, worse, no access to any money.

She'd tucked her bank card into her evening bag before she'd left her home in York last night, but she hadn't thought to bring it with her when she'd left Tariq's house. She'd been entirely too focused on getting out of there to think about such practicalities.

Once again, she was a fool.

All of the emotions that Jessa had been trying to hold at bay rushed at her then like a tidal wave, forcing her to stop walking in the middle of the crowded station. She thought her knees might give out from under her. She was nearly trampled by the relentless stream of commuters and holidaymakers on all sides as they raced through the building, headed for trains and destinations far away from here. But Jessa was trapped. Stranded. How could she possibly keep Jeremy a secret if she couldn't even take a simple train journey to somewhere, anywhere else? She was soaked through to her skin: cold, wet, miserable, and alone in Paris. She had no money, and the one person she knew in the city was the last person on earth she could go to for help.

What was she going to do?

She felt a hand on her arm and immediately turned, jostled out of the dark spiral she was in.

"Excuse me," she began, apologetically.

But it was Tariq.

He wore another dark suit, expertly fitted to showcase his lean hunter's physique, and a matching scowl. He held her elbow in his large hand much too securely. She did not have to try to jerk away from him to know she would not be able to do so if he didn't allow it. She had no doubt she looked pathetic—like a drowned rat. Meanwhile, he looked like what he was: a very powerful man at the end of his patience.

She hated the way he looked at her, as if she had done something unspeakable to him. When she had only ever acted to protect Jeremy! Hadn't she? She hated that he did not say a word, and only seared her straight through with that dark glare of his. She hated most of all that some part of her was relieved to see him, that that same traitorous part of her wanted him to rescue her, as if he was not the one responsible for her predicament in the first place!

Her eyes burned with tears. He only stared at her, his dark eyes penetrating, implacable. She felt her mouth open, but she could not speak.

What could she say? She didn't know whether to be relieved or appalled that he was beside her, even though he was what she had run from. She only knew there was an ache inside that seemed to intensify with every breath, and it had nothing at all to do with sex. It had to do with the way he looked at her, as if he was disappointed in her. As if she had wounded him in ways words could not express. She couldn't imagine why that should hurt her in return, but it did.

"Come," he said, his voice a powerful rumble yet curiously devoid of anger, which made the dampness at the back of her eyes threaten to spill over again. "The car is waiting."

The damned woman was likely to catch her death of pneumonia, Tariq thought darkly, which would not suit him at all, as she still kept so many secrets from him. As he stepped outside the station, two of his aides leaped to attention, umbrellas in hand, and sheltered them both as Tariq led her to the sleek black car that waited by the curb. Not that an umbrella would do her any good at this point. She might as well have jumped, fully dressed, into the Seine.

His driver opened the back door and Tariq handed Jessa inside, then climbed in after her, sitting so he could look at her beside him. He watched her settle into her seat and told himself he did not notice the way the soaking wet shirt clung to her curves, leaving nothing at all to the imagination. Not that he needed to imagine what he could still taste on his tongue and feel beneath his hands. He wordlessly handed her a bath towel as the car pulled into traffic.

"Thank you."

Her voice was hushed. Almost formal. She looked at the towel on her lap for a moment and then raised her head. Her eyes seemed too wide, too bright, and haunted, somehow. To his surprise, the anger that had consumed him earlier had subsided. Which was not to say he was happy with her, or had forgotten what she'd done to him—the lies she was still telling with her continued silence—but the fury that had seized him and forced him to walk away from her rather than unleash it in her presence had simmered to a low boil and then faded into something far more painful. Anger was easy, in comparison.

He didn't know why. He had been coldly furious all day, and doubly so when she'd left the house. He had had his people monitor her movements as a matter of course, and had seethed about it while he ought to have been concentrating on his official duties. When it became clear where she was headed and he had called for the car, he had felt the crack of his temper, but somehow the sight of her standing in the middle of the busy train station had gotten to him. She had looked so forlorn, so lost. Not at all the warrior woman with more fire and courage than sense who had made love to him all night long. Who had stood up to him consistently since he'd walked back into her life. By the time he'd reached her side, he had been amazed to discover that the angry words on his tongue had dissolved, unsaid.

Yet he still had the echo of what she'd said earlier ricocheting in his head, close as it was to something his uncle had said to him years before: *What kind of man are you?* The kind who terrorized women into risking pneumonia on the streets of Paris, apparently. The kind whose former lover defied him to her own detriment, throwing herself out into a cold autumn rain rather than tell him what had become of their child. What kind of man was he, indeed, to inspire these things?

He watched her towel off her face, then try to tend to the sopping mass of her hair. She shivered.

"You are cold."

"No," she said, but there was no force behind it.

"Your teeth are about to chatter," he said with little patience. Would she rather freeze to death than accept his help? *Obstinate woman.* He leaned forward to press the intercom button, then ordered the heat turned on. "See? Was that so difficult?"

She looked at him, her eyes dark and wary, then away.

"I hope you had a pleasant walk," he continued, his tone sardonic. "My men tell me you nearly drowned in a puddle outside the Louvre."

She looked startled for a moment. "Your men?"

"Of course." His brows rose. "You cannot imagine that a king's residence is left so wide open, can you? That any passerby could stroll in and out on a whim? I told you what would happen if you left."

"I didn't…" She broke off. She swallowed. "You have security. Of course you do." She shrugged slightly. "I never saw them."

Tariq leveled a look at her, lounging back against his seat, taking care not to touch her. Touching her had not led where he had expected it to lead. He had meant to control her and rid himself of this obsession, and instead had risked himself in ways he would have thought impossible. Felt things he was not prepared to examine. *Damn her.*

"If you saw them, they would not be very good at their jobs, would they?" he asked idly.

Silence fell, heavy and deep, between them. She continued to try to dry herself, and he continued to watch her attempts, but something had shifted. He didn't know what it was. Her desperate, doomed escape attempt that had proved her brave, if reckless? Or the fact that she looked not unlike a child as she sat there, as bedraggled as a kitten, her eyes wide and defeated?

"Why did you stop walking in the station?" he asked

without knowing he meant to speak. "You were nearly run down where you stood."

She let out a rueful laugh. "I have no money," she said. She met his gaze as if she expected him to comment, but he only lifted a brow in response.

"And what now?" she asked softly, that defiant tilt to her chin, though her hair was still dark and wet against her face, making her seem pale and small. "Am I your prisoner?"

There was a part of him that wanted to rage at her still. But he had not forgotten, even in his fury, even now, how she had somehow touched him once again, gotten under his skin. He, who had believed himself inviolate in that way. How he had yearned for her all of these years, though he had made up any number of lies to excuse it. How he had waited for her to wake this morning, loath to disturb her. He suspected that a great deal of his anger stemmed from that knowledge, that even as she defied him and lied to him, insulted him and dared him to do his worst, he admired her for it. It had taken him hours, and perhaps the sight of her dogged determination to get away from him in order to keep her secrets no matter what the cost to herself, to understand that truth, however uncomfortable it made him.

What kind of man are you?

And could he truly blame her for what she'd done, whatever she'd done? asked a ruthless inner voice. Given what she knew of him back then—a liar, a wastrel—why would she want to share a child with him? It was as his uncle had told him. He had not been a man. He had had nothing to offer any child.

"I need to know what happened," he said quietly. He did not look at her, watching instead the blurred Parisian buildings and monuments as they sped past.

"So the answer is yes. I am your prisoner." She let out a breath. "For how long?"

He could have said, for as long as he liked. He could have reminded her that he was a king, that he could have absolute power over her if he wished it. Instead, he turned to her and met her troubled gaze.

"Until you tell me what I want to know," he said.

"Forever, then," she said, her voice hollow. "You plan to hold me against my will forever."

"When have you been held against your will?" he asked, though his voice held no heat. "I do not recall your demands to leave last night. And I did not prevent you from leaving this morning."

"With no money," she said bitterly. "Where was I supposed to go?"

"If you are without funds, Jessa," he replied evenly, "you need only ask."

"I have my own money, thank you," she said at once, sharply.

"Then why didn't you use it?" he asked. She sighed and dropped her gaze to her hands. Again, silence stretched between them, seeming to implicate them both.

"Isn't this where you threaten me some more?" she asked softly, her attention directed at her lap. Yet somehow her voice seemed to tug at him. To shame him. "That you'll tear apart my whole life, make it a living hell?"

What kind of man are you?

Tariq expelled a long breath and rubbed at his temples with his fingers. When he spoke, he hardly recognized his own voice.

"You must understand that when I say I am the last of my bloodline, I am not only talking about lines of succession and historical footnotes that will be recorded when I am gone," he said, not knowing what he meant to say. Not recognizing the gruffness in his own voice. "I was orphaned when I was still a child, Jessa. I was not yet three. I don't know if the little I remember of my parents is real or if I have internalized photographs and stories told to me by others."

"Tariq." She said his name on a sigh, almost as if she hurt for him.

"My uncle's family was the only family I ever knew," he said, with an urgency he didn't entirely understand. She bit her lower lip and worried it between her teeth. "I thought I was the only one left. Until today."

"I don't know what you want me to say," she whispered, her voice thick.

"Do I have a child?" he asked her, appalled at the uncertainty he could hear in his own voice. He didn't know what he would do if she threw it back at him as he knew she could. "Is my family more than simply me?"

Her eyes squeezed shut, and she made a sound that was much like a sob, though she covered her mouth with her hand. For a long moment they sat in silence, the only sound the watery swish of traffic outside the car, and her ragged breathing. He thought she would not answer. He felt a new bleakness settle upon him. Would he never know what had happened? Would he be condemned to wonder? Was it no more than he deserved for the way he had behaved in his former life, the way he had treated her, the way he had treated himself and his family, his many squandered gifts?

But she turned her head to look at him, her cinnamon eyes bright with a pain he didn't fully understand.

"I don't know that I can make you feel any better about this," she said, her voice thick and rough. "But I will tell you what I know."

CHAPTER TWELVE

JESSA didn't know why she had said anything, why his obvious pain had moved her so much that she broke her silence so suddenly. She hadn't meant to say a word. And then she'd heard the raw agony in his voice and something inside had snapped. Or loosened. She had thought she might cry. Instead, she had spoken words she'd never meant to speak aloud and certainly not to him.

But the truth was, he hadn't meant to leave her, had he? His uncle had died—his whole family had died. What was he supposed to have done? It had occurred to her, somewhere out in all the cold and wet of the Paris streets, that somewhere along the line it had become important for her to keep blaming him for leaving her because it kept the attention away from what had happened after he left. From the decisions she had made that he had had no part in. Was that what she had been hiding from?

Tariq said nothing. He only looked at her for a long moment, his gaze fathomless, and then nodded once. Definitively. She expected him to demand she tell him everything she could at once, but instead he remained silent for the rest of their short journey to his grand house. Once there, he ushered her back to the suite of rooms on the top floor that she had run from earlier. Was it to be her prison? Jessa felt too raw, too exposed, to give that question the thought she knew she should.

No sign of their long, passionate night remained in the exquisite room. The great bed was returned to its ivory-and-gold splendor, and warm lights glowed from sconces in the wall, setting off the fine moldings and Impressionist art that graced the walls. Jessa stood in the center of the room, deliberately not looking at the bed, deliberately not remembering, and swallowed. Hard.

"You will wish to clean up, I think," Tariq said, an odd politeness in his tone as if they did not know each other. And yet, he anticipated her needs. He gestured toward the spacious dressing room that was adjacent to the palatial bathroom. "I have taken the liberty of having clothes laid out for you that will, I hope, fit."

Jessa looked down at the sodden mess of the clothes she wore, and swallowed again, not sure she could speak. She didn't know how to process his thoughtfulness. Perhaps he was simply tired of looking at her in such a bedraggled state. She was tired of it herself—her shoes so soaked that she could hear her toes squelch into them each time she moved. The room, for all it was large and elegant beyond imagining, seemed too close, too hushed around them. She was afraid to meet his gaze. Afraid she had opened herself up too far, and he would see too much.

Afraid that once she bared herself to him again, he would break her heart as surely and as completely as he had done before.

"There are matters that require my attention," he said after a long moment, still in that stiff way. As if he was as nervous as she was. "I cannot put them off."

"I understand," she managed to say, frowning fiercely at her wet, cold shoes.

"I will return as soon as I can." He sighed slightly and she risked looking at him. "You will wait here?"

Not run away, he meant. Not continue to keep her secrets. Stay and tell him what she'd said she would.

Share with him what should never have been a secret, what should have been theirs. Together.

"I will." It was like a vow.

They stared at each other for a long, fraught moment. Jessa could feel her pulse beat in her ears, her throat.

He nodded to her, so stiff and formal it was like a bow, and strode from the room.

It was already evening when a diffident maid in a pressed black uniform led Jessa through the maze of the house to find Tariq. He waited for her in a cozy, richly appointed room that featured a crackling fire in a stone fireplace, walls of books and deep leather couches. Tariq stood with his back to the door, his stance wide and his hands clasped behind him, staring out the French doors at the wet blue dusk beyond.

Jessa stood in the doorway for a moment, filled with a confusing mix of panic, uncertainty and something else she did not wish to examine—something that felt like a hollow space in her chest as she looked at him, his face remote in profile, his strong back stiff, as if he expected nothing from her but further pain. She shook the thought away, suddenly deeply afraid in a way she had not been before—a way that had nothing to do with Jeremy and everything to do with her traitorous, susceptible heart. She smoothed her palms along the fine wool of the trousers she wore, pretending she was concerned about wrinkles when she knew, deep down, that was not true. And that it was far too late to worry.

Tariq had been as good as his word. When Jessa emerged from her second hot shower of the day, she had found an entire wardrobe laid out for her in the dressing room, complete with more grooming products than she had at her own home in York. All of it, from the clothes to the hair bands and perfumes, had been specifically chosen with her tastes in mind. It was as if Tariq knew her better than she knew herself, a line of thought she preferred not to examine more closely. Not knowing what the night held, and not wanting to send the wrong message or make herself more vulnerable than she felt already, Jessa had dressed for this conversation in tailored chocolate wool trousers and a simple white silk blouse. Over that, she'd wrapped a sky-blue cashmere concoction that was softer than anything she had ever touched before. Now she tightened the wrap around her middle, as if it alone could hold her together. She'd even smoothed her heavy mass of hair back into a high ponytail, hoping it might broadcast a certain calm strength her curls would not.

"I trust everything fits well," Tariq said in a low voice, still staring out through the French doors. Jessa started slightly, not realizing he'd known she was there.

"Perfectly," she said, and then coughed to clear the thickness from her throat.

He turned then, and Jessa was lost suddenly in the bleakness she saw on his face. It made his harsh features seem even more unapproachable and distant. She wanted to go to him, to soothe it away somehow, and then wondered who she'd confused him for, who she thought she was facing. This was still Tariq bin Khaled Al-Nur. He was more dangerous to her now, she thought, than he had ever been before. She would be wise to remember that. Oh, it was not as if she had anything to fear from him—it was her own heart she feared. Perhaps it had always been her own surrender she feared more than anything else.

"Tell me," Tariq said, and she did not mistake his meaning.

She took a deep breath. Stalling for time, she crossed the room and perched on the edge of the buttery-soft leather sofa, but did not allow herself to relax back into it. She could not look at him, so she looked instead into the fire, into the relative safety of the dancing, shimmering flames.

There would be no going back from this conversation. She was honest with herself about that, at least.

"It was a boy," she said, her head spinning, because she could not believe she was telling him this after so long. A sense of unreality gripped her as if she was dreaming all of it—the luxurious clothes, the fire, the impossibly forbidding man who stood close and yet worlds away. "I called him Jeremy."

She could feel Tariq's eyes on her then, though she dared not look at him to see what expression he wore as he digested this news. That he was, biologically, a father. Swallowing carefully, she put her hands into her lap, stared fixedly into the fire and continued.

"I found out I was pregnant when I went to the doctor's that day." She sighed, summoning up those dark days in her memory. "You had been so careful never to mention the future, never to hint—" But she couldn't blame him, not entirely. "I didn't know if it meant I would lose you, or if you would be happy. I didn't know if I was happy!" She shook her head and frowned at the flames dancing before her, heedless of the emotional turmoil just outside the stone fireplace. "That was where I went. I stopped at a friend's flat in Brighton. I...tried to work out what to do."

"Those days you went missing," Tariq said in a quiet

voice. Jessa couldn't look at him. "You hadn't left, then, after all."

"It's so ironic that you thought so," Jessa said with a hollow laugh. "As that was my biggest fear at first—that you would leave. Once you knew." She laughed again in the same flat way. "Only when I returned to London, you had already gone. And when I saw who you really were and what you had to do, I knew that you were never coming back."

Jessa took a deep breath, feeling it saw into her lungs. It would get no easier if she put it off, she thought. It might never get easier at all. She blew the breath out and forced herself to continue.

"I was such a mess," she said. "I was sacked in short order, of course. I tried to get another job in the city, not realizing that I'd been effectively blackballed. My sister wanted me to move back home to York, but that seemed such an admission of failure. I…I so wanted everything to simply go on as if nothing had ever happened. As if *you* had never happened."

She heard a faint sound like an exhalation or a muttered curse, but she couldn't look at him. She couldn't bear to see what he thought of her. She was too afraid she would never tell the story if she didn't tell him now. From the corner of her eye, she saw him move and begin to prowl around the room as if he could not bear to stand still.

"But I was pregnant, and…" How to tell him what that had felt like? The terror mixed in equal part with fierce, incomparable joy? Her hand crept over her abdomen as if she could remember by touch. As if the memory of Jeremy still kicked there, so insistent and demanding.

"You must have been quite upset," Tariq said quietly. Too quietly. Jessa stared down at her lap, threading her hands together.

"At you, perhaps. Or the situation," she said softly. "But not at the baby. I realized quickly that I wanted the baby, no matter what." She sucked in a breath. "And so I had him. He was perfect."

Her emotions were too close to the surface. Too raw, still. Or perhaps it was because she was finally sharing the story with Tariq, who should have been there five years ago. She had almost felt as if he was there in the delivery room. She had sobbed as much for the man who was not her partner and was not with her as she had for the pain she was in as each contraction twisted and ripped through her. Now she pressed her lips together to keep herself from sobbing anew, and breathed through her nose until she was sure she wouldn't cry. This was about the facts. She could give him the facts.

"I had a hard labor," she said. "There were...some complications. I was depressed, scared." She had had postpartum depression on top of her physical ailments, of course, but it had not seemed, at the time, like something she could ever come out of whole. She snuck a look at him then. He had found his way to the couch opposite, but he did not look at her as he sat there, sprawled out before the fire. He aimed his deep frown toward the dark red Persian carpet at his feet.

Jessa wondered what he was thinking. Did this seem unreal to him? Impossible? That they could be sitting in a Parisian room, so many miles and years away from the heartache that they had caused together? It boggled the mind. It made her feel dizzy.

"I had no job, and no idea where I might go to get one," Jessa continued, ignoring the thickness in her voice, the twist in her belly. "I had this perfect baby boy, the son of a king, and I couldn't give him the life that he needed. That he deserved." Her voice cracked, and she sighed, then cleared her throat. "I thought at first that it was just hormonal—just first-time mother fears, but as time went on, the feeling grew stronger."

"Why?" Tariq's voice was barely a whisper, and still so full of anguish. "What was missing in the life you gave him?"

Me, Jessa thought. *You.* But she said neither.

"I was...not myself," she said instead. "I cried all the time. I was so lost." It had been more than she could handle. The baby's constant demands. The lack of sleep. The lack of help, even though her sister had tried. Had she not been so terribly, terribly depressed—near suicidal, perhaps... But she had been. There was no point in wishing. "And how could I be a good parent? The single decision I'd made that led to my being a parent in the first place had been..." Her voice trailed off, and her gaze flew to his.

"To get pregnant accidentally," he finished for her, so matter-of-factly, so coldly. "With my child."

"Yes." Something shimmered between them, a kind of bond, though it was fragile and painful. Jessa forged on, determined to get the rest out at last. "And I had had all this time to read about you in the news, to watch you on the television, to really and truly see that nothing you had ever told me was true. That I'd made up our relationship in my head. That I was a silly girl with foolish dreams, not fit to be someone's *parent*."

He raked his hands through his hair, his expression unreadable. But he did not look away.

"Meanwhile," she continued, her voice barely a thread of sound, "there were people with intact families already. People who had done everything right, made all the right choices, and just couldn't have a baby. Why should Jeremy suffer just because his mother was a mess? How was that fair to him?"

"You gave him up for adoption," Tariq said, sounding almost dazed. "You gave him away to strangers?"

"He deserved to have everything," Jessa said fiercely, hating the emphasis he put on *strangers*—and not wanting to correct him. "Love, two adoring parents, a family. A real chance at a good life! Not…a devastated single mother who could barely take care of herself, much less him."

Tariq did not speak, though Jessa could hear his ragged breathing and see the turmoil in his expression.

"I wanted him to be happy more than I wanted him to be happy with me," she whispered.

"I thought…" Tariq stopped and rubbed his hands over his face. "I believed it was customary in an adoption to seek the permission of both parents."

Jessa bit her lower lip and braced herself. "Jeremy has only one birth parent listed on his birth certificate," she said quietly. "Me."

Tariq simply looked at her, a deep anger that verged on a grief she recognized evident in the dark depths of his troubled gaze. Jessa raised her shoulders and then let them drop. Why should she feel guilty now? And yet she did. Because neither of them had had all the choices they should have had. Neither one of them was blameless.

"I saw no reason to claim a relationship to a king for a baby when I could not claim one myself," she said.

Tariq's gaze seemed to burn, but Jessa did not look away.

"I can almost understand why you did not inform me that you were pregnant," he said after a long, tense moment. "Or I can try to understand this. But to give the child away? To give him to someone else without even allowing me to know that he existed in the first—"

"I tried to find you," she cut in, her voice thick with

emotion. "I went to the firm and begged them to contact you. I had no way to locate you!"

"No way to locate me?" He shook his head. Temper cracked like lightning in his eyes, his voice. "I am not exactly in hiding!"

"You have no idea, do you?" she asked, closing her eyes briefly. "I cannot even imagine how many young, single women must throw themselves at you. How many must tell tales to members of your staff, or your government officials, in a desperate bid for your attention. Why should I be treated any differently?" She shifted in her seat, wanting nothing more than to get up and run, end this uncomfortable conversation. Hadn't she been running from it for ages? "It's not possible to simply look you up in the phone book and give you a ring, Tariq. You must know that."

His expression told her that he didn't wish to know it. He swallowed, and she didn't know how to feel about the fact he was clearly as uncomfortable as she was. As emotional.

"I went to the firm," she said again, remembering that day some months after Jeremy had been born, when she'd been desperate and on the brink of making her decision but wanted to reach Tariq first, if she could. "They laughed at me."

It had been worse than the day they'd sacked her. The speculation in their eyes, the disdain—they had looked at her like she was dirt. Like she was worse than dirt.

"They laughed at you?" As if he didn't understand.

"Of course." She found the courage to meet his eyes. "To them I was nothing more than the slutty intern, still gold digging. One of them offered to take me out to dinner—*wink wink*."

"Wink—?" Tariq began, frowning, and then comprehension dawned and his expression turned glacial.

"Yes," Jessa confirmed. "He was happy to see if he

could sample the goods. After all, I'd been good enough for a king, for a while. But he certainly wasn't going to help me contact you."

"Who?" Tariq asked, his voice like thunder. "Who was the man?"

"It doesn't really matter, does it? I doubt very much he was the only one who thought that way." Jessa shook her head and looked back into the fire, sinking further into the embrace of the cashmere over her shoulders. "I realized that I would have to make the decision on my own. That there was absolutely no way I could talk to you about it. We might as well have never met."

"So you did it." There was no question in his voice. Only that scratchiness and a heavy kind of resignation.

"When he was four months old," Jessa said, surprised to feel herself get choked up. "I kissed him goodbye and I gave him what he could never have if I kept him." She closed her eyes against the pain that never really left her, no matter what she did or what she told herself. "And now he has everything any child could hope for. Two parents who dote on him, who treat him like a miracle—not a mistake. Not something unplanned that had to be dealt with." She could feel the wetness on her cheeks but made no move to wipe it away.

"You don't regret this decision?" His voice seemed to come from far away. Jessa turned to look at him, her heart so raw she thought it might burst from within.

"I regret it *every day*!" she whispered at him fiercely. Unequivocally. "I miss him *every moment*!"

Tariq sat forward, his eyes intent on hers. "Then I do not see why we cannot—"

"He is *happy*!" she interrupted him, emotion making her forceful. But he had to hear her. "He is happy, Tariq.

Content. I know that I did the right thing for him, and that's the only thing that matters. Not what I feel. And not what you feel, either, no matter if you are a king or not. He is a happy, healthy little boy with two parents who are not us." Her voice trembled then, and the tears spilled over and trailed across her cheeks. "Who will never be us."

She buried her face in her hands, not entirely sure why she was crying like this—as desperately as if it had just happened, as if she had just accepted that it was real. It had to do with telling Tariq the truth finally. Or most of the truth, in any case—all the most important parts of the truth. It was as if some part of her she'd scarcely known existed had held on to the fantasy that as long as he did not know, it could not have happened. It could not be true. And now she had lost even that lie to tell herself.

Jessa did not know how long she wept, but she knew when he came to sit beside her, his much heavier body next to hers on the leather making her sag toward him. He did not whisper false words of encouragement. He did not rant or rave or rail against her. He did not plot ways to change this harsh reality, or ask questions she could not answer.

He merely put his arm around her, guided her head to his shoulder and let her cry.

It was late when Tariq got off the phone with his attorneys, having confirmed what he'd suspected but still didn't quite want to accept: British adoptions were relatively rare, and well-nigh irreversible. When the child came of age, he could seek out his parents through a national register if he chose, but not before. And British courts were notoriously unsympathetic to anyone who tried to reverse the adoption process—claiming they acted in the best interests of the child and sought to cause as little disruption as possible.

He left his office and made his way back to the small library where he'd left Jessa when she'd finally succumbed to the stress and emotion of the day and had drifted off to sleep. He found her curled up on the leather sofa, her hands beneath her cheek, looking more like a child than a woman who could have borne one. Much less borne his.

Some part of him still wanted to unleash the temper that rolled and burned inside of him on her, to hurt her because he hurt, but he found he could not. He looked at her and felt only a deep sadness and a growing possessiveness that he wasn't sure he understood. He knew he wanted to blame her because it would be convenient, nothing more.

The truth was that he blamed himself. He was everything his uncle had accused him of being, and while he had known that enough so that he'd altered his life to honor his uncle's passing, he had not understood the true scope of it until now.

He might have spent years haunted by her, but he had not wanted to deal with the young woman who had made his dissipated heart ask questions he hadn't wanted to answer, and so he had excised her when he left England just as he had excised everything that reminded him of his old life. He had transformed himself into the man his uncle wanted him to be, and he'd done it brutally. What would it have cost him to seek her out after the accident, even for something as little as a phone call? What kind of man left a young, obviously infatuated girl in the lurch like that? Had he allowed himself to think about it for even a moment, he would have known that she'd have been devastated first by his disappearance, and then by the shocking truth about who he was. How could he now turn around and blame her for making what she'd thought were the best decisions she could under those circumstances?

After all, she had not known how deeply she had touched him then, and how she had continued to prey on his thoughts for all of those years. Only he had known it, and he had barely allowed the truth of his feelings for her to register. He had buried them with his uncle, buried them with all the remnants of his former life, buried them all and told himself that he preferred his life that way. That Jessa herself was tainted by her association with his former, profligate self, and thus could never be considered a possible consort or queen for the King of Nur. The kind of woman who would fall in love with Tariq the black sheep was by definition unfit for the king. And if he woke in the night and heard her voice, or felt phantom fingers trail along his skin, no one had ever needed to know that but him.

And yet he had still gone to find her, breaking all of his own rules, telling himself any number of lies—anything to be near her once again. Had he known even then that one night could never be enough? Had that been why he had fought against it for so long?

He stooped to shift her from the couch into his arms, lifting her high against his chest and carrying her with him through the house, aware that something in him whispered that she belonged there, that she fit there perfectly. She nestled against him, her body easy with him in sleep in a way she would never be were she awake. He felt a sudden pang of nostalgia for the freely given love of the young girl he'd so callously thrown away. She felt good so close against him. She felt like his.

In his rooms, he deposited her gently on the bed, removing her shoes and pulling the coverlet over her. For a moment he gazed down at her, watching her breathe, and let the strange tenderness he felt wash through him. He did not try to judge it, or deny it. He thought of what it must have been like for her, to be so alone, abandoned and forced into so difficult a position. They were not that different, the two of them, he thought. Each of them thrust, alone, into positions they had never meant to occupy.

Without letting himself think it through, he climbed into the bed behind her, pulling her close, so her back was flush against his chest, her bottom nestled between his thighs. He inhaled deeply, letting her distinct scents wash over him, soothing him, letting him imagine that they could both heal. Jasmine in her hair, and something sweet and warm beneath that he knew was simply Jessa. Vanilla and heat.

She stirred, and he knew when she woke by the sudden tension in her body where before there was only languor. He smoothed a hand down her side, tracing the curves of her body, as if he could erase what she had suffered so easily.

"I did not mean to fall asleep," she whispered into the dark room. She moved under his hands, as if testing her boundaries, as if she thought she was his prisoner.

Tariq did not respond. He only held her and pretended he did not know why he could not let her go.

"In the morning," she continued, her voice much too careful, much too polite, "I will head home. I think it's best." She moved as if to separate from him, and he let his arm fall away from her when he wanted only to hold on, to keep her close, as if she was sunlight and he was an acre of frozen earth, desperate for winter to end.

"Tariq?" She turned toward him. He twisted over onto his back, aware of a different kind of need surging through him. A need for peace, the peace that only holding her close had ever brought him. "Should I find somewhere else to sleep?" she asked, her voice tentative. Scared. Of him. And why shouldn't she be, after the things he had done?

He could not bear it. And he refused to think about why.

And then, from that place inside him that he could not fully admit existed, yet could no longer ignore, he whispered, "I do not want you to go, Jessa. Not yet."

CHAPTER THIRTEEN

ONE week passed, and then another, and the subject of Jessa's departure did not come up again. Jessa had made the necessary calls home to her sister and to her boss, and had taken the long overdue vacation time she was owed that she had never bothered to take before.

"*Where* are you?" her sister Sharon had asked, shocked, when Jessa got her on the phone. "Since when do you run off on a holiday at the drop of a hat?"

"I had an urge to see Paris, that's all," Jessa had lied.

"I wish I could swan off to Paris on a lark!" Sharon had said. And then the time to mention who she was with and why she was with him had passed the moment Sharon put down the phone, so it had remained Jessa's secret.

It wasn't that she was trying to hide the fact that she was with Tariq from her sister, necessarily, but she wasn't planning to trumpet it from the rooftops, either. She told herself that there was nothing unusual in it; she and Tariq were simply giving themselves some space and time to process the loss of Jeremy together rather than apart. Who else could understand how it felt? They were being healthy, she thought, modern; and part of her believed it.

Jessa had all of Paris to explore each day, as Tariq spent

his time closeted in meetings or on the telephone with his advisors, political allies, and business contacts—tending to his kingdom from afar.

"Tell me what you saw today," Tariq asked each evening, and Jessa would relate stories of freshly baked baguettes, lazy afternoons in cafés, or walking tours of famous monuments. Each evening she tried harder to make him smile. Each evening she found herself more and more invested in whether or not she succeeded.

"I have always loved Paris," Tariq told her one night as they lingered over coffee out in one of the city's famous restaurants, where the service was so impeccable that Jessa almost felt compelled to apologize every time she shifted in her chair. "My uncle used this residence as a vacation home, but I prefer to use it as a base for my European business concerns." He leaned back against his chair in an indolent way that called attention to all the power he kept caged in his lean, muscled frame.

"What isn't to love?" Jessa agreed with a happy smile, propping her elbow on the table and resting her chin on her hand. She could look at him for hours. His face alone compelled her—all that harshness and cruelty tempered by the keen intelligence in his eyes. "It mixes magic with practicality."

It was as if she had forgotten they had ever felt like adversaries, though, of course, she had not. This sweet truce between them was far more dangerous than the wars they had already fought and survived. She was so much more at risk when he looked at her the way he did tonight, with something she so desperately wanted to call tenderness.

"Indeed," he agreed now, and their eyes caught, something more potent than the rich brew in their cups surging between them, making Jessa's pulse race.

"Tariq," she said softly, not wishing to break the spell between them but knowing she should speak, knowing she should acknowledge the truth of things, "you know that I—"

"Come," he said, pushing back from the table. "We shall walk home along the Seine and you will tell me which Van Gogh in the Musée d'Orsay you prefer."

"I cannot possibly choose," she said, but she let him pull her to her feet, exulting in the slide of his palm against hers. *Why not dream a little longer?* she asked herself. Who would it hurt?

"Then you must tell me about the Musée Rodin instead," he said, taking a moment too long before releasing her hand and stepping back to pull out her chair. "I have not been in many years."

Jessa had studied every luscious, supple curve of stone in the museum he mentioned, and had marveled at the raw sensual power of marble statues that should have seemed cold and dead yet instead begged to be touched, caressed. As she thought she might do at any moment.

But Tariq only took her arm and ushered her out into the soft Parisian night.

Sharing Jeremy's adoption with him had changed something, Jessa realized as they walked together along the banks of the Seine in a silence that was not quite comfortable—too charged was it with their simmering chemistry and the restraint they had shown in not touching each other in so long. Not since that first night.

Later, back at the grand house, when Tariq had politely excused himself and she was left in the lonely expanse of the bedroom suite, she thought more about the evening's revelation. Jeremy was not her private pain now, to hoard and to hurt herself with. It was theirs to share, and the sharing not only lessened the hurt, it removed all the walls she'd built around it. In place of those walls was something far too delicate and shimmering to name. She did not want to think about when she had felt this way before, and what had become of her.

"You are such a fool," she whispered aloud, her voice swallowed up by the ornate furnishings all around her.

But she also did not want to think about the one crucial bit of information she had withheld from him. The one small yet crucial fact about Jeremy she had not been able to bring herself to share. She could not quite trust him with it, could she? Not when she knew deep down that this was a fantasy she was living in, something that would not, *could not* last. Protecting Jeremy was forever. It had to be.

It was as if, Jessa thought as she changed her clothes for dinner a few nights later, having hurt each other so terribly and so irrevocably they were now both easing their way into enjoying each other's company, as if that might make the pain lessen. As if it could make it bearable somehow.

She twisted her hair into a chignon, gathering her heavy copper curls at the nape of her neck and pinning them into place, then looked at herself in the mirror of the dressing room. She felt like Cinderella. With her hair up in the casually elegant bun, she thought she looked a bit like Cinderella, too. It was so easy to get used to the life she'd been living these past weeks, without a care in the world, wandering Paris by day and exploring the many facets of Tariq's beguiling mind at night. The dressing room contained an array of clothes tailored to her precise measurements, all of which fit perfectly and made her look like someone other than Jessa Heath of Fulford: office manager in a letting agency and all-around nobody.

The Jessa she saw in the mirror was no ordinary Yorkshire lass. Tariq had mentioned the evening would be formal, and so she wore a floor-length satin gown the color of buttercream. It whispered and murmured seductively as she moved, the neckline plunging to hint at her breasts and the perfumed hollow between, then catching her at the waist before falling in lush folds to the ground. Her back was very nearly bare, with only thin angled shoulder straps to hold the gown in place. Though Jessa would have thought her very English paleness would look sickly in a gown so light, the color instead seemed to make her skin glow. Her freckles seemed like bursts of vibrant color rather than an embarrassment.

"You are lovely," a familiar voice said from behind her, causing Jessa to start, though of course she knew who she would see when she looked in the mirror. Her body knew without having to hear the words he spoke. It reacted to the very sound of his voice, the hint of his nearness, with the now familiar rush of wild heat that suffused her.

Tariq stood in the entry to the dressing room, mouth-wateringly debonair in his tuxedo, his long, strong body packaged to breathtaking perfection. His eyes seemed more green than usual, standing out from his dark hair and the black suit like some kind of deep forest beacon. His hard features seemed more handsome than fierce tonight, more approachable. Jessa felt a little stunned herself.

"Am I late?" she asked, feeling unaccountably shy suddenly in the face of so much steely male beauty. It was unfair that any one man could exude as much raw magnetism as he did, and so carelessly. She met his gaze in the mirror and then looked away, heat staining in her cheeks.

"Not at all," he said, and she knew he lied. There was a certain tenderness in his eyes that she could not account for, and could not seem to handle—it made it hard to breathe.

"Where are we going?" she asked.

The room around them seemed to contract and she pretended she was unaffected, that her nipples did not tighten to rigid points, that she could not feel the pull low in her belly. Sometimes he put his hand in the small of her back to guide her, or helped her out of a car, and though she felt even his smallest touch in every part of her being, that had been the extent of it. Though they had spent their first night together in every conceivable position, a vivid and carnal exploration of their passion, they had spent the weeks since merely talking—a curious inversion that was starting to make her shaky with need. He did not sleep with her at night and yet she knew with a deep, feminine certainty that he wanted her as much, if not more, than before.

"I must attend a benefit dinner," Tariq said, and shrugged. "It is of little importance. A dinner, a speech or two, and some dancing. You will be bored beyond reason."

As if that were possible when she was with this man. Jessa forced a smile, determined not to let the deeper emotions she could feel boiling within her spill over. This was a dream, nothing more. Cinderella went to the ball, and she would too, but that was all there was to it. The rest of the story did not apply, had never applied. She had no right to dream any Cinderella dreams, and she knew it.

"I am ready," she said, turning to him, and then stopped, caught by the arrested look on his face. As if he had been waiting for those words, but in a different context. Something unnamed but no less heavy crowded the room, narrowing the distance between them, making her pulse pound.

"Tariq?" Her voice was barely a whisper of sound.

He stood for a moment, his gaze consuming her, his mouth a flat, hard line that against all reason she longed to press her own lips against. Her heart kicked in her chest.

For a moment it seemed as if he might close the distance between them. His eyes dropped to caress her mouth, and Jessa felt it as surely as if he'd used his fingers. Her lips parted slightly, yearning for him.

"Very well then," he said, his voice rough, in his eyes all the things he had not done, all the ways he had not touched her. "Let us go."

Tariq bin Khaled Al-Nur's version of a party of no importance, Jessa found, was in fact a star-studded gala of epic proportions. Dignitaries, politicians and European nobles brushed elbows with cinema stars and international celebrities, in a shower of flashbulbs that overtook one of the famous arcades. The gala took place in a sumptuous hotel near the Place Vendôme and the Jardin des Tuileries, which Tariq confided had less historical significance than the hotel liked to admit. Jessa hardly knew where to look—from the frescoes adorning the ceiling of the reception room to the colossal gilt chandeliers that hung overhead to the rich red of the thick drapes and carpets. She felt as if she were in another world. A dream within a dream.

But this world was one in which Tariq was a king, and treated as such—not merely Tariq, her former lover. Jessa had known he was a powerful man, but she had never seen him in his element before except on television. Tonight, the fact that Tariq was an imperial power was made clear to her in a thousand little ways. It was the near-fawning deference he was shown, the deep bows he was accorded. It was the visible respect of the aides who ran interference for him, tending to his every wish and deflecting those whom he did not wish to interact with. It was the way everyone called him *Your Highness* or

Excellency, when they dared address him at all. Men Jessa only recognized from the news pulled him aside to whisper in his ear.

Once again, Jessa had the odd sensation that the world was shifting beneath her feet. It was one thing to know that Tariq was a king. What did that mean, in the abstract, shut up together in rooms where first and foremost she saw him as a man? It was something else again to really witness what it was for him to be a king, and, she could not help but think, that this was how he was treated in a country not his own. What must it be like when he was at home in Nur? Even among his peers, Tariq stood apart. He was harder, tougher. He was a warrior among bureaucrats.

She had no right to the fantasies that crept in, teasing her when she was less than vigilant. She knew her place in the world. Tariq was meant for a queen, not Jessa. Never Jessa.

"You seem unusually quiet," he said into her ear at one point, as they waited for dinner to be served. She could feel his breath fanning along her skin, teasing her nerve endings. She held back a shiver of delight.

"I am merely basking in Your Excellency's shadow," she replied, smiling at him. His hard mouth kicked up in the corner, surprising her. She snuck a look around the table. Here sat a recognizable head of state, there lounged an internationally acclaimed philanthropist; everyone exuded power of one kind or another.

"I imagine it must go to your head," she said.

He did not pretend to misunderstand her. "It is who I have become," he said simply, his gaze direct. Proud.

Had part of her been resistant to the very idea of his elevation in rank and status, even from a distance? Had she hoped, somewhere deep inside, that the doctor's son she'd loved so totally was the real Tariq and the wildly powerful king only a bad dream? Back then, he had simply been a man, however complicated. And now he was a king, and even more complicated. It was not only his job, his role. It was how he saw the world. It was who he was, every cell and every breath.

"Yes," she said softly. "I see that." She longed to touch him, but she did not dare. She did not know if there were rules of etiquette to follow, boundaries to observe.

"I cannot change the past," he said, and suddenly it was as if no one existed save the two of them. She forgot about rules, or other eyes, and drank him in.

"Neither can I," she replied without looking away.

So much loss. So many years wasted, a whole life created and given away to others. But could she honestly say she would change any part of it? Knowing that it resulted in a happy, thriving Jeremy? Something sharp twisted through her then, reminding her that she had not told him everything—could not tell him everything, even now.

"Perhaps it is time we stop looking back, then, you and I," Tariq said in a hushed voice, no less powerful for its low volume. It made something inside swell with a quiet kind of wonder, pushing all else aside.

"Where should we look?" She was in awe of what loomed between them, that made her fingers tremble and her eyes bright with a wild heat, though she refused to name it. She refused.

Tariq lifted her hand to his mouth and placed a kiss on the back of it, never breaking eye contact, not even when he sucked gently on the knuckle and made her gasp. Heat seared through her, melting her. The fire was never gone when he was near—it was only ever banked. Waiting for a trigger, a spark.

"I am sure we'll think of something," he said huskily.

* * *

Tariq turned to her the moment they crossed the threshold into the house, sweeping her into his arms and fastening his mouth to hers. He could not get enough of her taste, her heat, the soft and warm feel of her pressed against him. Jessa melted against him, her softness inflaming him, looping her arms around the column of his neck and arching into him. He tasted her again and again, exploring her mouth, feeling the kick of her immediate, uninhibited response flood through him.

Once again, he lifted her into his arms and carried her toward the bedroom, up the great stairs and toward their rooms on the top floor. Her fingers toyed with the ends of his hair where it brushed the top of his collar. Her eyes gleamed in the low lights of the quiet house around them while a secret, feminine smile curved her lips.

There were so many things he wanted to say, but he did not know where to start. He only knew that she had become necessary to him. Their tangled history was wrapped around him and growing tighter by the day, making it hard to breathe when she was not within reach. He found his way into the bedroom and set her down, unable to look away. One breath. Another.

She made a soft noise and reached out for him, her small hands framing his face, and pulled his mouth to hers. She tasted like honey and wine and went straight to his head, his heart, his aching hardness.

He set her away from him, turning her so he could look at the expanse of her creamy skin bared by the open back of her gown. He put his mouth, open and hot, on the tender nape of her neck, just to make her moan. He traced her spine with his fingers, making her shiver.

"All night I have wondered how soft your skin would be when I touched it," he told her in a low murmur, continuing to taste and touch. "You are better than crème brûlée, sweet and rich."

She let out a laugh, and the small sound ignited something in him, wild and hot and out of control.

He walked her over to the high bed, bending her forward until she braced herself on her elbows against the mattress. He heard the soft exclamation that she blew out on a sigh, or perhaps her breathing was as ragged as his. She turned her head, peering over her shoulder at him, her cinnamon eyes wide and inviting. Her lips parted, and he was certain he could hear the beat of her heart under his own skin. He held her gaze as he slowly pulled her gown up over her trim ankles, her shapely calves, her knees—

"Tariq, please…" It was a moan.

He knelt down between her open thighs, pushing the soft folds of material out of his way, marveling that her skin was softer than the satin of her gown. He pressed a kiss to the hollow behind her knee, the curve of her thigh, the crease where her thigh ended and her lush round bottom began. He curled his fingers into the soft scrap of material that covered her sex, and pulled her panties down and out of his way, helping her step out of them before he tossed them aside. He could feel her tremble. He ran his hands up her legs, testing her flesh beneath his palms. He leaned in close and inhaled the musky scent of her arousal and, moving forward to lick into her softness, tasted the wet, honeyed heat of her sex.

Tariq heard her cry out his name, but he was too far gone to reply. He knew only that he had to be inside of her, joined with her. So deep it would not matter what he could or could not say. He stood, his hands rough and desperate on the fly of his trousers. He sighed as he released himself, hard and pulsing with need. Stepping closer, he guided himself with one hand while he gripped her hip with the other, and drove into her depths.

It was perfect. She was perfect.

Tariq pressed his mouth against her neck, her shoulder, as he began to move, driving them both slowly insane with each sure thrust. He felt her stiffen, heard her cry out, and then she shook apart beneath him, moaning again and again. He withdrew, flipping her over even while she continued to gasp through the aftershocks, and settled her on the edge of the bed.

Her face was flushed, her hair in a mad tangle over one shoulder. Still she smiled at him and opened her arms, her eyes reflecting the man she saw in him—the man he wanted to be, and could be, when she looked at him that way.

Tariq moved over her, and slid back inside of her, making them both groan. She braced her hands against his chest. Still clad in his coat and dress shirt, he set a fierce, uncompromising pace. She locked her ankles in the small of his back and arched her breasts toward his mouth. He tasted her flesh, like salt and a sweetness he knew was all Jessa. All his.

When he hurtled over the edge, he took her with him. She shook around him, sobbing out his name like a song.

When he could think again, Tariq stood, pulling her to her feet and helping her out of the gown. Sleepy-eyed and deliciously naked, she crawled back into the bed, and curled on her side to watch him as he pulled off his formal clothes and tossed them in the direction of the nearest chair.

She was his. She belonged to him, whether it made sense or not, whether she knew it or not. She had survived their past and still made love to him with her whole self, body and soul. She had seen him in both of his incarnations, the shameful past as well as the present, and wanted him anyway.

There was more to it than possessiveness, a wide swathe of darker, deeper emotion, but Tariq pushed that aside. The possessiveness he understood. He could not give her up. Not again. He could not lose her unrestrained passion, her unstudied abandon when he touched her. He could not lose *her*. He did not want to think about it any further than that. He did not need to. He knew it to be true with a deep, implacable certainty.

"I must return to Nur," he said abruptly. He saw her tense almost imperceptibly and then drop her eyes to the mattress. "I have been putting it off these past weeks."

"Of course," she murmured, her voice even and yet distant, he thought. The hectic color faded from her cheeks as she stared at her hands. "We must all return to real life eventually. I understand."

How could she understand, when he was not sure he did? But he could easily picture her in the royal palace, wearing silks and jewels that enhanced her quiet beauty, while he made love to her on low pillows or feasted on her lush body in some desert oasis. He could see her against the bright blue skies and the shifting white sands, her eyes mysterious like his people's favorite spices, making him long to taste her over and over again. He saw her in his arms and immediately felt better. Safer, somehow, however illogical that seemed.

"I do not think you do," he said slowly, climbing onto the bed, holding her gaze with his as he prowled toward her on his hands and knees. "I want you to come with me, Jessa. I insist upon it."

"You insist…?" she breathed, but the color returned to her face, red and hot. Her eyes glowed.

He would never let her go again. *Never.*

"I am the king," he said, and pulled her to him once more.

CHAPTER FOURTEEN

"I WILL not hold you to what you said last night," Jessa told him the following morning, not quite meeting his eyes as she sat down at the breakfast table. "About going with you to Nur."

The morning was bright and unseasonably warm for Paris in autumn, which seemed to Jessa like a stark, strange contrast to inside the bedroom suite, where Tariq had taken her once again before she had fully come awake, pushing his way into her morning shower with that intense look in his eyes and driving her to ecstatic screams against the tiles. She was still quivering.

Tariq had called for breakfast to be served on the private balcony outside the bedroom, more secluded than the one she had seen that first night. He wore a dark button-down dress shirt over dark trousers, the coarse silk of his hair brushing the collar. She thought he looked like a warrior god pretending to be at rest, masquerading as some kind of businessman. The early morning sun teased the treetops and casement windows that lined the ancient street in front of her, and made her think she could do what she'd decided she must do in the shatter-ing aftermath of his lovemaking. She pulled her robe tighter around her and touched the wet hair she'd piled atop her head. She could act serene and calm and disinterested over rich black coffee and croissants so soft they seemed like clouds and butter. She could prove that she was no longer that infatuated, broken girl he'd left behind once before.

"Will you not?" He did not glance up from the papers he read, and yet the fine hairs on the back of her neck stood up in warning.

"Of course not," she said, feeling her temper engage and roll through her. Surely he should at least pay attention when she was attempting to be noble! She knew that if she went with him to Nur, she would not be able to maintain even a tenuous grip on the realities of their different situations in life. She knew she would be lost. "I have my own life to be getting back to, in any case."

Tariq laid his papers to the side of his plate and leveled a look at her. Jessa kept herself from squirming in her chair by sheer force of will.

"If you do not wish to accompany me to my country, then say you do not wish it," he said evenly. "But do not wrap it up in some attempt to release me from an obligation. If I did not want you to come, I would not have invited you."

"I was not—" she began, stung, though his words resonated more than she would have liked.

"We leave tomorrow morning," he said, rising to his feet. He crooked his brows as he looked down at her. "You must decide."

"Decide?" she echoed, her heart thumping too hard against her ribs. "Decide what?"

"If you will accompany me of your own free will," he said, his eyes gleaming, "or if I will simply take you."

"You cannot *take* me anywhere!" she gasped, but her

body betrayed her, her sex warming and melting as surely as if he'd touched her with his clever, provocative hands.

"If you say so," he said. He reached down and cupped her cheek with one large hand, his mouth unsmiling and his gaze intent, though still showing his amusement. And still it was as if he was branding her with his touch, his eyes. She felt small, safe and threatened at the same time— and more than that, *his*.

Completely and indisputably his.

His thumb dragged across her full lower lip, sending desire shooting through her body, tightening her nipples, wetting her sex further. Tariq smiled then, as if he could see her body's reaction. One dark eyebrow arched as color heated Jessa's cheeks. Point made, he turned away, disappearing inside the house and leaving her to her ragged breathing and her pounding heart.

He wanted to take her to Nur.

Part of her rejoiced for what that must mean, surely. It meant at the very least that he did not want this idyll in Paris to end any more than she did. But, of course, it was not quite that simple. Jessa drew her legs up beneath her on the chair, and stared out over the city she had come to love over the past dreamlike weeks, as if that could give her the answer.

She could not go to Nur. She could not continue to stay with him, ignoring reality while she played pretend. There were hundreds of reasons she should run back to York as quickly as she could.

And only one reason to stay.

Jessa rested her chin on her drawn-up knees and let out a shuddering breath as the shattering truth washed over her like the Paris sunlight, sweet and bright and unequivocal.

I love him.

She was in love with him. With Tariq, who had hurt her and lied to her. Who she was still lying to, if only by omission. Who she had made love to anyway, deliciously and repeatedly. Whose pain upset her, made her want to comfort and heal him, even when she was what caused it, and even when her own pain matched his. Their complicated, messy history should have made him the last man on earth she could ever have feelings for, but instead she felt closer to him because of it. As if no one could ever really understand her or what she'd been through, more than the man who grieved along with her.

Had she always loved him? Had she never fallen *out* of love with him? He had left and she had been forced to carry on, and she had had reason enough to be furious with him in the abstract, but she had still found her way into his bed within days of laying eyes on him again. She had told herself it was for her own purposes, but the reality was, she hadn't leaped into bed with anyone else. She had never wanted anyone else the way she wanted Tariq.

She wondered if on some level she had deliberately left her bag with her bank card behind when she'd set out for the train—because she hadn't really wanted to leave him.

She wanted to go with him wherever he wanted to take her, even though she knew it was highly likely that he would break her heart when he married someone more appropriate, but she couldn't find it in her to be as worried about that eventuality as she ought to be. It was clear to her now that she had been desperately in love with Tariq since the day she'd first seen him all those years ago, and there was no point in pretending otherwise. Just as there was no point attempting to be noble and leave him first—she might as well enjoy what little time with him she had, the better to hold on to in the lonely years to come.

Because Jessa knew that Tariq could never love her, not after what she had done in giving Jeremy away. How could he, when it was obvious to her that he had wanted his own family so desperately for all of his life? The truth was that she knew, deep down, that she had no right to him. She had been given the opportunity for a second chance, and she was not strong enough to resist it, even though it was clear to her that he would leave her once again.

Jessa uncurled from her chair and stood, staring out at the view but seeing instead his hard, proud face. He didn't have to love her. She would love him enough for them both. She was no stranger to hard love, love like stone, all immovable surfaces and impossibilities. She loved Jeremy more than she had ever thought it possible to love another person, and yet she had given him away, and knew with every breath and every regret that it had been the right decision no matter how much it hurt. She was used to love that bit back and left marks and forced her to be strong.

She could be strong for Tariq, too.

Her sister Sharon was a different story.

"Have you gone mad?" Sharon demanded down the telephone line, sounding scandalized—and uncharacteristically shrill.

Jessa had fortified herself with several cups of the hot, rich coffee from the breakfast service, but it seemed to have done nothing but make her agitated. Or perhaps she was already agitated. She had dressed with extra care, as if Sharon might be able to see her through the telephone and perhaps intuit what Jessa had been doing, but she found that the simple silk blouse and A-line skirt made her feel as insane as Sharon accused her of being. Was she dressing up, pretending to be someone else? Someone more sophisticated that Tariq could love? *Foolish,* she scolded herself, and adjusted her position, holding her mobile close to her ear.

"I don't know how to answer that," she told her sister, which was no more than the truth. She'd settled in for this conversation in the sitting room off the master suite, on the prim settee next to the windows, her back to the breathtaking view of Paris and angled away from the stunning Cézanne painting that took up most of the far wall—she wanted no distractions.

"I thought it was strange enough that you'd run off on a holiday with no advance warning," Sharon continued. "But to get mixed up with that man again? Jessa, how could you?"

"You don't know him," Jessa said evenly, feeling called to protect Tariq, even from her sister who could do him no real harm. Quite the opposite, in fact.

"I know quite enough!" Sharon said with a snort. "I know that he lied to you and left you! I know that men like him think they can swan in and out of people's lives as they please, with no thought to the consequences!"

"Tariq is not the same person he was then," Jessa said. She sighed. "And nothing is really as simple as it might have seemed back then."

"You can do whatever you like with your own life, no matter how reckless, but this isn't just about you, is it?" Sharon let out a ragged breath. "Selfish!" she half whispered, but Jessa heard her perfectly. She could even picture what her sister was doing—pacing the kitchen in her cottage with one arm wrapped around her waist, her face set in a terrible frown—as if she was there to see it in person.

Jessa told herself not to snap back at Sharon. Of course her sister was terrified by the prospect of Jessa with Tariq again. How could she not be? Jessa closed her eyes and lay her palm flat against her chest, just above her heart, as if she could massage away the ache that bloomed there. She could love Sharon, too, because she knew full well that beneath her sister's prickly exterior she loved Jessa in return. Sharon had always been there for Jessa. And wasn't that what love was for, in the end? To embrace others when they most needed it, whether they appreciated it or not?

"I would never do anything to hurt you," Jessa said softly, pinching the top of her nose between her fingers, hoping the headache that had bloomed there would fade. "Any of you. As you should know already. But I am going to go with him." She braced herself. "I have to."

"I can't believe this!" Sharon hissed. "What is it about this man that turns you so dense, Jessa? People don't change. He will hurt you all over again. That's a promise."

Jessa felt as if she'd been in suspended animation for years, with nothing but ice water and regret in her veins, until Tariq had roared back into her life and filled her with heat and life and love. How could she ever regret that, no matter what happened? But she couldn't share that with Sharon.

"I only phoned to let you know that I'll be traveling," Jessa said after a moment, fighting to keep her voice steady, and not to give in to the kick of adrenaline and insecurity that made her want to slap back at her sister. "I'm not asking for your permission."

She opened her eyes again and let them fall on the glorious painting on the wall across from her seat. It was a mountain scene, blues and greens and none of it soothing, somehow, with Sharon so angry.

"I cannot believe that you would risk so much on what? Your *hope* that things might be different?" Sharon made a bitter sort of sound. "I *hope* you haven't gone off the deep end!"

"I hope so, too," Jessa murmured, because there was nothing she could say that could make Sharon feel any better.

Sharon hung up the phone. Jessa let hers drop into her lap, and ordered herself to breathe. Her eyes were wide open this time. She had loved him when nothing about him was true, and she loved him now. Still. Did that make her the fool her sister thought her? Did she mind terribly if it did?

"Who were you talking to?" Tariq asked from the doorway, his low voice making Jessa jump in her seat as if scalded. Her eyes flew to his and she felt the blood drain from her face. She felt raw. Exposed. Had she said anything incriminating? Had she mentioned Jeremy?

"How long have you been standing there?" she asked, trying to sound calm, but her voice was far too high-pitched. Her heart pounded as if she'd just run a mile. It was too much—Sharon's frustrated anger and her own re-alizations about her feelings for Tariq. How could she face him before she had time to pull herself back together?

But it was too late—he was standing right in front of her, and Jessa was suddenly terrified that he could read her like a book.

Guilty. That was the look on her face, he realized after a moment of confusion. Guilty and pale.

"What is the matter?" he asked, searching her expression, all of his senses on red alert. He had finished a meeting more quickly than he'd expected, and had come here hoping to convince her to help him while away the time before the next meeting more pleasurably. He had not expected that he would find her secretive and jumpy. While he watched, she surged to her feet and held her mobile phone behind her, as if hiding it.

"Nothing is the matter," she said, but her voice was too uneven. Tariq felt his instincts kick in, the ones that served him well in politics as well as in combat situations. He moved closer to her.

"Who was that on the phone?" he asked again, this time with less curiosity and more command.

"No one," she said. Then she blinked and smiled, but it was not a real smile. It was far too strained. "It was my sister, Sharon, that's all."

"Did your sister upset you?" he asked. He searched her face. "With your parents gone, you must be close to her and her family."

She flinched, that guilty look stealing across her face again, though this time she tried to hide it. It was an absurd, over-the-top reaction, and he reached out a hand toward her, frowning, worried that something was truly the matter—

And suddenly, somehow, he knew.

The photograph he'd seen in her house flashed before his eyes, the one he'd snatched from the mantel and given only a cursory glance. The sister who looked like Jessa— the same copper-colored hair, the same chin. Her fair-haired, freckled husband.

And their olive-skinned, dark-haired child.

No. He felt himself freeze solid from the inside out, as if he'd been thrown headfirst into a glacier. *She could not have done this and not have told me, not after all of this*—

"Tell me," he said, feeling still, quiet, empty and bleak. "What is the name of your sister's child?"

It was as if he saw her from a great distance then. He saw her face twist into misery. Her hands clenched together in front of her. She was the very picture of distress.

"Tariq," she said, her voice heavy, and he knew it was true. "You don't understand."

All this time he had believed the child lost to him forever, believed that was no more than what he deserved—the reward for his wasted life. And all this time she had smiled so sweetly, made him feel as if she was the family he had longed for—all while knowing exactly where his child, *his son,* was!

"What exactly is it that I do not understand?" he asked her icily, his gaze boring into her. He held himself carefully, afraid that if he moved he would shatter into a rage so hot it would burn him, her, the whole house, the entire damned city. "Were you planning to tell me? Ever?"

"I couldn't," she said, her voice thick, her eyes bright with tears. "It is not my secret to tell."

"That excuse might work, Jessa, were I not the only other person on this earth who has a right to know *at least* as much about the child I never knew I had as you!"

"It is not about you!" she cried, throwing her arms wide. "It's about *him,* Tariq! It's about what *he* needs!"

"You let me think that he was lost to us forever. You *let me* think it!" His whisper was fierce, furious. He could taste the acrid flavor of betrayal in his mouth, feel it corroding him, turning everything he had believed about her—about the two of them—to burned-out husks and charred remains.

"This is exactly the reaction I was trying to prevent!" she cried.

"You have said enough." He silenced her with a slash of his hand through the air, and then he turned and stalked toward the door.

She had never planned to tell him. She had made love to him, comforted him, and had had no intention of telling him that all the while she knew where his son—his heir—was. He stopped walking when he reached the doorway, and stood there for a moment, fighting for control.

"Don't you think I would have noticed the resemblance at some point?" he asked, not turning back to her. "What story did you plan to tell me then?"

"When would you have seen him?" she asked after a moment, sounding genuinely confused. He turned then and stared at her in disbelief.

"Are you ashamed to be seen with me?" he asked acidly. "I think it is too late for these protestations, Jessa. You have been photographed in my company."

"I don't understand what you're talking about!" she cried. "I didn't think you'd ever lay eyes on him. Why would you spend time with my family?"

"I told you I was taking you to my country," he snapped at her. "What do you think that entails?"

"I'm sure you take a thousand women to your country!" she threw back at him, color high in her cheeks, her eyes dark.

"You are incorrect," he said icily, each word cutting. "I would never take a woman to my people unless I planned to keep her. Though that is no longer a subject you need concern yourself with."

She stared at him in shocked silence. He felt something move in him, but stamped it down. *No. Damn her.* Her pain did not, could not, matter—not anymore.

Tariq shook his head and turned back toward the door.

"Please..." she said, though it sounded more like a sob. "Where are you going?"

The look he threw back at her should have burned her alive.

"To see my son," he bit out.

And then he strode from the room before he broke something. Before she broke him any further than she already had.

CHAPTER FIFTEEN

OTHER than informing her that her presence was required only to assure him access to the child, Tariq cut her off completely. He did not speak to her on the plane, he merely sat in a thunderous silence that made Jessa ache in ways she would have thought impossible, though she would not let herself dissolve into tears as she wished. He did not speak to her in the car that took them from Leeds to York and then up the York Road toward the North Yorkshire Moors, and the small village along the way where Sharon had moved almost four years ago. Jessa could hardly stand to look at the cultivated fields that spread out on all sides, that intense British green against the cold gray skies. She could see only the coming heartbreak, the doom, the end of everything she had fought so hard to provide for the son she had loved enough to let go. She knew that no one could emerge from it unscathed, not her sister and Barry, not Tariq, not herself.

And worst of all, not Jeremy.

"I don't know what your plan is," Jessa said in a low voice as the car turned into the village and made its way along the high street. It was not the first time she had attempted to speak to him, but there was a desperation in her voice that had not been there before. "You cannot simply arrive at my sister's house and make demands!"

"Watch me," Tariq said, his voice vibrating with the same fury that had gripped him since Paris. He did not look at Jessa. He kept his brooding gaze fixed on the village that slid by outside the window, one elegant hand tapping out his agitation against the armrest.

"Tariq, this is madness!" Jessa cried. "My sister has adopted him! It is all quite legal, and cannot be undone!"

"You will not tell me what can and cannot be undone," he bit out, turning his head to pierce her with his dark, imperious gaze. He was angrier than she'd ever seen him, and all of it so brutally cold, so bitter. "You, who would lie about something like this? Who would conceal a child from his own father? I have no interest in what *you* think I should or should not do!"

"I understand that you're angry," Jessa said, fighting to keep her voice level. He laughed slightly, in disbelief. She set her jaw and forged ahead anyway. "I understand that you think you've been betrayed."

"That I *think* I have been betrayed?" he echoed, his eyes burning into her. He sat as far away from her as it was possible to sit in the enclosed space of the car, and yet she could feel him invading her space, taking her over, crowding her. "I would hate to see what you consider a real betrayal, Jessa, if this does not qualify."

"This is not about you," Jessa said as firmly as she could when she was trembling. "Don't you see? This has nothing to do with me or you. This is about—"

"We are here," he said dismissively, cutting her off as the car pulled up at Sharon's front gate. Tariq did not wait for the driver to get out of the car, he simply threw open his door and climbed out.

Jessa threw herself out after him, her chest heaving as if she'd run a marathon. Tariq paused for a moment outside the gate, and she knew it was now or never. After everything she had sacrificed—including, though it made her want to weep, Tariq himself—she could not let him wreck it all. She had to try one last time.

She lunged forward and grabbed on to his arm, holding him when he might have walked through the gate.

"Release my arm," he said almost tonelessly, though she did not mistake the menace underneath, nor the way he tensed his strong muscles beneath her hands.

"You have to listen to me!" she gasped. "You have to!"

"I have listened to you, and I have listened to you," Tariq said coldly, his eyes black with his anger. "I have watched you weep and I have heard you talk about how much you regret what you had to do, what you did because of me. I did not realize you were still punishing me!"

"It was not because of you!" Jessa cried as the wind cut into her, chilling her. "It was because of me!" She dragged in a wild breath, all the tears she'd been fighting off surging forth, and she simply let them. "I am the one who was so deficient that you left me in the first place, and I am the one who failed so completely as a mother that I couldn't keep my own baby! *Me.*"

She had his attention then. He stilled, his dark eyes intense on hers.

"But I did one thing right," Jessa continued, fighting to keep the tears from her voice. "I made sure he was with people who loved him—who already loved him—who could give him the world. And he is happy here, Tariq, happier than I ever could have made him."

"A child is happiest with his own parents," Tariq said.

Did she imagine that his voice was a trifle less cold? Was it possible?

Jessa stared at him, her fingers flexing into his arm, demanding that he hear her now if he heard her at all.

"He *is* with his parents," she whispered fiercely.

Tariq made a noise that might have been a roar of anger, checked behind the muscle that worked in his jaw. He shook her hands off his arm. Jessa let them drop to her sides.

"He is my blood," he snarled at her. *"Mine!"*

"His family is here," Jessa continued because she had to. Because it was true. "Right here. And he has no idea that he ever had any parents but these."

"Why am I not surprised that your sister would keep this secret as well?" Tariq demanded. "You are a family of liars!"

"He is a little boy who has only ever known *these* parents and *this* home!" Jessa cried. The wind whipped into her, racing down from the moors, and her hair danced between them like a copper flame. She shoved it back. "There's no lie here! They are his parents by law, and in fact. He loves them, Tariq. He *loves* them!"

His hard mouth was set in an obstinate line. "He is not yet five years old. He will learn—"

"You lost your parents, and so did I," Jessa interrupted, her heart pounding so hard in her head, her throat, that she thought she might faint. But she could not, so she did not. She searched his remote, angry face. "You know what it's like to be ripped away from everything you know. *You know!* How could you do that to your own child?"

The door to the cottage opened, and it was as if time stopped.

"Aunt Jessa!" cried the sweet baby voice. Jessa's heart dropped to her shoes.

"Tariq, you cannot do this!" Jessa hissed at him

urgently, but she did not think he heard her. He had gone pale, and still. Slowly, he turned.

And everything ended, then and there.

My son.

Tariq stared at the boy, unable to process what he was seeing. It had been one thing to rage about a child in the abstract, and quite another to see a small, mischievous-looking little boy, still chubby of cheek and wild of hair from an earlier sleep, toddle out the front door.

Tariq was frozen into place, unable to move, as the boy scampered down the steps. Jessa threw a look over her shoulder as she moved to intercept the child, scooping him up into her arms. She murmured something Tariq couldn't hear, which made the boy laugh and wiggle in her grasp.

The boy. Why could he not bring himself to use the child's name? *Jeremy.*

Another figure appeared at the door. Jessa's sister. She looked at the scene in front of her and blanched, telling Tariq that she knew exactly who he was. For a moment she and Tariq locked eyes, both struck still.

"Jessa," the other woman said, keeping her voice calm for the child's benefit though her eyes remained on Tariq, wary and scared. "What are you doing here? I thought you were on holiday."

Jessa shifted and put the little boy back on the ground. "I was," she said. She shrugged, half apology and half helplessness. "We thought we would stop by."

She looked at Tariq then, her cinnamon eyes swimming with tears. She put out her hand and cupped the top of Jeremy's head in her palm.

Jeremy, Tariq thought. *My son's name is Jeremy.*

"How lovely," the sister said, her voice strained. "You know how much Jeremy loves his aunt."

Jessa stood before him, still touching the little boy, her gaze silently imploring. Tariq felt something rip apart inside of him, and the pain was so intense for a moment that he could not tell if what he felt was emotional or physical.

Jeremy shook off Jessa's hand, his dark eyes fixed on the stranger he only just then seemed to notice standing before him. Tariq's heart stopped in his chest as the little boy moved toward him in his lurching, jerky dance of a walk, stopping when he could peer up from beneath his thick black hair. He was close enough to touch, and yet Tariq could not move.

His eyes were the same dark green as Tariq's. Tariq felt the impact of them like a body blow, but he did not react, he only returned the solemn, wide-eyed stare that was directed at him. Jeremy was as much Jessa's child as his. Tariq could see her in the boy's fairer skin, the shape of his eyes and brows, and that defiant little chin.

"Hello, Jeremy," Tariq said, his voice thick. "I am…"

He paused, and he could feel the tension emanating from both Jessa and her sister. He could almost hear it. He glanced over and saw that Jessa's sister had covered her mouth with her hands, her eyes wide and fearful. And then there was Jessa, who watched him with her heart in her gaze and tears making slow tracks down her cheeks. She stood with her arms at her sides, defeated, waiting for him to destroy everything she had worked so hard to protect.

She mouthed the word, *Please*.

"I am Tariq," he said at last, gazing back down into eyes so like his own, because it was the only thing he could think of that was not threatening to anyone, and was also true.

Jeremy blinked.

Then he let out a giggle and turned back around, to hurtle himself toward the door of the cottage and toward the woman who stood there, still holding her hands over her mouth as if holding back a scream. He buried his face against her leg, his small arms grabbing on to her in a spontaneous hug. Then he tilted back his face, lit from within with the purest, most uncomplicated love that Tariq had ever seen.

"Hi Mommy," Jeremy chirped, oblivious to the drama being played out around him.

Jessa's sister smiled down at him, then looked back at Tariq, her own face stamped with the same love, though hers was fiercer, more protective. But no less pure.

Tariq felt his heart break into a thousand pieces inside his chest, and scatter like dust.

Tariq stood by the gate, his back to the cottage, while Jessa carried on a rushed conversation with her sister. She kept sneaking looks at his strong, proud back, wondering what he must be feeling rather than paying attention to Sharon. When her sister finally went inside and closed the door, she hurried down the path to his side.

He did not look at her. He kept his eyes trained on the fields across the lane, that swept to the horizon.

"Thank you," she said, with all the feeling she'd tried to hide from Jeremy. And even from Sharon.

"I did not do anything that requires thanks," Tariq said stiffly. Bitterly.

"You did not ruin a little boy's life, when you could have and have been well within your rights," Jessa said quietly. "I'll thank you for that for the rest of my life."

"I have no rights, as you have been at great pains to advise me."

"I am sorry," she said. She stepped closer to him, forcing him to look at her. His eyes seemed so sad that it made her want to weep. Without thinking, she reached out and grabbed hold of his hand. "I am so sorry."

"So am I," he said quietly, almost letting the wind snatch it away. He looked down at their joined hands. "More than I can say."

She would not cry for him, not now, not when he held himself so aloof. She knew what that must mean—it was inevitable, really, after what they'd just been through. Jessa took a deep breath and forced herself to smile as she let go of him. She wanted to hold him and kiss him until the remoteness left him and he was once again alive and wild in her arms. She wanted to share the pain of leaving Jeremy behind, and make it easier, somehow, for both of them to bear. Oh, the things she wanted!

But she had always known that she could not have this man. Not for good. And she knew that he had lost something of far greater significance today than her. She could let him go just as she had let Jeremy go. It was the only way she knew how to love them both.

"You should return to Nur as you planned," she said, proud that her voice was even, and showed none of her inner turmoil. She could let him go. She could. "Your country needs you."

So do I! something inside of her screamed, but she bit it back, forced it down. He had never been hers to keep. She had known that from the start.

He seemed to look at her from very far away. He blinked, and some of the darkness receded, letting the green back in. Jessa felt a hard knot ease slightly inside her chest.

"And what about you?" he asked, something she couldn't read passing across his face.

Jessa shrugged, shoving her hands into her pockets so that the fists she'd made could not betray her. "I'll return to York, of course," she said.

The wind surged between them, cold and fierce. Jessa met his gaze and hoped hers was calm. She could do this. And if she broke down later, when she was alone, who would have to know?

"Is this your revenge, then?" he asked, his voice soft though there was a hardness around his eyes. "You wait until I am bleeding and then you turn the knife? Is this what I deserve for what you think I did to you five years ago?"

"No!" she gasped, as stunned as if he'd hit her. Her head reeled. "We are both to blame for what happened five years ago!"

"I am the one who left," Tariq said bitterly.

"You had no choice," Jessa replied. "And I was the one so silly she ran away for days. I left first." She shook her head. "And how can we regret it? We made a beautiful child, a perfect child."

"He is happy here." Tariq said it as if it were fact, a statement, but Jessa could see the pain and uncertainty in the dark sheen of his gaze.

"He is," she whispered fiercely. "I promise you, he is."

She didn't know what to do with the ache inside of her, the agony of feeling so apart from him. She was not the desperate, deeply depressed girl she had been when she had given Jeremy up. She was stronger now, and she knew that the way she loved Tariq was not like the infatuation of her youth. It was tempered with the suffering she'd endured, the way she had come to know him now, as the man she had always imagined him to be.

It might be that she could not bear to make this sacrifice after all.

He is not for you, she told herself fiercely. *Don't make this harder than it already is!*

"Come," Tariq said. He nodded toward the car. "I cannot be here any longer."

Jessa looked back at the cottage, so cozy and inviting against the bleakness of the autumn fields, and yet a place she would always associate with this particular mourning—the kind she imagined might fade and change but would never entirely disappear. She pulled her coat tighter around her. Then she put her arm through Tariq's and let him walk her to the car.

Jessa sat beside him in the plush backseat, feeling his grief as keenly as her own, as sharp as the wind still ripping down from the moors. Tariq did not speak for some time, his attention focused out the window, watching as fields gave way to villages, and villages to towns, as they made their way back through the country toward the city of York. Next to him, Jessa knew that his mind and his heart were still back at her sister's cottage, held tight in Jeremy's sticky little hands. She knew because hers were and, to some extent, always would be.

She had to hope that it would grow easier, as, indeed, in many ways it already had in the past few years. Seeing Jeremy thrive—seeing him happy and so deeply loved—healed parts of herself she had not known were broken. She hoped that someday it would do the same for Tariq.

"I do not know what family means," Tariq said in a low voice. He turned toward her, catching her by surprise, seeming to fill the space between them. "I have never had anyone look at me the way that boy looked at your sister. His mother." His gaze was so fierce then that it made Jessa catch her breath. "Except you. Even now, after everything I have done to you."

Their eyes locked. He reached over and tucked a stray curl behind her ear, then took her face in his hands. The warmth of his touch sped through her veins, heating her from within.

"I have already lost a son," he said, his voice almost too low, as if it hurt him. "I cannot lose you, Jessa. Not you, too."

Joy eased into her then, nudging aside the grief. It was a trickle at first, and then, as he continued to look at her with his face so open, so honest, it widened until it flowed—a hard and complex kind of joy, flavored with all they had lost and all the ways they were tied together.

She reached across the space between them, over her fears and their shared grief, and slid her hand up to hold him as he held her—holding that strong, harsh face, looking deep into the promises in his dark green eyes.

"Then you won't," she whispered as if it were a vow.

She would let the fear go this time, instead of him.

She would love him as long as he let her.

CHAPTER SIXTEEN

HE HEARD her laughter before he saw her.

Tariq strode down the wide palace corridor, past the ancient tapestries and archaeological pieces that told the story of Nur's long history in each successive niche along the way. The floor beneath his feet was tiled, mosaics stretching before him and behind him, all in vibrant colors as befit the royal palace of a king. When he reached the wide, arched doors that opened into the palace's interior courtyard, he paused.

Jessa was so beautiful, she took his breath away. She was a shock of cinnamon and copper against the brilliant blue sky, the white walls, and the palm trees that clanked gently overhead in the afternoon breeze. She seemed brighter to him than the vivid flowering plants that spilled from the balconies on the higher floors, and the sparkle of the fountain in the courtyard's center. She had set aside her novel and was watching the antics of two plump little birds who danced on the fountain's edge. She wore a long linen tunic over loose trousers in the fashion of his people, her feet in thonged sandals. Around her neck she wore a piece of jade suspended from a chain that she had found in one of the city's marketplaces.

She looked as if she belonged exactly where she was. *Mine,* he thought, not for the first time.

He crossed to her, smiling when she seemed to sense him and glanced around—smiling more when her face lit up.

"I thought you would be gone until tomorrow," she said, her delight evident in her voice, in the gleam in her eyes, though she did not throw herself into his arms as she might have in a less public area of the palace.

"My business concluded early," he said. He had made sure of it—he wanted to be away from Jessa less and less. In some sense, she was the only family he had ever known. What they had lost together made him feel more bound to her than he had ever been to another human being. And he could think of only one way to ensure that he never need be apart from her again. The birds chattered at him from their new perch on the higher rim of the fountain. "You have been here nearly a month and still you are fascinated by the birds?" He eyed her. "Perhaps you should get out more."

"Perhaps I should," she agreed. He watched as her gaze shuttered, hiding her feelings from him as she still did from time to time whenever any hint of a discussion of their future appeared. It was time to end it.

"As a matter of fact," he said quietly, "that is what I wanted to talk to you about."

"Getting out?" she asked, frowning slightly.

"In a manner of speaking," he said. He looked down at her, wanting to pull her into his arms and kiss his way into this discussion. That seemed to be the language in which they were both fluent. "I want to talk about the future. You and me."

Jessa went very still. The splash of water in the fountain behind her was all Tariq heard for a long moment, while her eyes went dark.

Then she lifted her chin, defiant and brave to the end. "There is no need," she said with a certain grace, drawing herself up and onto her feet. She picked up her book and tucked it underneath her arm with stiff, jerky movements. "I have always known this day was coming."

"Have you?" he asked mildly.

"Of course," she said briskly. "One of the first things you told me when you walked into my office was that you needed to get married. Naturally, you must do your duty to your country."

She held her head high as she skirted around him. She headed across the courtyard and up the wide steps toward his private quarters. Tariq followed, watching the sway of her hips in the soft linen and admiring the ramrod straightness of her spine. He followed her inside the palace and all the way into the vast bedroom suite, where he leaned against the bed and watched her look wildly around, as if searching for something.

"Never fear," she said in the same false tone, turning to face him. "I have no intention of making this awkward for either of us. I will simply pack a few things and be out of your way in no time."

She looked as if she might change her mind and bolt for the door.

"You are so determined to leave me," he drawled, amused. "It is almost a shame that I have no intention of letting you do so."

She froze in place, her face expressionless while her eyes burned hot.

"What do you mean?" she asked, her voice little more than a whisper.

"What do you think I mean?" he asked.

For a moment she only stared at him.

"I will not be in your *harem!*" she muttered, scandalized. "How could you suggest such a thing?"

"I am not planning to collect a harem." His mouth crooked up in one corner. "Assuming, of course, you behave."

"I don't understand," she whispered, though it was more like a sob.

"You do." He moved closer to her, so he could reach out and hold her by her slender shoulders. "You have simply decided it cannot happen. I do not know why."

Her mouth worked, and she flushed a deep, hot red.

"You must have a queen who is worthy of you," she said after a moment. "One who is your equal in every way."

"I must have *you*," he replied simply, leaning forward to kiss her. Her lips clung to his for a long, sweet moment, and then she pulled back to frown at him.

"No," she said firmly.

"No?"

"I won't marry you," she gritted out, and moved out of his grip. She rubbed at her arms for a moment, her head bent.

Tariq ordered himself to be patient. "Why not?" he asked, in a far easier tone than the possessiveness that clawed at him demanded.

She looked at him. Her lips pressed together, and her hands balled into fists at her side.

"I love you," she blurted out, and then sighed slightly, as if it hurt to say aloud, even as sweet triumph washed through Tariq—making him want to roar out his victory, shout it from the rooftops. When she looked at him again, her eyes were overly bright, but her chin was high. "I cannot marry a man who does not love me," she said. Bravely and definitively. "Not even you."

Tariq closed the distance between them, his expression unreadable. But this was not about sex, explosive as it had always been between them. This was about something bigger.

That must be why she wanted to collapse into sobs.

"Don't!" Jessa whispered, though she did not move— did not make any attempt to avoid him. "This is hard enough, Tariq! Please do not—"

He silenced her with his mouth upon hers, his hand fisting in the mess of her curls. He kissed her until she melted against him, soft and pliant against his hardness despite everything, until her arms crept around his neck and she kissed him back with a matching ferocity. He kissed her until she couldn't tell who moaned, who sighed, while the fire of their connection raged between them, incinerating them both in a delicious blaze.

"I love you," he told her in a low voice when he tore his mouth away from hers, his gaze dark and green and so serious it made Jessa gasp.

She searched his face, not daring to believe she had heard him right. She even shook her head, as if to refute it.

Tariq smiled.

"I have never loved another woman," he said. "I never will. How can you doubt it? I longed for you for five long years. I hunted you to the ends of the earth."

"York is not the ends of the earth," she said, absurdly.

He traced a line down her jaw, still smiling.

"That depends where you start." He sighed. "Jessa. What are you so afraid of? Did I not tell you what would happen if I brought you here?"

She remembered he had been angry, but she also remembered what he had said—that he would keep any woman he brought to his palace. But she could not seem to get her head around it. She could not seem to believe.

"That was a long time ago," Jessa whispered.

"I will marry you," he said, as if there had never been any other possibility.

"You cannot!" she cried, hard emotions racking her, fear scraping through her, leaving her trembling in his arms. "I do not deserve you! Not after—" Her eyes swam with tears, blurring the world, but she could still see him, so strong and intent. "I gave him away, Tariq. I gave him up."

"And we will miss him," Tariq replied after a moment, his voice thick with his own emotions. "Together."

Jessa let out a breath and, with it, something tight and frozen seemed to thaw, letting light and hope begin to trickle through her. Letting her wonder, *what if?*

He pressed his lips against her forehead. In a softer tone, yet no less demanding, no less sure, he said, "And we will have another child, Jessa. Not as a replacement. Never as a replacement. As a new beginning. This I promise you."

The tears spilled over now, wetting her cheeks. She touched his face, an echo of that cold day when Tariq had finally understood the magnitude of what she had given up, and why. Jeremy would be an ache they carried with them for the rest of their lives, day in and day out. But for the first time, she dared to hope that they would carry it together across the years, making it easier to bear that way. And someday, only if he wished it, they would tell Jeremy the story of how much he was loved, and how well.

"Yes," she breathed, her heart too full to let her smile. "We will be a family."

"We will," he said gruffly, and something powerful and true swelled between them then, and seemed to spread out around them to fill the room.

The thought of making a child with Tariq—deliberately—in joy and in love, and then raising that child together as she had always wanted to believe they were meant to do… It was almost too overwhelming.

Almost.

"I haven't agreed to any marriage," Jessa told Tariq then, with a small smile, while an intoxicating cocktail of hope and joy surged through her. She could feel it inexorably changing her with every second. Could dreams come true after all, after everything they had been through? After all that they had done? Was it possible?

Looking at him, she dared to believe it for the first time.

She was still twined around him, her legs astride one of his and her sex pressed intimately against his thigh. He moved slightly and made her groan as that sweet, delirious heat rocked through her.

"I suggest you get used to the idea," Tariq said, a smile in his voice, his eyes. "This is my country. I do not require your agreement." He kissed her again, capturing her lower lip between his teeth for a moment before releasing her. He smiled. "Though I would like it."

"Yes," she said softly, wonder rolling through her, making her feel as incandescent as the desert sun. Only with Tariq. Only for him. "Yes, I will marry you."

"You will be happy, Jessa," he vowed, fiercely, sweeping her up off the floor, high against his chest. She wrapped her legs around his waist and gripped tight to his shoulders, looking down at him as he held her. At the jade eyes that so consumed her that she had bought a necklace to match, so she might have something like him to look at when he was away. At this man she had loved for so long, and in so many different ways. Her playboy lover. Her king. *Her husband.*

"You will be happy," he said again, frowning at her as if he dared her to disagree.

"Is that your royal decree?" she asked, laughing as he whirled her around and tipped her backward onto the soft bed behind them. He fell with her, following her down and then bracing himself on his arms before he crashed into her.

"I am the king," he said, leaning over her. "My word is law."

"I am to be the queen," she said, shivering slightly as the idea of it began to truly take hold. She would have this man forever. She would be able to hold him like this, love him like this. She felt her eyes well up as she reached between them to trace his mouth, the hard planes of his face. Harsh, forbidding. *Hers.*

"So my word should also be law, should it not?" she asked.

"If you wish it."

Jessa smiled and lifted her head to kiss him, sweet and more sure than she had ever been of anything.

"Then *we* will be happy," she said and, for the first time, truly believed it, with all of her heart and soul. "Because I say so."